Tessa Barclay i_____st
who has written many succ_____m
the four-part Craigallan saga (*A Sower Went Forth, The Stony Places, Harvest of Thorns* and *The Good Ground*), the Wine Widow trilogy (*The Wine Widow, The Champagne Girls* and *The Last Heiress*) and the Corvill weaving saga (*A Web of Dreams, Broken Threads* and *The Final Pattern*), *A Professional Woman, A Gleam of Gold* and *A Hidden Beauty*. She lives in south-west London.

Her Father's Child

Tessa Barclay

HEADLINE

First published in 1994
by HEADLINE BOOK PUBLISHING

First published in paperback in 1994
by HEADLINE BOOK PUBLISHING

10 9 8 7 6 5 4 3 2 1

ISBN 0 7472 4577 0

Typeset by Avon Dataset Ltd, Bidford-on-Avon

Printed and bound in Great Britain by
Cox & Wyman Ltd, Reading, Berks

HEADLINE BOOK PUBLISHING
A division of Hodder Headline PLC
338 Euston Road
London NW1 3BH

Her Father's Child

Chapter One

Impossible to imagine, on that tranquil Sunday evening, that their world was about to be broken into little pieces.

The fire burned with a red and steady glow in its steel firebasket. The room's lighting was subdued except at the bridge table, where Lindon Tregarvon was experiencing some muted triumph at gaining the upper hand for once over his daughter and her partner.

Erica, for her part, was feeling more than a little irritated with her fiancé. His understanding of tactics was surprisingly poor. She couldn't help thinking to herself that if Gerald were going to be a success in the Foreign Office, he'd better train himself to pick up signals more promptly.

The distant sound of the doorbell hardly registered with any of them. None of their acquaintances would dream of calling after dinner on a Sunday evening, particularly in January. Whoever it was, Hurrock would deal with them.

'Our trick, I think, partner,' said Tregarvon with a glinting smile at his wife.

Amy made a note on her bridge pad. 'I think the rubber will be ours, dear,' she said, frowning as she did addition sums. 'That's fourteen shillings you'll owe us, Erica.'

'Gerald must pay,' her daughter replied, wagging an admonitory finger at him. 'It's all his fault.'

'Fourteen shillings! How could I ever have let myself be duped into playing with pirates like you?'

They were still chuckling politely at this sally when Hurrock came into the drawing room. He went to the master's side, bent, and murmured in his ear.

'Nonsense,' said Tregarvon. His roundish fresh-skinned features showed only perplexity. 'Tell them they'll have to come back some other time—'

Hurrock was seen to murmur yet again into the master's ear. It seemed to Erica that she caught the words, 'They insist . . .'

Insist? Who would dare 'insist' on intruding on the Sunday-evening privacy of a tycoon like Lindon Tregarvon? She felt a prickle of surprise, but her father was shrugging and rising from the chair.

'I suppose I must,' he said. 'Deal, my love, I'll be back in a moment.'

Amy Tregarvon gathered up the cards, shuffled, and began to deal. She had paid scarcely any heed to the interruption, her mind on the important topic of how the bridge game was going.

Outside in Park Lane cars whispered past on a roadway dusted with snow, the miniature bay trees at the front door wore white caps, and the wrought-iron rails of the first-floor balconies bore a trim of ice. A raw, cold night. But inside the house everything was warm and solidly comfortable – heavy blue velvet curtains to keep out the draughts, blue Aubusson on the floor, Hepplewhite card-table of walnut with a boxwood inlay, crystal decanter nearby with whisky for the menfolk.

2

Diamonds glinted. Amy Tregarvon had diamond studs in her ears and a brooch shaped like a seagull on the neckline of her dinner dress. Her daughter's engagement ring sparkled on her left hand. Across the table from Erica the man who had given her the ring collected up his cards, studying them with earnest blue eyes set in a handsome, Saxon face.

'No trumps,' announced Erica's mother.

'Father will be delighted to hear it,' Erica said.

'Will he?' her partner said, clearly longing to ask why.

'No chit-chat at the card table,' said Amy in mock rebuke.

Erica smiled encouragement at Gerald. One day soon after they were married, she would sit down with him for an evening of bridge and really teach him how to play. But of course you couldn't expect everybody to take the game as seriously as the Tregarvons did. For them it had passed many a long evening aboard ship on the business trips her father had deemed necessary to keep an eye on his fleet of liners.

A strange childhood, perhaps. She knew she wasn't quite like the other girls with whom she'd made her debutante's curtsey in the early summer of last year. The others, daughters of the aristocracy, of the landed gentry, of judges and haughty civil servants, had been boarders at ladies' colleges, had frittered away a year or so at finishing school in Geneva, Paris or Florence. To them, Erica's account of her life had seemed strange, too sheltered yet adventurous.

'You've been to New York? To Shanghai? But how *marvellous* . . .'

But she knew they thought her odd. At twenty, she was older than most of the debs of 1931; constant travel had made it difficult to find just the right sponsor for her presentation at Court. And not quite the sweetly-pretty type that was all the rage that year. The other debs thought her 'striking', which was a way of saying not really beautiful. They agreed among themselves that though her clothes were marvellous, her figure was a little too curvaceous for the long Patou line that was just coming in. Her rich brown hair looked good in the fashionable long bob and her brown eyes with their golden flecks were splendid – but rather apt to sparkle with impatience at their chatter.

All in all, they were impressed but not attracted. No bosom-friendships sprang up among them during the Season. And when her engagement to Gerald Colbert was announced, the debs said to each other, 'He's just right for her. *He's* got career prospects, *she's* got money, and he won't mind being bossed about so long as she pays for his polo ponies.'

Erica was thinking, as they waited for her father to return and resume the game, that if only Gerald could play bridge as well as he played polo, domestic bliss would be assured.

Her father did not return. Instead there was a hubbub outside the drawing room door. Raised voices, protests, a faint thud, which almost sounded as if someone had knocked over a chair.

'What on earth—?' exclaimed Gerald, throwing down his cards and half-rising.

'Lindon?' cried Erica's mother, turning in her chair.

'What's going on?' Erica said, and was at the door in a moment, throwing it open in alarmed inquiry.

Two men, tall and heavy-set, were standing either side of her father. They were not holding him, but gave the impression of crowding him. In the hall of the fine old house, a big wrought-iron lantern hung from the ceiling, and by its yellow light Lindon Tregarvon's face looked waxy white, shocked, almost dazed.

A chair had indeed been overturned. Hurrock was setting it upright as Erica walked into the hall.

'What are you doing?' she demanded, trying to get between her father and one of the big men. 'Who are you? What do you want?'

'Now, now, miss, no need to be concerned,' was the reply in a practised, soothing tone. 'This is just a little official matter—'

'On a Sunday evening? How dare you come here and—'

'Excuse me, miss, you are—?'

'I'm Erica Tregarvon. Father, who are they?' She turned to him for explanation.

Her father had always been the fountain of all knowledge for Erica. In all their travels, he had always been able to answer her eager questions. But now she was aware that he seemed at a loss. 'These men are from Snow Hill police station,' said Lindon Tregarvon in a voice strained and oddly muffled with tension. 'They want me to go with them.'

'Go with them?' It was Gerald, who had followed Erica out of the drawing room. 'To a police station?'

'I think it'd be best if you'd just come quietly, sir,' said the bigger of the two big men. 'No need to involve the whole family—'

'I'm not a member of the family, I'm Miss Tregarvon's fiancé,' Gerald broke in. 'And perhaps I should warn you

5

that I'm a Foreign Office official and don't take kindly to policemen barging into a respectable house.'

He was pulling rank and everyone knew it. There was scarcely any need. Gerald and Lindon in their beautifully tailored dinner jackets and gleaming starched shirtfronts were in considerable contrast to the two men from Snow Hill in their fifty-shilling-tailor suits and day-worn linen.

One of the two men put his hand in his breast pocket and produced a card which he held out towards Gerald. 'Chief Inspector Griffiths of Snow Hill, sir,' he said. 'This is Sergeant Lowry. We're here on legitimate inquiries.'

'No doubt, no doubt,' Gerald agreed, stepping down a little from his lofty Foreign Office attitude on hearing their titles. 'But if Mr Tregarvon is to be a witness in some case you're developing, surely you could have chosen a better moment than a Sunday evening—'

'Lindon, darling, you never mentioned anything to me about witnessing anything?' Amy's plump features creased in distress. 'Was there an accident or something? You never said a word—'

'No, no, my dear, no accident – nothing of the kind. I don't have the faintest idea what this is all about!'

'If you'd just come with us to the station, sir—'

'But I tell you I don't know anything about anything! I can't see what good it would do to—'

'It would help us with our inquiries, sir.'

'Inquiry into what?' asked Gerald, visibly startled at the phrase.

'I'm afraid that isn't a matter we could discuss.' The Inspector turned back to Tregarvon. 'You see how it's upsetting your family, sir. It really would be better to pursue all this at the station—'

'Pursue what? That's what I don't understand!'

'We would explain all that much more conveniently elsewhere, sir. With our files to hand—'

'Files? What files? What have they to do with me? I must insist that you either explain yourselves or leave my house! It's insupportable, to walk in and start talking in riddles about inquiries that don't concern me!'

'That's what we would like to discuss with you, sir.'

'What?'

'How our inquiries concern you.'

'But how can they possibly? If you have some crime or felony to investigate, it must presumably be something you suspect among the Tregarvon Line employees, and that could be done better either at the docks or the shipping office.'

'We could talk all that over at the station, sir.'

'I must insist that you come to my office tomorrow with any accusations about my crews. I know there's always talk of smuggling among crewmen, but the Tregarvon Line . . .'

'We don't want to talk about suspected smuggling, Mr Tregarvon.'

'I don't think you have any idea what you do want to talk about!' Erica cried in irritation. 'You keep going round and round in circles—'

'Quite right, miss, all we're doing is wasting time,' said Sergeant Lowry with a gruff laugh. He had a more genial air than his superior. 'Trust the ladies to see that men are making fools of themselves. But the fact of the matter is, sir, we've been sent to bring you in to Snow Hill and I'm sure you'll see how bad it would look for us if we went back without you.'

'Who on earth wants me brought to the station, then?'

'The Superintendent, sir. Strict orders. "Ask Mr Tregarvon to be so good as to accompany you back to Snow Hill." '

'Oh, good Lord, I can see this is going to go on for ever,' Lindon cried, giving up. 'All right then, I'll come with you. But let me tell you this, I shall have something to say to your superiors about the way you've carried out your orders.'

'Very sorry, sir,' said the Sergeant, with a grimace and a shrug.

'I suppose it means the end of the bridge game,' Lindon went on, turning in apology to Gerald. 'I'm very sorry, what a poor evening's hospitality—'

'We can continue when you get back,' suggested Gerald.

The Inspector cleared his throat.

'What?' demanded Lindon, recognizing it as a demurral.

'I don't think you should count on getting back in time to finish your card game, sir.'

'Not get back?' Amy cried, seizing her husband's arm in her two hands. 'What do you mean?'

'Well, madam, this might take a while.'

'A while? But it's only nine-thirty. Say you sort this out in an hour,' said Gerald in a tone of sweet reason, 'we could pick up the rubber again.'

'I don't think so, sir.'

There was an uncertain silence. Erica felt the hair on the nape of her neck begin to prickle.

'Is this likely to take a long time? Several hours?' Lindon asked.

'I think you could say several hours. Maybe more.'

'But . . . But . . .' Lindon stopped, pulled himself together. 'You're saying I might not get back until perhaps after midnight?'

'It's more than likely, sir. These things take time.'

'In that case—' He glanced about. 'Hurrock, bring me the telephone.'

'Who are you going to telephone, sir, if you don't mind me asking?' said Sergeant Lowry.

'My private secretary. I've appointments early tomorrow morning, he'll have to put them off for me.'

'I'd prefer if you didn't make any phone calls, sir,' said the Inspector, moving to intercept Hurrock as he advanced with the telephone in his hand.

'What? But I must! If you're going to keep me talking into the small hours, I shan't be on time at the office and Brandsworth is due to come in to discuss—'

'I'm sure your secretary will be able to handle it.'

'But I insist! Timothy will be at a loss to explain to Brandsworth – and he's a very important shipper—'

'I'm sorry, sir, it would be better if you came with us without contacting anyone.'

'This is outrageous!'

It was outrageous – and frightening. The two big men with their placid assumption that they would get their way, her father's bewilderment, Gerald's uneasy glance from one to the other . . . Nothing like this had ever happened to Erica before in her life.

She was at a loss. Life aboard her father's liners had always been so ordered, so well-governed. Almost nothing ever went wrong except the weather, the sea conditions, and even then within the ship there was calm and a controlled reaction from an efficient crew and experienced captain.

Here in the supposed safety of her own home she felt threatened. So did her mother. She could hear the fast, light breathing that so often foretold an asthmatic attack. She went to Amy to put a protective arm around her. 'It's all right,' she assured her, 'it's some silly mistake, Father will be back in an hour or two.'

They all followed out on to the porch to watch Lindon Tregarvon walk down the frost-rimed path between the two men. There a black Rover car was waiting. With a puzzled glance back at them, Erica's father allowed himself to be ushered into the car and driven away along the lamplit stretch of Park Lane.

Mrs Tregarvon was shivering in the chill of the January night. The butler waited while Erica shepherded her back indoors, then closed the door behind them with a firmness that seemed to imply, 'Let us get back to normal.'

Erica said over her shoulder, 'We'll have some hot coffee at once, Hurrock.'

'Yes, Miss Tregarvon.' He returned with a tray almost immediately, which seemed to imply that the kitchen had been on the alert. Erica reflected that he had probably given his impression of the two heavy-set men to the staff when he got back from showing them in.

Once her mother had drunk some coffee and Gerald had poured himself a brandy, Erica went on to the next matter. 'Father wanted Timothy told about this. I'll go and see to that now.'

'But . . . But, dear, those detectives . . . they said they would rather not . . .'

Erica shrugged in indignation. 'I don't care what they said. Father wants Timothy told and I'm going to tell him.'

As she made for the drawing room door Gerald said, 'Might be a good idea to give his lawyer a tinkle.'

That made her pause. She looked back at him. He met her glance. Frowning a little but saying nothing that might alarm her mother, Erica went to the study.

She had to look up Timothy Perriman's home number. He was a familiar friend to her, but only in the context of her father's business life. He lived in Maida Vale somewhere. She dialled the Elgin number, waiting with impatience while it rang. She had almost decided he was still away for the weekend when the phone was picked up.

'Timothy? Timothy, this is Erica Tregarvon—'

'Miss Tregarvon! What a surprise—'

'Timothy, the most awful thing has happened. Two policemen have just been here and they've taken . . . they've taken . . .' To her own surprise and dismay, her voice broke. Hot tears gushed from her eyes.

Until that moment she'd been too busy understanding what was happening, reacting with disbelief and indignation, to feel the shock. Now it struck her, a hot wound that made her waver at its pain. The walls melted and moved towards her, the contents of the room swam, the telephone earpiece slipped in her fingers and almost fell.

'Miss Tregarvon? What were you saying? What's the matter? Miss Tregarvon, are you there?'

She took a deep, searing breath. She swallowed hard.

11

With her free hand she wiped the tears from the rims of her eyes.

'I'm sorry. It just suddenly came home to me. I don't think I'd really . . . really taken it in . . .' She pulled herself together. 'Timothy, my father's been taken to Snow Hill police station to help with inquiries.'

'Help with inquiries? Into what?' cried Timothy, clearly aghast.

'God knows, they wouldn't say. They were terribly cagey. They just . . . kept insisting he must go with them, and when he said he wanted to get in touch with you before he left . . . because of tomorrow's appointments, you see, they wouldn't let him.'

'Wouldn't let him? You mean they actually—'

'No, no, they didn't actually *do* anything. They just kept pressing him to come with them.'

'But why?'

'To answer some questions.'

'But questions about what, Miss Tregarvon?' Timothy insisted, his voice rising as if speaking louder would get better results.

'I don't know, Timothy. It's a complete mystery. Father was utterly perplexed at the whole thing.'

'But he's gone with them?'

'Yes.' She caught at something in his tone. 'Do you think he shouldn't have?'

There was a tiny pause. 'I'm sure it wasn't necessary to take him to the police station. That's just being rough-handed. And it looks so bad . . .'

'How do you mean?'

'Well. "Helping police with their inquiries" . . . You know what that usually means when you see it in the papers.'

'No, what, Timothy? I don't understand you.'

'Well, it means . . . It's taken for granted by most people . . . It means they have a suspect in custody.'

'A suspect? My father?' Once again the room seemed to waver around her. But she frowned fiercely at it to make it straighten itself. She said, 'How dare you!'

'Miss Tregarvon, it's not what I think, of course it isn't. But people will say—'

'They won't dream of saying that about my father! It's unthinkable!'

'Of course it is. I completely agree with you. But—'

'But what?'

'I wish he'd refused to go.'

'Could he have refused?' she asked, thinking back over the scene. At the time the pressure applied by the two detectives had seemed irresistible.

'I think he could. I don't know too much about it. But unless they were actually arresting him—'

'Arresting my father?'

'Of course that's absurd. They only want to investigate something and he has information,' Timothy said. 'That's what it is. All the same I wish he'd said they must wait until tomorrow and come to the office.'

'That's why I'm ringing you, Timothy. He has appointments first thing.'

'But he'll be there in time for those—'

'No,' she said, and wondered at the mixture of fear and desolation she heard in her own voice. 'Those men said several hours, perhaps longer. I don't think Father will be in the office at the usual time so he wants you to reschedule his appointments.'

'Certainly. I'll see to it first thing. Don't give it another thought. I'll put everybody off until the afternoon. He has a lunch engagement – perhaps I'd better cancel that.'

'Gerald says he thinks . . .'

'What was that? What did you say about Gerald?'

'Gerald thinks I ought to call Mr Winkworthe.' She heard herself say it and knew she was asking Timothy to do it for her. She found herself hating the idea of saying all this again to the lawyer.

'I'll do that for you,' Timothy said at once. 'Leave it with me.'

'No.' No, it was her duty to see to it herself. No matter that the indignity of the explanation would make her wince, that the bewilderment of her first reaction was giving way to apprehension, she herself must speak to Winkworthe. She was her father's daughter, it was her duty to do everything necessary to help him.

'One thing,' Timothy remarked as she was about to say goodbye. 'We ought to keep this quiet.'

'Of course.'

'It could be bad for business confidence, you see. It's a silly mistake but you know how people are.'

'Yes,' she said with sadness, and broke the connection.

The maid at the Winkworthes' house said the master and mistress were spending the weekend with their son and daughter-in-law in Surrey. She supplied the telephone number. Erica redialled. After some delay and what seemed like reluctance, Mr Winkworthe came to take the call.

He was shocked out of his slightly irritated manner when he heard the news.

'And he went with them?' he exploded.

'Well, they made it seem . . . inevitable. And of course he knew it couldn't be anything really serious—'

'I'll be at Snow Hill as soon as I can. I'll set out at once. Miss Tregarvon, have you *any* idea what it's about?'

'Not the slightest,' she sighed.

'Did you get the impression it was a personal matter or something to do with business?'

'I've no idea. They could see Mother was getting upset and suggested it would be better to go to the station and . . . Oh yes, they said they would have their files at hand.'

'Files?'

'I think they said that.' She hesitated. 'Does that tell you something?'

'I was wondering if perhaps someone had been forging cheques on your father's account, or he had lost his wallet and it had been returned. Or some member of one of the ships' crews had been caught out in something.'

'Mother thought perhaps he'd been in some slight accident with the car.'

'But files . . . I'd better ring off, Miss Tregarvon, and telephone Snow Hill to let them know I'm coming at once.'

'Thank you, Mr Winkworthe.'

'Don't worry, child,' he said with unexpected kindness, 'it'll be sorted out as soon as I get there.'

Lindon Tregarvon didn't return to his Park Lane house during that night nor the next morning. When Erica came down to breakfast alone at nine, she found the morning paper folded by her plate. She had slept hardly at all, was heavy-eyed and depressed. While Hurrock poured her coffee she unfolded the paper.

The headline over the left-hand side of the front page leapt up at her. 'POLICE QUESTION TREGARVON. INSURANCE CLAIM IN DOUBT.'

The shock made her jerk the paper wider. Her hand hit Hurrock's. Coffee went all over the tablecloth and over the skirt of her soft wool dress.

'Oh, Miss Tregarvon, I'm so sorry—'

'Never mind, never mind!' She sprang up, retreating from his efforts to mop up the coffee with a napkin. She ran to the telephone in the study, the most private one in the house. As she reached for it, it rang.

'Miss Tregarvon? Is that you? This is Winkworthe here. May I speak to your mother?'

'Mother's not up yet, Mr Winkworthe. Last night was a shock to her, I persuaded her to take a little sedative.'

'Ah. Probably very wise. But the thing is . . . you see . . .'

'What is it, Mr Winkworthe?' she demanded, already sensing bad news in his manner.

'Your father needs his shaving kit and a change of clothes—'

'You mean he's being kept even longer?' she said in horror.

'No, no, in fact he ought to be home later in the day. No, he wants to tidy himself up and change out of his evening jacket before appearing in the magistrate's court—'

'But why? Why is he appearing before a magistrate?'

16

'He's being charged,' Winkworthe said baldly.

Erica stood like a statue. After a long moment she said, 'What is the charge?'

'The exact form is still being drawn up. The chief element in the charge is likely to be conspiracy to defraud.'

'That's impossible.'

'My dear, I'm afraid it's one of only several the police wish to bring. At the moment there are international points of law which are causing hesitation—'

'International points of law? I don't know what you mean! My father hasn't done anything wrong, in this country or anywhere else in the world! You know that as well as I do—'

'It's not a matter of what I know or don't know, it's a matter of what the Public Prosecutor believes. My dear girl, I must go, I've just got home from a most frustrating night at the police station and I have several other telephone calls to make. May I leave it with you to arrange the sending of Mr Tregarvon's toilet articles and a change of clothes?'

'Of course,' she said. 'I'll see to it. But my mother—'

'Yes?'

'Who's going to tell my mother?'

After a long pause the lawyer said gently, 'I'm afraid you will have to, Miss Tregarvon.'

Let her sleep, thought Erica. Let her sleep on in ignorance of this grotesque farce being acted out in police station and magistrate's court. Time enough to tell her when it was inevitable, when it was no longer possible to protect her from the facts.

She rang for Hurrock. 'My father needs a change of clothes

17

and his toilet things,' she said. 'Please pack them up and take them to him.'

'Take them to him? Where, miss?'

'Snow Hill police station, of course.'

Nothing about the butler changed. His face wore the same expression of polite attention that she was accustomed to. But somehow she was given to understand that Hurrock didn't wish to pay calls on a police station, that he felt it wasn't part of his duties and was lowering to his prestige.

A gust of anger swept through her. She was about to say something forceful to him. But then she recalled that to treat Hurrock with less than politeness always ended in some little obstructions from him: breakfast rolls brought in when they were no longer warm, the port shaken as it was brought to the dining table . . .

She said, 'I'd go myself, Hurrock, but I have to be here when my mother wakes up.'

'I understand, miss,' Hurrock said with an inclination of his silvery head. She could tell he was pleased that she'd had to explain herself. Is this what life is going to be like, she asked herself, until this stupid mistake is cleared up? Am I going to have to be diplomatic with the servants?

With that thought in mind she was careful how she spoke to her mother's personal maid. 'When Mother rings for her morning tea, Maitland, please let me know. I've some rather serious news for her.'

'Oh dear, Miss Tregarvon! About the master?'

Of course about the master, thought Erica with suppressed anger. Who else would it be, after last night's drama? She nodded and dismissed her.

Amy Tregarvon woke at about ten o'clock, sleepily rang for her maid to bring the tea, eyed the bedside clock and wondered why she was so late in rousing. Memory of last night's upset was just beginning to return when her bedroom door opened and her daughter came in. One look at her grave face was enough to make Amy struggle up against her pillows.

'What, darling? What is it?'

'It's about Father—'

'Yes, of course, if it's bad news I'd rather he came and told me himself—'

'He can't come, Mother. He's still at the police station, he has to appear in court later this morning.'

'What does that mean? What for? Does Winkworthe know?'

'Yes, it was Winkworthe who told me. He rang about an hour ago—'

'But why didn't you wake me? Why did you let me sleep on like this—'

'Mother,' said Erica, sitting on the side of the bed and taking her hands, 'please try to be calm. I let you sleep because you needed it. You were so worn and upset when you went to bed and it was pointless taking a sedative and then not letting it do its work. We'll talk about it, but you must promise not to get in a state.'

'I *am* in a state! I can't believe they're doing this to Lindon! Keeping him all night at the station – good heavens, do you think he's had any breakfast? And what sort of a bed would they give him? It's unbearable.'

'Mother, Mother, he's a strong healthy man, he can manage for one night with a hard bed and a bread-and-butter breakfast.

19

It's you I'm worried about at the moment. Please calm down, or you'll bring on one of your attacks.'

Amy had been subject to asthmatic attacks all her life. As a child she had been delicate, and it was from this that her reliance on card games had arisen; she'd whiled away many a long day on a sofa playing whist or cribbage with her governess. As she came into her teens her health improved but the tendency to asthma remained, always worse in summer and in the country. For this reason the doctors had recommended sea voyages. This was how it came about that Erica had spent so much of her childhood aboard ocean liners; Amy's health was better at sea but she was unwilling to be parted from her child, the more so as her first, a little boy, had died due to the complications of measles at the age of three.

There was a strong bond between Erica and her mother. They had been companions as long as she could remember, playing deck games together, listening to the gramophone in Amy's stateroom, and later playing cards as amiable opponents. As Erica became a keen bridge player, she began to surpass her mother. If they happened to cut so as to be partners, they made a formidable pair.

When Erica was being groomed for her debut and heard the other girls gossiping, their impatience and sometimes their actual dislike of their parents had puzzled Erica. If you didn't like your father and mother, who on earth were you going to like? Who else was there to turn to when you needed advice, support, comfort? But no, some of the girls seemed to think mothers were a necessary evil, to be put up with as long as you had to, to be disregarded as much as possible. Fathers, they seemed to think, were on the whole better: you could generally wheedle what you wanted out of a father.

To Erica it seemed bizarre. To her, her father was someone to be looked up to, admired and respected. It was true Lindon Tregarvon didn't spend as much time with his daughter as Amy did, but that was to be expected. Fathers were captains of industry, leaders of society, often called away on business. All the same, they were to be loved, because they were one of the two mainstays of the world.

Now Erica had to explain to her mother that Lindon Tregarvon, that honest, upright man, was by some weird misunderstanding to appear in a magistrate's court to be charged with some malefaction.

'But what? What can your father possibly have done wrong? They can't really mean it, they'll see how silly it is when they have to get up and talk about it in court. They will, won't they, Erica?'

'I expect so, Mother. We'll know soon.' She stopped as the door opened to admit Maitland with the tea-tray.

'Take it away!' cried Amy. 'I couldn't swallow a thing.'

'Yes, please, Mother – please, try to drink your tea and eat your biscuits—'

'It would choke me, I can't!'

'Just leave it, Maitland.'

The maid set down the tray. 'There, there, madam,' she said, 'don't you fret, everything will be back to normal when Mr Tregarvon gets back. And you wouldn't want him to see you in a state like this, now would you?'

'No . . . no, of course not . . .'

'Drink it while it's hot,' urged Maitland, pouring it. 'And

I'll draw your bath and put out your clothes. It's still very cold out, you'll be wanting to wear something warm. Shall I lay out the amber wool?'

Thus chatting and distracting her from her troubles, Maitland calmed her mistress into drying her eyes. She gave Erica a glance of sympathy as she went to turn on the bath.

Has it come to this, Erica thought to herself with dismay, the servants are sorry for us? Was that better than having Hurrock in a huff?

As she left Amy to begin her day, she grew angry with herself. What did it matter what the servants thought? Why was she letting it bother her? The important fact was that her father would be back in his home in an hour or two. And surely, surely, in the course of trying to frame the charge to be issued at the magistrate's court, the police would see how absurd it had all been.

Hurrock returned home, reporting that he had delivered the dressing case to a police constable at the station who said he'd see it got to its owner.

'You didn't see him?' Erica cried.

'There was no question of that, miss.'

'I hoped . . . I hoped . . .'

'Miss Tregarvon, I asked at the station and they said they didn't think they could frame the charge until tomorrow.'

'Oh no! That's impossible!'

'It's what the sergeant said, miss.'

Erica dashed to the telephone to call Winkworthe. At his sigh, she realized he had half-expected this. 'What can we do?' she demanded. 'We can't allow them to keep him there like this.'

'I'm afraid we can't prevent it, Miss Tregarvon. They say they have reasonable cause to hold him for questioning, and indeed from what I learned there's no doubt there's a very strong supposition of serious wrongdoing.'

'Not by my father!'

'Someone has apparently carried out a serious fraud. There are witnesses who have made statements that put it absolutely in the realm of fact. There's no way I can prevent the police from pursuing this inquiry, and to do so they have to question your father. That's the law, Miss Tregarvon.'

'I won't accept it! You *must* do something!'

'If I could, I would. But the police are within their rights. Mr Tregarvon went with them voluntarily last night. Since then they have facts which seem to implicate him.'

'That can't be true!'

'The Superintendent is adamant that they have a case, the only problem is how far to go with the framing of it. The law allows them to detain him until their inquiries are at a satisfactory state. I'm sorry, you must accept it, my dear. All we can do is wait.'

The rest of a day was a torment. Every time the phone rang Erica leapt to it, sure it would be word that her father was coming home. But it was always something else: first Timothy Perriman asking to be kept informed and saying he was keeping everything relatively smooth at the office; then friends inquiring if they had misread the newspaper; and at last the press, eager for background on the wrongdoer. They took it for granted Tregarvon was a criminal. 'Helping with inquiries' – what else did it mean?

Gerald rang to ask what was going on. 'Not back yet?' he

said in alarm when she told him. 'Good God, what's happening down there – a marathon?'

'Mr Winkworthe says the police are within their rights . . . But you said you had friends . . . ?'

'Ah,' murmured Gerald, 'ah, yes, at the Home Office. But you see, dear, if Winkworthe thinks there's nothing to be done . . . ?'

She understood that he no longer felt so certain about interfering on her father's behalf. The fact that he was being kept so long gave him pause. When she asked if he would come that evening to keep her company, there was another hesitation.

'I don't see how, dear. I'm promised to a dinner party at the Hastings'.'

'Oh, Gerald, please cry off!'

'I don't see how I can, Erica. It would put her table right out and she'd never get another man to fill in at this late hour. Besides, she's a cousin of my boss, I'd hate to get in her bad books.'

'I see. Of course.' They rang off with assurances of affection on both sides, but she felt a shiver of apprehension. It had dawned on her that Gerald might think his career was endangered by being engaged to a girl whose father was about to be charged with fraud, no matter how wrongly.

The day wore on to its end. Winkworthe returned to Snow Hill to ask for Tregarvon to be released but was met with a determined refusal. When he asked for temporary bail, the Superintendent said, 'We don't want to break up the thread of our inquiry, sir. We'd rather have Tregarvon here till the charges are clear in our mind, sir. Sorry.'

Charges? More than one? When Winkworthe came to tell her this, Erica was so shocked she couldn't speak. At last she said, 'Don't tell my mother. It's bad enough for her that they won't let him come home. She wanders about the house like a lost kitten, looking in all the rooms as if she expects to find him.'

Winkworthe's long, serious face creased into a tired smile. 'I can just picture it. Certainly, Miss Tregarvon, we needn't say anything about "charges" to your mother.' As he took his leave he pressed her hand. 'You're being very brave, my dear.'

Next morning at eight Erica went in a taxi with clean linen for her father. The case was taken from her by a constable who was formal, polite, but determined to tell her nothing.

'But I'm his daughter! I must know what's happening!'

'Sorry, miss, I'm afraid it's up to the detectives what happens and they don't let me know.'

'Then let me speak to one of them.'

'It wouldn't be no use, miss. I don't think they know themselves when they'll tie it up for the court.'

Amy Tregarvon was in the drawing room with her daughter when, at just before noon, her husband returned. With him came the lawyer. One look at Winkworthe's solemn expression was enough to tell Erica that her father had been brought to court on grave charges.

Her father's usually fresh complexion seemed grey, his eyes were red-rimmed with exhaustion, his shoulders were slumped.

'Darling!' cried Amy, rushing to him. 'You look worn

out! I'll have coffee brought . . . or brandy . . .'

'Told Hurrock I wanted a whisky and soda on the way in,' he said. He put his arms about her and patted her on the back. 'It's all right, Amy, don't let it put you in a tizz.'

'So it's all sorted out? Thank goodness for that! They must have been mad to treat you like that, and now it's all over I want you to take them to task. You know Gerald said he had friends in the Home Office or wherever it is.'

'Let's not think about that for the moment,' he said, releasing her and sinking into a chair. 'God, I'm tired! I need a bath and a nap—'

'Yes, of course, darling, but you'll have some lunch first?' Hurrock came in with the whisky. Amy held up a hand to him. 'Tell Cook we'll eat in a quarter of an hour.'

'But the veal pie has only just been put in the oven, madam.'

'Sweetheart,' said Lindon Tregarvon, 'why don't you go and talk to Cook about it? Something simple, that's all I want, when I've freshened myself up a bit.'

'Yes, yes, of course, darling. An omelette, that might be best. Cook never likes making omelettes but in the circumstances . . .' She hurried off with Hurrock, looking like a busy little tender at the side of a stately sailing ship.

Tregarvon motioned to his lawyer to sit down. Erica watched the two men with a sinking heart. 'What happened?' she asked.

Winkworthe hesitated.

'Go ahead, she has to know some time.'

'That's true, Tregarvon. Well, I'm afraid it's very bad—'

'Bad?' Erica whispered.

'Your father has been charged with conspiracy to defraud, some lesser offences against the mercantile laws, and . . . manslaughter.'

Chapter Two

Manslaughter. The word was so awful that Erica felt herself go cold. 'Somebody has died?' she faltered. 'As a result of something . . . something you did, Father?'

He shook his head to emphasize the vigour of his rejection. 'Certainly not! The whole thing is a lie from beginning to end! I would never have had anything to do with schemes of that kind.'

'Then how—?'

'Briefly, Miss Tregarvon, the case is this.' Winkworthe took it up. 'In the last two years, two cargo ships owned and insured by the Tregarvon Line have gone down at sea. In the case of the second, *Ganymede*, five of the crew drowned. It's concerning the death of those men that the charge of manslaughter has been brought.'

'But if ships sink at sea—'

'They're saying I arranged it,' her father said in a low, harsh voice. 'They're saying I conspired with the ships' captains to sink each ship and get the crew off, only in the case of the *Ganymede* something went wrong and only the first mate and the engineer got off.'

'No! No, that's horrible!'

'And it's not all of it,' Tregarvon went on. 'The police are "continuing their inquiries".' Swallowing the rest of his whisky, he pulled himself to his feet. 'I must get out of this damned suit – I seem to have been wearing it for a month. You'd better outline the rest of it to Erica, Winkworthe. She's got to know so as to be able to cope with what comes next.'

He went swiftly out of the room. Erica moved to stop him but instead turned to look with dismay at the lawyer. 'What comes next? What?'

'Bail was set at an extraordinarily high sum,' he sighed. 'Fifty thousand pounds. That reflects the feelings of the court on the seriousness of the charges. Not only is your father being held responsible for the death of five men but also for insurance fraud – the ships and their cargo were insured for very large sums—'

'But that's the basis of the whole thing, isn't it?' she cried, seizing on the point that seemed to her of most importance. 'What makes them think there was a fraud in the first place? Why can't the ship have come to grief in the normal way?'

Mr Winkworthe moved uneasily in his chair. 'I fear, Miss Tregarvon, that the engineer and first mate of the *Ganymede* have been heard boasting in their cups of the money they made over the loss of their ship in Darwin, Australia. An investigator working on behalf of an insurance company – nothing to do with the firms who insured the Tregarvon Line ships – heard of it, made some inquiries, and reported back to Lloyds of London.'

'But perhaps they were only making it up.'

'Perhaps,' Winkworthe said, but his tone let her know he felt it was not likely. 'They're being brought back to London to give evidence, but they've already made statements under caution. They say they were instructed to sink the *Ganymede* in the Torres Strait after landing its cargo at Daru—'

'I don't understand!'

'That's one of the purposes of the fraud, Miss Tregarvon. You insure a rather aged vessel and its cargo for a handsome sum, and then you tranship the cargo at some agreed port where the harbour authorities aren't too astute. The cargo is then sold on at its proper value, the ship is taken out and sunk, and the owner claims the insurance. It would be a very profitable venture.'

'My father would never do such a thing,' Erica said, feeling her cheeks go hot at the idea. 'He was a seaman himself during the War – he would never endanger crewmen like that!'

'There isn't supposed to be any danger to the crew,' said Winkworthe. 'They're supposed to get away in the lifeboats, and usually do. I gather that quite often the crew know nothing about the scheme. But to carry it out there must be complicity on the part of the officers – the captain and first mate, at least, and perhaps also the engineer. The police are at present looking for the captain of the *Lariette* – that was the ship that went down with a cargo of machine tools in the South Atlantic last year.'

'But I remember that! Father was very upset – the *Lariette* was one of the first ships he bought when he was building up the line.'

'Exactly. A very old ship, more or less due to go to the junkyard. The police are pointing out that she was insured for a surprisingly large amount.'

'But that was because the cargo was so valuable—'

'Quite true. And it appears some of the cargo of machinery has been found safe and sound and in use in a cotton-mill in New England.'

Erica turned to the window and back, to give herself time to think about what he was saying. 'You mean they've been investigating this for some time already?'

'Of course. It's a complex allegation. For more than six months a special squad of the City police have been building up a case.'

It made her shudder to think of it. All through the summer of last year, when she was enjoying her London season and being admired by gossip columnists, the police had been tunnelling away at the foundations of her happiness. They were trying to prove her father a swindler and a murderer – for if it were true that five men had died because of anything he had done it was murder, even if he hadn't himself killed them. But of course he hadn't had any part of it.

'Mr Winkworthe,' she said, 'I can see it's very serious. But my father had nothing to do with it and the police can never make a case against him.'

'Unfortunately they can. He signed the insurance documents and claimed the money after the loss of the ships.'

'But of course he would sign the insurance documents.'

'Then he is the one who benefits from the fraud, isn't that so?'

'But ships and cargo *have* to be insured. Couldn't someone else have arranged for the cargo to be stolen and then had the ships sunk to conceal the theft?'

'That, of course, is a possible defence,' Mr Winkworthe agreed in a dry voice, 'and is likely to be used by counsel when I brief him. Unfortunately McGuire and Lilton, the two men being brought home from Darwin, say that the instructions came from Mr Tregarvon himself.'

'They're lying!' she cried. 'They're simply lying!'

'Why should they?' Winkworthe countered.

She stared at him. 'How can you—?' And then, almost at once, 'You think he did it!'

'My dear, don't put words into my mouth. But you see how it looks? The case against your father is very strong indeed and once the press get a hint of it, it will look even worse. That was what he meant when he said you had to be prepared for what's to come. And there's your mother to think of.'

'Oh God,' Erica gasped. 'This will crush her.'

'No, no.' Winkworthe got up from his chair, to come and give her a fatherly pat on the shoulder. 'You'll find a way of protecting her.'

'How? It's sure to be headlines in the newspapers.'

'It was headlines yesterday, was it not? Perhaps that will be enough for Mrs Tregarvon.'

'Let's hope so. I'll tell the servants to keep the papers from her and not to gossip about it.'

He gave her a sad smile. 'I hardly think any instruction from you will prevent gossip, my dear. That may be the worst part of it for your mother.'

As he moved towards the door, Amy Tregarvon came in again, looking reasonably cheerful. 'There, that's arranged,' she remarked. 'Cook and I have come to an agreement about lunch. You'll stay, Mr Winkworthe?'

'You're very kind, but I had better not,' he replied. 'I have urgent business to attend to.' His glance at Erica let her know it was urgent business concerning her father.

She went with him to the front door. 'I shall be briefing one of the very best counsels,' he said. 'I already had a word with him by telephone – you may have heard of him, Speldon Banks?'

She shook her head.

'Well, he specializes in maritime cases, I dare say you wouldn't have paid much attention to those. Goodbye for the present, Miss Tregarvon, and keep a stout heart – we shall fight this case and win!'

She shook hands and closed the door on him. Fight this case – the words echoed in her mind. To tell the truth, she'd been sure all charges would be dropped. The idea that there was anything substantial against her father was to Erica absurd.

But if there was evidence of some sort, of course it was all based on a misapprehension. True, the cargo of machine tools had been found after it was supposedly lost at sea, but she knew from hearsay that crews of cargo ships sometimes engaged in moneymaking enterprises of their own: smuggling, either of goods or people, was quite common, and stealing from the cargo or the passengers' luggage was a constant worry.

Her *immediate* concern was what to tell her mother. She went back into the drawing room, searching for some comforting phrases.

Amy was fiddling with the dials of the radiogram. 'I want the one o'clock news, dear,' she explained, 'I want to hear what they're saying about your father.'

'Oh, you saw the headlines yesterday,' Erica responded in a calm voice that belied her feelings. 'It'll only be more of the same.'

'I do think newspapers are mean the way they always like to think the worst of people,' her mother said plaintively. 'You know they were absolutely horrid to Sybil Drewsley over her divorce, and anyone who knew anything about it could have told them Tony had been an absolute beast to her, so no wonder she went looking for comfort elsewhere.'

'What are we actually having for lunch?' Erica inquired.

'I thought an omelette would be rather light after all. I imagine there was nothing worth eating at that awful police station. Imagine it, dear, sandwiches as thick as doorsteps, made with margarine too, I expect. So I rearranged today's menus entirely, we're having the sole we would have had this evening and then the omelette, and tonight it could have been the veal pie but Colonel Pierce doesn't care for veal so Cook is ringing now to order steak—'

To her horror Erica remembered that they had guests for that evening. The engagement had been made over a month ago. She could think of nothing to say, but let her mother chat on about the menu. When her father appeared, changed into fresh clothes and looking more like himself, she left them alone to catch up on the last two terrible days.

She went to the telephone in the study to ring the Pierces. It was essential to warn them not to talk that evening about what they'd learned of the case through newspaper or wireless. But she found the warning wasn't needed. The Pierces were only too thankful to have the chance to withdraw.

'I'm sure you'd rather not have the bother of dinner guests,'

Mrs Pierce said with a great appearance of sincerity. 'With your father under questioning—'

'He's home now, Mrs Pierce.'

'Oh, he is? It's all sorted out?'

'He's on bail,' Erica said, not knowing how to express it more favourably.

'Oh, I *see*. Oh, in that case you will want guests even less – you'll have so much to discuss. Well, then, thanks for the phone call, Erica, Harold agrees with me that we're right not to inflict ourselves on you.'

'Thank you,' said Erica, and was in fact really thankful, though not for the way in which Mrs Pierce was only too relieved to get out of it.

When they sat down to lunch she mentioned she'd been chatting to Mrs Pierce on the phone. 'She was awfully nice,' she lied, 'she told me she knew we'd rather not have to cope with entertaining. So they won't be here this evening.'

'Thank goodness for that,' Amy said in all innocence. 'Lily doesn't play a bad hand of bridge but the Colonel always loses his temper.'

After lunch, during which conversation seemed to Erica to be weirdly divorced from reality, Amy went to have her afternoon nap. Lindon ordered the car to meet him at one forty-five, before joining Erica for coffee in the drawing room.

'I told her it would all be sorted out quite soon,' he said. 'I don't think she's able to understand the ins and outs of it, Erica, and I certainly don't want her worried by some of these ludicrous charges.'

Erica nodded agreement. 'It might be better if we went

down to the country for a week or so.'

'Can't be done. I have to be here to see the lawyers and deal with trouble at the office—'

'Trouble? Timothy said things were running quite smoothly.'

'That was when the business world hadn't heard the charges. All hell is about to break loose now.' He was grim, yet he seemed quite calm.

The phone had rung several times while they were eating. Now it rang again. Hurrock answered it, then came to the drawing room. 'It's a reporter from the *News Chronicle*, sir. There were several other reporters during your meal but I told them you were unavailable. They said they would ring back.'

'Thank you, Hurrock. Please tell the man that I have nothing to say at present but that if they want to contact me they must phone me at my office.'

'Yes sir.'

'And Hurrock—' Erica added.

'Yes, Miss Tregarvon?'

'If there are any phone calls from people wanting to speak to my mother about the case, tell them she's not at home.'

'Very well, miss.'

As he left, Lindon Tregarvon shrugged. 'It might work. But I don't think she can be shielded from it entirely. By and by some kind friend is going to get through and tell her the gory details.'

'Let's try to delay it as long as possible.'

'Right.' He rose to his feet, quite collected, ready for the day's work. 'I've got to go. Timothy is probably under siege by now, poor fellow. I leave you in charge here, Erica. Do your best to look after Mother.'

'Of course.' She kissed him on the cheek and went out with him to the hall. Hurrock came with his overcoat. As he opened the front door a man tried to shoulder his way in.

'Here!' exclaimed Hurrock. 'What're you up to?'

'Mr Tregarvon? Mr Tregarvon?' the man cried, looking eagerly past the butler. 'Can I have your reaction to the charges?'

'Get out of here!' said Lindon.

Erica had fallen back a little in surprise. Now she came up to stare at the intruder. 'Who on earth are you?'

'It doesn't matter who he is. Get out of my house!' shouted Lindon.

With Hurrock's help he bundled out the reporter, still calling inquiries as he slithered on the frosty tiles of the path.

'He's not going,' Hurrock said with indignation. 'And there's another of them out by the gate.'

'So much for a quiet afternoon at the office sorting things out,' Lindon said in a bitter tone, and stood a moment in thought. 'Well, I'm not going to let them stop me going about my business. I'll tell them what I told you, Hurrock. If they want me they must come to the office. And I'll get Winkworthe to think up something to say to them.'

He put on his hat, accepted his gloves from Hurrock, and went through the front door like a captain leading an assault. From the window at the side of the door, Erica was able to see him waylaid by three or four people. He shook himself free, said a few words, got into his car, and was driven away.

'If I were you, miss,' Hurrock said in a sympathetic tone,

'I'd go out the side way into the mews if you're wanting to get out. That bunch aren't going to go away, you can see that. They've been hanging about ever since Mr Tregarvon and Mr Winkworthe came home two hours ago, and it's freezing cold out there, so they're determined to get something by way of a story.'

Erica had no intention of going out at present. She wanted to stay near her mother for the rest of the day in case any new shocks were awaiting them. But by the time her father returned in the evening to fight his way indoors through the gang of watchers, she was dying to get away. She had the feeling she was stifling in the goldfish-bowl atmosphere of the house.

Gerald had rung earlier to ask if what he saw in the evening papers were true.

'That the charges have been made?' she answered. 'Yes, that's true enough. But of course there's nothing in them. You know my father well enough to understand he could never have been involved in a fraud.'

'Of course. It's a bit of a stagger, though, to see a thing like that in a headline.'

'Can you come this evening, Gerald? I'm longing to see you.'

'To the house, you mean?' There was doubt in his tone.

'Oh, I see what you mean, the reporters are still laying siege to us. And anyway,' she added, her brain moving to quick conclusions, 'we couldn't really discuss things in front of Mother.'

'She's taking it badly, I imagine.'

'Well, funnily enough, not. She just doesn't believe any of it.'

Gerald laughed. 'Good for her! Trouble is, old girl . . . others do seem to believe it.'

'That's just people who don't know Father,' Erica said with complete conviction. 'And anyhow, once these men from Australia are properly questioned they'll withdraw what they said and it will all be cleared up.'

'You think so?'

There were sounds from upstairs that meant her mother had awakened and was on her way down. 'Must ring off,' Erica said in haste. 'I'll tell you what, Gerald. Let's meet somewhere – at your place, for instance.'

This was considered not quite proper, even for an engaged couple. Gerald lived in an elegant but tiny service flat off Pall Mall. He said, 'I don't think that would be right, old thing. In any case, I thought you said the reporters were surrounding your house?'

'Yes, but I could slip out the side door. I could easily—'

'Let's have a drink somewhere quiet, that would be best, wouldn't it? Somewhere where no one would know us.'

'All right, where?'

He considered a moment. 'How about the Comedy Tavern? It's just at the back of—'

'A pub?' Young ladies of good repute did not go into pubs.

'Oh, it's not a spit and sawdust place. Theatre people use it a lot – you see the likes of Edna Best or Cicely Courtneidge.'

'All right, I'll meet you there, let's say nine-thirty?'

So after dinner, when her parents had settled down hand in hand on the sofa in the drawing room, she made her secretive way out of the side door into the mews, hailed a taxi, and was borne off to the Comedy Tavern.

The place was in fact rather attractive, with old theatre bills all over the walls and signed photographs of the famous. Gerald was already there, at a table in a quiet alcove. He rose as she joined him, and asked what she would like to drink.

'Oh, I don't know,' she said, wondering what you ordered in a pub. 'Would they have a glass of wine?'

'Port or sherry?'

'I meant table wine, something light.'

'No, 'fraid not.'

'All right then, I'll have sherry.'

When he had brought it and settled on his chair again, he said, 'It just struck me – aren't you having the Pierces to dinner this evening?'

'They cancelled.'

'Oh.'

'I think it's going to happen a lot,' she said. She twirled the sherry glass between nervous fingers. 'I'd no idea what it was like to be on the wrong side of the gossip column, until now.'

She waited for him to say, 'They'll soon see how wrong they were.' Instead Gerald looked unhappy and fidgeted with the knot of his tie. 'Fellows in the office were saying, when they saw the afternoon editions . . . It doesn't look good.'

'Of course it doesn't look good! All people see is the headlines: fraud, misrepresentation under the Freight Carriage Act, and then worst of all, the manslaughter charge. But what they don't understand is that the fraud charge is a parcel of nonsense and once Father has disproved that, the other charges just fall away.'

'He can disprove the first charge?' Gerald countered. 'I mean, Erica, the Fraud Squad don't take a case to court unless they're pretty sure.'

Erica stared at him. All at once his bony, high-bred face seemed less dear to her. 'What is this?' she demanded. 'You're not saying you *believe* any of that?'

'All I'm trying to say is you shouldn't think it can all be waved away as if it were a mistake, Erica.'

'But it *is* a mistake.'

'How can it be? Two ships went down, the cargo from one of them seems to have been found safe and sound, five men died on the other and the survivors were heard saying something about conspiracy—'

'I *know* all that! I know it better than you do, Gerald! What I'm saying is that my father had nothing to do with it.'

'Of course, darling.' His glance warned her to lower her voice. 'I'm only saying how it looks to others. And the chaps were saying this afternoon . . . you know . . . *cui bono*?'

'What does that mean?'

'Who benefits?' He shrugged. '*Something's* been fiddled and you can't blame people for seeing that it's your father whose bank balance has benefited.'

'Don't be absurd! Father isn't short of money.'

'He did say your London season was costing him more than he could afford.'

'That was a *joke*, Gerald! You do understand about jokes?'

'Oh, come on, old thing, don't lose your rag.'

A bubble of near-hysterical laughter rose in her. 'Is this the language of diplomacy?' she inquired. ' "Don't lose your rag, old thing"?'

He looked vexed. 'If you're going to pounce on every word I utter . . .'

'I'm sorry, I apologize. But I was hoping . . .'

'What?'

That you would comfort me, that you would tell me not to worry because you believed in my father. This was what she wanted to say. But she wouldn't plead for his sympathy. If he couldn't see without prompting that she was deeply in need of his help, what was the point? It meant they had less in common than she'd thought, and perhaps now was the time when it must be put to the test.

'I just can't understand why anyone – the men in your office, the writers in the press – seem to jump to the conclusion that Father would do something wrong just to make money! And don't they realize that by thinking of him like that, they're making it seem as if he's responsible for the death of those five men?'

'It's pretty awful,' muttered Gerald.

'Father was an ordinary seaman himself in the War. He'd never do anything to endanger crewmen.'

'I don't suppose many people remember that about him. They think of him as a shipping tycoon. And of course they think—' He broke off.

'What? What do they think?'

'Well, I dare say they think that a man doesn't make the kind of money your father's made without being pretty ruthless.'

'Ruthless?' she echoed, shocked.

'Well, I mean . . . In the past, perhaps. You probably haven't heard them, but when it's men only with the port after dinner, he tells some hair-raising stories.' He fell silent, aware he'd blundered into something that he should have left alone.

After a moment Erica said in a weary voice, 'You think he did it.'

'I never said that!'

'Not in so many words. But you've heard him tell tall tales after dinner so you think he could plot to deceive the insurance company and send innocent men to their death.'

'I don't think that!'

'You think he's innocent?'

'Of course I do.'

'And when any junior assistant secretary in your department says cruel things about him, you'll leap to his defence?'

'Yes, I will.'

'Did you, this afternoon? When someone said there'd been a swindle and only my father had benefited, did you stand up and say, "Lindon Tregarvon isn't like that"?'

'Oh, come on, Erica, you don't expect me to go round making speeches in his defence?'

She waited a moment. Then she said, 'If we were already man and wife, you'd have to speak up in his defence, wouldn't you? You couldn't let people say things about your wife's father.'

She saw the flicker in his brown eyes and knew he'd become aware of the pit yawning before him. If he married Erica Tregarvon now – whether or not her father was innocent – gossips were always going to say, 'His wife is Tregarvon's daughter – you remember, the man involved in that fraud case.'

44

'I don't know why you're going on about this,' he said, retreating into irritation. 'I've already said I think he's innocent and if anybody gets a bit out of hand when they talk about it, I'll choke them off. But I think you've got to accept that a fraud case can take a long time to come to court and once there the trial might drag on for weeks. You can't expect me to row with all my friends for the rest of the year. Be reasonable.'

'Oh, heaven forbid that I should make things difficult between you and your friends.'

'There you go again, getting on your high horse—'

'Silly of me, isn't it? I actually thought my fiancé would put me before anyone else.'

'Good God, what more do you want? I'm here with you now, aren't I?'

'Oh yes. In a nice quiet pub where nobody will recognize us. Wouldn't do to be seen out with the swindler's daughter, would it?'

'Well, sneer if you like, but not many fellows would want to be associated—'

'Please,' she said, holding up a hand. 'Don't let me be an embarrassment to you. After all, we're only *engaged*, aren't we? Nothing final about that. We can easily break it off if you think that's best.'

She watched him, and he went slowly red. He was longing to say, 'Yes, let's break it off,' but couldn't quite bring himself to utter the words.

She took the diamond off her left hand. She laid it gently in front of him on the table. 'Free,' she said. 'It's best, isn't it? You realize now that I'm not such a catch after all, and

I've discovered that I don't really like you much.'

'Now wait a minute, Erica—'

She was already rising to leave. 'It's all right,' she said, 'if you decide later on that you wish we still were engaged you can come to see me in a day or two and try to persuade me to take it back.'

But she knew he wouldn't.

On giving the taxi her address, she forgot to warn the driver to stop at the mews so that she could take the side entrance. The result was that the taxi pulled up at the gates in Park Lane and the waiting reporters saw her face before she could tell the man to drive on.

There was nothing for it but to get out and push her way to the door. But she'd made a big mistake because they worked out at once that she must have gone out through a side door. From now on they would stand guard over that way of escape too.

Her mother had gone to bed. Her father was in his study but came out as she made her way to the staircase. 'Well, lovey, did you have a nice chat with Gerald?'

'Very entertaining, yes.'

Self-absorbed, he missed the irony in her tone. 'Good, that's good. I've just been looking through my diaries. You know, when the insurance policies for the *Ganymede* were signed, it seems we were in the Bahamas. Remember?'

She tried to look back beyond the year of her debut, which now seemed like a foreign country, totally different from life as she was living it now. 'That would be . . . April of 1930?'

He nodded, studying the page of the day-book open in his

hand. 'April 22nd, it says here, "Policies signed and despatched with cheque". Perfectly normal. In fact, I don't remember anything about it.'

'Have you asked Timothy?'

'Of course! He and I have been over and over it, back and forth. We can't remember anything out of the ordinary. It's a company we often use, they've got insurance on four other ships.' He summoned a grim smile. 'Of course they're now challenging us about those, sending agents out to check that they're all right. I tell you, Erica, once people begin to think the worst of you, they get enthusiastic about it.'

'It's all nonsense,' she said, and reached up to kiss him. 'You'll see, when those crewmen get to London and are questioned, it'll turn out they cooked it up themselves.'

'Ye-es,' he agreed, patting her shoulder as she moved away, 'but you see . . . there's the other ship. That would mean two sets of ships' crews in my shipping line had the same idea independently. The police just find that hard to believe.'

She was too tired to be able to reason it out. 'Forget about it, Father,' she urged. 'Get a good night's sleep.'

'Yes, I must, I'm meeting Speldon Banks tomorrow, I must be in a state to talk sense to him. Goodnight, sweetie.' He paused and frowned. 'I'm so sorry, Erica. It's spoiled things for you, hasn't it, after that lovely season you had and being such a success.'

'Never mind about that. Goodnight, Father.'

'Goodnight.'

She was so exhausted that she fell into a deep sleep at

once. But at about three in the morning she was awake. Some slight sound had roused her.

After lying for a few minutes telling herself she'd imagined it, she heard it again. Someone was on the stairs.

She got out of bed, pulled on a dressing-gown, and hurried out to the landing. Her mother was creeping down towards the hall.

'Mother!'

Amy started, turned her head, then put her finger to her lips. 'Ssh,' she said, 'we mustn't wake your father.'

'What are you doing?' whispered Erica, joining her on the staircase.

'I can't sleep. I was just tossing and turning, and it was sure to wake Father. So I thought I'd come downstairs and play a game or two of patience.'

'Oh.' Erica put her arm around her and together they went down to the drawing room. There the fire was out but she switched on an electric heater and some shaded lights. 'What you need is some hot milk,' she said.

'Oh, Maitland made me drink some at bedtime! I do hate it, you only get it when something's wrong!'

'Well, then, some tea—'

'Don't ring!' her mother cried. 'The household's in enough uproar without getting the servants out of bed in the middle of the night—'

'But Mother . . .'

'Just leave me alone for a nice little game of patience.'

'Don't be silly, I'm not leaving you down here alone.' She could see there was nothing for it but to fall in with her mother's wishes. Cards had been their refuge many a time when her mother's asthma had made her unwell. 'All right, let's play a hand or two of solo whist.'

'No, no, you go back to bed.'

'We'll just use the folding table.' She installed her mother in a corner of the sofa, brought the little table, took the cards out of the bureau drawer, then set herself down opposite.

They cut for dealer. Her mother won. Erica smiled to herself at the eagerness with which she took on the deal – Amy loved the feel of the cards flicking expertly from her slender fingers. 'What goal are we playing for? Misere?' she asked as the deal ended.

'Whatever you like.'

'All right, let's make it misere, you're the caller.'

'All right.'

They played in companionable silence. Erica could see that her mother's whole attention was taken up with the game. Whatever it was that had kept her awake, she was able to forget it while she concentrated on the cards.

Erica wished she could follow that example but she had always been able to play cards and think of other things as well. Her mind seemed automatically to register what was going on, her memory to store which cards had been played and which were still to come. An American they'd met on one of the liners had said to Erica, 'You ought to take up poker, you've got the brains for it.' But she'd never wanted to play cards for the kind of money poker involved. To her bridge, her favourite card game, was an intellectual exercise, a matter of strategy and tactics, nothing really to do with the small sums in the wagers.

By and by her mother's attention began to waver, her head began to droop. 'I think . . . perhaps I'll just close my eyes a minute, dear . . .'

Erica eased her back among the sofa cushions, fetched an afghan from the hall cupboard, tucked it in around her. She debated whether to go upstairs to her own bed but then thought of the alarm her mother might feel if she woke to find herself alone in the drawing room. So instead she fetched another rug from the hall, wrapped herself in it, and curled up in the big armchair. And that was how the housemaid found them at six when she came in to clean the grate.

Soon after, Lindon hurried in, scared out of his wits at having found his wife gone from his side so early in the morning. Erica tried to silence his outburst but Amy was roused at his voice. 'Lindon? What's the matter?' she asked drowsily.

'That's what *I'm* asking! What are you doing down here at this hour?'

'What? I don't . . . Oh . . .' She was distressed and becoming tearful at the bother she was causing.

'Ssh,' said Erica, 'it's all right. Come along, come upstairs, you can have your morning tea as usual and everything will be back to normal.'

'Normal?' sighed her father. 'What's normal in this house at the moment?'

Amy went back to bed, to fall asleep again before the startled Maitland could bring the morning tea. Lindon took advantage of having got up so early to wash and dress and get out of the house before the reporters reappeared.

Thus the day started in a muddle and got worse as it went

on. The telephone rang ceaselessly. The reporters invaded the garden, peered through the ground-floor windows, kept ringing the doorbell.

And so it went on every day thereafter. The Tregarvons developed defensive measures against the onslaught but it wore them down. Erica saw her father becoming gaunt, her mother nervy and timid, the servants wary.

The discussions about the case with Speldon Banks seemed to be going badly; he was calling for all sorts of personal documents and records to build up a defence. Erica spent a lot of time in her father's study sorting out papers, sighing over the fact that their easy-going, vagabond life aboard ship was now causing so much trouble. It had been Lindon Tregarvon's way: he would do business from the stateroom of one of his liners, or from the saloon of his yacht in Nassau, or from a hotel in Florida. His secretary Timothy Perriman was always with them to keep record, to take notes, to send telegrams and wireless cables; it was an unusual business system but for Lindon it had always worked well. Until now.

Towards the end of January came the men from Darwin whose evidence had caused the police to act in the first place. Contrary to Erica's expectation, it appeared that they stuck to their story. The case against her father was not withdrawn. He was to appear before the magistrate on February 4th to hear the final charge. His counsel would answer on his behalf and ask for an early trial date so as to put an end to the harm being done to the Tregarvon Shipping Company by the doubt and uncertainty.

'But I thought it would be all sorted out?' Amy protested

in bewilderment to Erica. 'I thought you said it was all a mistake?'

'So it is, and it will be sorted out,' she soothed. 'Only it's going to take a bit longer than we thought.'

'But that man . . . the special lawyer . . .'

'Mr Banks.'

'Yes, he seems to think we'll all have to go to the Law Courts?'

'We don't know yet. He says he may want to call us.'

'Me?' gasped Amy. 'Say things in court? Before a lot of strangers?'

'Never mind, Mother. Mr Banks said he was still thinking about how to present the defence.'

On February 2nd, Lindon went out in the evening to have a long discussion with Timothy. Both men had been racking their brains to think what had happened to the documentation about the insurance, which was incomplete. After waiting up till midnight, Erica went to bed weary and depressed, without seeing her father to say goodnight.

Next morning she was roused by a tap on her door at seven. She sat up in bed, expecting the parlour maid. Instead Hurrock came in.

'Miss Tregarvon, I feel I ought to tell you. I went as usual a moment ago to Mr Tregarvon's dressing room to take his early tea, but Mr Tregarvon wasn't there.'

'He was very late home last night, he's probably not awake yet.'

'No, miss, I peeped in through the connecting door, he's not in the bedroom and in fact, Miss Tregarvon, he doesn't appear to have come home last night.'

She rubbed the sleep out of her eyes. 'Hand me my dressing-gown, Hurrock, then wait outside.'

'Yes, miss.'

She joined him in the corridor a moment later. 'You're sure he didn't come home?'

'Well, his hat and coat aren't in the hall.'

'He must have stayed overnight at the office.' This sometimes happened when there was a crisis in the shipping world.

She went down to the study, dialled the office number. There was always someone on duty there because shipping must be continually supervised. The night clerk answered the phone.

'Baillie? This is Miss Tregarvon.'

'Yes, miss, I recognized your voice.'

'Is my father there, please?'

'Here? No, Miss Tregarvon, there's only myself and the cleaners.'

'He's not there?'

'No, Miss Tregarvon.'

'Was he still there when you came on duty last night?'

'No, miss, only the switchboard girl and the day clerk.'

'Thank you, Baillie.'

Where could he have gone? He must be with Timothy. They must have gone home together after their long session yesterday evening. She dialled Timothy's number. The phone was picked up almost immediately.

'Timothy, is my father with you?'

'With me?' The surprise was clear in his voice. 'Certainly not, Miss Tregarvon.'

'He didn't go home with you after your evening together?'

'I beg your pardon?'

'You and Father – you were to spend the evening going over business records for the year before last.'

'What makes you think that?'

'But my father said . . . He went out after dinner last night to make a special search in the office.'

'Not with me, Miss Tregarvon.' Timothy's voice began to take on a tinge of alarm. 'What are you saying? That he's not at home with you now?'

'No, and as far as we can gather he didn't come home last night. I thought you might have offered him a bed for the night.'

'Oh, well, that would hardly be logical, would it? He lives closer to the office than I do. No, he's not here and we certainly had no appointment for last night.'

'What?'

'He said we had?'

'Yes, last night as he went out . . .'

Perriman didn't say anything.

'Timothy?'

'I'm thinking. Of course. He must be at his club.'

'Of *course*!' She almost gasped in relief.

But Lindon Tregarvon was not at his club. He was not at any of the places where Erica tried to find him. He did not reappear that day, nor the next.

The next day was February 4th, the day on which he was due to appear at the magistrate's court. Mr Winkworthe and Mr Banks arrived fifteen minutes before the appointed time, still hoping that Tregarvon might join them there. When his name was called, they went into the court.

The magistrate asked where their client was. They could only say they hoped he would come any moment. The court waited.

At ten-thirty it became clear that Lindon Tregarvon had skipped bail.

Chapter Three

For a few days more, Erica and her mother refused to believe it.

'He's had an accident!' wailed Amy. 'He's in a hospital somewhere, unconscious!'

But the police were looking for Lindon Tregarvon, a wanted man. They checked all the hospitals, checked all the accident reports, looked in all the places to which a man who had lost his memory might turn – Salvation Army hostels, cheap hotels.

The reporters searched. They had slacked off in their watch around the house as the day of the court appearance drew near, hoping for a gem or two on that occasion. So when Tregarvon went out on the evening of February 2nd, there had been no one to challenge him, no one to think of following him. So now the reporters searched, because now it was a *big* story.

Nothing.

'I'm afraid he's slipped off abroad, madam,' said Chief Inspector Griffiths, with something like pity in his broad face.

'He wouldn't! Not without telling me!'

He hesitated. 'Has he in fact been in touch, Mrs Tregarvon? Because if he has, it would be much better if—'

'He hasn't been in touch,' Erica intervened. 'We have no idea where he is.'

'Any friends he might have turned to?'

She gave him a bitter smile. 'At present the Tregarvons don't seem to have any friends.'

'Hm. Friends from the old days? He was an ordinary seaman himself, wasn't he? Anybody from that time?'

'Mother?' Amy shook her head helplessly. 'If he kept up with any of them, we didn't know of it,' Erica said.

'You see,' said the Chief Inspector, more to himself than to the women, 'a man like that . . . He could easily get himself a set of seaman's papers, get aboard a freighter . . .'

'But he wouldn't,' Amy insisted through her tears. 'Why should he?'

The answer was so obvious that no one felt like pointing it out to her. Lindon Tregarvon had gone on the run because he knew that if he went to trial, he would be found guilty and sent to prison.

The police view, after a few weeks, was that their man had got himself to Ireland and from there probably to the US.

'Do you know if he has funds abroad, Mrs Tregarvon?'

'Funds? I . . . I don't know anything about money. You'd have to ask Timothy.'

Timothy Perriman took the detectives through the books at the office. His long slender hands turned pages, his finger pointed. Erica watched him with admiration. He knew all there was to know about the financial situation, probably had it filed away in that narrow head of his.

'There are funds, as you see,' he murmured, 'but they could only be touched by using the firm's chequebook and

58

countersigned by our Chief Cashier. As to Mr Tregarvon's personal accounts . . .'

'We've checked with the bank. He hasn't made any large withdrawals.'

'In that case,' Timothy said with a lift of the shoulders, 'I can't be of any help to you.'

When the detectives had gone, Erica said, 'They think he put money aside somehow – in advance.'

'That's only supposition.'

'Do *you* think he's guilty of that shipping fraud, Timothy?'

'Of course not. Your father isn't a greedy man, Miss Tregarvon. There was no reason for him to plan a thing like that, just for the money.'

'The police think that a man who's made a lot of money wouldn't be too scrupulous about making a lot more.'

Timothy sighed. They were in Lindon Tregarvon's office in Bishopsgate, comfortable amidst the mahogany and rich Chinese wallpaper while a relentless February rain streamed across the windows.

'The trouble is,' he said, 'the police talk about his funds as if they were inexhaustible, but the way things are going . . .'

'The company's not in trouble?' Erica asked, startled.

'Not as yet.' He rose from Tregarvon's chair, to pace on his long thin legs across to the window and back. 'But of course people to whom Tregarvon Shipping owes money are beginning to demand payment. And I hear the insurance company is going to demand repayment for money it paid out for the loss of the two ships. And that will be a really severe drain on our reserves.'

'But everything will be all right? The company isn't in danger?'

He had his back to her. He said without turning, 'So far.'

'Timothy!'

After a moment he came to stare down at her. 'It's going to be difficult,' he said. There was anxiety in the downturn of his narrow lips, in the expression in the light grey eyes. 'I think you ought to prepare yourself for a rough time.'

'A rough time! What do you think this is now?'

He took her hand. 'It could get worse, Miss Tregarvon. I should move down to the country for a bit. You don't want to be where angry creditors can get at you.'

Erica was stricken at his words. She stood silent. He held her hand still.

'I'm thinking of your mother,' he said. 'Poor lady, she's not equipped to handle people such as bailiffs—'

'Bailiffs!'

'Let's hope it won't come to that. But I do really think you'd be wise to leave London. I'm sure the police would have no objections.'

'You make it sound so . . . I didn't think there was any possibility—'

'Even the greatest business can tremble,' he said in his cool voice. 'The management is doing all it can to keep an even keel but you must realize that your father was "the captain of the ship". There's a lot we're not able to deal with in his absence because we don't know exactly what his plans were. But we're doing all we can.' He pressed her hand. 'Try not to worry, Miss Tregarvon. Concentrate on looking after your mother.'

Erica needed no prompting on that score. Amy was in a state of collapse. Thankfully she accepted the suggestion that they should go down to the country house, and when later it was suggested that they sell the Park Lane home, she agreed without a tremor.

Tregarvon had bought the country house to give his daughter a base from which to meet the country set during her debut season. As yet they had made only acquaintances, no friends. But that suited Amy and Erica Tregarvon quite well. They didn't want visitors, awkwardly staying for the required twenty minutes and making stilted conversation. What was there to talk about, except the crime of Lindon Tregarvon?

Winkworthe visited from time to time, to keep them up to date with the legal situation. The police were still looking for Tregarvon, the case against him gaining in weight by his flight. But as weeks turned into months it became clear he was not going to be found.

'There are no more delaying tactics,' Winkworthe said with a shake of his grey head. 'The bail is forfeited. Because it was such a very large sum, the court was willing to wait but now the police authorities report that they have no more avenues to pursue. Your father has made a very good job of his disappearance, I'm afraid. He seems to have gone abroad. South America, perhaps . . .'

'He wouldn't,' moaned Amy. 'He wouldn't do that to me.'

'But he has, Mother,' Erica said, for once giving in to impatience. 'He's gone and he's left us to face the mess—'

'The court case, of course, has been abandoned for the present,' Winkworthe said, anxious to put as good a face on it as possible. 'The absence of Mr Tregarvon makes a trial impossible, and now the other men have withdrawn their statements. However, the insurance company has been before Mr Justice Jerdon in chambers and has been given the right of restitution. So there goes another very large sum . . .' He sighed. 'Money is just leaking away. Every creditor is pressing his claim. I'm afraid . . . I'm seriously afraid . . .'

'What?' Erica asked, frightened by his grave expression.

'I'm afraid you may be in difficulties over money before too long. And as it happens . . .'

She felt another surge of the angry impatience that so often seemed to seize her these days. Why couldn't he just come out with what he wanted to say, instead of all this head-shaking and hesitation?

But then she checked herself. Of course he didn't want to say things that would upset her mother. Amy was sitting with her head bent, her eyes fixed on her clasped hands. If she could, she would have put her hands over her ears rather than hear anything against Lindon.

'Mother, why don't you go and ask Maitland to make us some tea?'

Amy jumped up. Anything rather than sit here listening to unkind things about her husband.

When she'd gone, Winkworthe smiled at Erica. 'You take good care of her,' he said. 'I'm glad she doesn't have to face this alone.'

'What is this new thing we're going to have to face?' she replied, bracing herself for the words.

'We've had an offer to buy the shipping line—'

'Good God! Sell? That's ridiculous—'

'No, it is not, Erica. Money is going out faster than it's coming in and public confidence in the company has been so badly shaken that the banks won't extend any more credit. Your father was planning to buy two new ships; that order has of course been cancelled but there were penalty clauses which must be met over the cancellation. All the forward planning of the routes costs money; that is gone, utterly lost to us. At the present time, Tregarvon Shipping is only just staying afloat, but even so the ships are left at anchor, it seems to be impossible to get cargoes, and as for the passenger lines . . .'

Erica tried to envisage it. The ships she knew so well, tied up at the quay, empty, unused. It seemed impossible when she remembered the bustle and hurry she'd so often witnessed when they docked: quick, quick, cargo must be unloaded, passengers disembarked, so that the ship could sail with the next tide.

'Are you saying that we're facing bankruptcy?' she said at last.

'Not quite, but in a short time. But now, you see, there is this offer for the line—'

'A vulture sweeping down to feed on the corpse,' she suggested bitterly.

'It may seem harsh to you, but there's no sentiment in business, Erica. The Swiftway Line are making a fair offer. I would strongly advise you to get your mother to agree to it.'

'What does Timothy say?'

'It was Timothy who brought the offer to my attention. He has been working extremely hard, Erica. His loyalty is really remarkable, because I know for a fact that he's had at least one offer of a post in Hamburg which would have been very greatly to his advantage.'

'Oh! I never thought of that!'

'That Timothy's job with the Tregarvon Line has no future? Well, that's the fact, isn't it? He was your father's personal assistant. He can only remain where he is until someone else takes over and I really expected him to take up one of the offers that have come his way.'

'But he didn't. That's very good of him.'

'Indeed. Moreover he's taken pains to help keep things going, and made this contact with Swiftways, which will prevent a complete collapse. You will make your mother see that it's for the best, won't you?'

'Oh, she'll sign anything Timothy and I recommend.'

In this she was wrong. Amy Tregarvon had no head for business and very little trust in her own judgement, but she was certain her husband would never have sold his shipping line. She therefore took a stand.

'No, no, it can't be right. Your father would never hear of such a thing—'

'But Mother, he's not here—'

'Don't you think I know that?' Amy murmured through her tears. 'Every morning when I wake up I try to come to terms with the idea that I shan't see him today. I simply can't get used to it. I keep thinking I'll hear him whistling to himself in the next room, see him put his head round the door to say he's off to London . . .'

'Mother, dear, don't think about things like that. He's not here, and he's not going to be here so long as that court case is waiting to be tried—'

'But when they cancel all that, he'll be back. We can't sell the company!'

'The charge against him will always stand, Mother. He's never coming back.'

'Then we'll go to him! He'll get word to us and we'll—'

'You'd do that? Go and live a hole-and-corner existence abroad?' Erica was shocked.

'Oh, we met lots of people like that on our travels. There's nothing unusual about it: people who get sent abroad because of trouble at home. Remittance men, they call them, mostly,' Amy said, blowing her nose and sitting up a little straighter. 'You can live on quite a small allowance abroad, you know. So we must hold on to the shipping line so that we have something to live on when your father gets in touch—'

'But we can't hang on to it, Mother. It's losing money all the time, and very soon there won't be enough to pay the harbour and dock charges—'

'Don't be silly. People always need ships to take things to other countries and to get there themselves. A shipping company is always going to make money.'

'No, Mother, it's not so.'

But Amy was convinced she knew best. All her married life she'd travelled on ships with her husband, so to her they seemed a world of permanence and security. Nothing could happen to the shipping company; it had grown and prospered for twenty-five years, it must naturally go on doing so.

The year turned to autumn and then winter. Amy held fast to her refusal to sell. As 1933 dawned, the creditors of the Tregarvon Shipping Company made an application as a result of which the company was declared insolvent. Trustees were appointed under a committee of inspection to see what could be done to pay at least a percentage of the debts.

'I don't understand,' Amy said in bewilderment. 'How can they take the company away from us? It belongs to us!'

'I'm afraid not, dear lady,' Winkworthe said. 'It belonged to your husband and must now be sold to pay his debts. And so must this house, I fear.'

'The house? They can't sell my house!'

Patiently the lawyer and Erica explained over and over again that the courts had taken over, that the bailiffs would carry away everything in the house except their personal possessions, that it would all have to be sold because Lindon Tregarvon had jumped bail and left his business to founder.

'But where are we going to live?' Amy demanded. She had never really liked the country house, but over the months it had been her shelter. She couldn't imagine life without it.

'We'll go to a hotel.'

'Of course, a hotel, until everything is properly sorted out! We could go to Claridges, I always liked Claridges.'

But Erica had a better grasp of their financial situation. She chose an out-of-season seaside resort where she took rooms for them at the Wessex.

They weren't entirely destitute. Among their 'personal possessions' was a fair amount of jewellery. With Mr Winkworthe's help, Erica sold a pearl necklace given to her on her coming-out. With this money they had enough to live on for a few months. But it meant parting with the faithful Maitland, whose wages they could no longer afford.

'It's a sin and a shame,' sniffed Maitland as she finished packing for Amy for the last time. 'You're no more fit to cope with this hard world than a sparrow that's fallen from its nest. Mrs Tregarvon dear, I wish you all the very best, despite what your husband has done, and if ever you should want a personal maid in the future, you've only got to drop me a line and I'll leave whatever household I'm in, because I'd rather be with you than any other mistress I could imagine.'

'Thank you, Maitland,' Amy said, in tears herself at the parting, although she had never thought of her maid as a personal friend. 'Of course once all this terrible mix-up is sorted out, I shall want you back.'

'Yes, ma'am,' agreed Maitland, but her eyes met Erica's over the cabin trunk she was fastening, and they both knew it would never happen.

The Wessex in Chobsea was old-fashioned, quiet, and almost empty in the grey of February. There were one or two permanent guests who perked up at the arrival of two newcomers, the more so when they identified them as the wife and daughter of a criminal.

'I don't hold it against you for a minute,' Colonel Price said to Erica. 'You're not responsible for the sins of your father, that's what I say.'

'Thank you,' Erica replied, stifling the hope that he would be immediately seized with some plague which might silence his tactless tongue. She got her revenge at the bridge table, where almost every time they sat down to play she and her mother trounced the opposition.

She set about looking for a job. But the reverberations of the 1929 Wall Street Crash still rumbled on in a worldwide recession. Any jobs had to be offered first to the men and then, after that, women might try their luck. Erica had no luck at all. She was trained for nothing except the life of a lady. She could plan menus, arrange flowers, inspect table settings, write invitations, play good tennis and excellent bridge. These talents were not at all in demand.

'What I think you'd best do, miss,' suggested the proprietor of an employment agency, 'is get some training. If you could do shorthand and typing, for instance? Or perhaps you could train to be a nurse.'

'How long would that take?'

'Oh, to learn shorthand and typing . . . six months? Nurse training is three years residential, of course. But you could take a short course in nursery-nursing. That would mean living-in when you got a post.'

Nursing seemed out of the question. She couldn't leave her mother while she trained at a hospital, nor could she take a live-in post. Shorthand and typing seemed to be the answer. There was only one school of business studies in Chobsea, and from what Erica could make out from its dusty premises in a back street, it was not at all impressive.

'You might get a job here in Chobsea after you've trained,' she was told, 'but really all the best posts are in the big cities, like Southampton or Dover.'

As it was halfway through the term, she deferred a decision for the moment. She read the job advertisements assiduously, looking for something, anything, that might bring in some sort of an income. She'd realized she did have abilities after all: she could speak good French and Spanish, and might be able to find work translating.

But there was no one in Chobsea needing a translator. Once again, the employment chances lay in the ports. To get a job it looked as if they would have to move to Dover or Southampton, or back to London.

In any case, they must move soon. As the summer holiday season approached, the manager of the Wessex was hinting more and more strongly that they must either pay high-season rates or leave the hotel. So far Erica hadn't mentioned this problem to her mother who, always adept socially, was building up a friendship with the other guests and would be loath to leave them.

A parcel arrived. It came from Mr Winkworthe's office but, when opened with some trepidation by Amy, proved only to have been forwarded by him. The original sender was Gaynor Medcalfe of Nassau in the Bahamas.

'Dear Mrs Tregarvon,' he wrote, 'I dare say you remember me? Your husband and I raced against each other in the Inter-Club Round-Tour Pairs a year or two ago – he sent me a bottle of champagne when I beat him. I was sure happy to buy his yacht the *Margravine* from the receivers, though not of course about the reasons for her sale. She's a lovely boat, very comfortable of course you'll recall, and I'll take good care of her, I promise. Thought you'd like these few personal effects I found in a drawer in the stateroom when I took over as skipper. Best wishes from a fellow yachtsman, Buddy Medcalfe.'

'Oh,' gasped Amy, 'I thought it would have dreadful official documents and things in it . . . Oh, look – oh, Erica! Look!'

In the cardboard box were a set of hairbrushes backed with tortoiseshell, a folding silver photo frame with family photos, and a small silver cup engraved: 'Winner, New Providence

69

Invitation, 1929, Lindon Tregarvon.'

Naturally Amy dissolved at once into tears. Erica was hard put to hold back her own. These mementoes of happier times seemed to make their present circumstances so grey, so sunless.

She comforted her mother as best she could. 'Look, your wedding photograph, how nice the fashions were then . . .'

'Oh yes, that very slender look . . . Luckily I had the figure for it then. And your father . . . what a handsome man . . . And the only picture I had of Neville . . . Three years old when he died, poor little scrap . . .'

Erica looked at the once-familiar photographs, which had always stood on the shelf that served as desk by her father's chair in the yacht's saloon. In the centre of a triple folding frame of embossed silver were the smiling faces of the newly-weds, arm in arm outside St George's, Hanover Square; the tiny baby almost lost in his nest of lace-edged pillows and herself at about four in a sailor blouse and dark skirt were on either side.

'Poor little Neville,' wept Amy. 'We daren't have the usual photo on a sheepskin rug, he was too delicate to risk it. That's why I never wanted to be parted from you, darling, I wanted you near me all the time so that nothing could ever happen to you . . .' At this point, overcome by the thoughts of what had actually happened to her one remaining child, Amy threw herself on the bed and gave herself up to her sobs.

About half an hour later, when Erica had managed to dry the tears and still the grief, she began to talk about the future. This was a good opportunity; after one such outburst her mother was likely to be calm in the face of other blows.

'We'll have to be leaving the Wessex soon,' she observed.
'The rates go up at the beginning of July—'

'Do they? But why?'

'Because the holiday season starts then and Mr Abbot
needs our rooms to let to holidaymakers.'

'But if we pay what the holiday people would pay, then
surely—'

'We couldn't afford it, Mother. It's more than—'

'But Colonel Price? And Miss Rand? Are they leaving?'

'No, but Colonel Price has money besides his army
pension, and I gather Miss Rand has some very good
investments. So they can pay the extra, you see, and besides
there's a special rate if you make an agreement to stay for
two years.'

'Then couldn't we do that? Get a special rate?' Amy was
very unwilling to move. The last year had seemed restless
and frightening, but at least at the Wessex she'd started to
put down new roots.

'It's too late in the season now,' Erica explained. 'Mr
Abbot's allotted our rooms to people who've made bookings
for their summer holidays. In any case, Mother, we'd want to
move soon.'

'Would we?' Her mother's surprise was plain. Here they
were in shelter, in a hotel environment which agreed with
her. Why must they leave?

'I'm trying to get a job, you see, Mother. I think I'll have
to get some training.'

'Training? In what?'

'Well, I thought shorthand and typing. But to get that I'd
have to be in a bigger town than Chobsea, and besides I need

71

to earn some money to pay for the classes and the best chance seems to be translating, and there's no call for that here. But in Southampton perhaps . . .'

'Move to Southampton?'

'Or some other big town. Perhaps it would be better to go back to London.'

Her mother sighed. 'London in June . . . All the balls and parties . . . Trooping the Colour . . .'

'We wouldn't be involved in any of that, Mother,' Erica said, more curtly than she intended. 'We'd have to find a room somewhere cheap.'

'A hotel room, of course.'

'No, just a room, Mother. We'd have to do our own cooking and cleaning.'

'What?'

'Other people do, you know! They wash their own dishes and make their own scrambled eggs.'

'Of course I know that, dear. I know other people take an interest in cooking. There are articles in the newspapers about cooking, and dressmaking, and things like that. But . . . the fact is . . .' She broke off, her tear-stained features creasing in a frown. 'How exactly do you scramble an egg, Erica?'

Divided between laughter and tears, Erica threw her arms around her mother. 'Never mind, we'll learn!' she cried.

The main thing was, the idea had been put before her. In a day or two she would become accustomed to it, so that Erica could discuss it and urge her towards a decision. By the end of June they must vacate their hotel rooms, so Erica at once began to study the London newspapers for cheap accommodation, in preparation for the move.

But accommodation that they could afford, in a respectable area of London, wasn't so easy to find. Gradually Erica gave up the districts she already knew – Chelsea, Wimbledon, Hampstead – and began to think about such places as Walworth. Walworth – where on earth was Walworth? Or Stepney?

She was in the writing room of the Wessex, concocting a letter to an estate agent in Battersea who had a cheap one-bedroom flat to let, when the maid came in. 'A gentleman to see you, Miss Tregarvon.'

Erica looked up, astonished. She and her mother never had any visitors. 'Mr Winkworthe?' she hazarded, as being the most likely.

'A Mr Perriman.'

'Timothy!'

Although Timothy had kept in touch by letter and occasional phone calls, they hadn't actually seen Lindon Tregarvon's personal assistant since they had left London. It was perfectly understandable. In the first place he had been utterly swamped with work during the settling of the bankruptcy procedures. Those being at an end, Timothy had been without a job. No doubt he had been busy looking for something.

Just like me, thought Erica. And then added with grim humour, of course he's a hundred times better qualified than I am.

She said to Bessie, 'Would you tell Mr Perriman we'll join him in a moment, please, Bessie? And show him to the nook and then bring tea for three.' The nook was a corner of

73

the veranda where it was possible to entertain a guest in something like privacy – although nothing that went on in the hotel could be kept confidential for long.

She ran upstairs to tell her mother the news. Amy, who had been taking an after-lunch nap, roused up at once and began tidying her hair. 'Timothy! How nice! He's such a good young man!'

They went downstairs together. Timothy rose at once from one of the basket armchairs to greet them. Tall and slender and brown-haired, he wore the clothes of a City executive on a day off – a well-tailored suit of light grey worsted, a plain silk shirt, and brown shoes polished like chestnuts.

'Mrs Tregarvon! How lovely to see you again! You look so well. Miss Tregarvon, you too, it's been such a long time.'

They shook hands with great warmth. Amy even went so far as to give Timothy a little hug. He was something from the dear and familiar past, someone who had known and liked Lindon. Erica too was pleased to see him but didn't dream of hugging him. He had been her father's personal secretary, an acquaintance of long standing but not exactly a friend. In the hierarchy of their former life this had been betokened by the fact that she had called him Timothy, whereas he had always addressed her as Miss Tregarvon.

When they had settled themselves and Amy began to pour the tea, Timothy glanced about. 'I should imagine this is a fairly typical seaside hotel?'

'Oh, yes, it's quite nice. Colonel Price is a bit tactless sometimes, but Miss Rand—'

'Timothy doesn't want to hear about those old dodos,

Mother,' Erica intervened. 'It's not a bad hotel in its own quiet way. It was a lucky choice, I picked it with a pin out of a hotel guide.'

'Do you take one lump or two, Timothy? I forget.'

'No sugar, thank you, Mrs Tregarvon. So . . . What do you hear from Mr Winkworthe these days?'

'Not much, thank goodness! He sends awful legal papers from time to time. I'd no idea that these things dragged on so long.'

'I'm afraid there may be quite a few things still to sign,' he said with a sigh. 'It's been the same with me, I've gone over the books a hundred times with the various sets of auditors. Mr Winkworthe sends me things to sign too. By the way – ' he paused with his teacup halfway to his lips – 'he told me the dear old *Margravine* had been sold.'

Erica laughed. 'The dear old *Margravine*! You know you hated her!'

'Nothing of the kind—'

'Yes, you did, you were always seasick aboard her—'

'Now, now, Erica dear, just because you were practically born and brought up aboard ships, you shouldn't laugh at people who get seasickness. It's an awful ailment.'

'I can't deny it's been a handicap to me,' Timothy said, shaking his head in mock despair. 'Of all the people I had to choose as an employer, it had to be an ex-merchant seaman who loved the waves!'

'Hard lines for you,' Erica agreed. 'But when we were in port you could always stay at some shore hotel. I remember you were in the Monterosa in Rio.'

'Oh yes, the one with the marvellous dance-band.'

'I stayed at the Royal Palms the last time we were in Nassau with the *Margravine*.'

'So you did, they have that special Sunday buffet.'

'So who bought the *Margravine*, then?' he asked.

'Such a nice man! He sent me some personal things of Lindon's—' Amy broke off, the ready tears pricking her eyes. 'His hairbrushes, and that silver frame with the photographs.'

'Gaynor Medcalfe, do you remember him?' Erica took it up to give her mother time to recover. 'That big boisterous man with the blonde wife who always wears pink—'

'Medcalfe,' Timothy said, shrugging. 'I don't think I . . .'

'No, well, you didn't take part in the racing. Medcalfe is a mad-keen ocean racer. That's why he bought her, of course. She really should have been raced much oftener but Father . . .' Erica let it die away. It seemed so foreign to her now, the deep discussions of racing tactics, the planning to get to certain ports and there meet the *Margravine* and its crew so as to take part in the regatta.

'I bet he bought it for a song,' Timothy said with regret. 'That's the worst thing about receivers, they've no real idea of the value of special things. I'd love to see her again, the dear old *Margravine*. Any idea where he's taking her?'

'I don't know that he's taking her anywhere,' Erica said. 'He's Nassau-based, as far as I remember. If you're really keen to keep track of her, look in the yachting magazines – they'll have the entries for the various races and he's sure to race her.'

'Of course, I should have thought of that. Do you think of looking out for her yourselves?'

'The *Margravine*?' Erica was surprised. Although she had loved the yacht, there were other and more serious matters to take up her attention now. And she'd have thought the same was true of Timothy, who was no great lover of the wheel's kick or the wind's song.

Amy changed the subject by asking if Timothy had found a good post.

'Well, no, in fact, I haven't,' he said, turning to twitch a curtain to shield himself from the hot afternoon sun through the glass of the veranda. These days he had the untanned skin of the city-dweller. 'I may go into something of my own.'

'Set up on your own?' Amy cried in admiration. 'How marvellous! What kind of thing, Timothy?'

'Well, I thought . . . Trading consultancy. I know a lot about international shipping, you know.'

'Of course! Lindon thought the world of you. "Always has the information at his fingertips," he used to say about you.'

'That was awfully kind of him.'

'Nothing of the sort, it was true. I'm sure you'll be a huge success when you start up. And once you've got it all going, you can give a job to Erica.'

'Mother!'

'Nonsense, dear, why shouldn't I ask him? You need a job and Timothy might very soon have a business.'

'Don't be silly, Mother.' Erica was ready to die of embarrassment. 'If Timothy gets to the stage where he wants to employ others, he'll want better trained people than me.'

'Are you in fact looking for a job?' Timothy said, his shrewd brown eyes reading a thousand things from the manner of the mother and the reaction of the daughter. 'You're finding things a bit hard?'

'Hard! Erica had to sell her pearls. Well, of course, that didn't matter too much because she'd had no time to get fond of them, but if we have to sell some of my pieces, I know I'll cry my eyes out. Mind you, it might be better to do that than let Erica slave away at a typewriter in some dreary office.'

'Mother, please do stop.'

'You're looking for a job as a typist?' Timothy said, a little frown wrinkling his brow. 'Can you type?'

'Not yet. But I'm going to get lessons—'

'There are an awful lot of fully trained typists competing for jobs,' he remarked.

'I realize that, Timothy, but my choices are a bit limited. I thought if I could do shorthand and typing, and offer French and Spanish as well—'

'But business French and Spanish is quite different—'

'Don't I know it!' she agreed. 'I borrowed a book from the library and I couldn't understand one word in ten. You of course know it all already,' she said in envy. How strange to be envying Timothy.

He looked from one to the other. 'I wonder,' he said. 'I wonder if you and I could have a word alone, Erica?'

Erica was taken aback. Her mother, too, looked startled.

'What is it, Timothy? Some business thing? If it is, I'm trying to take part in all that. It's not fair to leave it all to Erica.'

'No, it's something personal,' Timothy said, his pale skin colouring up a little.

Personal? Erica was mystified.

He had risen from his chair. 'Could we perhaps go out into the garden for a minute or two?'

'Well . . . I suppose so . . .' With a shrug towards her mother, Erica led the way to the glass door and to the garden. On the far side of the lawn some pine trees offered an aromatic shade from the June sun.

'What's this all about?' she asked, blunt in her words because she was a little off balance. 'If it's something about my father, Mother will have to find out eventually.'

'No, it's not about your father,' he said, bending his head to examine the tips of his shoes as they scuffed gently at the pine needles. 'As a matter of fact, Erica, I came here today to propose to you.'

Chapter Four

If Erica had been off balance before, now she was completely staggered.

Her first thought was, This is some kind of joke. But he had called her by her first name – the first time he had ever done it. It implied a move to a new level of relationship. She was no longer Miss Tregarvon, daughter of his rich employer; she was Erica, someone he could speak to as an equal.

She found herself staring at him. Timothy Perriman. Tall, dark, reasonably good-looking, with calm good manners and a shrewd brain. What did she really know about him? If truth be told, nothing.

He had come to work for her father when she was about fifteen or sixteen.

He began to accompany them on their travels, sitting down to most meals with them in the dining rooms of ships and hotels. Their friends in overseas cities had often included him in their invitations to the Tregarvons.

Yet there had always been a distinction. They called him Timothy. He called them Mr Tregarvon, Mrs Tregarvon, Miss Tregarvon.

The silence after his announcement was lengthening uncomfortably. They stood under the pines, not looking at each other.

Timothy was thinking, I've bungled it. I shouldn't have blurted it out like that, without preparation.

But how did you prepare the boss's daughter for a proposal of marriage from a former employee?

He moved a little closer, took one of her hands. 'I'm sorry,' he said. 'This is difficult for me. I've never proposed before. I suppose I should have tried to be more romantic.' He sighed. He realized he hadn't even brought her flowers. What a fool. Especially as he'd been thinking about the matter for days now. Ever since Winkworthe had told him . . .

'I am a bit taken aback,' she said, not trying to withdraw her hand although it felt strange resting in his. He had scarcely ever touched her hitherto, except perhaps when handing her into a car or helping her up a gangplank.

'Are you? Surely you must have known I think the world of you.'

No, she hadn't known that. In fact, she had never stopped to think what Timothy felt about her. If anyone had asked, she might have replied that he probably resented her a little. She had been her father's darling, to whom he chatted about confidential matters in a way that an employee could never share. Sometimes she'd even been asked for her opinion on business, and though he'd laughed at some of her replies, Tregarvon had more than once been guided by her views. At those moments, if she'd thought about it, she might have felt that Timothy was put out over such things.

'I don't know what to say,' she muttered, embarrassed, and angry with herself because of her embarrassment. What was wrong with her? She'd been in enough trouble over the last couple of years to learn how to handle it, surely!

'Perhaps I ought to explain how I feel, Erica. Put the case to you, if I can use that expression. I want you to understand.' He paused. She made no response. 'Shall I go on?'

'Well . . . yes . . .'

'The way I see it, things have gone very badly for you and your mother and probably won't improve for a long time—'

'Oh!'

'I'm sorry, I know it sounds harsh, but after all the scandal—'

'That will die down.'

'Do you think so? You see, your name is so distinctive. If your father had been called Smith or Jones, you and your mother could get by without being noticed. But Tregarvon – people are going to remember it for a long time.'

He heard her sigh. She gave a slight nod.

'So the first good thing about marrying me is that you'd change your name.'

He could hear her take a breath, and knew she was going to say, I'm not going to get married just to change my name. He went on quickly, 'That's secondary, of course. The main thing is, it would mean you and your mother could have some security. I'm going to start out on my own, and I think I can make quite a thing of it. I've some money put by, you see, and I invested it at the bottom of the market crash and sold on the recovery so by now it's quite a sum. With that, I've got a good base, and though I don't expect to be able to keep you in the way you've been used to, it will certainly be better than life in a seaside hotel.'

'You're treating it almost like a financial problem.'

'Well, to a large extent it is, isn't it?' Surprising how

difficult it was to put it across. When he'd rehearsed it, he'd imagined she would say, Yes, I see that. He hadn't expected much resistance once the financial side was made clear to her. After all, she must surely be having a hard time, and as to finding a job, the idea was laughable. What was she trained for?

'What I'm trying to say is,' he began again, flicking through the card index in his brain for the key points, 'we've got to think of your mother. Her health has always got to be taken into account. It's a marvel to me she's survived so well thus far.'

'Of course I'm anxious about Mother,' Erica agreed. 'That's why I want to get a job, so as to give her some security.'

'But don't you see, that wouldn't be necessary! I could provide for her, she could live with us. There would at least be a roof over your heads, and by and by I hope to do better than that.'

'Timothy, it's awfully good of you—'

'It makes sense, Erica. And I want you to know that I've always . . . always . . .'

She was shaking her head now, and he felt her hand disengage from his. 'I never suspected you felt like this,' she said. 'I'm sorry, perhaps I was insensitive.'

'No, no, why should you be aware of it? I had to be careful not to show my feelings because of course it would have been very embarrassing, impossible . . .'

'Yes, it would.' Was that how it had been? Timothy hiding his affections because it would mean his dismissal, mean not seeing her any more? She felt a pang of sympathy. 'And then of course Gerald—'

'Oh, I always expected you'd get engaged to someone like that,' he said. He couldn't keep a faint tinge of scorn out of his voice. He'd thought Gerald Colbert a well-brought-up idiot. 'I was prepared for that. But now . . . Everything's different, Erica, and I thought that perhaps you and I might make a good partnership. I understand that you don't feel about me the way I feel about you, but after all, you weren't madly in love with Gerald, were you?'

Nor he with me, thought Erica. There was sense in what Timothy was saying. In the real world, happy-ever-after was only something you dreamed about. In the real world she'd been prepared to marry Gerald and be a good wife, a successful wife, a partner in his career, mother to his children, hostess to his friends. If she married Timothy it would be the same thing on a lesser scale. No grand Embassy balls, no glamorous overseas postings – yet there would be a house, and servants, and all the things her mother needed to feel safe again.

Timothy was waiting for her to say something. She found her tongue unprepared to say, Yes, I'll marry you. It was all too unexpected.

He nodded in understanding. He could see he had made his mark. No need to rush things, after all. Here she was, trapped in this stifling little seaside town by financial necessity. He could always come back tomorrow and again the next day, pressing the good sense of his offer, pushing her gently into acceptance. That was the way he'd planned it, really. No need to insist on an answer today. The business world had taught him the value of patience.

'Think it over,' he said. 'Talk it over with Mrs Tregarvon.

There's no hurry, although of course you wouldn't have to worry any more about job-finding, or in fact any other troubles of that sort.'

'Yes, Timothy. I see that. Thank you.'

'Good. Then let's go back in. I won't stay,' he said, offering her his arm. 'It might be a bit difficult if your mother wanted to know what we—'

'Oh yes,' she said thankfully. She felt a rush of gratitude. He was considerate. How strange, she'd never realized before that he could have qualities like that – generosity, consideration. She felt her eyes fill with tears as they went back towards the veranda. How self-centred she'd been in the past, how little she'd cared to know about anyone except herself.

Amy was eating a little iced cake when they returned. She set it down, looking from one to the other with curiosity. She thought Timothy looked solemn, and Erica was flushed and upset. But what about?

'I'll be going now, Mrs Tregarvon,' he said, bowing in farewell.

'But you've only just come! And you haven't had a cake!' Amy was flustered. Their first visitor, and he was leaving without proper hospitality.

'Thank you, some other time,' he said. He nodded at Erica. 'Today's Thursday, let's say I come back Saturday?'

'Oh . . . yes . . . yes . . . of course.'

In a moment he'd gone out of sight round the corner of the veranda towards the hall. Amy stared after him in astonishment. 'What an extraordinary thing! I suppose he came all the way from London to see us, and he didn't stay half an hour!'

Erica sat down, poured herself some tea. Her throat was parched. Her hand trembled a little as she put in the milk.

'What did he want to see you about?' Amy demanded. 'He said it was personal but I imagine it was some dreadful thing about Father, that he didn't want me to hear.'

'No, as a matter of fact, he asked me to marry him,' Erica said in a low voice.

'What?' Amy truly didn't quite hear. 'What did you say?'

'He asked me to marry him.'

'Timothy?'

'Yes.'

'Asked you to—' Amy broke off. 'Don't be silly.'

'It's true, Mother. He said he'd always thought a lot of me but had hidden his feelings. Now he thinks it would be a good solution to our problems if I were to marry him.'

She swallowed some tea. Over the rim of the cup she could see the changes in her mother's expression as she tried to come to terms with the news.

After a few moments a faint smile appeared. 'Well!' said Mrs Tregarvon.

'Does that mean you're pleased?'

'Well, sweetheart, it's good news at last, isn't it? Everything's been so dreary these last awful months, and though I didn't say anything at the time I thought Gerald behaved abominably.'

'That was all for the best,' Erica said, sighing to herself. 'I discovered I just didn't know him.'

'Well, you can't say that for Timothy. You've known him for years.'

'Have I?'

'What? Of course you have. Six or seven years at least.'

'I didn't mean that. I meant, do I *know* him? I was utterly taken by surprise when he started talking about marriage. I never for a minute suspected he felt like that about me.'

'I suppose it's a bit . . . But then of course, you *are* a pretty girl and he was with us day in day out.'

'But Mother, honestly, did you ever see him show anything except politeness to me? Or do any of the things people in love are supposed to do? I mean, like take anything of mine for a keepsake – a dance programme or a hankie – or seem sad if I went away, or anything?'

Amy pursed her lips. 'No, but then if he did, he'd have kept it secret. Your father would have given him his marching orders if he'd begun to get romantic.'

'Well, that's true, after all – I thought of that myself. Yet you'd think if he loved me, I'd have sensed it.'

'Why should you, darling? When he first came you were really very young, and we were always so much in the social round and so on. And then you went to finishing school, where I would have thought they did their best not to let you dream about romance except with people the parents had already approved of. And after that of course there was the Season. You couldn't be expected to think about Timothy when you were practising your curtsey for the Palace.'

Pushing away her cup, Erica leaned back in her chair and covered her eyes with her arm. 'It was so awful, Mother! I didn't know what to say!'

'What did you feel like saying?'

'I felt like saying, Let's forget you ever said this.'

'But you can't, of course. He's coming back on Saturday, he said. For an answer?'

'Yes.'

'What are you going to say?'

'What ought I to say?'

There was a long pause, so long that Erica took away her arm to look at her mother. Amy was nodding to herself. 'You think I ought to say yes?'

'I don't see why not, dear. He's a very nice boy, we know all about him, don't we? If I remember rightly, he went to one of the minor public schools. I met his parents once, Mr and Mrs Ralph Perriman, she was a Hickson, I believe, before her marriage. No money but a good family. The husband died of some bronchial complaint – I remember Timothy going to the funeral, that would be three years ago? I don't know what the mother did, I think he said she'd gone to live with a sister in South Africa.' Mrs Tregarvon drew a breath. 'And of course he's clever. That's important these days. He told us he thought he would do well with this business he's going to start, and I think he will. Oh, I think he's rather a good match, Erica.'

A good match. Why did it chill her to hear the words again? When they'd been said about her engagement to Gerald Colbert she'd been pleased, almost triumphant. Now they seemed cold and calculating.

She hesitated. 'What about affection? I can't seem to think of myself having any affection for Timothy.'

'Oh, good gracious, you weren't sighing romantically over Gerald, dear. You liked him and he was suitable and it was settled. The same thing with Timothy. You like him and he's offered—'

'But just because he's offered—'

'Erica, most women have to take the best they can get—'

'That's not true! You and Father were in love when you married! I've heard you talk about it often.'

'Ah.' Amy paused, to look back fondly at her young years. 'Ah, that was different. I was very, very lucky, dear. You know your father and I were from the same part of Cornwall and so Fate threw us together when he was just at the beginning of his career with the merchant navy. But you know, if he hadn't come along when he did, I was going to marry Harold Dudley, who had more or less asked me, and it was thought of as practically an engagement. Only he hadn't bought a ring or anything.' She fell silent, lost in her memories. Then she gave herself a little shake and returned to her argument. 'Not every girl can be as lucky as I was. And since the War, there's been such a shortage of men, a lot of girls have just been left on the shelf. No, no, it's important to seize the chance when you get it.'

Erica had heard her out with a growing sense of agreement. If she were honest, she didn't want to train to be a shorthand-typist and spend nine hours a day cooped up in an office. She didn't want to have to worry and pinch over money, she didn't enjoy genteel poverty. She didn't want to have to have the sole responsibility for her mother's well-being. Surely it would be better to marry a man who loved her, had loved her for years? She would learn to love him in return.

'I know you're right,' she said. 'It's just been such a surprise.'

'But you're getting used to the idea,' Amy said encouragingly.

'I suppose I am.'

'It would solve so many problems, Erica. You say we have to move out of the Wessex – well, you'll be going to your new home and I'm sure I can find a little place.'

'You'll be coming with us,' Erica said at once.

'Oh, I don't know, dear – newly-weds . . .'

Erica almost said, Don't be silly. She couldn't think of herself as a new bride in a new home with Timothy, wanting to be alone with him. Instead she said, 'Timothy specifically said he'd want you to live with us.'

'He did? Oh, that's so nice of him. He really is a very nice boy, Erica.' Beaming, Amy picked up the iced cake she'd abandoned earlier and began to nibble it. 'A summer wedding, that would be nice, wouldn't it? You'll wear white, of course.'

'I don't know . . . Perhaps it will be a registry office . . .'

'Good gracious, of course not! I quite see we can't have a grand affair with a lot of friends because of course . . .' She let it fall away. They no longer had any friends. 'But that lovely gown we had made for your debut. You ought at least to wear it for your wedding, it's just lying there folded up in a trunk.'

'We'll see.'

They were interrupted by Miss Rand, who came in fanning herself after an afternoon's croquet at the home of an acquaintance. She said, 'I hear you had a visitor?'

Erica groaned inwardly. Within an hour or so, it would somehow be known that she had a suitor, that a wedding was in the air. With a warning glance at her mother, Erica fled.

During the bridge game that evening, Erica's mind was often elsewhere. She slept badly. At about four in the morning she was wide awake, assessing her life.

If she married Timothy, the future was more or less assured. She would have a husband and perhaps a family. Certainly it would be better to be married than remain single; a single woman had a hard life and often ended up with that dreaded title, old maid. From her own personal point of view, she would be better off as a married woman.

Her mother, too, would benefit. Instead of the uncertain comforts of life in hotels or in a tiny flat, she would share a comfortable home. Her mother always made friends easily so, as the mother-in-law of a successful businessman, she would soon have a circle of companions from the neighbourhood. Perhaps the fact that she was the wife of the swindler Lindon Tregarvon might slip from notice.

It was a cosy, enticing vision.

Yet it had its jarring notes. She would be marrying a man she scarcely knew or, if she knew him, a man she'd never regarded as her equal. Of course that was wrong, she saw that now. All the same, she'd spent some eight or nine years of her life thinking of Timothy as someone to whom she could give orders. Was that a good basis for marriage?

Well, she could learn to honour him. That was part of the marriage ceremony – love, honour and obey. She must learn to do all three if the marriage was going to work.

The birds began to rouse themselves. A twittering of sparrows arose, and then the resident blackbird began his song. She sat up in bed. Her little travelling clock told her it was five o'clock. She got up and went to the window. Morning sunlight angled across the garden, the shadows of the pines stretched far on the green of the lawn.

She washed and dressed quietly. She unlocked the front door to go out into the silence of the Friday morning. The other houses of the broad residential road were still closed up tight. Her footsteps sounded loud on the pavement so she stepped on to the sandy road.

At the esplanade she stood leaning against the rail, staring out at the restless sea. The gulls swooped and swerved, screaming at each other as they scanned for baby mackerel in the bay. A fishing boat from the village to the west came chugging back to port with its morning catch.

I have to do it, she said to herself, staring at this tranquil scene. For Mother, particularly, it would be the best solution. After all, it might turn out to be a good marriage. She didn't notice that as she came to this decision, she was clenching her fists to bolster up her determination.

There wasn't an opportunity to tell her mother she had made up her mind. Amy always rose late, so late that she barely made it to the dining room before it closed, a subject of irritation to the staff. The other residents were up and about, picking up newspapers from the desk, looking at the morning's post, booking the best chairs in the veranda by leaving their books or their knitting on them.

At eleven morning coffee was due to be served. Erica's plan was to get her own and her mother's, take her to a quiet spot in the garden, and there tell her of her decision. But about half an hour before the coffee-tray was brought into the lounge, a big car could be heard drawing up outside. Erica, already on her feet because she found it difficult to sit still, went to the window to look out.

To her astonishment, a man she knew was getting out. It

was Captain Swinford of the *Langrovia*, the flagship of what had been her father's passenger fleet.

Her gasp of surprise brought Amy to her side. 'What is it, darling – oh!' Her gaze had gone past her daughter to the newcomer on the gravel drive.

Captain Swinford, unaware that they were watching him, glanced at the hotel's icing-pink façade, shook his head to himself, and was lost to sight as he came in under the canopy. A moment later Bessie looked in at the door of the lounge.

'Another gentleman to see Mrs and Miss Tregarvon,' she announced into the air.

'My, we are popular, aren't we?' said Mrs Eyott with envy.

With a vague smile in her direction, Amy hurried out with Erica at her heels.

Captain Swinford swung round as they appeared. 'Mrs Tregarvon! My dear lady! What a long, long time it is since we saw each other! And Miss Erica.'

Amy and Erica each took one of his outheld hands. He was indeed an old friend, captain of the liner they had loved the best. They'd voyaged with him often, had sat at his table for meals, had been entertained in his quarters with the elite of the passenger list.

A burly man, he looked strange in civilian clothes. They were accustomed to seeing him in spotless white ducks and a flat white cap with a shining black visor. Yet even in sports jacket and flannels he was imposing – over six foot tall, barrel-chested, narrow blue eyes in a weathered face.

The two women bombarded him with questions. How was Mrs Swinford? How were his children? Antony at university already – how amazing!

The maid appeared at their elbow. 'If you'd like to take your guest to the nook again, madam, I'll bring the coffee in a minute.'

'Thank you, Bessie.' Amy smiled in gratitude yet was quite well aware that Bessie would eavesdrop and report back.

When they were settled in the cane chairs, Amy asked the obvious question. 'But what brings you here, Captain?'

'Well, naturally, I wanted to see how you were faring. Mr Grahame and I have been wondering for some time—'

'But how did you know where to find us?'

'I telephoned Mr Winkworthe, of course. We've kept in touch regularly all through this long and miserable business of the bankruptcy.'

'It must have been a very anxious time for you,' Erica said, understanding that fact for the first time. All those employed by the Tregarvon Shipping Company must have gone through great fears for their jobs while the receivers threaded their way through the company's accounts.

'Well, that's all behind us now. You'll be aware that Bletcham Diamond have bought the *Langrovia*?'

Erica nodded. Bletcham Diamond Line had always wanted a ship of the *Langrovia*'s calibre but hadn't wanted to invest the money in having one built. 'Snapped up a bargain, didn't they?' she said with some sadness.

'Yes they did, but they shilly-shallied just like landlubbers do,' Swinford said with an angry grin. 'Waited as long as they could for the price to go down to rock bottom before they closed the deal.'

Bessie arrived with the tray of coffee. She spent some time setting out cups and clinking spoons into saucers, but all she heard was chat about the buying and selling of ships. Nothing at all interesting to tell Miss Rand and Mrs Eyott.

'However, in the end, the deal was struck and we've kept the ship's crew almost entire,' the captain ended. 'We lost a couple of the younger men, who couldn't hang about waiting for the transition, when they'd got to keep at sea to earn their officer's papers. But on the whole it's the same old *Langrovia*.'

'That's lovely,' sighed Amy, looking back with nostalgia at that wonderful life in the luxury of a big ship. All the ship's officers had been known to her, she'd taken an interest in their careers and their families. She went on to question Swinford about some of them. Where was Alan Cowan? Did Dinsdale Bryant make it to second mate?

'With a record of serving aboard the *Langrovia*, you're likely to get the next step up,' Swinford said with permissible self-satisfaction. 'But the chief officers are still with her. Mr Grahame, Mr Tonsley and me in particular.'

Mr Grahame was the first mate, or First Officer as he was more grandly known aboard the liner. Mr Tonsley was Ship's Engineer. These two men were the chief assistants of the Captain, and headed a crew of something over five hundred and thirty, although of course many of these were stewards and waiters. The officers each had specific duties to perform: some were concerned with navigation, some with the passengers' accommodation, some with the loading and unloading at ports and the stowage of cargo, with the ship's engines, or with entertainment, or medical welfare, or a hundred other aspects of life on a floating city.

Amy had seen men enter the service of the ship, work

their way up, and move on to captain other vessels. To her they were a sort of extended family. She listened eagerly to all that the captain had to report about them.

'But what I chiefly came to say was,' he ended, 'that no matter what's happened, we shall always be proud to have served on Mr Tregarvon's ships and especially the *Langrovia*. If there's anything we can do for you two ladies . . .'

Amy's eyes misted with tears. 'Nobody can do anything,' she faltered. 'It's all decided now. My husband is a criminal on the run, and Erica and I just have to make the best of it.'

Captain Swinford took refuge in his coffee cup. Erica said, 'One of the hardest things to come to terms with is that Father could do that to us. He left us to face the music all on our own. Do you understand that, Captain? You knew him well.'

Swinford pursed his lips. 'It surprised me, I tell you that for nothing. But under pressure, you know . . . A man might do anything.'

'What's so hard to bear is that he didn't even leave us a little note,' Amy sighed, 'and I keep hoping with every post that I'll get a letter . . . To say where he is, to ask us to join him . . .'

'That's not likely, ma'am. Put the police right on his trail, wouldn't it?'

Amy was silent. Erica said, 'It's Mother's notion that he's gone somewhere where he couldn't be extradited.'

'Oh, yes, very possible, you and I have seen a lot of places like that in the course of our travels, haven't we, Mrs Tregarvon? Well, well, even if he were to get in touch in the end, what are you doing in the meantime?'

Amy looked at Erica, waiting for her to say she was

probably going to get married. Erica avoided her eye. She didn't want to talk about that to anyone except her mother as yet.

'We can't do anything on the money side,' Swinford remarked, with a clearing of his throat. 'But we've been talking the last few days, Mr Grahame and Mr Tonsley and I, and if you thought of getting away from it all . . . You know, just to draw breath and have time to think . . . Well, my officers and I want you to know that there's a stateroom aboard the *Langrovia* waiting for you if you want it.'

Amy clasped her hands together in delight. Erica, too, was for a moment dazzled at the idea. A return to comfort and the dear, familiar surroundings.

Common sense prevailed. 'We couldn't possibly afford—'

'No, no, that's understood,' said the Captain. He picked up a biscuit to crunch between his strong white teeth as he arranged his thoughts. 'If you understand me, Bletcham Diamond haven't exactly got to grips with the business of running the *Langrovia* yet. Mustn't be disloyal to my new employers, of course, but they made a bit of a mess of the publicity for this cruise we're about to do, so we're running with a half dozen of empty berths. Doesn't make sense, does it, to have them going across the Atlantic empty if you'd like to use a couple?'

'An Atlantic cruise,' breathed Amy.

'I don't want to dwell on sensitive matters but it wouldn't cost you anything. The three of us would foot the bill and, as you know, when crew members buy tickets for friends or relations they get reduced terms anyhow. So you don't have to worry about the cost.'

'How kind,' sighed Amy.

'It's a long cruise – Southampton to South America and then north – Pernambuco, Trinidad, Belize, New Orleans, Miami and New York. Most of them places you know well, ma'am.'

'Pernambuco,' remembered Amy.

There was a pause. 'You haven't said anything, Miss Erica,' the Captain observed.

Erica was too overwhelmed to speak. It had dawned on her like a revelation that she could get away from the difficulties of life in England. She need not marry Timothy after all.

It might only be a temporary escape. But the mere chance of it had taught her something. She very much didn't want to marry Timothy Perriman. Why it should be so, and why it should only be clear now, she couldn't tell.

Early this morning she'd talked herself into thinking it was a good solution to their difficulties. Yes, of course, no need to take a poorly paid job in a field where she was a beginner, no need to find a poky little flat and eke out an existence with her mother. No, her mother would be provided for, and she herself would be an accepted member of society again.

But the moment a door was opened to another escape route, she understood how impossible it all was. She didn't know Timothy, and the little she'd gathered in the old days had never tempted her to make a friend of him. He was all right, of course, a dependable assistant to her father, self-contained, alert, trustworthy. But a very buttoned-up type, a businessman first and foremost. To think of him as a lover was impossible.

The Captain was waiting for a reply. 'What do you think, Mrs Tregarvon?'

Amy was incapable of saying what she thought. She was too beguiled by the idea of getting aboard the dear old *Langrovia* and sinking into its bosom to be able to weigh the pros and cons. 'What do you think, darling?' she quavered to her daughter, deathly afraid her sensible child would say no.

'I think we should go,' Erica replied. 'It's a lovely idea! Thank you so much, Captain Swinford, I can't tell you what this will mean to us!'

'You'll come?' He was delighted. 'That's great, really great. Oh, Mr Grahame will be pleased! He wanted to come with me to put forward the idea, but he's needed on board to oversee preparations for the cruise. I'll telephone him to say you've accepted, if I may. There's a phone?'

'Yes, a public telephone in the hall,' Erica said, and rose to show him the way.

'That's all right, I think I can navigate my way to a phone box, my dear.' He strode off.

'Oh, Erica,' cried Mrs Tregarvon, rocking back and forth so that her basket chair creaked, 'just think of it! It'll be like going home!'

'Won't it though?'

'I thought you might want to say no.'

'No, no, it's a marvellous idea. I wonder when she's sailing?'

'Clothes!' cried her mother. 'Erica, we've nothing to wear!'

'Good Lord, we've got trunks of clothes in the basement here—'

'But they're two years out of date!'

Laughing, Erica shook her head. 'We'll just have to put up with that. In any case, we were always in the forefront of fashion, most of the other passengers will only just have caught up with us so we'll be on equal terms.'

'Couldn't we just have a couple of new things?' Amy said on a breath of longing. 'It would be so lovely to go into Hardy Amies—'

'We haven't the money.'

'I could sell that little diamond brooch.'

'No, Mother, come on, we've been given a wonderful present, we mustn't cancel out all the benefits by spending money in a silly way. But . . . we may need to sell your brooch. You can't go ashore at the calling points without a *little* spending money.'

'I suppose that's true.' She paused. 'And then there's the bridge tables, we couldn't play bridge aboard ship without losing money sometimes.'

'All right, so we'll sell the little brooch. But no new clothes.'

'Just as you say, dear.'

Captain Swinford came back to report that his First Officer was delighted, that the ship's Purser would put their name on the passenger list, that they should be ready to board tomorrow week at Southampton. 'I needn't tell you which quay, you know your way around Southampton passenger terminal. We sail at six, so see you around five.'

'It's so lovely!' cried Mrs Tregarvon as she shook hands in farewell. 'You just don't know what this means to us! We'll tell Reception at once, shall we?' she added. 'They're anxious to know if they can let our room to somebody else.'

'And the wonderful thing is,' added Erica in some triumph when Captain Swinford had gone, 'because we're giving a week's notice, we shan't have to pay another week's rent penalty.' She marvelled at the words as she said them. How extraordinary that she should be so delighted at saving six guineas.

Then her mood of elation faded. 'I'd better ring Timothy,' she said.

'Timothy!' Her mother had just remembered what that meant. 'You won't be able to marry Timothy until September at the earliest.'

'I shan't be marrying Timothy at all.'

'Not at all? But darling—'

'I realized when Captain Swinford offered us the chance to get away, it was an escape route from marrying Timothy.'

'Darling, that's a silly way to look at it.'

'No, it's true, Mother. I don't love Timothy.'

'But we talked about that—'

'And what's more,' Erica surged on, 'I don't think I even like him.'

'Oh, now, come, Erica—'

'Do *you* like Timothy?'

'Of course I do. I've known him for years.'

'That's not what I asked. Do you like Timothy?'

'Yes, I . . . Well, I . . . Yes, I suppose . . .' Flustered, Amy took refuge in what she thought was an unassailable argument. 'Your father liked him.'

'Did he?'

'Of course he did. He trusted him absolutely.'

'In business. But did you ever hear him discuss anything personal with him?'

'Of course I did. Certainly I did, many times.'

'What, for instance?'

'Well, I . . . I . . . I don't exactly remember . . .'

'No, and that's because it never happened. I look back now, and I can never remember Father speaking or acting towards him as more than a respected employee. Don't you think that means something? If in a relationship of over eight years they never got on close terms, perhaps it means that Father didn't have any strong feelings for Timothy. Nor do you. And as I'm the one who was going to marry him, I'm the one who sees it as important. So the wedding's off.'

Amy hesitated, was about to speak, changed her mind, and stood silent.

'You're not going to argue me out of it?'

'No . . . You know, funnily enough, in a way it's a relief!'

'A relief? Oh, Mother!' Erica laughed and patted her on the shoulder. 'Well, wish me luck. I'm going to ring and tell him no.'

But strange to say she hadn't thought to ask Timothy how to get in touch. She had his old telephone number at his flat, but there was no reply from there. What his business number might be, she'd no idea.

She rang Mr Winkworthe. Mr Winkworthe was at the magistrate's court. His secretary looked up Mr Perriman's number. 'It's a small place in Gracechurch Street, Miss Tregarvon,' she said. 'Mr Winkworthe has noted against it, "temporary".'

There was no reply from the Gracechurch Street number. Later, at an hour of the evening when she thought he'd be at home, she rang his flat again. A strange voice answered. 'May I speak to Mr Perriman?' she inquired.

'Ah, Mr Perriman. He left. Wait a minute, I had a number in case anyone should ring.' But the new tenant couldn't lay his hands on it. 'Sorry,' he said ruefully, 'it was over six months ago he gave it to me, I'm afraid I must have thrown it out.'

She tried the Gracechurch Street office again just for luck, but there was no reply at eight in the evening. There was nothing for it but to wait for Timothy's visit next day.

He arrived at a little before lunchtime. Erica had taken up position by the window so as to see him as he walked up the drive. She went out to meet him.

'Hello, Timothy.'

'Hello there. On the watch, were you?' Timothy smiled a little at the thought. He was pleased she felt him important enough to watch out for.

'Let's walk round into the garden again,' she said. 'I have something rather difficult to say to you.'

'Difficult? What do you mean, difficult?'

She offered him a wrought-iron chair on the edge of the lawn, then sat down next to him. 'Mother and I are going on a cruise on the *Langrovia*,' she said.

'You are?' He wrinkled his brow. How could they afford that? 'Rather an expensive undertaking, isn't it?'

'Captain Swinford has invited us as his guests.'

Timothy looked at this piece of news from various angles, then gave up. 'I suppose that was very kind of him,' he acknowledged. 'Why are you telling me, though?'

'Because we're going straight away, Mother and I.'

'But . . . wait a minute . . . You can't go. You're going to marry me!'

She was shaking her head. 'No, I see now how unfair that would be, Timothy. I'm tremendously grateful to you, but I don't love you.'

'What does that matter?' he cried. 'We talked about that when I asked you. We both know you're not head over heels with me. But you must see it's a good arrangement. You need someone to provide for you and your mother and I'm willing to do that—'

'Willing?' she broke in.

Something in the tone of her voice warned him to stop and think. He said, 'I mean, I want to do that. You know I want to do everything in the world for you. I'll make you happy. Your mother will have security. You're not going to throw all that away just to go on a cruise?'

'No, of course it's not like that. There are all sorts of reasons. One is that when the captain suggested the idea, Mother looked as if the Gates of Paradise were opening for her, and I realized it was just what she needed to give her back some of her confidence—'

'But that would be a temporary thing! What is it, after all – four weeks, five – on a ship that you know and have always liked. I understand that, of course, Erica, but from the point of view of everyday life, it's nonsense. What happens when you come back?'

She shrugged. 'We'll face that when we come to it.'

He struggled for a moment with the sense of rejection and

anger, then made himself say, 'I'll still be here when you come back.'

'No. No, it's very, very good of you, Timothy, but I must definitely say that my answer about the marriage is no.'

'But why? What's made you change all of a sudden? When I left on Thursday, you were almost committed to the idea, I know you were.'

'I've just come to understand that it would be a big mistake.'

'No it wouldn't! You need me, Erica! How are you going to manage without me? You don't know anything about the real world, you've never had to learn.'

'I'm learning,' she said, puzzled at his fervour. 'The last eighteen months have taught me a lot.'

'Oh, have they! What have you learnt? Not much if you'll throw away a good chance like this so as to go swanning off on a liner! It doesn't make sense, and of course it's typical—'

'Typical? You mean, it's an example of my frivolous outlook?'

He caught himself back. He wasn't handling this well. But he'd been so sure she'd say yes. In his mind it had been a settled thing ever since their conversation the day before yesterday. At the time she'd been surprised by his offer, but a little nub of common sense within her head had urged her to acknowledge the good sense of it. Now, for some unknown reason, she'd changed her mind.

'Listen, Erica,' he began again, 'I'm making a mess of this, I know I am. But I do so terribly want you to understand how important it is. Don't throw everything away just on a whim.'

'It's not a whim.' She smiled at him, and he understood

she was sorry for him. Sorry for him! How dared she! But she was going on. 'I esteem you, Timothy, I value you for your loyalty to my father who, God knows, didn't deserve it. But I could never settle down into a marriage with you, no matter what you say. I'm being honest about it, you see, there was quite a temptation at first to grab at the chance because it *would* have meant a lot to Mother. But that wouldn't be fair on you and so—'

'Fair on me! What does that mean? Is it just a fancy way of saying you don't think I'm good enough—'

'On the contrary, it's a way of saying I'm not good enough for *you*. You deserve someone who loves you and wants to make a go of—'

'I'm the best judge of what I want! Don't you understand that I thought it over before I ever asked you? Do you imagine I would have come here without thinking it through? Of course not. Give me credit, Erica, I'm not a fool, I thought of all the disadvantages – that you probably had never thought of me as husband material, that there was a certain handicap in being married to a Tregarvon—'

'Oh, thank you very much! That's very complimentary—'

'No, wait, I didn't mean it like that, I'm only telling you so you'll know how strongly I feel about you.'

'I'm beginning to understand that. And frankly I'm puzzled. I'd have thought you had too much good sense to keep on like this when you can see it's no use.'

'But why is it no use? I mean, after all, Erica, what else are you going to do? You aren't really going to learn shorthand and typing, stop fooling yourself.'

He saw the colour rise and knew he had gone too far. But

that was because nothing had gone to plan. He hadn't expected this long argument: he'd truly thought she'd jump at the chance of a nice safe marriage.

'Timothy,' she said, getting to her feet, 'I'm not so totally without resources that I have to grab at a chance of getting married, particularly when it's to someone I now find I don't even know. I'll manage somehow.'

'Oh really? How? Jobs don't grow on trees these days, you know, and as for grabbing at marriage, who else is going to ask you?'

'Thank you,' she said coldly. 'Now we know where we stand.'

He'd wrecked it. As soon as she had said the words in that icy tone of voice, he knew he'd put an end to any chance of staying close to her. And it was important to stay close to Erica Tregarvon. She was his one link with the Tregarvon family now that the shipping firm had been wound up. As her husband, he could have had access to anything that might be turned up about her missing father.

Now she would keep him at a distance for ever. He had somehow made her dislike him – and his plan had been quite the opposite, to get her to like and trust him, to put her in his debt so that she would turn over to her darling husband any information about Tregarvon, any papers of his that came to light . . .

'Erica,' he began, in one last attempt to repair the damage.

'I'd like you to leave,' she said. 'You know your way to the front of the house.'

'But we can't part like this.'

'Oh, I think we can,' she said. 'I find I don't like you, and it now seems you don't like me. So that's an end of it.' She walked away across the lawn, head high and back straight. He stood by the wrought-iron chairs watching her reach the house and go in through the veranda doors.

All right, there must be other ways of keeping in touch with news of Lindon Tregarvon. Pity, though. Being husband to the Tregarvon daughter would have given him a lot of authority.

With an angry sigh and a shrug he walked back to the drive and on to the station for the journey back to London.

'How did it go, dear?' Mrs Tregarvon asked nervously when Erica came in.

'Badly,' was the reply. But then the gong sounded for lunch and Amy felt she need not pursue this touchy subject.

That evening a huge bouquet of flowers was brought to Erica in the lounge after dinner. Inside the tissue wrappings was a card: 'Forgive my clumsiness this morning. Please be in touch before you leave on the *Langrovia*.' Timothy's signature and his address were at the bottom of the card.

'A love token?' suggested Miss Rand coyly.

'Hardly.' Erica tore up the card and dropped it in the nearest wastepaper basket. Then to the astonishment of all the other residents of the Wessex Hotel she marched into the hall with the bouquet.

'Here,' she said to the receptionist. 'Here's a bunch of flowers for you.'

'For me?' Miss Doyle stared at the long-stemmed red roses. 'But Miss Tregarvon – they're clearly from someone who thinks a lot of you!'

'No,' said Erica. 'Quite the contrary.'

Chapter Five

A lowly fourth officer stood by the opening of the baggage hold, superintending the trundling aboard of the passengers' luggage. He'd been instructed to keep a special eye open for the luggage of the Tregarvon ladies and, since junior officers always obey orders handed down from the commander of the vessel, he did so.

Efficiently, but without enthusiasm. He knew the name Tregarvon. Naturally, for the Tregarvon Scandal had swept through the merchant fleet about eighteen months ago, and for some weeks little else had been talked about.

The man Tregarvon had caused the sinking of two good ships, and the deaths of men, just so as to claim the insurance. In the eyes of seafarers he was a rat, who like a rat had scuttled off to hide somewhere rather than take his just deserts.

Why Captain Swinford should be troubling himself in the slightest about these two women, Hobart Crosley couldn't imagine. Besides making sure their cabin trunks got to their stateroom, he'd been tipped off to look after the ladies in a general sort of way during his 'socializing hours': make sure everything went smoothly for them, introduce them to pleasant people, that kind of thing. The Old Man seemed to have a soft spot for them.

Bart Crosley had no such feelings. They were the wife

and daughter of a swindler and a murderer. And as for all that rubbish in the newspapers about being left friendless and penniless, if they were penniless, how could they afford a stateroom? Only rich people went for lengthy cruises on ocean liners in staterooms.

In his short career on the great ships, Bart had seen plenty of those. On the whole he was beginning to think he preferred life on a freighter, where passengers were few and of a less demanding kind. On an ocean liner, passengers seemed to think the ship's officers were there simply to look after them; it seemed scarcely to occur to them that they had duties concerned with the safety and progress of the ship.

Yet he'd been pleased to transfer from the liner *Princess Julia* to this job aboard the *Langrovia*. To serve under Captain Swinford would always stand a man in good stead when applying for promotions. One day Bart, having already got his master's certificate, intended to get a ship of his own. So when an opportunity arose to join the *Langrovia* he'd leapt at it. Whether he'd have been so keen had the ship still been part of the Tregarvon Shipping Company he wasn't sure, but that had not been in question: by the time the vacancies were being advertised the ship had been sold to Bletcham Diamond Line.

The Old Man had hung on to his post, you bet! Commander of the *Langrovia*, with eight executive officers under him; it was a plum job, and he deserved it. Much further down the scale came Bart's job: he was officially the Senior Second Officer which made him number four in the watch-keeping hierarchy, after the Chief Officer and the Senior and Junior

First Officer (the Staff Captain, deputy to the Commander, didn't stand watch).

In other words, he was among those who most often got the dog watches, the most difficult times at sea: the hours of half-light, the hours of changing from day to night and back again, dawn or sundown. These were the watches given to the men of middle ranking, men of experience yet without sufficient seniority to be allowed a full night's sleep.

'Shan't be there to hand round cocktails to the Tregarvon ladies,' he'd observed to the Staff Captain when he saw the rota on the officers' noticeboard.

'Oh yes you will, my lad. You'll do the four-to-six dog. Your junior and the Senior Third will take the six-to-eight. And see here, Crosley, don't take it so lightly. The Commander wants these ladies to have a smooth passage.'

'Aye aye, sir,' said Bart. Better to keep his thoughts about them to himself.

A glance at his watch told him it was time to go and make himself useful on the First Class decks. Any minute now the liner would be leaving Ocean Dock. At such times people became tearful, or panicky when they felt they'd forgotten to pack some vital article, or apprehensive when they thought of the waves ahead. Or, on the other hand, tiddly from too much farewell champagne.

Bart went to the cabin he shared with Yates, the Junior Third Officer. He changed his working jacket for a spotless white, gave his hair a bit of a brush, and surveyed himself as best he could in the inadequate mirror.

'Gorgeous,' Yates commented, coming out of the bathroom.

'That's more than I can say for you, Ike. Did you stay up drinking ashore all night?'

'Very nearly.' Yates surveyed him out of bloodshot eyes. 'You, on the contrary, look too fit and healthy to be true.'

'I *am* fit and healthy,' said Bart. 'It's all that clean living and brushing my teeth regularly.'

He was in fact the picture of health. Tall, tanned from eight years of the seafaring life, fairish in an unspectacular fashion, brown-eyed, spare and muscular, he was good-looking enough to seem attractive to the women passengers but not enough to make crewmen think him a ladies' man. On the whole his crews had approved of Officer Crosley. He was easy-going when things went well yet could crack the whip when things were going badly. On the *Langrovia* he had yet to make his mark, which was one reason he didn't fancy the assignment of dancing attendance on two silly women.

He felt the tremor as the great ship, as big as a city block, moved away from the quay. The orchestra was playing sprightly tunes over the loudspeaker system. Cheers and a chorus of goodbyes could faintly be heard as he made his way up to the top deck.

The four funnels had a plume of smoke, the engines on quarter power. They would not use them at anything like full power until they had passed the Swinging Ground in Southampton Water. Then they would head into the Channel, gaining speed until they were at about twenty knots. No need for full power on this voyage since this was mostly a cruise: no Blue Ribands to be aimed for, no fastest crossings attempted.

Some of the passengers stayed at the rail to watch

Southampton fade into the distance. Among those who turned away earliest were a middle-aged and a young lady. Passing them as they stepped into the lounge, Bart heard the elder say to the younger, 'I don't feel the least desire to watch until it vanishes from sight. It can't vanish quickly enough as far as I'm concerned.'

Erica took her mother's arm in a gesture of support as they walked through the lounge and on towards their quarters. So far they had not met any of their fellow passengers. It was difficult to know how they would be greeted. They had decided to give the cocktail hour a miss, choosing to face the ordeal at dinner. For at dinner they would have the support of the captain, at his table.

When they had first walked into their stateroom on A Deck, for Amy it had been like coming home. For Erica too there had been pleasure, a sense of relief, in being once more in these well-remembered surroundings. The same walnut panelling on the walls, the same rich blue and brown carpeting, the silk spreads on the twin beds, the matching silk lampshades, the ample mirrors reflecting the evening sunshine from the ports . . .

It was the tradition not to change for dinner the first evening of a cruise. However, most women took account of that in what they wore on coming aboard. Both Amy and her daughter had chosen a late-afternoon frock from among the finery so long stored in the trunks in the hotel basement. Amy was in powder blue, with fine silk stockings and court shoes in grey. Erica was in jade, a colour that set off her chestnut hair to its best advantage.

Both of them took trouble with their hair and make-up.

Amy had never quite managed the art of doing her own hair so Erica helped her pin it up into an iron-grey crown. As she did so she thought with regret that there had been no grey in her mother's hair before that dreadful evening when the police came for her father.

For herself, Erica had adopted the fashionable Joan Crawford style, lots of long thick tresses carefully curved into deep waves, with curls at the front of the crown tumbling on to the forehead. Luckily she had a natural wave, and so was spared the indignity of overnight curlers. Even so, a fair amount of tactical pinning-up was necessary.

The two women surveyed each other. 'Well?' asked Erica.

Amy nodded. She felt sure no one would ever know they were practically penniless.

The First Class dining saloon of the *Langrovia* was decorated in the style of sixteenth-century France: panelling of silver-grey ash helped along by silver-grey paint, chandeliers mimicking real candles, tapestry chairs at the white-clothed tables. As Erica and her mother went in, most tables were already full. Heads turned at their entrance, not with any particular interest but because Captain Swinford rose as they approached.

'Good evening, ladies. I hope everything in your cabin is to your liking?'

'Beautiful, thank you, Captain,' said Amy. A steward was already pulling out her chair, helping her to settle, flipping out her napkin to drape it across her lap. To the other diners this was a signal that the captain had warned the steward to give particular attention to these two passengers.

When they were seated and had been given menus,

Swinford made introductions. 'Mrs Tregarvon, may I introduce Mr Lewis Simmons? His wife Mabel. Mr Simmons is Dean of Gerlinburg College in Arizona. Mr and Mrs Kletscher, from Vienna. Mr Kletscher you already know, I'm sure – the composer? Mr William Johnson, who will tell you about his business better than I can since it's to do with punch-card machines. M de La Metterie, the publisher. Miss Tregarvon, I include you in the introductions, of course.'

Everyone nodded over their vast menus. If one or two had already noted the name in the passenger list, it had clearly meant nothing to them. Or, if they knew it, they took the captain's lead by reacting with the usual polite friendliness of the first night at sea.

However, others in the dining room weren't so immediately under the captain's eye. Erica could hear a little whisper at nearby tables, and out of the corner of her eye could see heads going together as gossip was exchanged.

Well, so be it. Some time or other it had to become known that they were wife and daughter to the infamous Lindon Tregarvon.

Erica looked at her menu, apparently engrossed in choosing her first two courses. In her heart she was damning yet again that thoughtless, heartless man whom for over twenty years she had adored. It was his fault that people were whispering about them. It was his fault that from now on – for years and perhaps for ever – they would be tainted with the memory of his crimes.

The dinner went by quite agreeably. Dean Simmons talked about the difficulty of attracting a good football coach to his college, Ed Johnson explained his punch-card machines, Frau

117

Kletscher proved to have three children whose exploits she reported, M de La Metterie insisted on speaking French so that his conversation was mostly with Erica.

At the moment when the dessert plates were removed, Captain Swinford turned his head and signalled. Two of the officers at the watch-keepers' table obediently rose.

'Ladies and gentlemen, let me present Mr Bailes and Mr Crosley. You'll meet all my officers in due course, but I want you to know that until you become accustomed to the faces of the crew, these two gentlemen are at your service to give you any information or help you may need.'

'Thank you.'

'How kind.'

'How d'you do, young men.'

Amy and Erica were a little surprised. They couldn't remember ever having two 'helpers' introduced before. Generally passengers learned to know a few of the officers almost at once because, as soon as feasible after the first meal aboard, there came a boat drill. Being directed around the decks to the lifeboats was as quick a way as any to learn who was who.

These two officers came with them when they adjourned to the lounge for coffee. It seemed to Erica that Mr Crosley tried to attach himself to her. She neatly deflected this attempt by sitting between her mother and M de La Metterie.

Bart Crosley duly gave his attention to Mrs Simmons, who wanted to know if she should go fetch a wrap before boat drill was called. He tried to give half an ear to the Tregarvon ladies. The girl was chattering away in French to the publisher, showing off, he thought, scattering her conversation with references to names of French writers. The mother was listening rather kindly to Mrs Kletscher's long story about how Klara had gone on the helter-skelter six times at the Prater and not been the least bit frightened.

When coffee had been cleared away, the alarms rang for lifeboat drill. Some of the passengers were old hands but some couldn't help being a little at a loss and even rather afraid. Tourist Class seemed to give the boatswains a lot of trouble.

'Let me show you the way—' Bart began, giving Mrs Tregarvon his arm, and offering the other to Erica.

'Thank you, we don't need help,' Erica said with some sharpness.

'No, that's right, thank you, Mr . . . Crosley, is it? We've done this before, you go and look after Mr and Mrs Kletscher.'

Foiled again, thought Bart, and left them. One thing was sure: it wouldn't be hard making himself agreeable to the mother, but Erica Tregarvon struck him as stuck-up and snappish. Too bad, because in her way she was rather a looker: not beautiful, perhaps not even pretty, but with a vitality that gave her sparkle and light.

After the fuss of the drill, everyone repaired to their respective lounges and bars for restoratives. The ship's Purser, Colin Ridgeford, approached with an elderly lady in tow. 'Now, Mrs Tregarvon,' he said in the tones of old acquaintance, 'I hope you're ready for the battle? May I introduce Miss Maugren, who'll give you a run for your money.'

'Oh, so soon, Mr Ridgeford? Perhaps we ought to—'

'Do come and play,' urged Miss Maugren, 'I've heard so

much about you, I'm longing to try my hand in a game with you.'

'Really?'

'You perhaps don't remember her – my sister, Mrs O'Rourke? She and her husband played bridge with you over a season in Buenos Aires—'

'Of course I remember! Margaret O'Rourke! And her husband – Henry? Harold?'

'Harold. How nice of you to remember. Margaret spoke so often about those games, she said she'd never been so much on the *qui vive* in her life as when she was in a foursome with you.'

'Then, of course, we must play,' said Amy.

To tell the truth, she needed no urging. She too had been aware of the whispering in the dining saloon and, at this moment, could feel someone studying her with avid interest. She longed to take refuge at the card table, to see the friendly faces of the kings and queens and jacks, to lose herself in the rigour of the bridge game.

It didn't occur to her to ask if Erica would rather do something else, talk with people her own age, or go dancing. She led the way to the card room with her daughter in her wake. They settled themselves at the table. The steward brought the fresh deck of cards, the notepads and pencils.

'Well, now . . . A penny a hundred?' suggested Mr Ridgeford, glancing about.

A penny a hundred! Bart, seeing them settle down to this high-stake gambling, shrugged to himself and withdrew. No use the Old Man telling him to look after the Tregarvons if they were going to immerse themselves in a bridge game with two old fuddy-duddies like the Purser and Miss Maugren. Relieved to have the rest of his evening free, Bart Crosley repaired to the ballroom to find himself a pretty blonde partner and dance the foxtrot.

During the voyage to their first port of call, a routine was established. Erica would rise early and swim for half an hour or so while she had the pool to herself. Amy as always had breakfast in bed and rather late. They would be together for part of the morning and for lunch. In the afternoon Amy napped, Erica played deck games or chatted or simply watched the sea change from cold North Atlantic grey to soft tropical turquoise. In the evenings there was bridge, that sure refuge from barbed remarks and scornful glances.

The Crossing-the-Line ceremony was held for those who wished to undergo it, the island of St Paul was duly sighted and honoured with a sounding of the ship's siren. The colour of the sea changed as the outflow from the Amazon tinged its waters. Next day would be Pernambuco, or more properly Recife, the main city of the region of Pernambuco.

Amy and Erica had been here on a previous occasion but, though it was referred to in the ship's programme as 'The Venice of Brazil', Erica didn't remember it as being particularly appealing. It had some lovely old churches and a huge street market, but she seemed to recall a good deal of cement dust in the humid air.

But it was a pleasant shore excursion. So was Trinidad and then Belize. She and her mother spent very little money, though other passengers would come back on board with straw hats, crocodile handbags, coral necklaces, and other such trophies.

Often on these shore trips, Mr Crosley would seem to be at their elbows. Erica couldn't understand what he thought he was up to. If he was trying to get a date with her, why didn't he ask her? In which case she'd have said no and got rid of him. She always remembered her mother's commands from her girlhood: 'Never get involved with any of the officers.' Looking back now, she supposed the converse was true: the officers had been told, 'Don't get involved with the boss's daughter.' But now things were different, she wasn't the boss's daughter any more, fair game for any romantically inclined male on board the *Langrovia*.

The liner sailed north towards the United States. Erica began to have a private worry. What, actually, were they going to do when the ship reached her final destination, New York? When she and her mother had accepted Captain Swinford's invitation, Erica had closed her eyes to what might come after. Just at that time it had been enough to get away – from the Wessex Hotel, from England, from Timothy Perriman. Now they were nearing Miami, and after that came New York, journey's end.

Were they going to stay in New York? If so, what were they going to do for an income? If not, were they going to return to England? How? They could hardly expect Captain Swinford to extend yet another invitation to be his guests aboard the *Langrovia*. He could do it once without attracting too much criticism from the new owners but even the commander of a great liner has to explain unnecessary expense to the directors.

Luckily, none of these questions seemed to be troubling

Amy. Only Erica thought about it and, as she'd learned to do, she kept her worries to herself.

Captain Swinford had thought about the matter, though. At an afternoon tea-party for favoured passengers in his quarters, he sought her out.

'Are you intending to come on to New York with us?' he inquired. 'Or are you thinking of stopping at Miami?'

Erica looked up at him. He was such an old friend, she could be entirely frank with him. 'To tell the truth I don't know what to do next,' she confessed. 'We were so grateful to get away from the problems facing us that we didn't really look much further. But the fact is . . .'

'The fact is New York at the beginning of July is not very inviting. Quite. Why not stop off in Miami?'

'Well, it's hot in Miami—'

'But there's always a pool where you can cool off.' He smiled, taking a seat next to her. At his nod, a steward hastened up to offer Erica fresh tea. Cake was brought, a little table was arranged for her use. When the bustle of activity was over the captain went on. 'If you remember, one of your mother's friends has a house in Miami.'

'Really?' She frowned, racking her brains.

'Mrs Harry Oakes,' prompted the captain. 'Perhaps Harry bought it after you went off to finishing school. I know for a fact that La Marmora is usually empty except for the servants. Half an acre of sea-front, ten rooms, a pool and a path to the beach – why don't I send Mrs Oakes a cable and ask her if you could use it for a month or so? She's in Canada now, I'm pretty sure.'

The friendship between Amy Tregarvon and Mrs Oakes

went back a long way. One day in Sydney a newly married couple had come aboard a Tregarvon Line ship in which the owner and his wife were voyaging that summer. Tregarvon already knew Harry Oakes, famous for having made his fortune by finding gold *under* the lake at Kirkland in Canada. Harry had chosen to marry a young bank teller who found the role of millionaire's wife a little daunting. In her usual kindly way, Amy befriended Eunice Oakes.

For the following ten years they had met intermittently as their husbands travelled across the world on business. They weren't bosom friends, but there was a warmth in their relationship that absence and distance couldn't quench.

Erica's spirits rose. Of the few people from their past who might be pleased to hear from them, Eunice Oakes stood out as one of the foremost.

Swinford duly sent his cable. Within hours came the response: a cable to the captain himself thanking him for putting forward the opportunity of doing something for Mrs Tregarvon, and one to Amy. 'Please do drop in on my house in Miami and see if all is well. You would do me a favour by staying a while if it suits your plans – houses need to be lived in! All the best from Eunice Oakes.'

'La Marmora!' cried Amy. 'I remember reading about it when they bought it. The decor is by Mamel, and the pool is Carrara marble. Erica, do say you agree to leaving the ship and staying a while in Miami.'

'Of course, Mother, if you'd like to,' Erica agreed, greatly relieved. At the Oakeses' house they would live rent free, looked after by the Oakeses' staff and with the use of a car if they wanted it. It was another respite from their troubles –

yet already she was aware that they couldn't go on for ever living on the bounty of others. Some day soon she must give serious thought to the matter of earning a living.

And a little seed of an idea had already been planted. Among the passengers on the *Langrovia* was a Texan oil tycoon and his wife, Harcourt and Delona Nellbrond. Harcourt was a mad-keen bridge player and though his style didn't quite appeal to the Tregarvon ladies, he had his successes. His wife Delona, however, was a very poor player.

'I've tried to teach her,' he groaned as yet again she lost him a rubber. 'God knows I've spent hours at it, but I can't seem to get it across to her that you have to use your head.'

'He shouts at me,' Delona said with a droop of her marcelled head. 'I know I could learn if only he'd keep his temper.'

Erica had been on the verge of saying, 'I could teach you.' But she had held her tongue, because in the past when she'd taken on the role of teacher she'd had scant thanks. Older people who didn't play well resented being shown their shortcomings by someone as young as Erica.

Now, though, things were different. If Mrs Nellbrond wanted to learn without being shouted at – and was prepared to pay for the lessons – Erica Tregarvon was ready to take her as a pupil.

The Nellbronds too were leaving the ship at Miami, where in a few weeks' time there was a bridge tournament, which Harcourt wanted to drop in on as a spectator. Suppose Erica were to suggest that Mrs Nellbrond might take a few lessons to pass the time before the tournament?

Delona seized on the idea with rapture. 'Oh, honey, if you

can just explain the values at bidding so I could understand what the heck to do at the outset, I'd be *so* grateful.'

'I think I could do a bit more than that, Delona. I think I could teach you to play with some confidence.'

Delona shook her head. 'Erica, if you were playing with Harc as your partner, you'd be undermined from the outset.'

'Not at all! Anyhow, what do you think? Would you like some lessons when we stop off at Miami?'

'I'd love it!'

'There's just one thing, Delona. I'm afraid I'd have to ask for a small fee—'

'A small fee! Baby, if you could just show me how to avoid making a fool of myself, I'll give you one of Harc's oilwells!'

They laughed, and a fee was arranged, not exactly an oilwell, yet more than Erica would have thought of suggesting if she'd been asked to name a price.

They disembarked at Miami, saying grateful farewells to Captain Swinford and his officers. Once again the ubiquitous Mr Crosley was to be seen supervising the removal of their luggage from ship to shore. Erica thanked him nicely and dismissed him from her mind. Mr Crosley watched her go with her mother into the arrivals lounge with some perplexity.

'If you want my opinion,' he murmured to Ike Yates, 'I think those two women are living on next to nothing.'

Ike was on his way back from sending the mail bags ashore. He glanced over the rail. 'Who? Oh, the Tregarvons . . . Can't be right, old chap. They were in a stateroom on B Deck.'

'All the same . . . I was around when they made shore trips. They spent almost nothing. And that girl was up all hours playing high-stakes bridge with the men in the card room.'

'Well, there you are. You don't play for high stakes unless you have the money to pay your losses.'

'But she almost never lost! In fact, I think she made quite a bit.'

Yates, who until that moment hadn't been paying much attention, now looked sharply at his colleague. 'You're saying she played for the money?'

Bart hesitated. He had watched Erica, as he'd been instructed. And what he'd seen had been rather unexpected. The two women, although in one of the luxurious First Class cabins, seemed to have almost no financial resources. They never ordered drinks in the bar except when it was socially necessary. Ashore they avoided all the tourist traps, didn't even pay for a meal in a restaurant as a change from the ship's dining saloon. Their tips to their cabin staff had not been by any means munificent, although oddly enough no one was complaining.

And when Erica played cards, it was with a care and attention that impressed him. He himself played bridge, because it was expected of him as a social asset, but he was nowhere near Erica in ability. And almost from the first he understood that she had no intention of losing. He'd thought it was because she was the sort of girl who liked to be a winner, but he soon began to sense that there was something more involved. She couldn't *afford* to lose. On the contrary, it was important to win because the stakes in the late-night games could be quite substantial.

In other words, she needed the money.

He avoided answering Ike's question. Ike, thinking it over,

shrugged. 'A bit of an adventuress, is she?' he suggested. 'Learning to live by her wits now Daddy's skipped and left her to fend for herself?'

That sounded harsh. Bart found himself almost ready to defend her. After all, what was wrong with learning to fend for yourself? But people who lived off their earnings at cards were not on the whole greatly loved by the officers of cruise ships.

Yet there was hardly likely to be trouble over bridge. Poker, yes, there had been fights before now over accusations of cheating at poker. But bridge was a nice respectable game. He sighed to himself. He wished now he'd entered more into the spirit of Captain Swinford's orders, and tried to be a friend to Erica Tregarvon. Too late now, she had gone to live in some swish house in Miami, on the charity of some rich acquaintance.

Chapter Six

They were playing cards in the shade of the veranda at La Marmora. A covering of trumpet vine, keeping the roof cool, allowed its bright orange flowers to peep in at them. Great hanging baskets of fern swayed gently in the breeze from Biscayne Bay.

'Now you should play the ten of diamonds,' said Erica.

'I haven't *got* the ten of diamonds,' replied Delona Nellbrond in despair.

'Yes you have. You played the six and the seven, and now you should play the ten.'

'How can you possibly know what I have in my hand? It's like black magic.' Delona had found the ten of diamonds and now obediently played it, understanding at last as she did so that she couldn't possibly win the trick and must let this card go for nothing.

'I have a good memory,' said Erica.

The Mexican housekeeper looked at the English señorita with awe. Memory? Perhaps the American señora was right, perhaps there was something of black magic in it. Under her breath, just for safety's sake, Mrs Domingo murmured a little incantation against the evil eye.

This was the third afternoon she'd been pressed into service to make a four, and with each session her respect for the young

129

lady grew. As for the American señora, she might one day play as well as Mrs Domingo, which wasn't saying much since the housekeeper had only learnt her game at church socials.

What Erica said was true. It was simply a matter of memory. She'd always had the ability to memorize every card as it was played, which meant she could make a good guess at what remained in the hands of her partner and her opponents. Because of course people played what they had according to certain predictable impulses – I'll part with *this* and hope to gain with *that* later, I'll bid my long suit because this hand is so unbalanced – Erica could almost hear the thoughts as they ran through their heads. Naturally, good players sometimes foxed her. But that was part of the fun of it.

However, there was precious little fun in trying to teach Delona. Harcourt Nellbrond could certainly never have married her for her brains, for she seemed unable to concentrate for more than ten minutes at one time.

Erica was partnering Delona, her mother was partnering the Oakeses' housekeeper. There had been some progress over the three afternoons: Delona was now at a stage where she could take her turn to deal without going into a panic. But whether she would ever develop the precious instinct known as 'card sense' was debatable.

'You are going to enter the tournament, señorita?' inquired Mrs Domingo.

Erica, concentrating on her own cards and on Delona's, shook her head.

'Oh, but you should, honey!' cried Delona. 'It's quite a

big affair, the prizes are quite worth going after.'

'I've never played tournament bridge—'

'Why ever not? You're a natural.'

'It's a fairly new thing, public competition. Mother and I have won little silver cups aboard ship, of course, but as for entering for a money prize . . .'

'Gee, I'd love for you to win! It would be such a poke in the eye for Harc! He thinks women can't really play bridge, he says they're too emotional.' Delona laughed. 'I am, of course – I'm a bundle of nerves when I play with Harc. But you're so cool, Erica, ice-cool . . . I bet you could give those guys at the Esmeralda Hotel a run for their money.'

When Harcourt had called to collect his wife, Erica looked at her mother. 'Shall we go down to the Esmeralda after dinner and take a look?' she asked.

'Erica, you're not thinking of taking part in the tournament?'

'Why not? "Prizes worth going after", Delona said. We could do with the money.'

'I don't know . . . Do you think it's ladylike?' Amy asked in slight distress.

Erica didn't know the answer to that one. She had wondered about her taking part in late-night sessions aboard the *Langrovia*, she the only woman in a bridge game, taking it all rather more seriously than her fellow players. And she had gained what these days was to her a substantial sum, almost fifty pounds. Perhaps at the Esmeralda there was even more to be won.

At her request, the houseboy brought the Oakeses' Pontiac round after dinner. Erica drove her mother along palm-lined roads, past the University at Coral Gables, and into central Miami where the big hotels spilled their lights and their noise into the quiet streets. The Esmeralda was in the Spanish-grandee style – heavy black oak furniture, wrought-iron lampshades, and a good many fringed shawls cast over banisters and grand pianos.

As they crossed the lobby to the lounge, a big bill on a stand gave them some of the information they were seeking. 'Hotel Esmeralda Hosts State of Florida Bridge Tournament! Open Competition! Elimination Matches July 10th & 11th. Register Now!'

Amy glanced at the board but went on without checking her step. Erica would have liked to stop, but fell in with her mother's action. Perhaps it wasn't 'ladylike' to show an obvious interest in a bridge competition.

In the lounge they ordered coffee. While they waited for it to come, Erica sauntered to the side table where magazines and newspapers were available for guests. As she'd expected, there were leaflets and brochures about the hotel's activities. Among them was an entry form for the bridge tournament.

The entrance fee was twenty dollars. Players were asked to enter the eliminating heats in the ballroom on Monday and Tuesday. There would then be a break. Then on Thursday and Friday the main tournament would be run, still in the ballroom. The finalists would play for the prizes on Saturday evening after dinner in the sun lounge. The prizes, when she came to them at last, were worth trying for. Two hundred dollars, five hundred dollars, and one thousand dollars plus a silver cup. With the exchange rate at four dollars to the pound, it meant that the first prize was worth £250.

Two hundred and fifty pounds sterling. It would have to be split with her partner, but she and her mother could live on a hundred and twenty-five for a year.

Amy had poured the coffee by the time she got back. She saw the folder in her daughter's hand and said with a sigh, 'That's about the tournament.'

'Yes, and I'm going to fill in the entry form and hand it in at the desk before we leave.'

'Erica . . .'

They sat looking at each other. 'I know, Mother, you think it's not quite "done". I'd have said the same a year ago, but things are different now. It just happens that I have this ability to play the game of bridge. And I could make over a hundred, perhaps. We could use that money.'

'I suppose that's true.'

'You're not going to enter?'

'Oh no. I can't quite explain how I feel . . . It would make me feel – a bit disreputable. It's a bit too like living by your wits, Erica.'

'But what else have we, Mother?' Erica said bitterly. 'Our wits, and our ability to fit into a certain social setting.'

'But you know what we've always said about those people we've seen on ocean liners, people who always try to make money out of the ships' sweepstakes or let others pay for their drinks.'

'Mother, just because I'm going to play in a bridge tournament doesn't mean I'm going to become a demi-rep!' Erica said, laughing. 'I'm going to play honest bridge. What's wrong with that?'

'Nothing, I suppose . . . It's just that I never thought of

having to rely on cards for a living. Are you sure it's . . . quite respectable?'

'I'll regard it as respectable until I learn different,' Erica said. And Amy, who had come to rely on her daughter for almost everything, accepted this view with no more demur.

When they had paid for the coffee Erica led the way to the lobby. There she found pens and inkstands. She filled out the form, took it with two ten-dollar bills to the desk, and was given a receipt together with an envelope containing a card with her number and a typed instruction sheet.

Today was Saturday. July 10th was next Monday. It would have been nice to sit down with some keen players and sharpen her wits, but she was honour-bound to go on with the lessons for Delona. Sighing to herself, she drove back to La Marmora.

'Señorita, a phone call for you,' said Mrs Domingo as she took her evening wrap. 'From New York.'

'Really?' Who could it have been? No one knew they were in Miami except Captain Swinford and people who had seen them leave the ship. Even so, only the captain was likely to have the telephone number of the Oakeses' house.

'Did you take a message, Mrs Domingo?'

'No, señorita, he say he will ring back.'

'What is it, dear?' asked her mother, looking about for her copy of *American Ladies Journal.*

'A phone call. Very odd. Must be Mr Swinford, I suppose.'

'Oh, how nice! I suppose he's just about to leave New York for the return trip. What a kind thought, to ring us to say goodbye.' Smiling to herself at the kindness of their old friend, she went up to her room to read in bed.

Erica stayed downstairs, restless because of her decision

to enter the tournament. Bridge, invented in the United States in 1925, had grown in popularity all through the Twenties, until now it was perhaps the most popular social card game in the Western world, ousting whist from which it had derived. It had seemed logical that as players became more expert, they would want to test their skill against others. Thus half a dozen different entrepreneurs had tried the idea of open competitions.

As yet, no one was quite sure how to run them. Rules varied from country to country, and in fact from region to region. Strict supervision must exist to eliminate any chance of cheating, and the rules were 'according to Hoyle' – that's to say, they followed the rule book named after an English writer on card games.

But the organization still differed from place to place. Some tournaments allowed partners to enter and play together all the way through. Others felt that this opened the way to communication by secret signs and winks and nods, so insisted all competitors should draw cards for partnerships.

The competition at the Esmeralda was 'partners by draw'. A lot could depend on whom she had as a partner. All the same, as the tournament progressed the no-hopers would be weeded out until at the final only the first-rate players would be left.

Typically, it didn't dawn on Erica to doubt that she would be there at the final.

The phone rang about ten-thirty. Mrs Domingo answered it then came into the drawing room. 'Your gentleman from New York, señorita,' she said, and brought the phone in on its long extension cord.

Erica was so sure it was Swinford that she said in greeting: 'Captain? Safely in port, I gather.'

'Erica? Erica, what are you doing in Miami? I came here to meet you off the *Langrovia*—'

It was the last voice she expected. She was so astounded she felt as if cold water had been dashed in her face.

'Timothy?' she gasped.

'I couldn't understand what had happened! Why didn't you come to New York?'

Surprise held her speechless.

'Are you there? Erica? Erica?'

'Yes.' It was as much of a reply as she could muster.

'I had to ask Captain Swinford what had become of you. I was so worried!'

Now at last her tongue was able to form words. 'What on earth has it got to do with you where I am?' she said in amazement.

'But I asked you to be in touch before you sailed.'

'Don't be silly. I had nothing to say to you.'

'Erica, how can you speak to me like that?'

Very easily, she thought. Amazement changed to something like curiosity. 'What do you want, Timothy?'

'I want to see you, of course. I came to New York on purpose.'

'On purpose to meet me off the cruise?' Once again she was surprised. Startled too. Of course it was easy for him to reach New York before the *Langrovia* – he need only have taken one of the fast trans-Atlantic liners which completed the trip in four days. But why should he go to so much trouble?

'I must see you, Erica. Everything went all wrong when I

talked to you before. I lost my temper.'

'You certainly did. And let me know your true opinion of me.' At the recollection, her cheeks burned. 'I don't think we have anything further to say to each other.'

'But we have, we have! I'll come to Miami, I can catch a plane—'

'No, don't.'

'But I *must*—'

'If you come here I'll tell the servants to close the door in your face.' She paused. 'How did you know where we were?'

'Captain Swinford told me, of course.'

Too bad. It hadn't occurred to her to say that she didn't want Timothy Perriman to know her whereabouts. Why should it? She had regarded that conversation in the garden as the end of their acquaintance – acquaintance, not friendship – it had never been as close as a friendship. So why was he seeking her out again?

'Don't come here, Timothy. It wouldn't do any good.'

'But what are you going to do in Miami?' he demanded. 'What are you going to live on? You can't stay there for ever.'

'It's none of your business!'

'Even someone as generous as Eunice Oakes isn't going to want you there as a permanent house guest.'

'Your interest in our welfare is very touching but your lack of tact is staggering!'

'I didn't mean it like that,' he said, flustered, and went on to make it worse. 'I meant, after all, you've no real claim on her except occasional holiday encounters, and you could hardly ask her for cash money to get by on. I suppose there's jewellery you might pawn but that would only last so long.'

'Mr Perriman,' Erica said dangerously, 'be quiet! Stop interfering in our affairs, stop bothering about what doesn't concern you. I can look after my mother without resorting to the pawnbrokers, thank you. And don't come here, there's a tough young Mexican houseboy who'll throw you out if you do.' She put the phone down with a bang. She found to her astonishment that she was trembling, partly with rage, partly with distress.

But after a minute or two, wonder got the better of those emotions. What on earth had prompted Timothy to cross the Atlantic? Why was he even imagining she wanted to see him here in Miami?

She went slowly upstairs. Her mother was sitting up in bed reading her magazine. When Erica came in, she made as if to get out. 'Is it Captain Swinford?' she said. 'I heard the phone, I'd just love a word—'

'Don't bother to get up,' Erica said. 'It was Timothy.'

'Timothy? Perriman?' Amy was as astonished as her daughter. 'But it's the middle of the night in London!'

'He isn't in London, he's in New York.'

Amy's blue eyes widened in surprise. 'What on earth is he doing in New York?'

'Meeting us off the *Langrovia*, he thought.'

'Timothy Perriman went to New York on purpose to meet us when the *Langrovia* docked?'

'Yes.'

'But that's absurd!'

'I thought so too. But he made it even stranger by saying he'd fly here to Miami to see us.'

a friendly game was quite in order but not in a competition for a cash prize.

The competitors were asked to look for their names on place-cards already set out on the tables. These had been drawn by lottery earlier in the day. Erica found herself with two men, one clearly a young businessman on holiday, one an elderly retired Miamian. The fourth player was a plump woman of about thirty.

The decks of cards were ceremoniously brought in on silver trays by white-gloved waiters. At each table there was a draw for partners. Erica found herself partnered with the retired man, to her relief. She'd already read in the eyes of the younger man a too-confident superiority, and the plump lady was by now perspiring with nerves.

It was a tedious morning. As rubber succeeded rubber it became clear that most of the competitors were of a low standard, entering only because they thought they might as well have a try at the money. There was too much chatter, too much effort to bolster up poor technique with distractions and desperate dashes.

The lunch break was a welcome relief. A 'Competition Special' was on offer in the dining room, where Erica met her mother. They sat down to shrimp bisque, salad, cold ham, ice-cream, and coffee. Erica fell on each course hungrily.

'So how's it going?' Amy asked, watching her daughter devour a second helping of salad. She marvelled at her healthy appetite. She herself, waiting in the lobby for the morning session to end, had been so beset by nerves she'd almost given herself one of her bronchial attacks, and still couldn't bring herself to eat.

'Well, they're no great shakes. My first partner wasn't bad – Sidney, his name is, he was a textile foreman in Hertford before he retired to Miami. He brought off a useful take-out double – he had the king, jack, seven and six of spades on a one-diamond opening bid – but he's handicapped by a poor memory. I don't think he'll survive the afternoon unless he gets good partners.'

Erica, of course, expected to survive, and did, with her first partner, a shrewd thin lady in blue linen. Together they trounced the opposition and were lucky enough to draw each other at the next rubber. They played on, doing well again. At the end of the afternoon Erica was pleased to see Jane still among the survivors, as she was herself.

Tuesday was a repetition of Monday, with the standard of play higher and a greater quiet in the ballroom – less chat, no giggling, more concentration. Erica was able to spare a glance of commiseration when Jane, her partner of yesterday afternoon, was eliminated in the last rubber.

Wednesday was a free day. Erica spent it swimming in the pool at La Marmora, reading, listening to the radio. She didn't think about bridge at all, until in the evening she passed a quiet hour or so with her mother, Delona, and Mrs Domingo. She told herself you could hardly call it practice – Delona played so badly it was more like torment.

The real competition started on Thursday afternoon. The competitors had been thinned down to eight tables. The winners would play again on Friday afternoon, then again on Friday evening. The third-best score of Friday evening would gain third prize, two hundred dollars.

On Saturday evening there would be one table. The players

were to be allowed either the suspense or the blessing of day-time leisure. The winners of that evening's play would receive one thousand dollars and the cup, the losers would receive five hundred dollars.

Until she left the table on Friday evening as one of the surviving quartet, Erica had been in no doubt that she would win the main prize and the cup. Now it seemed less certain. One of the four remaining players played at least as well as she did, and only if she drew him as partner could she be sure of winning.

'You know who he is?' she said to her mother. 'Mitchell Harrowford.'

Amy had been unable to nerve herself to go to the hotel since Monday. The strain of that first day had been too great for her. Now she drew her brows together and tried to think. 'Mitchell Harrowford? Do I know him?'

'We saw him once or twice – he was on the *Sinclaire* when we went on the Australia run three or four years ago, and I think he was aboard the *Corfu* the year before. A tall, thin man, always impeccably turned out – plays a quiet game with very few signals but lets his partner know when to switch suits—'

'By a high card – yes, of course, Harrowford.' Amy smiled and then frowned. 'We didn't entirely approve of him. He plays for money—' She broke off, looking confused for a moment. 'Of course, that's what the competition is, a game for money. How silly I am! So he's doing well?'

'He's with me in the final four. I don't know how it's going to go tomorrow evening if I don't draw him as partner. A rubber of two games played against him.'

'But darling, a lot depends on who *he* draws—'

'No, I think he could win with just a mediocre partner. And the four of us that are left are by no means mediocre.'

'Don't worry about it, my love. You're in line to win something.'

'Yes,' sighed Erica, 'but I'd set my heart on my share of that thousand dollars.'

It was not to be. Erica drew Sam Lutsky as her partner, Mitchell Harrowford drew Winthorp Hayes. Lutsky was a square, quiet, grey-haired man who smoked non-stop while he played, unaware that sometimes his intake of tobacco smoke gave hints of his state of mind to anyone astute enough to notice.

And Harrowford was astute enough. He sat in his white tuxedo, a carnation in his buttonhole, relaxed and apparently at ease. His dark brown eyes seemed to give casual glances at the other players and at the cards on the table.

Erica wasn't deceived. He could read Lutsky like a book, and she was afraid that he could read her also, although she was always an unshowy player and not given to trying to direct her partner.

Harrowford and Hayes won the first game, but only just. Lutsky said comfortingly to Erica as they sipped iced tea, 'We'll whip the pants off them in the second game.'

She gave a little half-shrug. She was on the verge of saying, 'Mr Lutsky, could you give up smoking until we've finished playing?' But that would be useless. He was so accustomed to having a cigarette on an ashtray-rim at his elbow that he would probably flounder without it. Yet every time he drew on his cigarette, he was telling his clever opponent what he felt about the state of play.

The evening was very warm. Her cerise taffeta evening dress was sticking to her back. She would have given anything for a cold shower and a change of clothes. What had possessed her to wear taffeta, why hadn't she chosen something softer?

The sun lounge had been arranged so that the guests of the hotel and competitors from previous sessions could stand around the table to watch the play. The presence of this small crowd raised the temperature around the players, nor were the fans so effective as in the ballroom. The fresh deck felt cool to the fingers at first but soon lost its pristine freshness.

Lutsky played well in that last game. He had a quick brain, and a rapport had grown between him and Erica in the first round. She had warmed to him, and they survived a neat little finesse from Winthorp Hayes.

But halfway through she understood they weren't going to be the winning pair. A little better luck with their hands, a little less ability in their opponents – one or other of these chances would have given them the advantage needed. But Harrowford was a first-class player, Hayes was very good, and the cards ran in their favour.

As the second game drew to a close, the scores on the pads told their tale to the invigilator. He went to murmur to the hotel manager, who in his turn went to fetch the President of the Chamber of Commerce to present the prizes.

On his return the last trick had been played. Mitchell Harrowford reached across to shake hands with Hayes. 'Well done, partner.'

'Thank you. And thank you, Miss Tregarvon and Mr Lutsky, for a nerve-tingling game.'

They shook hands politely. Erica made herself smile as she rose. The invigilator had taken their score pads to the manager, who cast his eye over them, signed them, and consigned them to the reporter from the *Miami Herald*.

Drinks were brought. Erica drank hers gratefully. She looked for Amy, who proved to be sitting in a cane settee, fanning herself. She waved, Amy waved back. No need for any words, Amy knew Erica and her partner had come in second.

'Ahem. May I have your attention, ladies and gentlemen?' The manager was addressing the public access microphone on the table in the bay window of the sun lounge. 'Ladies and gentlemen, I give you our hardworking and renowned Reynold T. Culdon, President of the Chamber of Commerce of our flourishing city. Reynold T. Culdon!'

Applause greeted the sunburned man who came forward at the introduction. 'Thank you, Mr Vinesci, for that warm-hearted introduction. Ladies and gentlemen, thank you for supporting the first All-Comers Bridge Tournament of the State of Florida. I think we've all witnessed some thrilling play during this past week, and I would like first to present the prize for third place, which was won last night by Mrs Rebecca Upnalt and Mr Thomas Sigimo. Mrs Upnalt and Mr Sigimo!' He produced a large envelope edged with gilt and lettered in green, the colour of the Esmeralda Hotel. The two third-prize winners accepted the envelope, opened it excitedly, and sorted out the crisp ten-dollar bills it contained.

'Now our second prize winners. Anyone who watched the play this evening will know how gallantly they battled with some very poor cards. Let me hear your tribute to Miss Erica

Tregarvon and Mr Samuel Lutsky!'

Applause and some cheers. Erica and her partner accepted
the same kind of envelope. 'You open it,' Lutsky urged. She
did so, but found herself too shy to divide up the money.
Lutsky grinned, took it from her, and counted out the two
sets of twenty-five ten-dollar bills. 'That pays for my trip
and a bit over,' he said with satisfaction. 'Okay by you?'

'Yes, thank you. And thank you for a good game.'

'Huh . . . I've a hunch you'd have done better with one of
the others, but that's the way it goes. No hard feelings?'

'Of course not.'

The President of the Chamber of Commerce was now
calling upon the winners to come forward and receive their
cup. Erica joined the applause as Winthorp Hayes accepted
it. She couldn't help noticing that Harrowford was very careful
to take hold of the envelope containing the money prize. It
struck her that the cup meant nothing to him.

Champagne was brought, toasts were made, and about an
hour later it was all over. Erica went to find her mother for
the drive back to La Marmora, reconciled to the fact that she'd
only won the equivalent of sixty-odd pounds. Still, that wasn't
bad for a week's work.

'Excuse me.'

She paused on her way across the lounge.

'Miss Tregarvon, I just wanted to say that you and Mr
Lutsky could have won. You in particular, you played
extremely well.'

'Thank you. But of course you played better.'

'Well, I won't deny that, but I had a better partner. If you
had been lucky enough to draw either myself or Mr Hayes,

you would have been one of the winning pair.'

She smiled and said nothing. She knew it was true.

'I have a feeling we've seen each other before?'

'Yes, I was saying so to my mother last night. You were aboard the *Sinclaire* a few years back.'

'The *Sinclaire*. Ah yes, Sydney and Melbourne . . . Forgive me, I don't recall if we played bridge together?'

'No, but we watched you in play a couple of times. We admired your style.'

'That's good of you. And may I return the compliment. I admired yours – you really have a lot of talent.' He hesitated. 'Have you ever thought of taking it up professionally?'

'Professionally?'

He smiled. 'Don't be so surprised. There's a living to be made out of playing first-class bridge. There are tournaments like this one, and in bigger cities there are bigger prizes—'

'Oh, I don't think—'

'And then on liners, there are always passengers who want to while away the time with a game or two. You must have played on board?'

'Yes,' she admitted.

'But not for money?'

'Well . . . in fact . . . on our last trip . . . yes, I played for money.'

'And won?'

'A bit.'

His smile lit up his thin face very briefly. He wasn't a man who smiled easily. 'I believe . . . I've deprived you of a rather useful sum this evening.'

'Well, yes. Although I wasn't interested in the cup,' she said, smiling.

'Me neither. I sold my share in it to Hayes for twenty bucks – he wanted it as a memento.'

'Sold it!'

'Sure. I always sell cups and trophies – you can't eat them.' He looked faintly apologetic. 'It *is* my living, you understand.'

'I understand.'

'If you decide to use your talent I think you could do well. I wish you luck.'

'Thank you.'

'Perhaps our paths will cross again?'

'Perhaps. Goodnight, Mr Harrowford.'

'Goodnight, Miss Tregarvon.'

As she joined her mother Amy said, 'What was he telling you?'

'That I ought to play bridge professionally.'

'That's what he does, of course.'

'And it's what I'm going to do.'

'Erica! You couldn't!'

'Why not?'

'I explained all that to you. It might be all right for a man but . . . a girl . . . No, no, it's impossible.'

'Mother,' Erica said, 'it's a way of making a living. If Harrowford can do it, I can do it.'

'No, no, darling!'

But even then Amy Tregarvon knew that she was wasting her time. They needed an income and her daughter had found a way to earn it.

Erica wasn't the kind to learn shorthand and typing then

be an office girl in some junior position. She was the kind that wanted to excel in what she did.

Unconventional though it might be, insecure, lacking in respectability, Erica was going to play cards for a living.

Chapter Seven

A sweet, enticing scent of oranges drifted on the air. The cruise ship *Vincenta* lay in her berth in the deepwater harbour of the Schottegat. Along the quay the pastel-coloured buildings glowed in the early evening sun – sugar pink, pistachio green, coffee beige, mint blue. Dutch gables with elaborate plasterwork topped the houses, the doorways were surrounded with carved stone, the doors themselves were heavy mahogany and wood, deeply panelled and with splendid brass fittings. For this was Curaçao, the jewel of the Dutch Antilles.

The passengers of the *Vincenta* were preparing to go ashore for an evening's pleasure. The shops in Willemstad would stay open as long as they wished to buy bottles of the orange liqueur that bore the island's name, and also embroidery, lace in a style reminiscent of the Flemish, wallets and handbags of sharkskin, baskets, carved whalebone, and perfumes distilled from the tropical flowers.

'Oh, Miss Tregarvon, Miss Tregarvon, you said you knew Willemstad, you said you'd been here several times before. Miss Tregarvon, could you show me the best place to buy amber? My mother particularly asked me to bring her a string of amber beads.'

Mrs Achtov, talking as ever nineteen to the dozen,

151

descended the gangplank some two or three yards in front of Erica, turning her head to beg for help without regard to the danger of losing her footing.

Sighing, the seaman on gangplank duty grabbed her elbow as she tottered on to dry land. He exchanged a long-suffering glance with Erica.

Everyone on the *Vincenta* had suffered from Mrs Achtov ever since they left Miami. They all knew she was recently widowed and, without her husband to tell her what to do, at a loss. In the course of evening bridge she had told Erica not once but a dozen times the story of her life with Rudi. 'I wonder if Rudi would have liked me to wear black? I feel guilty about going out of mourning but my mother said I couldn't wear black on a cruise.' Either her husband or her mother had told her what to do all her life, and only a broken leg had prevented her mother from coming with her on the cruise to give her her daily instructions.

Erica perforce joined her on the quay. 'The shops are a little further along the bay,' she told her. 'It's not far, and it's cool enough now for you to walk if you feel like it.'

'Should I? Or should I take a cab?' Mrs Achtov glanced about. 'But there's a crowd waiting for the taxis. I'll walk, shall I? Are you going to walk, Miss Tregarvon? Let's walk together.'

'I'm sorry, Mrs Achtov, I have an engagement—'

'Here? In Willemstad?' Mrs Achtov turned her plump, bewildered face this way and that as if to see whether this foreign port could possibly contain any respectable person with whom Miss Tregarvon had an engagement.

'Oh yes, it's a date I made a long time ago,' Erica said,

lying wildly. Anything, anything, to get Mrs Achtov off her neck.

The Tregarvons, mother and daughter, had chosen the *Vincenta* for their first excursion into professional life because it was the first cruise ship leaving Miami after the Florida Bridge Tournament. Moreover, the oil tycoon Harcourt Nellbrond knew someone on the board of directors of the shipping line. With his introduction Erica had been able to arrange a double cabin for herself and her mother at somewhat reduced rates, on the understanding that she was to consider herself an auxiliary to the entertainment staff of the ship.

She was to play bridge every evening after dinner until eleven if passengers wished to play. She was to ensure that the rubbers were properly run. If there was money involved, it must only be for small sums, a dime a hundred. Sums played for in late-night sessions weren't the concern of the management, however. If she gave bridge lessons, the fees were by arrangement between herself and the passengers.

Mrs Tregarvon was not bound by any of these responsibilities but it was expected that she would play bridge often. Since nothing pleased Amy more than a good rubber of bridge, it was no hardship to her.

For Erica, it had its drawbacks. In times gone by, she could choose whom she would play with. Now that was no longer so. Whoever wanted to play must be given a game, and it was up to Erica to see to it. There were usually at least three bridge tables each evening, but it wasn't always possible to off-load the bores or the troublemakers on to the other foursomes.

Mrs Achtov was a minor problem compared with some.

One of the male bridge players was amorously inclined, and one of the women was envious of Erica's clothes and therefore inclined to be bitchy. But on this evening ashore in Curaçao, both of these passengers had other plans. Only Mrs Achtov was at a loose end and intent on clutching Erica to her ample bosom.

Erica was sorry now she hadn't elected to stay on board with her mother. Amy had chosen to wait until the next day before going ashore.

'Where are you meeting your friends? In town? We might as well go along together—'

'Thank you, Mrs Achtov, but really I'd better wait here. Look, the taxi queue is almost gone, you could get a car now.'

'I do wish you'd at least come with me and point out the shops, Miss Tregarvon, since after all there's no one here expecting you.' Mrs Achtov surveyed the quay once more. No one who looked like a suitable escort for Miss Tregarvon could be seen. 'You're sure you were to meet them *here*?'

'Oh yes, quite sure.' Erica too glanced about. If she could happen upon any respectable-looking woman, she would buttonhole her and start a conversation until Mrs Achtov got into a cab.

'Are you going to spend your whole evening with your friends?' asked her tormentor.

'I'm afraid so.' Go away, she was saying inside herself. Go away, leave me in peace.

'I do think it's bad of them not to be here to meet you if they promised,' Mrs Achtov complained loudly. 'How long are you going to hang about waiting for them?'

'Oh . . . a while yet . . . You go along, Mrs Achtov.'

'I wouldn't feel right about leaving you on your own in a strange port.'

'No, no, that's quite all right.'

'Your friends live here, do they? Perhaps we could go together to their house.' This was a splendid idea as far as Mrs Achtov was concerned. It would take care of her whole evening, because of course the friends would be sure to invite her to spend it with them.

'Erica!' cried a hearty voice. 'Sorry I'm a bit late.'

Erica whirled.

From behind a stack of crates, a somewhat familiar figure had stepped. It was Hobart Crosley, fourth officer on the *Langrovia*.

'Mr Crosley!' she gasped.

'Have you been waiting? I got held up in the post office.' He was in civilian clothes, white linen jacket, cotton trousers, a Panama hat. He raised the Panama to Mrs Achtov. 'Good evening,' he said.

'Er . . . Mrs Achtov, this is Mr Crosley, a . . . a friend of mine. Mrs Achtov is a fellow passenger on the *Vincenta*.'

'How do you do.' The tone was polite, but there was a hint of farewell in it. Here was a young man meeting his lady-friend, it seemed to imply. Why was Mrs Achtov hanging about?

'Oh . . . well . . . I guess I better take a cab . . .'

'Let me get one for you, madam.' Bart stepped to the kerb, signalled a driver and handed Mrs Achtov in. 'Where shall I tell him?'

'Ah . . . the shops . . . I want to buy some amber beads.'

'Tadeus Huystens,' Bart said to the driver, who smartly pulled away.

Erica was waiting for him with a smile of gratitude when he came back. 'Where did you appear from?' she asked. 'And how did you know I needed help?'

'Oh, damsels in distress are my daily lot,' Bart said.

He had seen her from along the dock and thought to say hello, and then hesitated behind the packing cases, because Miss Tregarvon had never seemed particularly welcoming on board his ship. But the conversation he was listening to told him the older woman was hanging on like a limpet. As he himself suffered from troubles of this kind, he felt an immediate fellow feeling. But he was less certain now. 'Have you in fact an engagement?'

She shook her head. 'That was just to get rid of her.'

'Would you . . . er . . . would you like to have dinner with me?'

'But haven't you got arrangements of your own?'

'Only with the postal authorities.' He shrugged. 'Some registered mail's gone astray, I'm supposed to sort it out and rejoin the *Langrovia* with it tomorrow at Kralendijk.'

Kralendijk was the port of the next island in the Dutch Antilles, Bonaire.

'You're cruising back from New York to Southampton?' She stifled a sigh. It would have been so lovely to be aboard the *Langrovia* again. The *Vincenta* was a comfortable ship, fitted out for wealthy passengers, but it was a one-class ship with none of the aristocratic elegance of the *Langrovia*.

'How about it? Are you hungry?'

'Not very, but I'd be glad to have dinner with you.' She'd

never imagined herself saying so to Mr Crosley, who had rather annoyed her on the passage out by his habit of appearing at her elbow when she didn't want him.

Bart whistled up a taxi. It took them to a fine old house set on a promontory. This was the Kronprins Hotel, whose restaurant was well-known for its fish dishes but not glamorous enough to figure in the cruise brochure. There was no danger of meeting Mrs Achtov here.

Over the meal Bart brought her up to date with news of the *Langrovia*, such as it was. A well-run ship seldom had any great events to report. Erica, rather reluctantly, explained what she was doing aboard the *Vincenta*.

'Playing professionally?' He raised his eyebrows. 'Was that what you were doing aboard the *Langrovia*?'

She frowned and shook her head. 'Not consciously. But I did win money, and I won some in a tournament in Miami. So I realized it was a way of making a living – and we do need to have some sort of income.'

That thought had already come to him in the last days of her cruise with the *Langrovia*. 'Your father skipped without leaving you enough to live on?'

She flinched at the word 'skipped'. She said nothing.

'I thought on the westward trip . . . you seemed not to have much in the way of cash.'

'No.'

'Left you with nothing?'

'The liquidators took everything.'

'Oh, but . . . Shrewd financiers make provision for that kind of thing. They put things in their wives' names, I hear.'

'No.'

'He didn't do anything like that?'

'No.'

'What a rat.'

It was said flatly, as if it was an opinion long held. She understood that among seamen the affairs of Lindon Tregarvon would have been discussed often and with bitterness. All the same she felt she must make some defence. No daughter ought to sit by and hear her father spoken of like that.

'I don't think he ever expected to have to run away,' she began, her voice uncertain.

'Otherwise he'd have made some arrangement for funds for you and your mother?'

'No! I didn't mean that! My father never expected to . . . to . . .'

'To be found out? No, I suppose he didn't.' He looked back on many arguments among his fellow officers. 'It was a clever swindle, probably would never have been uncovered if those crewmen in Australia hadn't got drunk and talked too much.'

'Don't,' she said, the hurt echoing in her voice. 'I can't bear to think of it. Men died . . .'

Bart closed his lips on the next thing he'd been about to say. He understood that she was suffering at the mere memory of her father's wrongdoing. What a fool he was, blundering in on her troubles. He changed the subject. 'If you're really going to travel the sea-routes playing bridge for a living,' he said, 'we'll probably run across each other here and there. The *Langrovia*'s new owners are keen on the cruising business, we're likely to be on luxury trips rather than bread-and-butter runs across the Atlantic.'

'You don't approve of that?' she guessed. His tone had implied it.

'I'm beginning to think I'm not cut out to serve aboard big liners. Perhaps in a year or so I'll go back to cargo ships.'

'Is that where you started, in the freight lines?'

'Oh yes. *My* father would have laughed me out of the house if I'd ever said at first that I'd try for a post on a passenger liner. He thinks all that is cissy.' He grinned, thinking of his father at home with his pipe smoke curling around his head and his slippered feet up on the end of the sofa while he read his paper.

'He's a merchantman?'

'Trawler owner. Tough as old boots,' he replied fondly. 'He took me to sea almost from the moment I could toddle. My poor mother had fits, imagining I'd get washed overboard in the first high seas. But I look back now and realize he only ever took me out at first when it was calm. I worked on board the trawler in my school holidays – Christmas was almost always spent going after cod.'

'No Christmas tree? No turkey and mince pie?'

'Mum saved that up for when we got back. Fish run in the winter, you see . . .' He broke off. 'You don't want to hear all that.'

'Yes I do, it's fascinating. Why did you leave fishing and go on the freighters?'

'That was Dad's idea. He says fishing's all right for a man with medium brains but anybody a bit bright ought to have the sense to get out and do something better. So I went to a school for the merchant service – in Blackfriars – and learned all about navigation and sea law and so forth. And then on to the *Baricron*, shipping timber to and from the Baltic. And from there to a Greek line touching all the main ports of the Med. And so on, taking exams as they came, until I got my master's and could apply for the *Langrovia*. Dad doesn't know whether to be proud or ashamed that I'm on the *Langrovia*.' He laughed.

'He sounds great fun, your father.'

'Yeah . . .' He let the word sigh away, studying her. 'That's why I can't help wondering . . .'

'What?'

'Have you ever tried to find Tregarvon?'

'Tried to find him?'

'Don't you keep wondering all the time, how he is, how he's doing?'

'No,' she said, shaking her head with vehemence. 'I never think of him.'

'Never? I find that strange.'

'I don't know what you mean.'

'Didn't you love him?'

'Of *course* I did! That's why it was so . . . so . . .'

'If my dad disappeared,' Bart said, thinking about it, 'I'd never rest till I found him. I'd be wondering all the time – where is he? How is he? Is he well? Is he getting three square meals a day, is anybody looking after him?'

To his consternation Erica Tregarvon leapt to her feet, her cheeks flaming. 'Why don't you mind your own confounded business!' she cried, and throwing down her napkin, walked out.

By the time Bart had disentangled himself from the table and paid the bill, she'd gone. The doorman said she'd told the taximan to take her back to the *Vincenta* A glance at his watch told him it was growing late. A fast cutter was to take him to Bonaire overnight so that he could rejoin the *Langrovia* as arranged at Kralendijk – he couldn't spare time to go on board the *Vincenta* with his apology.

How could he have been so tactless? Thinking aloud about how he'd feel in her place – what business was it of his? But he hadn't expected her to take it so much to heart, because she had always seemed so controlled, so in charge of herself – he hadn't understood until that outburst how much the scandal wounded her. Yes, she had indeed loved her father, but only by wiping him out of her mind could she keep control of her feelings about him.

Bart walked down to the town from the hotel. He found a flower shop, went in, and ordered a bouquet of Sobralia orchids, the delicate narrow-flowered white kind that he'd always liked better than their more flamboyant sisters. He wrote a note to go with them: 'Sorry for rushing in where angels fear to tread. I promise to do better next time we come across each other. Best of luck, Bart Crosley.'

The flowers were delivered by the steward soon after Erica was back aboard. She was in the bathroom taking a shower, to cool both her skin and her temper. Her mother tapped on the bathroom door, calling above the rush of the water: 'Darling, someone's sent you some flowers!'

'Huh!' grunted Erica, shampooing her chestnut hair vigorously.

'I'll put them in water, shall I?'

Throw them overboard, thought Erica. But that was silly. 'All right,' she called.

'There's a note.'

'Just a minute,' she said, turning off the water and wrapping herself in a towel.

She was ready to tear the note up and stamp on it. But somehow it disarmed her. She sat with the words blurring in front of her eyes, foolish tears rising for no reason that she could think of.

'What is it, dear?' Amy asked in anxiety.

'Oh, nothing. I just got angry with someone this evening – silly of me.'

'With who, dear?'

'Bart Crosley. Remember him? From the *Langrovia*?'

'The tall young man with the determined chin?'

'I think that describes him.'

'Why were you angry?' Then Amy stiffened. 'He didn't—?'

'No, no. In fact, he was a perfect gentleman and I ought to have been very nice to him because he rescued me from Mrs Achtov.'

'So why did you get cross?'

Erica got up, finished drying herself, and wrapped herself in a dressing-gown of Chinese silk, bought in the long-off happy days when money meant nothing to her.

'Mother,' she began after a hesitation, 'have you ever wondered where Father went when he ran away?'

Amy gave a gasp, threw her hands to her cheeks, and sat down abruptly on the dressing-table stool.

'I'm sorry!' Erica cried, at once remorseful. She never

spoke of her father to Amy because it always brought tears to her eyes. She put an arm about her mother's shoulders. 'Don't cry.'

Useless to say that. Amy wept quietly for a few moments, then sought out a handkerchief and dried her eyes. 'I have wondered, darling – yes, I have. I've sometimes longed to know where he is, just to know that he's all right.'

'That's what *he* said.'

'Mr Crosley?'

'Yes, he was talking about his own father and said he could never rest easy until he knew he was all right, was being looked after.'

'I thought he'd get in touch with us,' Amy said. 'I was sure of it.'

'Did he say he would?' Erica asked, and held her breath, for if her mother had known beforehand that Lindon Tregarvon was planning to skip bail, it would mean her mother had connived in his wrongdoing.

'No, nothing like that. He didn't talk much after the first shock. At first he kept saying it was all a mistake, it would all be cleared up, he was sure it was a plot on the part of the shippers. But then in the last few days he was a lot less certain. He . . . he seemed in a sort of a daze . . .'

Erica hugged her mother. 'Don't talk about it if it upsets you.'

'Well, darling, it does upset me, but now you've asked the question – where is he? How is he? I keep wondering about that.'

'Didn't he give the slightest hint of where he was going?'

'No, the police asked me all that, over and over. It was all such a terrible shock, my mind was a blank most of the time. I just kept telling them that he almost never talked about business with me. Timothy was his business confidant and Timothy had no idea either, though the police questioned him a dozen times.'

'You say Father gave up the idea that it was all some silly mistake?'

'Oh yes. At least, he realized it wasn't just nonsense. But he was sure there was some mistake and he said he ought to be able to clear it up.'

'How?' Erica asked eagerly.

'Oh, it had something to do with documents . . . I forget exactly . . .'

'What documents?'

'I'm sure I don't know, dear. I know Father was astonished at some of the documentary evidence the police had got hold of, but he couldn't argue with them on some points because you know, dear, that last year or so, while you were going through your London season, he let things slide a bit. He used to do business here and there all over the world. You remember, he'd telegraph the London office from Rio or Hong Kong, just as if he was telephoning across the street. But when we settled in England for your debut he didn't do that so much. He took such an interest in all that, you know, sweetheart. He was so proud of you!'

'Don't, Mother,' Erica begged, feeling her throat choke up at the words.

'It's true. And he was so happy when you got engaged. That's why it shattered him so when the detectives came with their awful accusations. Then after he'd thought it over during that first week, he seemed to cheer up a bit. He said he was going to clear his name. I was so pleased to see him looking less unhappy although of course I couldn't help thinking it was only a day-dream. Still, day-dreams can make you happy.'

'Clear his name?' Erica repeated. 'Did he actually say that?'

'Oh yes, dear. That was just before he went away. He seemed more hopeful and determined, and he said . . . he said . . .' She faltered into silence.

'He said what?'

'I don't know . . . That there was a thread he could follow, that would clear his name. That there was something in the past that he ought to follow up. Lots of little things like that, trying to make himself believe he could sort it out, but not based on anything solid, you see. Like saying he only had to get to the *Margravine* and everything would be different.'

'The *Margravine*?'

'He was always happy aboard the *Margravine*,' Amy sighed.

'But Mother . . . why didn't you tell me this before?'

'What, dear?'

'That he said he wanted to get to the *Margravine*.'

'But it was only wishful thinking, my love.'

'Mother, don't you see? That may be where he went – to the Bahamas, to board the *Margravine*.'

Erica took her arm from around her mother's shoulders, got to her feet, and stared down at her. Amy Tregarvon stared back.

'You think he went to the Bahamas?'

'Well . . . why not?'

'But the *Margravine* . . . It's been sold. To Gaynor Medcalfe, to help pay off the creditors . . .'

'That's true, Mother, but that doesn't mean that Father didn't go to the Bahamas. There's no knowing how long it might take him to get there, having to do it under an assumed name, I suppose. And, of course, when he got there he'd find an order posted about the boat having passed into the hands of the liquidators.'

'You think he might be there? In Nassau?'

'It's possible,' she said slowly.

The *Vincenta* completed her stay at Curaçao, then headed on through the Caribbean on a round tour that would take her at last back to Miami. This time the two Tregarvon women had a little money in hand. They took a room at a motel, not wishing to claim any more hospitality from Mrs Oakes. When they had left on the *Vincenta*, telegrams had flown back and forth between the two families, Eunice Oakes insisting that they must feel free to use La Marmora any time they were in Miami. But they couldn't go on for ever being in debt to friends for a place to stay.

The day after they'd settled into the motel, Erica looked up 'Inquiry Agents' in the phone book. At random she chose an address on Raintree Street, called for an appointment, and presented herself that afternoon as arranged.

The office was a severely practical place, all filing cabinets, plain deal desks, and whirring electric fans. Daltry Clarbrook rose to greet her. 'Miss Tregarvon? Good afternoon, pleased to meet you. Can I offer you anything. Coffee? Iced tea? Juice?'

'Nothing, thank you.' Now that she was here, she didn't know how to begin. She'd said her inquiry was about how to find a missing person, but now she realized it meant telling this stranger something about her father, and the whole idea seemed uninviting.

Clarbrook however had met this frame of mind before. He was an ex-policeman from a northern force, retired to Miami for the climate, but glad to implement his pension with some inquiry work.

'Just take your time,' he soothed. 'I haven't any other visitors coming for the next hour or so and I don't have to be anywhere until six this evening.'

'Thank you.' He was a big man, grey-haired, a little too fat, but with shrewd eyes. Haltingly she told him about the disappearance of Lindon Tregarvon.

The shrewd eyes grew a little unbelieving. He'd expected something about a missing husband. International ship-owner? Abandoned wife and daughter? Find out if he's been to his yacht? Her yellow linen dress was of exceptional cut and her beige sandals, although recently mended, were handmade. And even if it wasn't all strictly true, her money was as good as anybody else's.

'The trail's kind of cold by now,' he pointed out.

'I'm afraid that's true. I'm sorry.'

'The terms are fifty dollars a day plus expenses, first day's fee in advance,' he said, and saw her flinch. 'It won't take very long, probably,' he added quickly, 'and expenses will be mostly phone calls. I won't hit you for fares or hotel bills or anything like that.'

'Oh . . . Well . . . In that case.' She took out her notecase, counted out fifty dollars, and took the receipt. 'When can I expect to hear something?'

'Couple of days. Let me have your address and phone number.'

There was a one-day bridge tournament in Palm Beach from which Erica and her mother, playing as a partnership, returned with five hundred dollars. Then they were contacted by the owners of the cruise line to ask if they would like to join a trip to Buenos Aires, same terms as before.

The day before they were due to sail, Erica rang Daltry Clarbrook to say they would not be in Miami and that in any case she couldn't afford to continue his fees.

'I've got a little something for you,' he said, 'if you care to drop by.'

'You've found him?'

'No, it wasn't likely to be that easy, lady,' he said with some sympathy. 'But there's something.'

She went by taxi into central Miami, heart beating unexpectedly fast. The office seemed just as plain and uncomfortable as before.

Clarbrook took a folder from a wire basket on his desk. 'You understand this is all telephone inquiry,' he began. 'Whether there's more to learn if you're there on the spot, I can't tell. I started this investigation by associating with the *Margravine*, since that was supposed to be the reason your father might go to Nassau. You told me the boat had been sold to Gaynor Medcalfe.'

'Yes.'

'Medcalfe has been entering her in regattas and so forth. He's taken her away from Nassau a lot. The people around the quays remember your father well, from the old days. And of course they read about the insurance case in the papers – it was covered in the *Nassau Guardian* and the *Tribune*. They say definitely he hasn't been around since the scandal broke.'

'But he might have been using an assumed name?'

'Yeah, I thought of that. No one answering his description has been around.'

'But of course he might not look quite the same . . .'

'He's grown a beard, you mean? Something like that? Could be. But the fact is, no one's been showing any particular interest in the *Margravine* – except for one man.'

'Who?' asked Erica, tense with suspense.

'You mentioned your father's personal secretary? Perriman?'

'Yes!'

'He's been aboard the *Margravine*.'

'Aboard her!'

'Yeah. Does it mean anything?'

'Timothy Perriman went to Nassau?'

'No, seems he met Medcalfe in New York earlier in the year. Medcalfe was in an event off Long Island soon after he bought the boat from the liquidators—'

'Yes, I saw it in the yachting magazines—'

'Perriman got in touch with him through the Long Island Yacht Club. Medcalfe invited him aboard, for old times' sake. Took him sailing for a couple of days off Montauk Point.'

'Timothy went *sailing*?'

The detective sat back in his wooden armchair to study her with interest. 'Shakes you?'

'Timothy's a rotten sailor. He gets seasick moored to the quay!'

'You don't say . . . Well, I must admit it made me sit up and look around when his name came up. Your father was talking about the *Margravine* before he took off, and now his personal secretary turns up aboard the boat.'

'It's very strange,' muttered Erica.

'Well, see, Miss Tregarvon, that's as far as I can take it. It's just possible Perriman expected to meet your father somewhere where the *Margravine* was in port, but it seems it wasn't Nassau and it wasn't Long Island, because nobody on the boat-slips at Easthampton recalls anyone who fits your father's description. This guy Medcalfe likes to race the boat, so he takes her all over the place. You'd need a coastguard service to keep track of her, practically. You got that kind of money?'

She shook her head.

'I'm sorry. We seem to have reached the end of the rope.'

'Well, thank you for what you've found out, anyhow. I'll pay your bill, if you'll give me the total.'

'Yeah, sure, here it is.' He pushed over a sheet of paper on which she saw every phone call painstakingly itemized.

When she had counted out the money he said, 'What're you going to do now?'

'I don't know. There isn't much I *can* do, because my mother and I are setting out for Buenos Aires tomorrow.' At his startled look she added with a smile, 'We work aboard the ship – on the entertainment side.'

'I get you. Well, if there's anything else you want me to do, let me know. Always at your service.'

'Thank you. But perhaps I'll try ringing Timothy Perriman when I get to the motel.' She glanced at her wrist. 'It's about three in the afternoon in England. If I can get his office number from International Directory.'

'What's England got to do with it?' Clarbrook said in surprise.

'He lives there.'

'He lives in New York,' Clarbrook said. 'He's got an office near Bowling Green. Here's the telephone number.'

Erica took the slip of paper from his hand. 'In New York . . .'

'Sure. You didn't know that?'

She shook her head. 'Although in fact when he rang us some weeks ago, he was speaking from New York. But I thought . . . he'd just come on a flying visit.'

'No, Mr Perriman's a solid citizen. He's got all the right permits and he's doing well. Shipping consultant, whatever that may be.'

'Thank you,' said Erica, shaking hands. 'You've given me a lot to think about.'

And think she did, without coming to any sensible conclusion. Besides, they had to go aboard the *Southwind* a few hours later and take up their duties.

Six weeks went by before they returned to the home port of Fort Lauderdale. Once again they booked into a motel to rest and sort out their plans.

'I'm going to New York for a few days, Mother,' Erica said. 'Want to come?'

'New York in November?' She shuddered. 'No thanks! And why on earth *you* want to go, I can't imagine.'

171

'I want to get my hair properly cut,' she said. It was a poor excuse, but her mother accepted it without demur.

She hadn't told Amy about her approach to Daltry Clarbrook or what he had found out. She didn't know whether what she was doing would have any results and hadn't wanted to raise false hopes. Moreover, now that Timothy had reappeared in the scheme of things, there was even less reason to speak about it. She knew her mother half-regretted the fact that Erica had turned her back on him.

She took the overnight train to New York, booking into a quiet hotel near the station. She looked up the phone book to check the number and sure enough there it was: Timothy Perriman, Shipping Consultant, Barharb Building, Bowling Green. A young woman's voice answered.

'Perriman Consultants.'

'May I speak to Mr Perriman please?'

'Who is calling please?'

'Miss Tregarvon.'

'In connection with what matter?'

'It's a personal call.'

'I'm sorry, ma'am, Mr Perriman is very tied up.'

'Would you please just tell him Miss Tregarvon is on the line.'

'I assure you, ma'am—'

'Just tell him. If he says no, that's an end to it.'

There was a short delay, a series of clicks, and then Timothy's voice, sounding uncertain. 'Erica?'

'Yes, it's me, Timothy. How are you?'

'I'm well, yes, I'm well. How are you?'

'Fine, thank you. Timothy, can I come and talk to you?'

'Where are you?' he asked, bewildered.

'Here in Manhattan.'

'You are? When did you get in?'

'I'll tell you all that when I see you. Could I come to your office?'

'When? Now? I'm afraid I have appointments for the rest of the day.'

'Tomorrow?'

'Tomorrow's pretty busy too.' She could hear him turning pages to and fro in his diary. 'I'll tell you what, are you free this evening?'

'Well . . . yes . . .'

'Would you have dinner? I'd be through here by seven. Shall we say eight o'clock?'

She hesitated, but then shrugged. What did it matter where they met so long as she could ask him the questions she had been brooding over for weeks? 'Where, Timothy?'

'The Fontaine, it's near Columbus Circle, any taxi driver will know it.'

'All right then, eight o'clock.'

She went to her former hairdresser to have her hair cut. It was an extravagance, but she felt she needed the boost to her morale. She hadn't brought evening clothes with her, but her dark skirt and a soft silk blouse would have to do. Her topcoat was one of the good things of long ago, a fine windproof twill lined with quilting, warm enough for even the coldest Manhattan November.

And she was glad of it, because the weather was vile, a strong cold wind blowing sleet along the boulevard.

Erica shivered as she stepped into the cab outside her hotel.

173

But it wasn't from the cold. It was with a mixture of apprehension and excitement. She was going to speak to the man who might be able to tell her something about her missing father.

Chapter Eight

Predictably, the Fontaine had a fountain. It also had pale blue walls and white panelling, lots of gilt-edged mirrors, and a maitre d'hotel in a blue silk evening jacket.

Timothy was waiting in the bar, a little nook with painted grey tables and velvet-cushioned chairs. He rose to greet her, taking both her hands effusively. For one awful moment she thought he was going to attempt to give her a welcome kiss but she avoided that by shaking hands and sitting down.

The head waiter gave them menus, summoned the bartender with a flick of the finger. They ordered their drinks.

'Well,' said Timothy, 'you didn't go home with the *Langrovia*?'

'No, for the time being we're based this side of the Atlantic.' She could see he was about to ask where, so to forestall him she said, 'And so are you! I passed your office earlier today. A very imposing building.'

'That's important here,' he said. 'In London you can get away with operating from a dusty cranny but in New York you have to have a good business ambience.'

'You're doing well?'

'Not bad,' he said, looking pleased.

His financial well-being was evident from his appearance. He had always been well-dressed; Erica's father had insisted on that, arranging for his secretary's suits to be made by his own tailor. But now in addition Timothy's narrow dark head was beautifully barbered, his evening shirt had black pearl studs, his evening shoes were handmade. Everything about him spoke discreetly of success, and the attention he received from the restaurant staff confirmed it.

He asked after Mrs Tregarvon. 'She's well,' Erica said. 'So long as we're near the sea, her bronchial condition is no problem.'

'But you're not at La Marmora.' She shrugged, and since nothing else was forthcoming he said, 'I tried to ring you there, they said you'd gone.'

'Oh yes. As you said, we couldn't stay there for ever.'

He had the grace to colour up a little at the reminder. Luckily, because the last thing she wanted was to get on uneasy terms, the head waiter came to say their table was ready.

They ate New England lobster, duck bigarade, tarte de cerises, with Vichy water to drink. Respectable restaurants served no alcohol. America was still enduring Prohibition. They talked about what they'd been doing since last they met. Timothy agreed that he was doing well: 'I just happened to notice a niche in the business world that needed filling.'

When he asked what she was doing she said, truthfully, that she had been teaching bridge to beginners. When he asked for her address she said vaguely, 'Oh, we move about a lot,' and if he thought it was in search of yet cheaper lodgings, she didn't disabuse him.

When they reached the coffee and petits fours, she felt it was safe to embark on the real business of the evening. 'Life has certainly been very different for both of us since my father vanished,' she said musingly. 'Mother and I were saying a while back, I wonder where he went to?'

'Goodness knows,' Timothy said, crackling the paper container of his petit four between thin fingers.

'Did he ever say anything to you that could have given you a hint?'

'The police asked me that a hundred times. I've no idea.'

'There was a suggestion that he had money put by in some spot where he could get at it?'

'Not that I knew of. And if it's money that's a problem, Erica, you know I would always—'

'No, no. Mother and I were wondering . . . really . . . how he is, if he's all right.' She waited.

Timothy eyed her. 'Why do you say it in that tone of voice, as if I might know the answer?'

'Do you know, Timothy? Not where he is, perhaps, but how he is? Does he contact you?'

'Not at all!' He was very vehement. 'I know nothing about him! What on earth makes you say a thing like that, Erica? I'm as baffled as you are as to his whereabouts.'

'But you were so much in his confidence. If he were to contact anyone it would be—'

'I can't have you saying things like this,' he interrupted, colour rising under sallow skin. 'You're implying that I'm in touch with a man who's wanted by the police! That would be extremely damaging to my reputation if it got around. I can't let you go on like that, Erica. I must ask you not to speak to me on the subject again.'

Methinks the lady doth protest too much, thought Erica.

'Did he go to the Bahamas?' she asked. 'Was that it?'

She thought he flinched. 'Why the devil should he go there?'

'To get to the *Margravine*?'

This time there was no doubt. His expression changed fractionally, he pressed his lips together. Then he rallied. 'He had other things to think of than a luxury yacht! Wherever he went, it wouldn't be anywhere where he'd be recognized the minute he showed his face, now would it?'

There was truth in that. All the same, the mention of the yacht had rattled Timothy. It dawned on Erica, accustomed to summing up opponents at the card table, that Timothy was the kind of man who liked things to go according to plan. He wasn't at his best when taken by surprise.

So she said flatly, 'Why did you go aboard the *Margravine*, Timothy?'

Now she had him really startled. The flush of colour left his cheeks, he went perceptibly paler. 'What gave you that idea?'

'Oh, I heard it . . . Sailing people, you know, in Miami, who'd been to the Easthampton Regatta. It's a small world, the sailing world.'

'Oh, yes. I see. Well, I was . . . I happened to be there . . .'

'In Easthampton?' Her tone implied, You never liked sailing communities.

'I was in New York, and I happened to see that the new owner was sailing the *Margravine* in the competitions, so I . . . It was just for old times' sake.'

'But you never liked yachting, Timothy. I can't think why you'd bother.'

Unfortunately at that moment, when he was totally off-balance, the waiter arrived to ask if they would like more coffee. Timothy had their cups refilled, waited while sugar and cream were offered. Then he said, much more relaxed, 'If you think about it, Erica, the relationship between your father and me was much more than employer–employee. There was a friendship there. The *Margravine* was one of the things he was fond of. It's perfectly natural I'd want to take a look at her.'

She was about to say, 'But you sailed in her – you know you're always seasick.'

But the waiter reappeared.

'Excuse me, sir.' He bent to speak quietly in Timothy's ear. Timothy glanced across the restaurant at another table. He rose.

'Excuse me a minute, Erica. Some important clients of mine . . . They just want a word.'

He threaded his way among the tables. The group who had summoned him numbered eight people. Erica examined them with some surprise and great interest. Four of the men were dark-haired and olive-skinned, almost certainly Italian or of Italian parentage. They were what her father would have called 'flashy', too much satin edging to their dinner suits, too much gold in the way of cuff-links, watch-chains and rings. There was one other man, more quietly turned out but rather coarse in looks. The three women were exquisitely gowned, with perfectly waved hair and make-up applied by an expert. Everything about them said 'high-price cocotte'.

Well, well, she said to herself. So this was the niche in the business world that Timothy happened to notice?

After a moment or two Timothy came back. As he resumed his seat he looked uncomfortable. She knew he wished she hadn't seen his clients.

'We have a business meeting tomorrow,' he muttered. 'They just wanted to alter the timing a little.'

'They look . . .'

'What?' he said with some apprehension.

'As if they have money,' she ended. She'd been going to say they looked ruthless.

'Oh yes! And of course, you know, Americans like to let people know they're successful.' He was apologizing for their showiness, for the fact that he'd had to hurry across the room at their summons.

Erica wanted to get the conversation back to the matter that interested her but Timothy had had time to make his own change. He said, 'I want to use this chance to say I'm sorry for the tactless things I may have said long ago. I hope you understand that the scandal and your father's exodus . . . well, they had their effect on me too, you know. I know I didn't approach you in the right way.'

'Let's not talk about that.'

'But I want to! That's why I was so glad to hear your voice this afternoon! I wanted the chance to explain to you.' He paused. 'You made me very angry, you see, when you rejected me.'

'But Timothy, you couldn't really have expected—'

'Yes I did. In the first place it seemed such a sensible solution to your problems, and then I . . . well, you'll think me a fool but I really couldn't believe you hadn't guessed my feelings and perhaps felt something for me too.'

'No,' she sighed, shaking her head. 'But that's all in the past.'

'I've never met anyone who could hold a candle to you, Erica. Couldn't we go back and start again?'

'Start what again? Seriously, Timothy, there was never—'

'Just tell me I haven't absolutely ruined things. Say we can at least be friends.'

'Yes, of course.' It was terribly embarrassing. She simply wanted to end the conversation and get away.

'I'd like you to know that if ever you need anything, if you need help making ends meet—'

'No, no, everything is fine, thank you. It's kind of you, Timothy, thank you, but really there's no need.'

She let him put her into a taxi and was driven away. When the taxi had taken her about two blocks she tapped on the window. 'Would you take me back, please? I've left my gloves.'

Her gloves were in her handbag. She asked the taxi to wait, went back into the restaurant, told the maitre d'hotel she'd left her gloves in the powder room, and went into it.

The kindly black woman in attendance looked up in surprise at her reappearance. 'Leave something, honey?'

'No, I wanted to ask you something. You've taken the wraps for three ladies this evening, one is a tall blonde in a blue chiffon gown with diamond earrings, one's shorter with a ruched oyster-coloured gown, and the third is darker with a double row of pearls and I think wearing green.'

The attendant's eyes went to three fur wraps hanging on the coat-rack. 'Oh yeah.'

'Do you know anything about them?'

'They with the Italian gennemen.'

'Yes.'

'I dunno nuthin about them.'

Erica took a five-dollar bill from her purse. 'I don't want names or anything. I'd just like some idea what business the gentlemen are in.'

The bill disappeared like magic into the pocket of the frilly apron. 'Honey, you don' wanna get mixed up with those fellas. It's a twitchy time for them, what with the Bill going through the House.'

'What Bill?' Erica said in bewilderment.

'Repeal of Prohibition, dearie. Where you bin?'

'Repeal of Prohibition?'

'Yeah, and all the gennemen that's made a fortune in the last ten years selling hooch is wondering where their next plate of spaghetti is comin' from.'

'You mean they're *bootleggers*?'

The black woman shrugged. 'The Bassania brothers,' she said in a low voice. 'They spend a lot here recently, try to look respectable, you know? But it's the same for them as the rest. What they gonna do with all those trucks, those ships that anchor off some little place on the coast?'

'Thank you,' Erica said, and hurried out to her taxi.

Shipping consultant! No doubt Timothy's clients had a big problem for him to solve. Bootleggers out of a job, with a fleet of vessels both large and small for which they must now find a use.

Marvelling at this information Erica went back to her hotel, packed, paid her bill, and returned to her mother in Miami.

* * *

Their next voyage was to be a short Christmas cruise from Miami to Havana and thence across to Vera Cruz. Christmas Day in Havana was pleasant enough but most of the passengers of the *Magnolo* spent it gambling in the many casinos. In Vera Cruz harbour, to Erica's delight, she saw the *Langrovia* at anchor. How long was she staying? Until the day after tomorrow, to allow the passengers time to see the religious dances in front of the cathedral.

She sent a message aboard. About an hour later came the reply. 'Off duty this evening from nine p.m. Meet you in the Coronado Restaurant.'

She got there too early, but was quite happy to wait. The restaurant proved to be on a jetty built out over the water, a little removed from the city itself. The lights of Vera Cruz twinkled, she could hear the faint echo of the guitars and trumpets from the dancing in the plaza.

When Bart Crosley arrived he was in uniform whites. 'I didn't stop to change,' he said. 'Hope you don't mind.'

'Not at all.' But the uniform brought forcefully to mind the old warning: never get involved with the ship's officers. That was all right, of course. She wasn't 'involved' with Bart Crosley. Yet, oddly enough, he was the nearest thing she had had to a friend since she'd had to rebuild her life.

They ordered cocktails, and the fiery Mexican tortillas to follow with an accompaniment of sea-breeze cooler, a drink very popular on board the cruise ships.

Bart had been glad to get her note, because he'd never known for sure whether she'd accepted his apology.

He said, 'You didn't stay angry with me then?'

'Not for long.'

'How have things been going with you?'

'Not bad. There are some very wealthy passengers on these American cruises – the men like to play bridge for stakes that "make it worthwhile".'

'And you win all the time?'

'Most of the time. Enough so that I always come out ahead. So far,' she added, putting her cocktail glass aside.

'Yes, so far. It's sort of unstable as a livelihood, isn't it?'

'It's the only one open to me. I'm not trained for anything else.' She had never dreamed she would ever admit such a thing to anyone except her mother. Her own words surprised her. She looked at him, and to her relief when he nodded there was understanding in his brown-eyed gaze.

The tortillas came. Bart, who'd hurried ashore without going to the dining saloon for a meal, made inroads on the pile of neatly rolled pancakes filled with a mix of beans, a little meat, and various kinds of searing hot peppers. Erica watched him in wonder. It would have taken the skin off her throat to eat them so casually.

In any case, she wasn't hungry. Half the time on board ship seemed to be given up to meals of one kind or another. And she'd asked him to meet her for a specific reason.

'You remember what you said about wondering where my father had gone?' she began.

'I remember.'

'When I got back to the ship that night I asked my mother what she thought.' She cast her mind back to that scene. 'She got upset, she always does if we talk about Father. But after a bit she murmured something about our yacht.'

'Our yacht,' Bart echoed, and laughed.

Erica blushed. 'Well, we did have a yacht, once. She's called the *Margravine*. Father kept her at Nassau.' She saw he was still amused at her phrase so she went on defensively, 'Father was a merchant seaman originally, you know! He wasn't always a shipping magnate. He loved the sea, really loved it, that's why we spent so much time on it, much to the discomfort of many of his staff.'

'It's a sailing yacht, the *Margravine*?'

'A converted brigantine built in Salem. Father used to skipper her himself at first, but later he didn't have time to sail her much. But he always kept her in good trim and we had a crew we could call on any time we were in the Bahamas.'

'What was it your mother said about her?' he prompted, seeing that it made her sad to look back on those days.

'She said Father had talked about wanting to get to the *Margravine*, just before he ran off.'

Bart finished the last of his tortillas, drank a great draught of sea-breeze, and then asked, 'Why are you telling me this?'

'I . . . I'd like your opinion. Something rather odd came out of it.' She explained about hiring an inquiry agent to find out if Tregarvon had been seen in Nassau and the lack of success on that point. 'But then Mr Clarbrook told me that my father's former private secretary had looked up the new owner of the *Margravine* and gone aboard her.'

'And that means something to you?'

'It puzzles me. Because, you see, Timothy is the world's worst sailor. Even aboard a big liner he'd begin to look queasy if the weather got rough. And aboard the *Margravine* . . . In fact, he only ever came aboard when she was moored at the dockside. He'd never go out in her. Yet he made a special trip to Easthampton and went out for a two-day cruise with Mr Medcalfe.'

'Well now, that's odd.'

'The weather was rough – I had Mr Clarbrook check back on it. Timothy was seasick all the time. Apparently everybody was laughing about it after they got back.'

The waitress came to clear away the sticky plates. Bart ordered coffee, making sure it would be American and not the mud-like beverage the Mexicans seemed to like.

'Why do you think this unseamanlike private secretary went in search of the *Margravine*?'

'I wondered if it was some point of contact with my father. I thought, perhaps, they'd made an arrangement to meet somewhere, wherever the *Margravine* might be.'

Bart felt a shock at her words. He half-shook his head. 'That would mean this chap colluded with your father in making his getaway.'

'Yes.'

'Erica, that's a very serious charge.'

'That's exactly what Timothy said when I asked him—'

'You asked him?' Bart was startled.

'Yes, I went to New York to see him in November and asked him straight out if he knew where Father was, and he got very agitated.'

'No wonder. Look here, Erica, you can't go around accusing people of things like that. If he did in fact help your father make a run for it, he could be in serious trouble with the law.'

'Not now. In England, yes, he could be charged with something or other – conspiracy to pervert the course of justice or something. But not in New York.'

'Now listen to me,' Bart said in a severe tone, frowning at her over the coffee pot, 'don't make accusations like that. It's libel or slander or something.'

'Don't worry, he's not going to sue me,' Erica replied, tossing her head. 'He's got himself nicely set up in New York as a shipping consultant and the last thing he wants is to remind everybody he was connected with a man who got caught out in a gigantic fraud.'

'Shipping consultant? What's his line – cargo handling? Passenger transport? Mail contracts?'

'I didn't find out. I saw a group of men he said were his clients, though.'

'At his office?'

'No, in a smart restaurant in Manhattan. You should have seen them, overdressed thugs, they looked to me. The cloakroom attendant told me they were bootleggers.'

'Bootleggers!'

'Well, ex-bootleggers, of course, now Prohibition's been repealed. I suppose there's a fortune to be made, advising people like that what to do with all the things they used for their rum-running.'

'Erica, it's no joke! Do you realize what those fellows are like? Good God, *Al Capone* is a bootlegger.'

'The cloakroom girl said the bunch at the restaurant were the Bassanias.'

'Some other branch of the Italian Brotherhood,' Bart said, thoroughly alarmed. 'If your friend Timothy's got himself mixed up with the Mob, he'd better know what he's doing.'

'He's no friend of mine,' Erica responded indignantly.

'Thank God for that.' He had listened to the gossip, and was well aware that many crews and captains had been deeply involved in illegal shipping of liquor, be it rum, French wine and brandy, Dutch gin, Scotch whisky. Now these men were on the beach – unemployed. The ships were laid up until some new use could be found for them, but the syndicate which owned them wouldn't be happy for long in idleness. Anyone who got mixed up in that kind of thing was either asking for trouble or knew his way around.

Which brought him to the question, Did this Timothy know his way around? Was he after all the kind of man who might have helped a crooked financier to arrange his disappearance?

He was now beginning to regret telling Erica she ought to want to know where her father had gone. If the answer lay with this dubious character in New York, the farther away she stayed from him the better.

'The chap Timothy, will you be seeing him again?'

'It isn't very likely.' She didn't say, because he keeps on trying to persuade me to marry me, and it's all too embarrassing.

'It's better you don't see him,' Bart said. 'He has some very odd clients.'

'I'm not interested in his clients,' Erica burst out. 'If he knows where Father is, why doesn't he tell me?'

It would make him an accomplice, that's why, thought Bart to himself. 'What's he like, this Timothy?'

'Oh . . . businesslike . . . efficient on the whole, though he gets rattled if his advance planning is messed up.'

'Devoted?'

'I beg your pardon?' The question took her by surprise.

'Devoted to your father. A faithful retainer,' Bart suggested.

'Oh no. No, although he claimed—'

'What?'

'That there was friendship between himself and Father.'

'But you think not?'

'We-ell, they were friends. Of course. Father wouldn't have kept him on if he disliked him, now would he? Father took an interest in him, but then he did with all his staff.'

'You're talking about how your father felt towards Timothy. How did Timothy feel towards your father, in your opinion?'

That was much more difficult to assess. Erica cast her mind back to those days, now so distant, like something seen through the wrong end of a telescope.

Timothy had always been around. He was included in their social activities, had gone on most of the long sea trips, had stayed ashore at the ports when Tregarvon wanted to go sailing. He'd been with them in Paris, in Genoa, in Rio . . . He'd been at the coming-out party for Erica. He'd gone with them to Ascot, to Henley, to Cowes.

He'd enjoyed it all. She could picture him now, springing to his feet to offer a light for the cigarette of some businessman, fetching a wrap for some pretty debutante. She could hear his voice: 'Are you in a draught, Mme Lelonge? Shall I close the window? Let me get you another drink, Mr Berkimedes.' And replying to her father: 'Yes, Mr Tregarvon. No, Mr Tregarvon.' What had been in his voice? Respect, compliance, attention. Affection?

'I don't think Timothy felt much for my father,' she

ventured, 'beyond what an employee would feel for a good-hearted employer.'

'No devotion?'

'That's the second time you've used that word. What are you asking?'

'I was thinking . . . a man who'd help another man evade justice in a big scandal like the Tregarvon case must have strong feelings of loyalty and affection—' He broke off suddenly, seeing Erica shake her head with vehemence.

'No. Timothy didn't feel like that about Father.'

'A bit of a cold fish, is he?'

'Oh no! He's capable of emotion.' She thought of his anger when she turned down his proposal. 'He's got pride, a lot of self-regard.' She paused, but decided not to say that he claimed to be in love with her. She was sure it wasn't true. At that moment it came into her head that perhaps Timothy wasn't capable of love.

Bart thought it over. 'I've never met him, of course. But the man you describe doesn't seem likely to take a risk like helping your father escape.' When she made no response he went on, 'You don't agree?'

'Why is he interested in the *Margravine*, then?'

Bart shrugged. 'Idle curiosity? Ghoulishness?'

'Ghoulishness?'

'Well, there are people who like to go to the scene of an accident, or who bid at auction for the belongings of, for instance, Mata Hari.'

She laughed. 'Mata Hari!'

'I'm serious. A chap on my last ship paid fifty pounds in Jamaica for what was reputed to be the cutlass with which

Blackbeard the Pirate cut down four men.'

'And was it?'

'Oh, very possibly, if Blackbeard bought cutlasses stamped "Made in Sheffield".'

The elderly waitress who had served them watched them, envying their laughter. A handsome couple, the man tanned and imposing in his uniform, the girl alight with amusement. When they rose and went out into the tropical darkness Rosita was thinking, a lovely night, a night for lovers.

There was a little breeze off the Gulf of Camperche. Erica shivered in her sleeveless silk dress.

'Cold?' Bart said, and put an arm round her to keep her warm.

She was grateful for the protection of that arm and its strength as they made their way off the uneven planks of the jetty. If her high heels had caught in a crack, she might have fallen. But he steadied her, and she leaned against him more closely.

'Shall I whistle up a cab?'

'No, let's walk.'

The harbour lights of Vera Cruz were not far off. Music could still be heard from the plaza. The little restaurant was lost to view by a turn in the road. Soft light from the infrequent street lamps cast their shadows before and behind them as they walked. The fragrance of the red frangipani filled the air. Above, the stars glowed like sequins on a blue velvet gown.

They came to a little park with benches. Without having to speak a word they turned into it, sank down on the nearest bench, and went into each other's arms. His kiss was different from any other, demanding yet tender, urgent yet soft. His mouth caressed her throat, the skin of her upper arm. Then he had pulled aside the soft silk, and she felt his lips upon her breast.

She wound her arms more fiercely about him, bringing him closer, ever closer. For a time they were lost in each other.

Then she felt him draw back. He said hoarsely, 'I'd better take you back to your ship.'

'No!'

'Erica, we're heading straight for—'

'I know where we're heading, Bart, I'm not a fool, I know what I'm doing.'

'Sweetheart, it's the tropical night, the music—'

'That's not the reason.' She put her hand to his cheek. 'Don't say it has to end, darling. Not now that we've just found each other.'

'Erica, are you sure?'

'I've never been so sure of anything.'

'We could go . . .'

'Where?'

'There's a beach house, a friend of mine owns it.'

'Where, darling?'

'Not far.' He hesitated. 'Erica, I want you to be sure.'

'I'm sure.'

A five-minute walk took them to a track leading down to the shore. A cabin could just be discerned in the starlight. Bart took a key from under a flowerpot by the door.

'There's no one here?' Erica asked.

'He's gone home to his family in Seattle for Christmas.

Wait a moment.' He unlocked the door. She could hear him thread his way to a table. A match was struck, and he lit an oil lamp. 'The simple life,' he said with a smile in his voice. 'He's an artist.'

The room was untidy, with canvases stacked around the walls and a folded easel over a chair. Bart opened a door on the far side and stood, waiting to see if she would cross its threshold.

She went past him into the bedroom. The bed was spread with a multicoloured serape which could only just be seen in the faint glow from the studio's lamp. Erica stepped to the bedside, turned, and held out her arms to Bart. He unfastened the foolish little hooks and eyes of her dress. The soft silk whispered as it fell to her feet. She in her turn unbuttoned the stiff uniform tunic with its gold stripe. His skin burned to her touch.

Soon they were lying side by side, touching, kissing, exploring. She felt the frisson of his fingers along her spine. He let himself come alive to the brush of her lips on his chest. Little by little the exploration became more urgent, more frantic.

And then they were enveloped by an overpowering wave, a devouring flame. One moment they were seeking, longing, demanding. The next they were one, together as never before, a part of each other, a part of creation, of the universe, of eternity.

Afterwards they lay drowsing, sometimes speaking, sometimes merely snuggling against one another. Later they made love again, still learning about one another, finding the ways of delight in each other's bodies.

About three in the morning Erica sat up, tousle-headed, smiling, but with some recollection of the ordinary world. 'I have to get back to the *Magnolo*. Mother will be wondering where I've got to.'

'Erica . . .'

'Yes, darling?'

'Erica, I had no idea that . . . that . . .'

'What, my love?'

'It was the first time for you.'

'Oh yes.'

'Erica, darling . . .' There was something in his voice, regret, guilt . . .

She laid fingertips on his lips. 'It's all right. I'm glad. I'm glad it was with you. Oh!' She giggled.

'What?'

'I might have gone to bed for the first time with Gerald!'

'Who the devil is Gerald?' he growled, pausing as he tried to sort out his uniform from the tangle of clothes on the floor.

'The man I was engaged to. Good heavens, it doesn't seem possible.' She tried to imagine herself flying to seventh heaven in Gerald's arms, and the idea was so ridiculous that she seized Bart round the waist, fell against him, and laughed aloud.

When at last she went aboard the *Magnolo*, it was to find her mother sound asleep in their cabin. She undressed quietly, showered and crept into her own bed. But she didn't sleep. She was looking back over the miracle that had happened.

In the morning her mother slept on, as always. At about nine-thirty Erica took a tray to her, a habit developed so as to save the steward any trouble. Amy, waking unwillingly, sat up to allow the tray to be placed across her lap.

'Were you very late last night, dear?'

'Rather, I'm afraid.'

'Where did you go? Anywhere nice?'

'Oh, just to a little Mexican restaurant.'

Innocently, Amy asked about the food. The idea that her daughter had anything more interesting to report never crossed her mind.

'What are you going to do today, Mother?'

'Mr and Mrs O'Brien have asked me to go sightseeing with them. There's quite a lot of sixteenth-century architecture, I hear. And they want to go to a convent up in the hills to pay for a novena – a novena, is that right?'

'I dare say. What about lunch? Are you coming back to the ship?'

'No, no, the O'Briens are hiring a car and taking a picnic basket. We shan't be back until dinner.' She looked anxiously at her daughter. 'You won't be bored on your own?'

'Not in the least, no. I'll take a swimsuit and go swimming.'

She did in fact take a swimsuit and swam from the beach by the artist's cabin while she waited for Bart. He had the afternoon off, due back on duty for the dog watch at four, although watch-keeping was something of a formality in port.

When he came she was wrapped in her beach towel, drying her hair in the sun. He ran his hand through the damp tresses. 'You smell of salt and seaweed.'

'The water's lovely, just a bit prickly to the skin.'

They went into the cabin. The afternoon passed in the newlydiscovered pleasures of the flesh, continually astonishing and rewarding to her.

They were both aware that they only had a little time before

Bart went back on duty. He opened the bottle of wine he'd put to cool in a bucket of sea water, poured it into chipped cups, and then looked at her seriously over the rim of his. 'We ought to talk.'

'What about?'

'The future.'

'I'm still trying to catch up with the present!'

He laughed. 'You're a constant surprise to me! To think I used to consider you a conventional, bossy girl!'

'I am bossy,' she admitted. 'I boss my mother about.'

'I won't hear a word against you.' He leaned over to kiss her on the tip of the nose. 'What are we going to do?'

'What about?'

'Us.'

'I don't think we need to do anything. We're perfect.'

'Be serious, Erica. The *Langrovia* sails for Pernambuco on the 28th. I have to go. If I don't I'll have jumped ship.'

'Of course you have to go, darling.'

'But then . . . what about us?'

'We'll meet again, my darling. Let me know the *Langrovia*'s schedule and I'll pick cruises that bring us to the same port.'

'That's not so easy.'

'No, but we'll manage somehow.'

'Listen, Erica, I'm not going to be with the *Langrovia* after this cruise. Remember I mentioned that I wasn't really cut out for serving aboard luxury liners.'

'Oh-h,' she said slowly. 'I remember.'

'I've got a berth aboard one of the Argentine Circle line, the *Carico* – first mate.'

'Oh, well done.'

'No, but listen, sweetheart, it's not exactly a good time for us to be thinking of getting married.'

She set down her drink. His words sent shock waves through her. She hadn't thought ahead – at least not beyond the next time they could meet and make love. 'Married?' she repeated.

'Well, that's what you'd want, isn't it?'

'I don't know . . .' Marriage. Could she ask him to take on so much? He was at the beginning of his career, and life wouldn't be easy for him because the shipping world (like everything else) was experiencing a slump. If he married her, he would get not only Erica, but her mother.

The home port of the Argentine Circle ships was usually Buenos Aires. What would it be like for her mother to live in some inexpensive little flat in Buenos Aires? How would Bart like it if he had to share his home with an ailing mother-in-law?

Erica had seen both the gilt and the gingerbread by now. She knew how hard life could be, how uncertain. Happiness such as she and Bart had shared could easily be wrecked – for instance, if the shipping line decided to lay up some of its vessels and Bart therefore lost his job. Or if her mother had one of her more serious attacks and ran up doctor's bills.

Bart felt he had to offer marriage. She understood his reasoning. It was his duty to make her this offer – only a cad takes a girl to bed and then, when it suits him, walks away. Of course he loved her, wanted her to be his wife, but if she were not so alone in the world, so friendless, he wouldn't feel the need to get married at once.

'What are you thinking?' he demanded, watching her serious expression.

'I'm thinking it certainly isn't a good time to be talking about marriage,' she said at length. 'And darling, there's no need. We know we love each other, and surely we can wait a bit.'

'But I hate to think of leaving you, and not seeing you again for weeks.'

'But that would be so whether we're married or not, wouldn't it?' she said in a faintly teasing voice. 'A sailor's wife has to get used to the long absences, right? So you see, you needn't worry on that score.'

'But I do worry! The kind of life you lead, it's got its dangers.'

'I can handle them, Bart. I've learnt a lot in the last year or so.'

That didn't comfort him in the least. He took her in his arms and held her close, and for a long time they clung together without words.

They had one more day of happiness. On December 28th the *Langrovia* sailed for Pernambuco, and on the following day the *Magnolo* set out for the return trip to Miami.

'See you in Buenos Aires in February,' they told each other as they kissed in farewell.

But it didn't happen. Although Erica came in on one of the *Magnolo*'s longer cruises and stayed four days, the *Carico* never made it. Engine trouble kept her in Bahia Blanca until the beginning of March.

The Depression caused a cut-back in the number of luxury

cruises. Erica and her mother stayed in Miami most of the time, barely getting by, running a little bridge club from their motel. Bart was sailing between South America and Liverpool.

They wrote often. Yet after a time the ache of longing became less insistent, and the days and nights of Vera Cruz began to seem dream-like. It was almost as if they had happened to two other people.

And perhaps, Erica thought, it was better that way. Better to remember it as a golden dream, perfect for its time, but too precious to survive the harshness of reality.

Chapter Nine

The *Providence* was a new ship. To be offered the chance of sailing aboard her on her maiden voyage was an honour. Besides, they needed the money.

'But to Cherbourg, darling,' murmured Amy Tregarvon, shaking her head. 'In the autumn.'

'She's like a floating palace, Mother. You won't feel a thing even if we get an autumn storm.'

Her mother was still shaking her head. 'Cherbourg is so dismal in wet weather,' she said.

'But it's only for the turn-around. We'd only be there four or five days.'

Amy looked out of the window at the view. Miami was changing. Where there had been a row of small Spanish-style apartments, there was now a high-rise block of offices. The garden of the building in which the Tregarvons lived was to become a used-car lot.

Certainly it would be nice to go sailing away on the new American liner. To leave their cramped apartment, to set aside the constant anxieties over money, even for a month or so.

The Eastern Seaboard Line were offering them a job in the entertainment department for this maiden voyage. First-class cabin, reasonable salary, no restrictions on extra earnings from special lessons to passengers: an exceptionally good offer, because the rich and famous would want to travel on the beautiful new ship. The rich and famous were notably generous with money even in these hard times. The Tregarvons might make enough from this one trip to see them through beyond Christmas.

Erica was watching Amy's eyes travel over the unlovely view. 'Not very attractive,' she agreed, although Amy had made no criticism. 'And it's going further downhill, I hear. Perhaps when we get back, we'll find a better place.'

'The thing is, Erica . . .'

'What?'

'The thing is . . . I don't think I want to go.'

The words were a shock. Never before had her mother resisted the idea of going to sea.

'But why ever not?'

Amy sighed. She turned away from the uninspiring view to study the solitaire game laid out on the card table. After a moment she moved a five of diamonds.

'Why not?' Erica insisted, very worried. Amy's face was set in a strange, determined look she'd never seen before.

'Well, it's this way, Erica . . . I think I'm getting too old for our kind of life. Struggling to make ends meet when we're in Miami, always having to be conversational and good-natured to one set of strangers after another when we're aboard ship . . .'

Erica couldn't find a quick response. What her mother said was true. It wasn't an easy life.

'We'd find it hard to dress well enough for the *Providence*,' Amy went on. 'Fashions have changed a lot in the last few years, all our clothes are out of date, even if they once were high couture.'

'But we could go to Second Best again.'

'Oh, I hate that!' Amy burst out in unexpected anguish. 'Having to wear somebody else's cast-offs.'

'Yes, I know, I know, but they *are* good quality.'

'But they don't look like *us*! That marocain dress, I'd never have had a thing like that made for me in the old days—'

'But what else can we do, Mother? Buying new at that quality is quite out of the question.'

'This trip on the *Providence* – truly, Erica, do you think our clothes are going to look right in the first-class dining saloon, no matter how careful we are at Second Best?'

'Well . . .'

'It's not so bad for you,' Amy went on, 'you're young and pretty enough to carry off anything. But I'm beginning to look like an old frump.'

Erica allowed herself a little grin. 'So that's what this is all about? You're worried about what to wear.'

'No, it's *not* that! I'm being serious, Erica. I've been thinking for a couple of months now . . . longer, in fact . . . I've been thinking . . . I think I'd like to settle down permanently in some little place ashore.'

Erica gasped. 'But you always loved shipboard life.'

'It's the packing and repacking,' Amy cut in. 'And the queuing up at Customs. And the sorting out and ironing when we get home. In the old days I never had to do any of that. It was always easy, always enjoyable. But now . . . I'm so tired of it, Erica. I don't want to do it any more. I want to settle down.'

'But where, here in Miami? You know it's been difficult this summer, trying to make a living here. We'd really have to go somewhere with a steadier clientele. Where would we go?'

There was a long hesitation. Then Amy said, 'I didn't mean both of us, dear.'

The conversation so far had been a surprise to Erica. Now she was reduced to utter silence.

Amy continued. 'It's a strange sort of life in the first place, roaming about the seas playing cards. But for a grown girl to have her mother tagging along all the time—'

'Oh, Mother, you know I love having you with me.'

'But it's not right, dear! After all, you're twenty-four. It must put all the young men off, seeing me at your side all the time—'

'Now that's nonsense.'

'No, it isn't. Don't tell me it didn't spoil things for you with that nice young man from the *Langrovia*.' She paused. 'You don't seem to get so many letters from him nowadays?'

'No . . . Well . . . A year's a long time without seeing each other,' Erica said, with a little shrug that rejected sympathy.

'But you might meet someone else,' Amy said, smiling, 'if you didn't have Mummy at your heels all the while.'

'Let's not even discuss that,' said Erica curtly. 'I'm not out there looking for a husband, you know.'

'Darling, I was only joking. It's just that . . . that . . . shipboard life isn't the same for me any more. It's all been spoiled. It used to be such a pleasure, everything easy, something to look forward to every day. Now every day's an effort.'

'Oh, Mother!' Erica cried, stooping to put her arms around her. 'I'm so sorry.'

'Now, now, child, it's not your fault,' her mother said. 'Everything's changed, I know that. But it seems to make it that little bit harder, having to live a totally different kind of life aboard ship. So I've decided . . . at least I want to discuss it with you . . . I've pretty much decided not to go to sea any more.'

Erica straightened to look down into her face. 'But what would we—'

'I told you, not "we", just me.'

Erica stifled a sigh. It was all so unrealistic. Hard enough earning a living when they were both employed, but if her mother was to stay ashore and have to be supported by Erica's earnings, it became impossible.

'Let's just stop and think about it. The rent here—' Erica began.

'But I shan't be staying here.'

'But wherever you go, the rent—'

'But I've thought of all that—'

'Now, listen, Mother, hold still a minute and be sensible.' To her surprise her mother gave a sudden little chuckle. 'What?' Erica said. 'What have I said that's funny?'

'It's not what you said, it's the way you said it.'

'Well, what? What was funny about the way I said it?'

'You sounded just like your father.'

Erica frowned.

'Don't look like that about it, dear. I know you don't like to talk about him, but he's often in my thoughts. And sometimes you have a way of speaking or holding your head . . . It's so like him.'

'I'm not like him,' Erica said with quiet anger.

'But you are. In so many ways, Erica, you're so much your father's child.'

Erica rose, paced about the cramped living room, picked up a book and put it down again. 'Never mind all that,' she said. 'We were talking hard facts a minute ago. You have to face it, Mother, I can't earn enough on my own for both of us.'

'But you wouldn't have to.'

'What do you mean? Are you planning to starve?'

'No, on the contrary,' Amy said with quiet satisfaction, 'I think I'll probably be living rather well.'

'Living rather well? On what?'

'On my salary.' There, she'd said it. Amy was pleased with herself.

'You . . . You've got a job?'

Amy nodded.

'Where? Doing what?'

'Being a hostess in a hotel.'

'Mother!'

Hostesses in some hotels in Miami were ladies of dubious reputation. If they didn't themselves cater to the needs of male guests, they provided ladies who would do so, and for a fee. The idea of her mother in any such role was ludicrous. And as for the better-class hotels, why would any of them take on Mrs Tregarvon when they could get a young, pretty woman with plenty of energy to look after the holidaymakers?

'It's all right, dear,' Amy hastened to explain. 'It's not

here in Miami. I know how difficult it might be here. No, no, this is something quite respectable. Mrs Oakes suggested it.'

Amy had kept in touch with the wife of the multi-millionaire ever since they had been given the use of the Oakeses' house. Pride had kept the Tregarvons from accepting further hospitality, yet Amy and Eunice Oakes had written to each other with a certain regularity.

'You see, Harry has bought all sorts of property in the Bahamas and now he owns the British Colonial Hotel. You remember, dear, it's *the* hotel in Nassau. Eunice says that to help the employment situation – which is as bad there as anywhere, oddly enough – Harry's decided to run it with only Bahamian staff. Only Harry feels he needs a couple of people to just . . . you know . . . look after the holidaymakers, especially the more sedate kind.'

'Mother, this job is in Nassau?'

'Yes, dear.'

After a little hesitation her daughter said, 'He isn't there, Mother. If he ever was there, he's gone now.'

Amy stared down at the cards on the table. After a moment she gathered them up and began to shuffle them aimlessly. 'I know that, Erica. I've come to terms with the fact that your father's gone underground somewhere and may never try to get in touch. Taking this job at the British Colonial has nothing to do with that.'

'So what has it got to do with?'

'It's a place to settle down, Erica. A place where I've got a friend, well, not a *close* friend, but Eunice and I go back a long way. And I know Nassau, I always loved it when we put in there for a stay. So that's why I'm taking up the offer.'

207

'Which is what?'

'Oh, to run around after the fifty-plus travellers, take them to see the stately colonial homes on the old estates, play cards with them, put them in touch with dressmakers or tropical tailors, that kind of thing. I get a room in the hotel and my board, plus a small salary.'

'Just like what we've been doing aboard ship.'

'Except that I shan't have to keep packing and unpacking, and I'll have Mrs Oakes to turn to if there are any problems.'

In fact it did sound a good offer. Life aboard ship had its strains and stresses. Nassau was a relaxed place, easy-going, civilized. With the implied protection of Mrs Harry Oakes, her mother would be in a somewhat privileged position.

They talked it through for most of that day and the next. Erica had to give a yes or no on the chance to sail with the *Providence* by the end of the week. She rang Eastern Seaboard's head office to say that if she accepted, this time she would be travelling without her mother as a companion. After some discussion the manager of the entertainment division remarked that it made little difference to him, he could easily hire someone else to fill the gap left by Mrs Tregarvon if necessary.

So it was settled, not without some misgivings on Erica's part. Her mother was tired and frailer than she used to be. Perhaps she was right to settle down. Yet she had never had to cope on her own in life so far. Mrs Oakes would be there to help her, however. Eunice Oakes was well-known for her kindness and good works. Let Mrs Lindon Tregarvon be one of those good works, if it must be so.

Erica made the Bahama crossing with Amy to see her

settled in at her new job. The hotel had been redecorated, so that the room allotted to her was bright and fresh, if not very large. The manager was an American, newly imported for the post. All the rest of the staff – assistant managers, housekeeper, maitre d'hotel, chef, and the throng of maids and waiters – were Bahamians, inexperienced as yet, but eager to make a success of the hotel. Mrs Oakes took the trouble to drop by to welcome the hostess, a fact noted by the rest of the staff.

The hotel was busy. The sticky-hot season being over, life was resuming on Grand Bahama. People were coming in from their big houses to wine and dine, to see what the British Colonial looked like with its new decorations, and to find out what the new management planned for the winter.

Others had come perhaps for business reasons. Erica, sitting under a big umbrella in the Palm Garden after a swim, was surprised to see some familiar-looking men gathering by the pool.

Familiar-looking, not in themselves, but in their style, their type. Resort clothes, a trifle too exaggerated: linen trousers, short-sleeved shirts in loud patterns, gold identity bracelets, gold rings, gold cigarette lighters. They were just like the men she'd seen Timothy Perriman speaking to at the Fontaine Restaurant in New York.

'Are they anybody special?' she asked McDermot, the manager, when he joined her for a pre-lunch drink.

He let his glance drift towards the group of men and their girlfriends, but tactfully. 'Oh,' he said. 'The would-be owners.'

'Owners of what?'

'Of this hotel. Mr Oakes beat them to it.'

'But surely, he bought the place at the beginning of the year? Why would the would-be owners still be hanging around?'

'They didn't hang around. They went away, and then they came back. I hear they're trying to talk Mr Oakes into selling.'

Erica looked at her drink and frowned. She didn't fancy the idea of her mother being employed by people like that.

'Don't worry,' McDermot said, hiding a satisfied grin behind a meaty hand, 'Mr Oakes isn't going to sell. Especially not to them. They're why he bought the hotel in the first place.'

'I don't follow that,' said Erica.

'It's widely believed they're from the Outfit.'

'The Outfit? Oh, you mean those ex-bootleggers.'

'That lot, yes. They're a collection of separate gangs, grouping together to do business in different areas now that rum-running has died.' He paused to look back into the past. 'I hear there was a lot of rum-running through the Bahamas in those days. Handy, d'you see? Handling alcohol on British territory was no crime, but it was only a few miles off the coast of the US. I hear fortunes were made.'

'By the Italian gangs?' Erica asked with a faint nod towards the men now ordering drinks from a harried bellboy.

'Oh yes, by them, but also some supposedly very respectable families of the Bahamas.'

'No!'

'Oh yes. Hands clean, of course – they imported the booze into the Bahamas and sold it on – no business of theirs where it went after it left their warehouses.'

'Good gracious.' Erica was genuinely surprised. Often as

she'd been here in the past on visits, she'd never suspected there were any disreputable characters among the members of the Yacht Club.

'Well, that's all over now. Naturally, people who've been making easy money look around for a way to do it again. Some people here on New Providence thought it would be a good idea if our friends there were to buy the British Colonial.'

'Buy the hotel? I don't see what they'd gain, particularly—'

McDermot nodded his big head lazily. 'A casino, Miss Tregarvon. Easy money. Like Havana, you know? Off the American coast, easy to get to, tropical climate, beautiful girls, and gaming rooms open from sundown to sunrise. But,' he raised a finger to emphasize his point, 'Mr Oakes doesn't approve of gambling. So he got in first and bought the old BC. And our Italian friends were *not* pleased.'

Erica sat up under the pretext of putting on her sun hat. The group by the pool had been served their drinks. One of the girls in a low-cut swimsuit was kneeling by one of the men, holding his cocktail to his lips so that he could drink. It had something of the look of a harem slave tending to her master.

'Are they staying for long?'

'I think they'll be leaving almost any day. Mr Oakes told me to look after them well but not to let them get away with anything. Day before yesterday his lawyer dropped by to talk to them. I think he told them they were wasting their time. So I expect they'll be packing up soon. Thank goodness,' he added.

One of the girls, exquisitely lovely, rose to her feet, posed ostentatiously, then dived into the pool. A moment later she emerged, her dark hair sleek against her scalp. Knowing her swimsuit was clinging to her figure provocatively, she sauntered back to the lounging chairs, only to be shoved so hard she staggered.

'Keep off, you dumb broad! Do I want to be dripped on?'

'Charming,' murmured Erica. She couldn't help wondering if Timothy knew them.

Timothy, as it happened, didn't know this precise group. But he knew others who had business connections. At a planning session in New York, mention was made of the failure of the Nassau deal.

'Some old fool bought the place out from under us,' Manzini remarked. 'He intends to run it as a resort hotel, for God's sake.'

'But in any case, there was still the problem of the gaming licence,' Timothy said soothingly. 'Until we get that solved, we can't even start thinking about a casino.'

'We'll get a licence.'

'The Assembly have always voted that down.'

Manzini pursed thin lips. 'Such things can be arranged.'

'But not easily, Mr Manzini.'

'Easy takes a few minutes. Difficult takes a few years, that's the only difference.'

Privately Timothy thought the matter of getting the staid Assembly of the Bahamas to alter their laws about gambling was likely to be a little more than 'difficult'. But he had learned not to argue with Giancarlo Manzini unless he had sound business reasons.

'We'll continue to look out for a site in Nassau?' he inquired.

'Oh, sure. But I won't send any of the family to look. The way Enzo tells it, people get a funny look when they see guys like us. What we want is a perfect English gentleman like you, Perriman.'

'You want me to go?'

'Go take a look.'

'I ought to point out, Mr Manzini – land purchase isn't my speciality, I know more about shipping and international shipping regulations.'

'Yeah, yeah, I wouldn't expect you to do the buying. We'll hire a local guy to make the deal for us. Thing is, to find a spot and buy our way in.'

'I don't see the point, if you'll excuse me, Mr Manzini. Without a gaming licence you can't open a casino, and except for a casino you've no reason to buy land in the Bahamas.'

'Let me worry about that. What I want is that you should just go there and see what's available.' He paused to light a cigar, then added, 'Tell you one thing,' smiling and shrugging, 'Enzo says, don't stay at the British Colonial – it's as dead as George Washington. Snooty old dames with grey hair and their husbands with a heart condition – they come tottering off the cruise ships. Enzo says the average age is sixty. They even got a "hostess" practically that age to look after them, some classy old broad in black lace and pearls called Tregarvon.'

'I beg your pardon?' Timothy said, looking up from the papers he was gathering for his briefcase.

'What?'

'What name did you say?'

'What name what?'

'You said a hostess, or something of that kind. Tregarvon?'

'Yeah, I think it was that.' Manzini raised thick black eyebrows. 'A girlfriend of yours?'

'Hardly,' Timothy said. 'Not at that age. But I used to know someone of that name.'

' "Hardly",' mocked Manzini. 'I love your English accent. From what Enzo said, it's "hardly" worth your trouble to look her up while you're there.'

Timothy Perriman arrived in Nassau off the Pan American plane from Miami two days later. His mind was chiefly on the matter of looking at property suitable for the building of a casino, but he was interested to know what Mrs Tregarvon was doing in Nassau. He could never forget that Erica had asked him specifically about the yacht, the *Margravine*. What did she know? What could she possibly know? And if she knew anything, did her mother know too? Was that why Mrs Tregarvon was here in Nassau?

He signed himself in at the Montagu Beach Hotel, and spent the first day being driven about the island simply looking at land. Plenty of good sites, especially with the modern building techniques which could deal with the sandy subsoil. Plenty of silvery beaches, plenty of sheltering palms . . . Everything perfect except the straitlaced outlook of the governing council.

And of course the question of whether the land was for sale. He couldn't come out and ask openly. The moment he let it be known why he was here, opposition would harden from those who disapproved, and those who approved would raise their prices sky-high.

So he spent his second day chatting with the businessmen of Bay Street, the men who controlled the money and the government. They were nicknamed the Bay Street Boys, otherwise known as the United Bahamian Party, the party which was usually in control of the electorate. To them Timothy made no mention of building a casino. He murmured about finding a place for a fish-processing plant backed by money from the United States. Yes, indeed, Mr Perriman, several prime sites. Let us show you some maps.

He decided he would go to the British Colonial for dinner that evening. To his great surprise, one of the first people he saw was Erica Tregarvon. Manzini had never mentioned Erica. Timothy had somehow taken it for granted that Amy Tregarvon would be on her own here. But here was Erica in the bar, in a soft silk-muslin gown of Nile green, with her chestnut hair piled up in big soft tresses on top of her head and topped with a hibiscus flower.

Her presence threw him into a panic. Last time they'd spoken, she'd questioned him about the *Margravine*. And Nassau was where the present owner of the *Margravine* lived. Had she sought him out, spoken to him? What had she learned?

Timothy was debating whether to beat a retreat when Erica noticed him. She was as startled as he, perhaps more so. She rose from her chair to greet him before she thought whether she wanted to speak to him.

He came forward, his surprise quite natural after all, his smile growing as he surveyed her. 'Erica! How wonderful to see you! And how wonderful you look!'

'How are you, Timothy?' She gave him her hand. He was perspiring. Not to be wondered at, for it was a warm evening. All the same, he was nervy, she felt. He had never liked anything out of the ordinary, anything that altered his arrangements. Her presence here had shaken him.

'What on earth are you doing here?' she asked. A natural question, but he seemed unprepared for it.

'Oh . . . Business, you know.'

'What was it, shipping consultancy?' She recalled what she'd been told. 'There's something worth doing here?'

Idiot, he told himself. He should have said he was on holiday. 'Oh, no, I'm . . . er . . . taking a look at property.'

Are you, she thought. She remembered what Derrick McDermot had said about 'the Outfit' looking out for a place to house a casino. The Outfit, men very like those who'd summoned Timothy across to their table. 'I didn't know you were in the property business?'

'Er . . . No, I'm . . . thinking of buying a house here.'

'You're going to live here?' Now she was really puzzled. Timothy wasn't a tropics man. He liked cool climates, city surroundings. He certainly couldn't be thinking of Nassau for its sailing advantages: he wasn't fond of the sea.

'No, as an investment,' he said. 'It . . . er . . . would be advantageous.'

'Oh, I see.' She didn't believe a word of it, but she didn't let him see that. 'Well, I hope you find what you want.'

'Is your mother with you?' He'd just remembered he wasn't supposed to know about Amy's post as hostess.

'Yes, she's working for the hotel.'

'Really? In what capacity?'

She gave him a brief sketch of Amy's duties. He smiled politely, and she suddenly had the feeling that he'd already been aware of what she was telling him. Was that why he was here? Because someone had told him Amy Tregarvon was here?

No, she scolded herself, that's paranoia! Surely Timothy can come to the Bahamas on business without my reading something underhand into it.

But his next words threw her back into alarm. 'Now you're here, I suppose you've taken a look at the dear old *Margravine*.'

'The *Margravine*!'

'That fellow who bought her.'

'Gaynor Medcalfe.'

'His home was Nassau, wasn't it?'

'Yes, but he sold her on to someone else, I gather.'

'He did?'

Was that relief in his tone? She couldn't tell. He'd recovered enough so that his voice was under control.

Amy came into the bar at that moment. Her astonishment at finding Erica talking to Timothy Perriman was almost comical. She spent several minutes exclaiming, asking how he was, how he was faring, regretting the fact that she had hostess duties this evening to prevent her from spending it with him. She took it for granted that he would have wanted to dine with them. Erica was thankful when the four passengers from the cruise ship arrived to be taken in to dinner.

'But we'll see you tomorrow?' Amy urged, taking his hand and pressing it in leave-taking.

'I'm afraid not. I'm flying back to Miami.'

'Oh, dear, so soon?'

'I have to be in New York again by tomorrow night. I'm so sorry, Mrs Tregarvon. Perhaps if you're ever in New York you'll look me up.'

'Of course, of course. Though it's not very likely . . .'

Timothy hurried away to dine in his own hotel. Everything had gone wrong; he'd intended to find Mrs Tregarvon, get her alone, and just sound out the situation: find out if she ever thought about Lindon and where he might be, that kind of thing. He hadn't expected to meet the shrewd eyes of the daughter.

Erica Tregarvon . . . He never had known how to handle her. He'd got it wrong every time he tried. It was worrying. What were they doing *here*, in Nassau? The *Margravine* had been sold, Erica said. To whom? Should he try to find out? Did Erica know? He could have asked her. Yet he mustn't talk to her about the *Margravine* – it always made her suspicious.

Suspicious, yes. What did she suspect? Should he let it worry him?

Mr Manzini had friends here in Nassau. Perhaps before he left tomorrow Timothy would ask them to keep an eye on the Tregarvon ladies.

Erica, dining with her mother and the four newcomers from the *Tropic Rainbow* cruise, had to give her attention to cheerful conversation. Yet part of her mind was worrying at the problem of Timothy.

She was sure he was somehow involved with the gangs who used to make money from bootlegging. Sometimes she saw articles in newspapers suggesting that the gang bosses had 'turned legitimate', and were now investing in respectable businesses.

A casino was a legitimate business. She thought of the sedate enterprises she'd seen on her travels – Monte Carlo, for instance. All Edwardian gilt and crimson velvet. If the 'Outfit' wanted to start a casino in Nassau, it would be perfectly legal, supposing they could get a law passed allowing it.

If that was why Timothy was here, he had a perfect right. There was no reason to be suspicious about it. Yet it seemed so strange. Why should he turn up at the British Colonial where she and her mother were staying? And why once more had he dragged the *Margravine* into the conversation? She couldn't make sense of it. All she had was an indefinable unease.

But there was nothing to be done about it. In a few days she would be leaving her mother to her new role at the British Colonial, and herself setting out for New York to board the *Providence*. And as for looking up Timothy, not for a million dollars. Because for some reason that defied logic, she found she mistrusted Timothy Perriman.

Chapter Ten

The passenger list of the *Providence* contained, as expected, the names of the rich and famous. It also contained a name that startled Erica. Mitchell Harrowford. Since the bridge tournament at the Esmeralda, he hadn't crossed her path, and Erica now realized that he must only play on the trans-oceanic liners.

On the *Providence*'s first night out, there was the usual Captain's Cocktail Party for the more notable passengers. Erica had long since grown accustomed to being left out of such invitations. In the old days, of course . . . But that was all in the past.

Her duty this evening was to round up any passengers who seemed at a loss before dinner. She walked slowly through the first-class lounge picking out those who looked as if they needed company, but there were few passengers here who were unsure of themselves; most of those present were rich by inheritance or by their own efforts, or they were foremost in their professions; stars of stage and screen, painters, writers.

She saw one man on his own, and a middle-aged couple not quite at ease. Before rounding them up for a pre-dinner drink, she looked into the bar to see if there were any lonely males drowning their sorrows there. She discovered a group of about seven men, sitting round a table, much at their ease, talking and laughing contentedly. And one of the men was Mitchell Harrowford.

He saw her. Before she could quietly withdraw, he raised an eyebrow at her and, with a little jut of his chin, indicated he wanted to speak to her. As she went out he was excusing himself to his companions.

He joined her in the deck-passage outside, offering his hand. 'Hi there. We have met, but I don't suppose you remember—'

'Indeed I do. Mitchell Harrowford from the Esmeralda Hotel, almost three years ago.'

'Right! And you're Erica Tregarvon, with special concern for the bridge parties aboard.'

She nodded.

'I'm the same, only it's understood I'll also make sure any games of poker are run honestly.'

'You play poker too?'

'Not with the same enthusiasm as bridge. Poker's a game that's all tactics, no strategy. I may say I'm also stand-in for your mother. I understand you and she usually travel together?'

'Not any more.' Erica still couldn't feel reconciled to the fact.

'Well, look, Miss Tregarvon . . . don't mind my saying this . . . it's a little different, being a woman on her own. You understand what I mean.'

'I don't think I do,' she said, her chin coming up a little at the implication.

'You've probably had little or no trouble up till now. A

girl travelling with her mother – well, it's a guarantee of . . . of . . .'

'Respectability?'

Harrowford drew back a little. 'Gee,' he said, 'I can tell I'm putting my foot in it! Okay, I withdraw what was going to be an offer of help.'

'Oh no.' Immediately she was contrite. 'I'm sorry! Of course I'd be glad of any help. This is a very sparkly sort of passenger list, not like the easy-going bunch I'm used to on cruise ships.'

'Only too true. Some very big "temperaments" aboard. Let's hope none of them want to play cards.' He was smiling down at her from his slender height. He was an elegant man, with dark hair touched with a little grey at the temples, dark eyes under dark brows, about fifteen years her senior.

'Well, the crossing only takes five days. They can't throw much of a temperament in that time.'

'You'd be surprised. I could tell you tales . . .' He let it die away. 'I'd better get back to my bunch. I'm spreading the word that I can be called upon if anyone wants a game. How about you, have you found any bridge fans?'

'Not so far, but we'll see what we find in the card room after dinner.'

'I'll see you there.'

He went back into the bar with his long easy stride. She for her part collected up her three lost lambs and set about putting them at their ease. A complimentary drink soon soothed their tensions. The middle-aged couple were making the maiden voyage as a silver-wedding celebration. The lonely male was travelling to a promotion in his firm's French department. None of them was interested in bridge. She saw them safely introduced to the others at their dinner tables and went to take her own place.

After the meal she went to the card room. Some of the tables were already occupied, games already commencing. By and by about a score of people were looking at each other, trying to decide how to divide themselves up. Erica took it in hand, introduced them to each other, sorted them out at vacant tables, and at last had six leftovers. She was just deciding she would have to fill one table and then somehow entertain the two surplus players when Mitchell Harrowford came in.

'Ah,' she said. 'Mr Harrowford . . . I wonder if you'd be so good.'

'Certainly, certainly.' With accustomed ease he collected up three of the six and took them off to a table. Erica took the remainder. The room settled down to play.

So it was next day when, in the afternoon, squalls of rain kept most of the passengers off the decks. Harrowford seemed to be at hand whenever she turned in need of him. She gathered from the stewards that he had been up half the night in a long and serious poker game, yet he showed nothing of it in his appearance: easy-going, elegant, unruffled.

The trouble with unpleasant weather is that if the passengers can't go on deck to play shuffleboard or sunbathe, they have to amuse themselves under cover. It necessarily meant that some of them passed the time in the bar. That evening Erica found herself being pursued by a film star who, a good deal the worse for drink, was convinced she must want to go to bed with him.

'C'mon, dearie,' he slurred in her ear on a gin-sodden

breath, 'don' play hard to get now, y'know y'all want it, y'keep writing me fan letters to say so . . .'

'I've never written to you, Mr Cookfield. Take your hands off.'

'C'mon, pretty li'l thing, always liked li'l brown-haired girlies.'

'Let *go*!'

'Wha's the big fuss for? What else are you here for, eh?'

'Not for this, Mr Cookfield,' said a voice from the companionway behind them, and Mitchell Harrowford came down the steps with unexpected speed. 'Miss Tregarvon is in charge of the bridge-playing, not the bed-hopping.'

The actor whirled unsteadily. 'Where you come from?' he demanded in surprise. 'Genie out'f a bottle?'

'You've had more than enough out of a bottle. Come on now, there's a good guy, let's go to your cabin.'

'Not without my li'l girlie! I need some comp'ny! All on my own and lonesome.'

'Isn't that sad, now? I know how you feel. Why don't we go to your cabin and talk about it, huh?' All the while, imperceptibly, Harrowford was leading the drunken star a little more towards the entrance to the staircase that would take them to the first-class cabins.

Left alone, Erica sagged against the rail for support. Her velvet wrap, which Cookfield had almost dragged off her shoulders, seemed to have no warmth in it. She shivered, uncertain what to do next. She was expected in the card room, but she felt a sudden desperate need of something, a moment of comfort, of kindness, after the startlement of Cookfield's attack.

Next moment she heard a footfall. She turned quickly, ready for flight.

'It's only me. I handed him over to a steward. Did he scare you?'

'No, of course not! Well . . . I . . . Yes, I must admit I'm a bit shaken.'

'Come on, I'll buy you a drink.'

'No, I ought to be in the card room.'

'Oh, for heaven's sake, don't be so conscientious! If they can't settle themselves down to a game of bridge without guidance, they're beyond saving.'

She let him take her to the bar. There they settled on an upholstered corner bench. After a few sips of brandy and soda, Erica began to feel better.

'I see now what you meant by needing help,' she murmured.

He sighed and shook his head. 'There's always at least one on every passenger list,' he said. 'He takes it for granted that a woman on her own, a divorcée for instance, or a widow . . . And the trouble is, to some extent it's true, there are women who like a bit of a fling in the circumstances of an ocean crossing.'

Erica managed a smile. 'Mother and I used to watch them,' she acknowledged. 'We'd call them "sea-butterflies". But I never thought I'd be taken for one.'

'Cookfield was too drunk to know what he was looking at.'

'What a good thing you happened along.'

'I didn't happen along. I've been keeping an eye open for you.'

'Good heavens!'

'Look, I'll level with you,' he said, 'I've got a lot of interest in you. I don't suppose you remember, but I told you at that tournament that you played very well indeed.'

'I do remember,' she said. 'I was very flattered.'

'Well, it was true then, and it seems to me you're playing even better now. And you seem to be on your own these days?'

'Yes.' She couldn't keep the regret from her voice. 'Mother's decided she'll go no more a-roving.'

'Well then.' He took a moment to sip his drink and arrange his thoughts. 'How would you like to go into partnership?'

'I beg your pardon?'

'With me. Oh—' as he saw an objection forming on her lips – 'strictly business! But you've seen for yourself, on a trip like this there are a lot of card players who want a game at a high level, and the longer the voyage the higher the level becomes. On this trip, of course, we'll be saying goodbye to them in three days, but you see, if you make the trip regularly you tend to meet the same people – business people, mostly crossing back and forth. It builds up, you get to have a sort of following. You can make money from that. And of course you can give lessons, and run tournaments, and so on.'

'Yes,' she agreed, 'Mother and I have given lessons in hotels ashore.'

'You have? Then you know what I mean. It's not a bad life, earning a living by doing what you enjoy, but I think perhaps you've seen that for a woman on her own, there are pitfalls.'

'You may be right.'

'What d'you say then?'

She hesitated. 'Have you had partners before?'

'Oh, sure. I had a guy I used to team with on the Pacific crossing. We'd stop off in Hawaii and run a bridge school in one of the resort hotels for a few months, then come back to San Francisco, and so on like that. But he fell in love and wanted to settle down in Brisbane.'

'You're not married?'

He shook his head.

'Never have been?'

'No. Why do you ask?'

'I'm asking because you said "strictly business". I'd need to know where I stand.'

'That makes sense. Well, if you're asking whether I'd want to extend my interest beyond the business area, the answer's no. I'm not . . .' He paused. 'I'm not a very affectionate type.'

Erica looked back to the travelling years with her parents to recall what she'd seen of Harrowford. The little cameos she had of him revealed him at the card table, well-kept hands dealing the cards, calm dark eyes surveying his partner – the partner sometimes a man, sometimes a woman. She couldn't remember ever seeing him talking and laughing flirtatiously with a woman.

That was good. If she were going to go into a partnership she didn't want to be burdened with emotional demands. Her mother might have romantic notions of finding 'Mr Right', but the memory of the golden days with Bart would always act as a barrier in her thoughts of any man.

She put on her most practical manner. 'So what would this partnership involve?'

He laughed. 'Where did you learn that tone of voice?

Sounds like a business executive talking to a dealer on the phone.'

'Never mind the tone, answer the question.'

'Okay. You'd get protection.'

'Protection!'

'I guess that word has gangster overtones.' He was still amused at her starchy manner. 'What I mean is, we'd let it be known that we're a pair. You'd be protected from the wolves.'

The word 'wolf' was just coming into fashion to replace 'ladykiller'. Erica said, 'You mean that after one scare with a drunk like Cookfield—'

'Listen, Erica – may I call you Erica? – that won't be the last, believe me. You'd find it a comfort to have someone on hand to boff them for you.'

'Are you much given to that? Boffing people?'

'And damage my hands? Are you kidding? No, but men don't hit on women so much if they think they've got someone to stand up for them. Believe me, I know, I've seen it a hundred times. Passenger ships, resort hotels, night clubs. Some men think a woman without a partner is there for only one reason. If you had me hovering about, you'd be safer.'

'I see. So you'd be my bodyguard, that's what I get out of it. What do you get out of it?'

'I get part of what you win at the bridge tables.'

'That's your idea of partnership? I split my earnings with you?' She was indignant.

'Hey, hey!' Once again he was laughing. 'I know your father was a big businessman, I guess you've inherited something from him – you zoom right in on the flaws. Did I say I was going to take your money and you weren't going to get any of mine?'

She frowned at him. 'Didn't you?'

'No, no. I meant we'd put our winnings together and split them fifty-fifty.'

She sat up. 'Including your poker winnings?'

This time he threw his head back and laughed in delight. While he was still laughing he signalled to the barman, who hurried across. 'Let's have some champagne,' he said, calming down. 'I think we're going to have something to celebrate by and by. A bottle of Krug,' he ordered, and when the man went bustling off he turned to Erica. 'Listen, honey, I admire you for your chutzpah. But we only split the money we both have a claim to. Until you sit in on a poker game and make a killing, I think we'll keep our arrangement for the bridge game only.'

She'd expected that reply because, after all, the gains at poker could be very large indeed. It would have been totally unfair to expect him to share them if she played no part in winning them. As she had no intention of ever learning to play poker she shrugged slightly and let it go.

While the waiter brought the champagne in its silver bucket of ice and set two glasses before them, they talked finance.

Erica realized that one way and another their winnings at the bridge table were more or less equal. Mitchell tended to win larger sums in the games he played, but he played fewer than Erica, transferring to a high-stakes poker game late at night. Erica on the contrary stayed at the bridge tables for late-night games with serious players, who were prepared to back their skill with serious money. Sometimes she won, sometimes she lost, but on the whole she came out well ahead financially.

But if the two of them played as partners, there wasn't a doubt they could do very well indeed, especially if they played in tournaments.

'But tournaments are generally ashore,' she pointed out. 'Are we going to stick together ashore?'

'Why not?'

She shook her head. 'When I get back from Europe I have to go to see my mother. I couldn't travel around to places like Saratoga Springs or Atlantic City.'

'Okay, we'll agree that when we touch home base you go your way and I go mine. But let's say we travel together and while we're abroad we stick together until after the return trip. How's that?'

'Who's to choose which ships we go on?'

'I think I ought to choose. I've been at this a long time, Erica.'

'How long, actually?'

'All my life.' She waited, and seeing she expected more he said, 'You don't want the story of my life, it's boring. Let's just say I started playing cards when I was a kid and began to earn a living from them as soon as I saw how to do it.'

'Always honestly?'

'More or less.'

'I don't want to be mixed up in anything dishonest. I've always despised card sharps.'

He nodded. 'Me too, but when you're desperate about your next meal you sometimes have to say goodbye to your principles. I'll tell you this, I only ever did it when I was desperate, and that hasn't happened since I was twenty. Okay?'

After a long hesitation she said, 'Okay.'

'Partners?'

'Yes.'

He took the champagne from among the ice, opened it dexterously, and poured some into the glasses. He slid the bottle back into the silver bucket so that it made a little triumphant crunching sound.

He raised his glass. 'To us.'

'To us, Mitchell.' It was the first time she'd used his first name. It was a significant step, more significant than the agreement or the champagne toast.

She had accepted him as partner and friend. She knew he had flaws, he admitted them without shame: he'd lived by his wits, he'd been a cheat, he looked at life very coolly. Perhaps if she'd been asked to find a partner, she would have looked for someone different. But Fate had brought her Mitchell Harrowford.

After a long period of being the protector of her mother, the leader and provider, she would be able to relax a little; she had someone she could turn to now. Not the Mr Right her mother had hoped for, but someone.

The *Providence* docked at Cherbourg. Erica and Mitchell removed to the Hotel Heloise to await her return trip. Erica had a moment of sudden panic when they presented themselves at the reception desk, but Mitchell asked for two single rooms. 'Adjoining rooms, m'sieu?' asked the reception clerk with an arch glance.

'Not necessarily,' Mitchell said.

So that was all right. He didn't have any designs on her.

The return trip was more enjoyable than the west–east crossing. Once again there was a full passenger list of the rich and the famous, yet they seemed easier to handle. Erica had to admit to herself that having a man at her elbow was very useful, particularly with ardent Frenchmen.

What was more, they made good money. It dawned upon her that Mitchell now came in on the late-night bridge parties, instead of moving off to some corner of the smoking room to play poker.

'It was very good of you,' she said as they divided up the funds as the *Providence* sailed past the Statue of Liberty once more.

'Nonsense. There weren't any big spenders among the poker players this trip. Don't count on the same thing next time around.'

They'd already agreed that Mitchell should choose the next ship. He'd said he thought they'd go for a long voyage next time, so they looked at the shipping pages.

'How about the *Verdona*?'

'The *Verdona* . . .' Her eye followed his pointing finger down the columns. 'Singapore and Hong Kong via Southampton?'

'She'll be full of British civil servants from Southampton eastward,' he said in his tone of cool amusement. 'They're the keenest bridge players in the universe. What do you say?'

'Well . . . All right.' The sailing date was two weeks ahead, which gave her plenty of time to fly from New York to Nassau and back. 'What will you do in the meantime?'

'Oh, there's always a poker game in New York. I shan't be wasting my time.'

'You wouldn't like to come to Nassau with me?'

'What for?'

'To see Mother.'

He gave her a wry glance. 'And what would Mother think if you brought a man home to meet her?'

'Oh!' She hadn't thought of that. 'Well, never mind then, though what she'll say when I tell her about you, I can't imagine.'

Her mother's views were quickly stated. 'I can see it's better for you to have someone as a colleague,' she said in a tone of doubt, 'but really, you know . . . Isn't there something rather improper in it?'

'Not in the least,' said Erica in some annoyance. 'It's a business partnership.'

'But is that the way the other passengers see it?'

'What do I care about that?'

'Erica dear, you can *say* that, but it never does a woman any good to have her reputation put in doubt. I mean . . . if a nice young man came along, what would he think? What would that nice Hobart Crosley think?'

'Mother, I haven't heard from him in months. So it hardly matters, does it?'

'Is this . . . Is this going to be a permanent thing?'

'Who knows? I once thought I was going to marry Gerald Colbert and live in permanent contentment – but it didn't happen.'

Mrs Tregarvon fanned herself with a palm-leaf fan and

held her peace. She was tired, the Nassau evening was hot, and Erica wasn't in the mood to listen. She could only hope that this unsuitable relationship would end as quickly as it had begun.

Her daughter returned to New York, rejoined her partner, and sailed off to the Far East on the *Verdona*. From there they sailed round-trip to San Francisco and thence to Hawaii. And after that to Europe again.

It was on the return trip from France that Mitchell Harrowford proposed to Erica. 'It makes sense,' he remarked. 'It would cut down on expenses. We could share a cabin or a hotel room—'

'Two can live as cheaply as one?' she quoted.

'I've never believed that,' he acknowledged. 'But certainly a pair can live cheaper than two singles.'

They were in the quiet writing room of the *Providence*, a place where passengers went in search of tranquillity. The lighting was subdued, targeted over easy chairs and writing desks. A huge flowering azalea masked them from the few other occupants. Here it was warm and pleasant, in contrast to the grim grey skies of December outside. This was the winter of 1936, with the Great Depression still gripping the entire world.

Everything seemed headed for chaos. The financial situation remained uncertain, the political situation even more so. The Abyssinian War had ended in May when the Italian Fascists captured Addis Ababa, yet the rest of the world had hardly had time to draw a thankful breath before another war had begun, this time in Spain – Spanish

Fascists against the elected government.

As if that were not enough, there had been worldwide gossip about the British monarchy: the former Prince Charming of the nations, now Edward VIII, was rumoured to be in love with an American divorcée and to be insisting she be acknowledged as Queen when they married.

In a universe so at odds with itself, it seemed strange to hear Mitchell talking about altering their partnership.

'What has brought this on, Mitchell?' she asked.

'Well, the money hasn't been as good this last month or two.'

'But we always knew there would be ups and downs.'

'I guess so, but . . . These are funny times, Erica. I thought maybe you'd like to be married – be a married woman, I mean.'

'But why?' She was really puzzled. It was he who in the first place had put forward their relationship as a purely business arrangement.

'Well, you know how men talk . . . In the bar or the smoking room.'

'What about?'

'This business about Edward and Wallis Simpson. The jokes . . . I mean, it suddenly made me wonder. Do women talk like that when they get together? And if they do . . . do they say things about *you*?'

'Mitchell! You're worried about whether they're calling me bad names?'

'Don't laugh it off, Erica. If the women are anything like the men, reputations get torn to shreds in ten minutes flat. So I thought, perhaps you'd like to get married?'

She thought about it. Mrs Mitchell Harrowford. Did she want that?

'In what way would things be different?' she said carefully. 'I mean, you're not saying you're in love with me now, are you?'

He met her gaze. Their eyes held for a long moment. Then he shook his head and looked away. 'I don't think I'm capable of being in love, Erica. But that's not the point. I was thinking more of your side of it. I'm pretty sure a lot of folk take it for granted that you and I go to bed together. Okay, so some don't mind a bit and some think the less of you for it, but what I'm saying is, it's not necessary to subject you to that kind of speculation. You could be my wife and that would quiet all the wagging tongues.'

'That's kind of you, Mitchell.'

He looked quickly again at her, but she meant it quite sincerely. It was kind of him. He wasn't the marrying kind, she knew that full well. Sex seemed not to interest him. She'd never seen him look covetously at a woman, nor at a man either, if it came to that. He was simply self-contained, with no need for a passionate involvement with another person of either sex.

On the other hand, he was capable of friendship. He had been a good friend to her, and was proving himself even more so by this offer.

'We could be married in New York. I think you need a blood test first, I'm not sure.'

'I don't know, Mitchell.'

'Think about it,' he urged.

Chapter Eleven

During the night Erica woke. For a moment she was at a loss. She sat up, stretching out a hand as if to touch someone. But there was no one there, no one to touch. She was alone.

A sense of loss overwhelmed her. A moment ago she had been happy, enveloped in warmth and love. Now there was nothing, no one.

A dream. Her mind snatched after it, trying to remember its message. But already it was vanishing, wraithlike.

She was alone. Nothing new in that. What made her huddle into herself now, feeling loneliness like a cold tide engulfing her? If I marry Mitchell, she said to herself, I shan't be alone.

But was that true? With Mitchell, could she ever have a sense of belonging? She was willing to give herself, yes, to be less and yet more than herself in a total union with another person. But was Mitchell willing? Could he do it? Did he want to 'belong' to anyone, he, so self-possessed, so detached from passion?

So many doubts . . .

She remembered herself as she was at her debut – so sure of herself, quite convinced she had only to find a suitable man and she could be happily married for the rest of her life. Gerald's departure had hurt her very little, and now she knew it was because she'd had no deep feelings for him.

Timothy, whom she could have married, was a man she felt she could never trust. Mitchell was quite different though. She felt she could trust him completely and she had respect for him. Affection, too – yes, though he never asked for it and would never have stirred himself to return it, she gave him affection.

Respect, trust, affection – were these enough for a marriage? Would these keep loneliness at bay?

She had not let herself think about Bart Crosley. It was useless to think she could find with someone else the physical rapture he had given her. She had loved him eagerly, carelessly, and grieved at their parting. But she mustn't measure other men against Bart Crosley; little chance that she would ever meet another like him. And as for Bart himself, where was he now? Oceans away, living his own life, perhaps regretting their separation but knowing as she did that the golden dream was over.

I ought to marry Mitchell, she told herself. It's the sensible thing to do. If I'm so much my father's daughter I ought to weigh the pros and cons, as he would have done, and be decisive.

But then her father's decisions had been wrong. He had thought only of himself in the end. She had to think not only of herself but of her mother. Would her mother approve if she became Mrs Mitchell Harrowford?

No. Not at all. Because Amy Tregarvon had married for love. However much events had mocked her, however great the betrayal that followed, Amy Tregarvon still believed in love. It was true she'd wanted her daughter to accept Timothy but that was because she imagined Timothy had been secretly in love with Erica for years. She would be appalled if Erica told her, 'Mitchell doesn't love me and I don't love him, but we're getting married.'

Yet there was comfort and companionship to be gained in the marriage. More respect from fellow passengers, the status of a married woman.

I don't know, I don't know, her heart cried.

In the end she lay down again and closed her eyes. She need not give Mitchell his answer immediately. She would wait, and perhaps the spirit of her dream would return, bringing with it understanding, certainty, self-knowledge.

Next day Mitchell made no inquiry. She understood he was leaving her to come to her own decision in her own time. The day after, they would reach New York.

The morning of that day, December 11th, the ship's newspaper contained as usual a summary of the previous day's events, as gathered by the ship's radio officer. Erica unfolded the duplicated sheet to read while she drank her early morning tea.

'The King Abdicates,' said the headline.

Abdicates? Startled, she read on. It seemed that the scandal known to the rest of the world but concealed so long from the British people had at last ended. Edward VIII had given up the succession to his brother so that he could marry the woman he loved. In an emotional broadcast the previous day he had renounced all claim to the British throne.

Erica sat staring at the sheet of paper as if it was giving her a message no one else could understand. A king had given up his throne so as to marry the woman he loved.

Was this what marriage demanded – a love that could face

so great a sacrifice without tremor? By comparison her own musings seemed petty, almost prosaic. How dared she think she could embark on a life with Mitchell based on nothing but the wish not to be lonely.

When at last she left her cabin to start the day, her mind had been made up for her. She would tell Mitchell she preferred to go on as they were, that she liked her independence, that she didn't care if others looked askance at her as of dubious reputation. She wouldn't tell him she'd been influenced by the Duke of Windsor's decision: it would probably amuse him, make him call her a romantic. And perhaps she was, perhaps she was still hoping for some more perfect love to come her way. Whatever the reason, her resolution was made. She would be a partner to Mitchell Harrowford, not a wife.

He accepted her decision almost without argument. 'I suppose you're right,' he murmured, 'I'm no great catch.'

'It's not that, Mitchell.' She was distressed he should think so. 'I thought it over . . . I thought about it a lot. But then I decided . . . I decided . . .' She didn't know how to account for her decision without being hurtful. She didn't want to say 'I don't love you', or 'A marriage like that seemed such an empty thing'. So she said, 'I decided I liked my independence, even if it does bring me some nasty looks.'

'I understand.' The light voice held no resentment, no anger. 'Okay, we go on the same as always. So what are you going to do when we get to New York if you're not going to go before a justice of the peace with me?'

'I have to go to my mother's. It's Christmas, after all, Mitchell.'

'Right. Where would you like to be headed in the New Year?'

'I leave that to you.'

'How about we do the Australia run and then when the weather turns better again we do another trans-Atlantic?'

'Whatever you think.'

'Just one thing. If we go on a liner to Australia, I'm going to have to play poker a lot. Australians are the most ardent gamblers in the world except the Chinese.'

'That's all right.' She understood he was saying that her share of the earnings would go down. But she would get by, because on a long voyage it was almost always possible to pick up pupils for a series of bridge lessons.

Christmas in the Bahamas was quite an experience. Although the Tregarvon family had touched on the islands often in the old days, they'd never been there for Christmas. The white population celebrated more or less in the ordinary style, with imported pine trees dressed up in tinsel and baubles, carols, and Father Christmases collecting money for charity. There was a Christmas Regatta during which the yachts of New Providence were trimmed for a sail round Hog Island and back, with much merrymaking en route. There were dances and balls and paper hats.

The black population had its own ideas. In the run-up to Christmas they contented themselves with braiding the manes of the carriage horses and threading ribbons through the wheels of their bicycles. But Boxing Day was a dress rehearsal for Junkanoo. This was a supposedly Christian festival, and was justified by the claim that it celebrated the journey of the Three Wise Men. But with its loud music and drum rhythms, its columns of parading dancers, its masked men and outrageously bright costumes, it had more the effect of some African tribal custom.

The dancers trooped in and out of shops, hotels and public offices, scattering flower petals, coloured shells, fake paper money, all 'gifts' of the Wise Men. In return they received drink, cake, and real money. They pranced through the lobby of the British Colonial Hotel, up the stairs, through the ballroom where a dinner-dance was in progress, and out again chanting and waving farewells.

'My, they're noisy,' Erica said in astonishment.

'So spontaneous,' said Amy. 'You can't imagine a British crowd behaving like that.'

'I suppose not.' Erica wasn't quite so enamoured of the Junkanoo parade as her mother: there was so much excitement and so much drink that she feared it could easily turn to trouble. But no, the night of Boxing Day passed peacefully if you discounted the drums, the banging of frying pans and dustbin lids, and the occasional outburst of the trumpets. This time Erica's slight feeling of unease was groundless: but on a future occasion she was to see the Nassau crowd in a more frightening aspect.

In the morning she went for a farewell walk before catching the flight to Miami. It was very early, scarcely a soul was stirring. Yet she had an odd feeling, as if someone were padding along parallel with the path she was taking along the beach.

She paused in the orange gleam of the rising sun to listen. Nothing. Imagination, or some cleaning-woman on her way to the shopping district to tidy up after Junkanoo. Or a dancer, wearied out and with a sore head, picking his way home after the long night of parading.

She stood watching the waves foaming against the pink coral reef. A fishing boat was edging along the narrow channel between the harbour and Hog Island. One mistake on the pilot's part, and the hull would be ripped open by the razor-sharp edge of the coral. Seabirds flew in attendance, waiting for the fish scraps to be thrown overboard, dipping and swerving, the white of their wings occasionally brilliant against the dark green of the forest on shore.

A beautiful place. Her mother was happy here. While it wasn't exactly an ideal life for her, it had its advantages – the sea air and the soft climate which were beneficial for her bronchial condition, the lack of urgency in the lifestyle, the friendliness of the people. If anyone here knew that she was the deserted wife of the wicked millionaire Lindon Tregarvon, no one spoke of it to her.

Not that there were no scandalmongers in Nassau; there were always tales of who was visiting whom late at night, whose car had been glimpsed parked in a spot where it ought not to have been, whose gambling debts were growing too big to handle. But on the whole they were a tolerant society. Harry Oakes (now Sir Harry as a reward for the good work he had carried out for New Providence) was perhaps one of the few Puritans. He disapproved of unfaithfulness, of drinking if it got out of hand, and of gambling.

If Timothy Perriman's intention had been to find a place for his ex-bootlegging friends to start a casino, he would never succeed while Sir Harry Oakes was influential in the Executive Council. Erica smiled to herself and shrugged. Timothy and his friends . . . what a strange thing that was. Timothy Perriman, so buttoned-up and British, at the beck and call of a gang of flashy gangsters.

At that moment a friend of one of Timothy's friends – a fetcher and carrier who could be called upon for menial tasks – was squatting behind the scarlet bougainvillea edging the beach, watching the English lady. Why he was doing so he had no idea. He'd been given an instruction: keep an eye on her, see what she does, who she meets. But there was nothing to report. Miz Tregarvon's life was an open book. Walks and chats with her mother, bridge games in the hotel, afternoon tea with little cakes, early to bed. If the man who sent down the instruction expected to find out that Miz Tregarvon had a lover, he was in for a big let-down.

But orders were orders. He padded back to the hotel behind Erica, and didn't give up until at last she was driven to the airfield later in the morning to fly back to the mainland.

His report, when it eventually reached Timothy Perriman, was filed away with the others. It had given him some comfort. It seemed Mrs Tregarvon was in Nassau simply because she had been given a job there, and it seemed Erica went there to visit her mother. Nothing more, nothing less. Neither of the women made any effort to find the *Margravine*. So much the better.

Erica, unaware that she was a continuing source of interest to Perriman, journeyed on to San Francisco for the voyage to Australia. The ship this time was the *Cavalier*, elderly, comfortable, steady in the face of the inevitable rough currents around Tahiti and the Tubuai Islands.

At the beginning of May, without thinking too much about

the political situation in Europe, they were in New York again to board the *Portland*, bound for Cairo. There was to be a bridge tournament lasting a week at the King David Hotel and, flatteringly, they had been invited to take part.

It didn't occur to them to consider that the Civil War in Spain was now raging fiercely, because they had no intention of landing in Spain. True, the *Portland* would anchor off Bilbao in northern Spain to take on mail and supplies, but tourists had been warned it wouldn't be sensible to be ferried ashore in view of the fighting between government forces and Spanish rebels near the port. It was only after they were aboard and well on their way that they learned that farms north of Bilbao had been destroyed by bombing from the air.

Bombing from the air? Whoever heard of such a thing! There had been some wild tales about the Japanese bombing of Chinese cities from the air the previous year, but you couldn't believe a word of what you read about China, and besides, it was a long way off. But bomber planes in action in Europe?

Luckily it hadn't needed to concern the passengers on the *Portland*. They would not be landing at Bilbao, they would not be taking the slightest risk of getting involved in any of the fighting between the two factions.

A misapprehension. The passengers and crew of the *Portland* might not have had the least intention of getting involved in the fighting, but the German pilot of the fighter-bomber changed all that.

He had nothing against the *Portland* itself. To him it was just a tiny shape resting on the silvery floor that was the sea beneath him. But, having flown from a base in Spain held by the Fascist rebels, he was now in trouble. He had been unable to release his cargo of bombs because of losing his place in the squadron's run-in. He had circled back for a second attempt. An anti-aircraft gun of the government's defence force scored a lucky hit.

His tail-fin damaged, he was having problems steering. If he couldn't get rid of his load he wasn't going to make it back to base in Italy.

He pulled the release on the instrument panel before him. The stick of six bombs went screeching seaward.

It was a morning promising warmth to come. Heat haze coiled here and there about the sea surface. Erica was in the ship's pool for her morning swim.

Her swimming cap masked the noise of the first explosions. She felt them, though, as two giant fist-thumps in the water. She paused in the middle of her third length, treading water, listening in puzzlement.

Two more enormous drum-beats, bigger than before. Harder, with a shuddering after-call. She dragged off the swimming cap to listen.

To her astonishment she saw that the water in the pool was tilting, as if the hand of a god had seized it for a drinking goblet. She began to back-stroke away from the declining edge but found that the force of the water, like some weird tide, was pushing her into it.

She thrashed her way to the side, pulled herself up and out. As she tried to stand up, she staggered: the tiled edge of the pool was at an angle of thirty degrees. She clutched a steamer-chair for support. It fell over, taking her with it. She went slithering down the incline, grazing bare legs on tiles made uneven by the shock waves.

All this had taken a moment. She heard two more explosions. This time they attacked her ears, shuddered in reverberation through the ship and through her body. Great spouts of water roared up past the glassed-in walls of the poolhouse, one almost alongside, one towards the stern.

What was it? What? A tidal wave? An earthquake?

The water of the swimming pool began to pour over the rim like wine from a carafe. It hit the wall of glass panes, splashed back, and began to mount in a triangular pond. The ship was keeling over. The water gathered in the ditch made by the floor and the glass wall. Then, as Erica watched in fascination, the weight broke the glass and the water went pouring through.

She was holding on to the rail which guarded the steps down into the shallow end. She heaved on it, got herself upright, grabbed at the handle of the door to the poolhouse. The door was difficult to open, warped and grating against the jambs. It was now leaning at more than thirty degrees.

My God, thought Erica, the ship's sinking!

She ran along the passage. The passage smelt of smoke and dust, she could feel dust settling on her damp skin as she ran. She could hear noises and shouts from all over the *Portland.*

The pool had been built over the cargo hatches aft of the ship. At the end of the passage was a lounge, and beyond that a staircase down to the cabin rows. People still in their night clothes were scrambling up the tilting staircase, there were people pouring along the deck outside, from the dining saloon, from the cabins in the forward area, from the games room.

Everywhere was dust, grit, a strange smell of burnt chemicals, charred paper, little chips of wood, particles of broken glass.

'We've been hit!' 'Passengers to lifeboat stations please!' 'Let me past!' 'Where's Johnny?' A babble of voices, and over it the blare of the ship's alarm system, the shrilling of the bo'sun's whistle.

Someone seized Erica as she pushed her way through. 'Don't go that way, the water will sweep you—'

'I must, I must!' She pulled free, struggled on.

First of all she must get some clothes. She was clad only in a green swimsuit. Then she must find Mitchell.

Her cabin was fourth along the row. Luckily her key was pinned to the strap of her suit, a habit her mother had drummed into her since childhood. She unlocked her door, shoved and pushed against obstacles until she got it open.

Everything in her cabin had fallen over or was tilting. She climbed across to the wardrobe, seized a dress, a coat, some shoes.

Her handbag? Locked in a drawer. She couldn't find the drawer key. She'd left it on an ashtray. The ashtray was now buried out of sight beneath a fallen bureau.

For a moment she looked wildly about, trying to think where the key might be. Her mind seemed in a time-lock. Her eye lighted on something silver. She dived at it. A silver-backed hairbrush. Her hand was closing round it when the door was swung wide on its hinges.

Mitchell came lunging in. 'Come *on*! What the hell are you doing down here? The lifeboat—'

'I can't find my purse.'

'The devil with your purse.'

'Mitchell, what's happening?'

'We're sinking, that's what.'

'Did we hit something?'

'Something hit us.' He was dragging her out by an arm.

Now she could hear a strange sound, a deeper thrum beneath the tattoo of running feet on the boat deck, the calls and shouts and orders. 'What's that?'

'Never mind, let's get the hell out of here.'

She just managed to snatch up the coat and shoes before they were out in the passage. There was *water* in the passage. She stared at it in horror. It was seeping under doors on the side opposite Erica's cabin.

This was what she'd heard, the sound of water gushing in at open doorways on the port side, running through cabins and bar rooms, carrying stools and little tables on its current, knocking against walls and doors.

She looked at Mitchell in terror, but he was concentrating on keeping them both upright. He was wearing a cashmere sweater and trousers over pyjamas. He'd clearly been in bed when the emergency began.

But he'd known at once what was happening. 'We're sinking.' He had said it. Now she knew it was true. The *Portland* was going down. Going down fast. Going down with two holes in her, caused by the middle two bombs of the stick of six.

Two had landed in the sea to starboard, two had hit her more or less amidships, two had gone into the sea on the port side. These were the two water spouts Erica had seen. She had felt the vibration of the others through the water of the swimming pool. She still couldn't understand what they had been.

Now she could hear the creaking and straining of the ship as she heeled over. As they staggered along the tilting passage there were occasional crashes as something big was wrenched from a bulkhead, hit the deck, and skittered down the slope of the tilting ship.

There was a crowd on the stairway. No pushing or jostling: clearly one of the officers was organizing things at the top of the stairs. One or two children were passed overhead to go first into the boats. One was crying wildly, a second was enjoying himself as if it was a funfair.

And all the while the *Portland* was settling deeper into the water, still heeling over to the port side.

'Put your coat on,' Mitchell commanded. 'You're shivering.'

She hadn't even noticed. But now he said it, she saw her skin was blue with cold. He helped her into the coat, steadied her while she pushed damp feet into shoes.

In a minute or so they were at the top of the stairs.

'Know your lifeboat station?'

'Yes.'

'Make your way there.'

They moved on, but the order was easier given than carried out. Their lifeboat station was on the port side towards the stern. The port side was well down now, the deck almost to the water level. Even scrambling along on hands and knees, it would have been impossible to get there.

They and the rest of the group stopped, irresolute, frightened. They could see the uniform of one of the ship's officers a little ahead. He was shouting orders that were inaudible to them. But he was pointing with an urgent gesture, that implied 'Away, away!' And, away from the *Portland* on the waters, they could see little boats bobbing about as fishermen and bumboatmen came out from Bilbao to help.

'That's it! We must get to the rail, jump over, they'll pick us up!' The idea was put into words, passed on. Mitchell shoved Erica ahead of him to the rail. Below, about forty yards away, a little rowboat was standing off in expectation.

'Go!' shouted Mitchell.

'You too.'

'I'm coming. Will you for God's sake get up on the rail?'

She did as she was told. Mitchell helped her up, held her steady as she turned on the top to take a deep breath for the jump. Next moment she was flying through the air.

The water hit her like a blow. It seemed icy cold. She went down for what seemed like for ever, but kicked out and fought her way up. Head out of the water, she looked towards the *Portland*. Mitchell was climbing up on the rail.

She spat out sea water. 'Jump! Jump!' It was urgent. Now she was a few yards away, she could see how severe the ship's damage was, how low the rail was tilted as the *Portland* keeled to her grave.

Now Mitchell gathered himself for the jump. Just as he launched himself, a bench from the promenade deck came slithering down and dropped on him. It forced him off the rail, into the air, coming with him, entangling him as they hit the water together.

'Oh, God!' cried Erica. But whether aloud or within herself, she couldn't tell.

She struck out towards him. Behind her someone was yelling in Spanish, 'No, no, lady, it's too dangerous!'

If she heard, she paid no attention.

The bench, mostly of wood, floated. Mitchell was beneath it, held down. He seemed not to be struggling.

'Mitchell! Push it away!'

Still no movement. He was unconscious.

Without another thought Erica dived. She came up under the floating bench, alongside Mitchell. She had thought to push the bench away, but it was surprisingly heavy.

She took hold of Mitchell's head, to hold it up out of the water. A moment later something was under the bench, dragging at it.

A boathook. While the hook pulled, she held Mitchell with one arm, shoved upward with the other. The bench began to lift slightly. Mitchell came free. She pulled him down and under, swam with him two or three yards, and came up again.

They were in clear water. The bench was being carried away by the current set up by the sinking ship. The rowboat was coming towards them. Erica threw up an arm to wave, but it splashed helplessly back into the water. Her strength seemed to have gone.

She was aware of being lifted by rough hands, of voices saying, '*Despacio, despacio, hay tambien un hombre.*'

For a while she lost track of what was happening. Something was draped about her – a blanket. A rapid exchange in Spanish. Something heavy was brought aboard. The creak of the oars. Motion. Smells of the harbour, coal smoke, tar, fish. The crying of gulls, the rattle of a chain and grab, a shunting engine.

'Come, señorita, step up. Look, your foot here . . . let me help you . . .' She roused herself. She rose as a hand came under her elbow. Childishly obedient, she was about to step out of the boat on to the quay.

She stopped. 'Mitchell?'

'*Su hombre*.' A gentle nudge. 'All will be well, señorita. Please go on, we bring him.'

She clambered ashore. The docks of Bilbao were strewn with dazed figures, sitting in exhaustion on crates and bollards.

Ambulances were already drawing up along the quay. When Erica saw them, she looked back frantically for Mitchell. He must go in an ambulance. He had been unconscious in the water.

A makeshift stretcher was being handed ashore. She ran to grasp his hand, but one of the seamen put her gently aside. 'Careful, señorita, he is hurt.'

'Mitchell! Mitchell!'

But the lips made no move to form a reply, the eyelids remained closed over the brown eyes. 'Mitchell, can you hear me?' And then, to the men who so gently carried him towards the ambulance, 'What is it? What's wrong?'

'I don't know, señorita. The doctors will say.'

Two attendants transferred the unconscious figure to a hospital stretcher. It was put aboard an ambulance. Erica made as if to climb after.

'No, señorita, no—'

'But I must!'

A flood of explanation in Spanish. At first it all went babbling past, but then she realized that if she could only stop her mind from tumbling about in hysterical bewilderment, she could understand, she could respond.

'We need the space in the ambulance for the injured,

señorita. Are you hurt? No? Then you must go to the church. See? The church? The good sisters will look after you.'

'But where are you taking him? Don't take him!'

'We must, señorita. He is your husband?' A glance at her left hand. 'No. Your fiancé perhaps? What is his name?'

'Mitchell Harrowford.'

'Write it, if you please, on this label.'

With clumsy fingers she took the pencil, wrote Mitchell's name on the luggage tag, saw it tied to a button of his pyjamas.

'Let me go with him—'

'Impossible. Come later. Please, señorita, you are keeping us from the work.'

She realized she was being selfish, stupid. Stretchers were waiting to be loaded. She fell back. As the men loaded them aboard and climbed into the vehicle she called, '*Donde? Dicame, donde va?*'

'*Hospital, el centro commercial, avenida Bajarego.*'

She was still calling questions as the back doors closed and the vehicle drew away, its alarm bells ringing.

A group of women passengers was being conducted towards the spire of a church. One of them, a fellow bridge player, took her by the arm. 'This way, dear.' She went along, understanding that for the moment it was best.

In the church volunteers and sisters from the Convent of St Marina were already offering hot drinks and dry clothes to the shipwrecked women. Erica's wet coat was peeled off by kindly hands. If there was a shocked gasp at her skimpy swimsuit, it was quickly stifled. She was helped out of it, given a worn towel with which to scrub herself dry.

Clad in hideous linen underwear from the convent's own

stock, she was offered the choice of a print dress four sizes too big or a skirt and blouse that had seen better days. She chose those, pulled them on. She put on her own shoes, soaking wet though they were.

A middle-aged woman with a notebook and pencil was threading her way among them. She was asking questions and receiving puzzled responses. She climbed on a chair. She called a demand. Above the babble of voices, it was hardly possible to hear her.

'What does she say?'

'Dunno. Something about "*habla espanol*".'

The woman was asking for an interpreter.

'*Hablo espanol, yo,*' called Erica.

Afterwards she almost regretted it, for she was kept at the church for hours acting as interpreter. But it was impossible to refuse help when women were anxiously asking for their husbands and children. And even more important to do what she could when she discovered that five people had died on the ship, three had drowned in the water, and eleven were still missing.

At noon a meal of bread and soup was provided. Consuls appeared to deal with the various nationals: English, American, French, Belgian, Dutch, German. Now at last Erica learned that the *Portland* had been sunk by bombing.

'But why? The *Portland* was a neutral ship.'

'We don't know. We may never know,' said Jack Mesonero, the British consul. 'The aeroplane was probably a German fighter-bomber based at an Italian airfield.'

'A German? But how is that possible?'

'Oh, it's Mussolini's way of helping his brothers-in-arms.

We hear there's a squadron from Germany, flying attacks on the Spanish government's defences. It's to back up General Franco in his campaign to take north-eastern Spain.'

'But . . . but . . . how can that be allowed? Why doesn't someone stop them?'

'Stop who?' asked Mesonero from behind the smoke of his little cigarillo. 'Germany denies the squadron exists, Italy says they've made no airfields available, and the Spanish government hasn't got the resources to send up fighter-planes to defend its air space even if they knew an attack was coming. There's nobody can stop a bombing raid if somebody wants to make one.'

'But that's absolutely unforgivable! You mean these planes can just fly over and bomb innocent civilians?' cried Erica.

'Well, you see,' Mesonero replied with a cynical grin, 'Franco doesn't regard the civilians of northern Spain as innocent. They're holding out against him. It makes him cross.'

'It's not funny!'

'No, and I'll tell you something that you'll like even less. The British government's made an immediate protest to Italy, Germany, and the high command of the Falangist troops. But nothing will come of it. They'll all deny responsibility.'

'But they've killed at least eight innocent people.'

'They've killed a lot more than that. Early this morning they practically demolished the town of Guernica.'

Erica was stunned into silence.

After a moment the consul resumed. 'I don't think you'll ever get any compensation for anything you lost on the ship. As to your present predicament, I'll give you some money but you understand that Bilbao is under siege. There's precious little to buy and the currency I'm giving you may very soon be worthless.'

'What do you mean?'

'When Franco's troops take over—'

'Take over? They're not going to take over? Surely the government is going to hold—'

Mesonero was shaking his head. 'Nobody says so outright, but we all know the government forces here can't hold out. Franco's got almost all the armed forces on his side. All the Republic's got is a few companies of soldiers and some foreign volunteers. It's a lost cause.'

Erica didn't want to believe him. She knew nothing about Spanish politics but she didn't want these kindly people to be defeated.

But Mesonero was proved right. Two months later, on June 18th 1937, the Nationalist forces of General Franco marched in to take over Bilbao.

By then Mitchell was out of hospital. Not because he was fully recovered, but because the hospital had needed all its beds for the casualties of the bitter fighting.

The American consul had made funds available. A room was found for Mitchell, but not in the same hotel as Erica. She was glad of it in some ways for the Hotel Cristal wasn't very comfortable. But neither was the Rosario: both were in the Old Town, on the right bank of the Nervion River, with few of the amenities brought about by the twentieth century.

Neither the British nor the American governments could make money easily available in a siege. The consuls on the spot had to do the best they could, and it was at least a blessing that Mitchell's room at the Rosario was on the first floor. There was no lift and he found walking up and down stairs very difficult.

The doctors had been somewhat vague to Erica in their diagnosis of his injuries. First of all, she wasn't a relative, not a wife, not even a fiancée. So to discuss his case with her was unethical. When it became urgent to discharge him, they had to change their minds, for someone had to take responsibility for him. And it seemed Señorita Tregarvon was the only person willing to do so.

'*Bueno*, there was some injury to the spinal column, just below what you would call the nape of the neck, no?' At Erica's expression Dr Assunto added hastily, 'No, no, I don't speak of a broken neck, but there was a partial fracture of two of the vertebrae – you understand, vertebrae?'

'Yes, please go on.'

'This has caused pressure on the nerves. You will understand that now the brain's messages to the nerves are interrupted a little. Señor Mitchell sends the message to his legs to move, the nerves don't pass on the message. So this accounts for the slight drag when he walks and the fatigue, for it is a big effort, no, to get legs to move when the messages are faint.'

'Will it get better?'

'Oh yes, in time,' said Dr Assunto with so much optimism that Erica at once knew improvement would be slow and perhaps unlikely. 'Well, also, this partial fracture is responsible for the headaches. You have noted that Señor Mitchell suffers sometimes from severe headache.'

'Of course, but I thought—'

'These are not serious, señorita, all he needs at such times is rest and quiet, and of course *aspirina*.'

'I see.'

'But there were internal injuries, you understand, Señorita Tregarvon. The lungs were damaged. We have made repairs, and with rest and good food everything in time will be reasonable.'

'Reasonable? What does that mean, reasonable?' Erica broke in.

'*Pues*, he will probably be short of breath if he exerts himself too much. What kind of work did Señor Harrowford do? Was he active physically, was there much physical stress?'

'You're asking all that in the past tense,' she said in alarm. 'Are you telling me Señor Harrowford is going to be an invalid?'

Dr Assunto looked down at the papers on his desk. He clasped his hands to stretch his fingers, unclasped them, then looked up to meet her eyes.

'Señor Harrowford is . . . *cuantos anos tiene?* . . . how many years?'

'He's forty-two, I think—'

'Forgive the impertinence, but has he enough money to retire from business once he is at home again? This would be a good time to retire.'

After a moment Erica said, 'I see.'

There followed some discussion about making good arrangements for Señor Harrowford once he was home again, and when he would be fit enough to travel, and whether it would be possible for foreign nationals to leave Bilbao while the Nationalist forces had the city under siege. No one could leave Bilbao without permission from the commander of Franco's army. But on the whole, said Dr Assunto, it was likely that permission would be given to foreigners.

They both knew that permission one way or the other was unimportant at the moment. First Mitchell had to regain some strength; under present conditions in Bilbao that wouldn't be easy. The 'good food' recommended by Dr Assunto was simply unobtainable unless one had strong contacts with the smugglers who brought in goods over the Pyrenees from France. Even if you had the contacts, you needed money, and the amount doled out from the consulates was only just enough to live on. Though Erica had a little something in reserve, she preferred to keep that for a real emergency.

She escorted Mitchell to his room at the Rosario when he was discharged. There were no ambulances available because of an influx of wounded due to the almost continuous shelling. The American consul had to pay for a taxi – a very high fare but then prices for everything were very high. With the help of Señor Carillo, the hotel owner, she got him to his room: small, rather shabby, but sparkling clean. From the window there was a good view of the street below; Mitchell spent a lot of time sitting at the window watching the day-to-day life of the citizens of the Old Town.

If she could, Erica would have moved in with Mitchell, to save money. But the hotel bills were paid directly from the consulate. When she proposed to Jack Mesonero that it would be cheaper to share a room, he was shocked.

'But you and Harrowford aren't married!'

She sighed. 'That's a known fact.'

'You wouldn't really move in with a man you weren't married to?'

'It's a bit unusual, I agree, but these are unusual days, Mr Mesonero—'

'I couldn't possibly make money available from my funds for such a thing,' he said. 'Besides, Señor Carillo would never allow it.' The idea of an unmarried woman living with a man was beyond his understanding. The Church forbade it, society forbade it, common decency forbade it.

So Erica had to pay one of the maids at the Rosario to give Mitchell some help and attention. Señor Carillo approved of the arrangement and got ten per cent even of that small amount from Consuelo.

Slowly, Mitchell began to improve a little. When the besieging army wasn't shelling the city he and Erica would go out for walks in the sunshine, sometimes down to the banks of the Nervion, sometimes to the local market if the traders had anything to lay out.

By June 10th it was clear the Nationalist guns were on the outer rim of the new industrial section on the left bank. There were two destroyers off the river mouth blockading the harbour, the Spanish Navy having gone over to Franco. Erica found the politics hard to understand; usually, in history books, the 'Nationalists' were the government and the 'Republicans' were the people trying to overthrow it because it was ruled by a monarch. Here in northern Spain, the 'Nationalists' were the rebel forces, mostly the army, and the 'Republicans' were the remainder of the officially elected Spanish government.

Scarcely a fit male Bilbaoan was to be seen; all the men

were at the barricades trying to keep out the infiltrators. The enemy artillery was never quiet; the shriek of shells in the air, the thunder of their arrival on target, the smashing of masonry, all formed an almost constant background to the ringing of alarms and the rushing of ambulances.

'Lucky for us we're in the Old Town,' Mitchell remarked as they sat sheltering in the hotel's cellar making a glass of poor but expensive wine last a long time.

'Yes, Franco's out to take the new part with all the steel mills and so forth, I suppose.' She let a little time go by and then asked, 'What do you think will happen to us when the *Nationalistas* get here?'

'Nothing much, I imagine. Franco's in enough trouble with other governments. He won't want to make things worse by behaving badly to innocent foreigners.' Mitchell smiled, a faint curving of thin lips in a wan face. 'This is a bit different from the luxuries of Cairo, huh? I'm sorry, Erica.'

'Good heavens, it's not your fault! Nobody could have expected a passenger ship to be bombed.'

'It's not just that. I know I'm a burden.'

'Now don't let's have any of that,' she said in a schoolmistress tone. 'You just need a bit of time to get back into shape.'

'Is that what I need?' he sighed. 'I wonder. I tried playing a game of double solitaire last night, Erica, and d'you know, when it wouldn't work out and I checked back, I found I'd made a mistake in the fourth row.'

'Oh, Mitch, anyone can make a mistake!'

'I used not to. I used to be able to remember every card once it was played. I can't concentrate any more.'

'It'll come back, dear.' But she wasn't sure of that. The Mitchell Harrowford who had left the hospital wasn't the same confident, self-contained man who had sailed with her from New York. Whether he would ever reappear, she didn't know.

In the week that followed, the enemy troops took street after street of the industrial area. The naval vessels bombarded the breakwaters at the river mouth to make sure no small vessels ferried in men or supplies. The Old Town came under fire, the civil rescue teams were out all the time burrowing into the rubble of wrecked buildings for survivors. Food became almost unobtainable, the drinking water supply was reduced, electricity was only sometimes available, the telephone system – always sporadic – closed down. Rumour had it that the *Nationalistas* were in the new town.

It was almost a relief when trucks filled with troops roared over the bridges into the Old Town. There was no fighting from rooftops in the old quarter, the men had hidden their weapons and taken off their military armbands. Some had been able to melt away into the Basque countryside by finding a gap in the perimeter at night.

Nationalist soldiers jumped down from the trucks, sergeants marshalled them into platoons, they marched off to take up guard. It was over. Bilbao had fallen.

For three or four days Erica and Mitch stayed indoors, as ordered by loudspeaker vans which toured the streets. They had no way of getting in touch with each other. On June 26th restrictions were eased; the population of Bilbao was allowed to go to church.

Erica flew along the cobbled streets to the Hotel Rosario. She was met in the narrow hall by Consuelo, the maid who looked after Mitch. 'All is well, señorita, but there is trouble to come.'

'What do you mean, Consuelo?'

'The *insurgentes* are conducting searches, you have heard?' At Erica's nod she went on, her dark eyes fiery with indignation. 'They are looking for our fighting men. I hear they have been told there is an injured member of the International Brigade in the area.'

'And is there?'

'Señorita! By this the informer means Señor Harrowford! You know there are many *Americanos* in the *Brigada*. This snake thinks to make money out of a mere suspicion. Señor Harrowford is *Americano* therefore he must be *brigadista*.'

Erica felt herself go cold with fright. 'Consuelo! Who's the informer?'

'God knows, and may God punish him! So far this *canalla* has eluded us so we cannot silence him. But luckily the *insurgentes* have much to do concerned with loading steel and tyres on trains to take south. They do not work too hard as yet at following up the tales of the informer.'

'How long before they get round to it?'

'Who knows?'

'We must get the señor away, Consuelo.'

'I agree, and the sooner the better.'

'But how?'

Consuelo sighed and made the sign of the cross. 'God will help you,' she said.

Mitch was at the door of his room when Erica got there. 'I heard your voice down in the hall. My God, Erica, I thought they were never going to raise the curfew!'

'How are you? Consuelo tells me you've had no trouble.'

'No, but how about you?'

'Someone was arrested last night in a house two doors down. It sounded serious.' She shrugged. 'They searched the Cristal too but nothing came of it.'

'We've got to get out of here,' Mitchell said, frowning and shaking his head. 'It's no place for you.'

'It's no place for anybody at the moment, love, the *insurgentes* have got scores to pay off against Bilbao. But as soon as I can arrange it, we're going to pack up and go.'

'How long d'you think that might be?'

'I don't know,' she answered. 'Not long.'

'I gather we'd have to have travel permits.'

'Franco won't want to feed useless mouths.'

In that she was right. Franco didn't want to waste food on Bilbao. As to innocent foreign nationals, they could go if they wished, but they were not to use trains or ships, which he needed for transporting supplies for his troops.

'We'll have to go by car,' Erica said.

'By car? We haven't got a car.'

'I'll get one.'

'How?'

She smiled. 'You know that coat I was wearing when we dived off the ship?'

'Yes, don't tell me you're going to sell that for a car? Even English flannel isn't worth that much.' He was smiling, and she felt a little surge of pleasure, for these days he scarcely had energy for even the smallest of jokes.

'In the pocket there was a gold necklace.'

'Erica!'

267

'I remember how it got there. I was wearing it one evening when I went on deck for some air, and the clasp at the back kept catching in the lace of my dress, so I took it off and stuck it in my pocket.' She put her hand under the collar of the cheap blouse she was wearing, to pull the chain into view.

'You mean that was still in your pocket after diving about in the sea?'

'It appears it was caught on the pocket lining. I told you, the clasp sticks out a bit. And the nuns found it when they dried my clothes, and they just handed it back to me, angels that they are.'

'It looks as if it's worth a few bucks,' he said, fingering the heavy links.

'One of the few remainders from the days of wealth and luxury,' she agreed, stifling a sigh. 'It's eighteen-carat gold. I'm going to take some of the links out of it and swop them for a car.'

His glance was sceptical. 'Do you think anyone will sell?'

'Yes, I do, because nobody except the *Nationalistas* has the petrol to run a car any more.'

'Oh, great, so you buy a car without gas.'

'I'll get some, in the *mercato nero*, with another link from the chain. We only want enough to get us across the border into France, Mitch.'

'Haven't the *Nationalistas* commandeered all private cars?'

'Not yet,' Erica said with a rueful grin, 'but I think they're going to any minute, so we've got to get moving on this.'

She could tell he wasn't entirely willing. His resources of energy were low. And since he had no idea he was being mistaken for a member of the International Brigade, he didn't have her sense of urgency. 'Are you sure you won't get into trouble?' he asked. 'Are you allowed to buy and sell transport? I'd have thought there'd be some law—'

'Mitchell Harrowford, do you want to sit here like a waxwork while these arrogant bullies strut around making life unbearable? Do you want to be a drag on people like Señor Carillo and Consuelo, who have enough troubles?' She didn't add, And who might be arrested too if they were suspected of harbouring a *brigadista*.

'No, of course I don't want to be a drag.'

'Then let's do it.'

Only half persuaded, he let her go on with her plans. Truth to tell, she had many reasons for wanting to leave Bilbao. Mitchell was losing ground again, through lack of food, lack of proper rest, lack of medical attention. She had to get him out of here.

Finding a car that was for sale and could be afforded took her two days. Haggling with the owner took another day. Petrol was difficult but by the first week in July she had enough in the tank of the car to get her to Irun.

Meanwhile the consuls had supplied temporary passports. The *commandante del distrito* issued travel permits on presentation of the passports and letters of credence from the consuls. On July 6th, three weeks after the *insurgentes* drove in, Erica Tregarvon and Mitchell Harrowford drove out.

They were on their way to the French border and civilization.

Chapter Twelve

Erica had been warned that the roads to the northern frontier would be difficult, thronged with refugees. What no one had told her – because no one knew – was that the government forces were launching a counter-attack against the Nationalists round Brunete.

Immediately outside Bilbao the car was stopped frequently by road patrols. At first by Nationalists, who examined their papers and directed them off on to side-tracks to leave the main road clear for military traffic. After that there was a kind of No Man's Land. Sometimes they glimpsed men skirmishing on the hillsides. At some of the crossings, machine-gun posts had been set up. Civilian traffic was being allowed to pass but anything remotely like a military vehicle was stopped. Who was conducting the searches was a matter of luck: sometimes it was a group in the uniform of the Nationalists, sometimes men with the Republican armband.

By and by the Nationalist uniforms disappeared. It seemed they had crossed into Republican-held territory. Farms wrecked by bombing raids stood empty among the fields, cattle were bellowing to be milked from ruined cow-sheds.

Erica had intended to follow the signposts – Durango – Deva – San Sebastian – Irun. But on the minor roads there were few signposts and moreover the roads weren't merely thronged, they were clogged. From the steep mountain tracks into the lower foothills came whole families – on foot, on carts, riding donkeys, driving a milk cow before them, with hens in baskets – trying to save what they could to live on while the war raged in their region.

Erica felt impelled to pick up a family she passed sitting exhausted by the roadside: a mother, a grandmother, and three small children. Speech with them was impossible, their only language being Basque. But it was easy to understand, by their graphic gestures and the despair in their eyes, that their village had been destroyed. And with their help Erica was able to keep edging north towards the frontier.

They came at last to a recently erected control post on what seemed to be a traffic road for the district, one that would eventually join up with the Pamplona–Bayonne road. Here there was a long queue. Some of those waiting spoke Spanish. Yes, this was the frontier with France. Yes, this was a newly made frontier post. Yes, this was in Republican hands. Yes, one could cross into France. But not speedily. There was nothing to do but wait.

The day wore on, night came. The frontier post couldn't function at night, there was no light by which to examine papers; no electricity of course, but also no paraffin for oil lamps.

The scant accommodation of the nearby hamlet had long been commandeered. The waiting crowd gradually settled themselves down to sleep where they could, some wrapping themselves in blankets under a tree, some creeping under a cart for shelter from the fine rain that began to fall, some in the lee of a boulder or a bush.

The car Erica had bought was an ancient Citroën, perhaps once the pride of some small businessman and built around 1926. During its hard life it had been adapted to use as transport for a wine merchant, readapted for family use with a hole cut out to make a sun-roof, seen service with a smallholder to carry fruit and vegetables, and finally been the transport of a trio of factory workers.

In the back of this Erica settled down to sleep, with the mother of the Basque family sharing the seat. The children were tucked up in the front. The grandmother rigged up a tarpaulin strung from the door handle and under this, with every appearance of contentment, she composed herself for the night. Mitch was offered a share in a makeshift tent.

The early morning light saw the queue, once more, slowly moving forward. Erica awoke with a raging thirst and a crick in her neck. The children were sitting up looking hopefully towards the grown-ups for breakfast. The grandmother was building a fire and had fetched water for coffee in a battered kettle.

Cleansing and sanitary facilities were non-existent; one disappeared into the nearby trees for privacy, and washed in the brook. When Erica rejoined the Basque family, breakfast was being served: weak coffee and some very stale bread, but nevertheless very welcome. By and by Mitch limped up to join them, supporting himself on a makeshift stick. One look at him told her he had had a very bad night.

At about eleven in the morning Erica's rickety Citroën edged up to the frontier gate. Mitch and two of the children had got out to ease the aches in their limbs. The Basque sergeant took the passports and travel permits of Erica and

Mitch. After a few moments he summoned his colleagues; they stood conferring over the papers.

'Oh dear,' muttered Erica to Mitch out of the open window, 'is something wrong?'

'Who's to know? I don't understand a word they're saying.'

Next moment, to her astonishment, the soldiers were embracing Mitch heartily.

Mitch was too good a poker player to let himself be taken aback. He shook hands with the men, smiled acknowledgement when they patted him on the back, restricted himself to '*No comprendo*' when they asked questions, accepted the glass of fiery spirits they presented, and was ushered back into the car with much applause.

'What on earth was all that about?' Erica asked as they drew away.

'I think they thought I was a wounded American fighter from the International Brigade. I didn't tell them different.'

'Good Lord!'

Erica drew up in No Man's Land between the Basque post and the French post to await the Basque family. But time went by, and the bedraggled group didn't come through. Finally, the mother of the children looked towards the Citroën, raised her hand in farewell and, turning, gathered the family around her to shepherd them back the way they had come.

'Aren't they letting them through?' cried Erica, preparing to get out and argue.

'Don't,' Mitch said, holding her back.

'But Mitch—'

'They haven't any papers, Erica. Even if they were let

through on this side, I don't think the French would accept them.'

'But—'

'Don't worry,' he soothed, seeing her distress. 'What d'you bet they walk two miles into the hills and cross somewhere where there isn't a guard?'

'Do you think so?'

He frowned. It was clear he had a fierce headache. 'We can't do anything about it. Go on.'

He was right, of course. Reluctantly Erica set the car in motion and, in a minute, was waiting to go through the French control.

Their papers were taken, once more there was a conference. This time there was no show of approval. On the contrary, the sergeant in charge went into his office to telephone.

'*Il y a un problème?*' Erica inquired of the corporal under whose eye they had been left.

'*Bien sûr. La France ne veut pas de brigadistas.*'

So now the presumption that had acted in their favour on the Basque side was a real liability. 'France doesn't want *brigadistas*' – troublemakers who left their own countries to fight for a regime that had all the appearance of becoming Communist.

After a short telephone conversation the sergeant returned. He asked them to follow him to a hut where a few benches, a table and a chair formed an interrogation office. His questions, as they now expected, were about Mitch's background.

'You are a *brigadista*?'

'No, I'm a tourist.'

'A tourist? From a theatre of war?'

'That was accidental. We had no intention of stopping in Bilbao.'

'You fought in Bilbao?'

'No, I'm not a soldier.'

'But you walk with a stick. You have been injured?'

'Yes, on board the passenger ship, *Portland*. It was bombed in the river mouth of Bilbao in May.'

The name *Portland* gave him pause. 'Ah, the *Portland* . . . And mademoiselle? You were also a passenger?'

'Yes, sergeant.'

There was a little break in the questioning. The sergeant conferred with the corporal. Erica caught the words 'infiltrator' and 'spy'. It seemed the frontier guard had been warned not to allow troublemakers or spies into France.

'This is foolish,' Mitch said through gritted teeth to Erica. 'The Nationalists wouldn't have let us leave Bilbao if they'd thought we were Republican spies.'

'I know, I know . . . These poor men are just scared of doing the wrong thing.'

'Well, we'll have to help them make up their minds. Never let your opponent settle into certainty,' said Mitch the champion bridge player.

When the soldiers turned back to them, he was ready with a suggestion. 'Messieurs, you could contact the British and the American consuls in Bilbao to certify our papers.'

'We cannot get through to Bilbao,' the sergeant said. 'The Republicans have cut the lines in preparation for this counter-attack.'

'Ah . . . But you can telephone, for instance, Biarritz? Or perhaps even Paris?'

'Well . . . It might be possible . . .'

'If you would be so good as to telephone Paris, and ask your superiors to contact the Paris office of the New England Shipping Line, they would tell you that the names of Mademoiselle Tregarvon and myself were on the passenger list of the *Portland*.'

'Hm . . . But is it likely the Paris office would have such a list?'

'Messieurs, five died on the ship, others are still missing. Relatives are probably still seeking information about the missing. You can be sure that the Paris office would have such a list.'

The sergeant was a worried man. He didn't want to cause trouble to people who, although they looked poor and dishevelled, might well be millionaires such as travelled on cruise ships. On the other hand he would be reduced to the rank of private if he let in Spanish *agents-provocateurs*.

'*Eh bien*, there are others waiting to pass through the control. Please be seated, please wait. I will send a telephone message to Paris about the *Portland*.'

There was no guard, but when they left the hut a soldier of the frontier contingent kept them under surveillance. At midday, at Mitch's suggestion, Erica asked for something to eat and drink. 'The French always respect people who respect their stomachs,' he said.

Food was brought: French bread, local cheese, a small carafe of wine. When she offered to pay, she discovered that the currency of both the Spanish official government and the Nationalists were invalid.

'But never mind, mademoiselle,' said the young private

with a wink at Erica, 'you could pay me with a kiss, eh?'

For a moment she didn't know what to do. But he was only a boy, and his open cheerful face told her he meant no harm. She gave him a sisterly peck on the cheek, he winked again, and went away.

This lad was their friend from now on. He kept them abreast of what was going on. Sergeant Deneuve had put through a call to HQ at Pau, Pau was contacting Paris. Communications weren't good, other calls had priority: of course Paris was keeping an eye on everything that happened on the border now that the fighting was so close.

The young private offered to lend them his paperback book to pass the time. 'Thank you, but what I'd like better is the pack of cards from my valise, Patric,' said Mitch.

'Cards? You play cards?'

'With enthusiasm.'

'Leave it to me.' He came back half an hour later with the cards and watched with interest when Mitch and Erica settled down to a game of two-handed whist.

'*C'est le bridge*?' he asked.

'No, it's whist. Are you interested in bridge?'

'Not me, the sarge. When he's at home him and his wife, they play.'

'Is he any good?'

Patric watched with admiration as Mitch's hands expertly dealt the cards. 'Not like that,' he opined, and went out.

Evening came. The border ceased business for the night. Their friend Patric brought them dinner: sausages, locally made, tomatoes locally grown, more bread and wine.

'And the call to Paris?' asked Mitch.

'Still no reply on that. And I'm afraid . . . you know . . . the shipping office would be closed now until the morning.'

'No,' said Erica out of long experience, 'shipping offices always have a night staff.'

Patric looked embarrassed. 'Well, you see . . . the government offices are closed now anyway.'

'You mean we're stuck here for the night?'

'I'm sorry, mademoiselle.'

As he was leaving Erica went with him to the door. 'Could you get some aspirin for my friend?' she asked.

'Aspirin?'

'He suffers very severe headaches due to the injuries to his spine.'

'But surely he carries aspirin.'

'I think he's used them all up.'

Later Patric came back to take away the dishes. He brought with him a phial of aspirin, and an invitation. 'The sergeant wondered if you and the lady would like a game of bridge?' he inquired.

'Bridge?' echoed Mitch.

'Well, he would like to get in some practice. If you want to know what I think, his wife is better at it than he is.'

'Tell the sergeant we'd be delighted to play.'

'Oh, no need to send messages. If you're ready, it's this way.'

He led them back to the office in which the telephone was housed. Here the sergeant was waiting in a mixture of embarrassment and impatience.

'It's very kind of you to give me this pleasure,' he said with great formality. 'I haven't been playing long, I hope you won't find me too stupid.'

'Who's making up the foursome?'

'Private, tell Corporal Seplet to come.'

They settled down round his desk. A bottle of wine was provided, the paraffin lamp was lit to offset the early mountain twilight. They played bridge.

It was one of the worst games Mitch and Erica had ever had to endure. Sergeant Deneuve was anxious and over-cautious, Corporal Seplet had to be prompted, while the two experts were hard put to it to conceal their ability. Only the fact that Mitch was suffering from a blinding headache kept them from winning every trick.

Corporal Seplet had to remind his sergeant that it was time to change the guard when ten o'clock came. They played for another hour but then weariness forced an end. The sergeant shook hands gratefully and ushered them personally back to the interrogation hut.

'I'm sorry there are no comforts,' he apologized, taking in the look of the interior as he stood with them at the doorway, holding up an oil lamp to light their way. 'I'll send over some cushions and blankets. It's the best we can do for bedding. We're not equipped to hold people overnight.'

'Thank you all the same.'

'*Bonne nuit.*' He put the lamp on the table and left.

Although theoretically they should have been more comfortable than the previous night – since at least they were under cover – neither of them slept much. Erica could tell Mitch was in pain, for he moved constantly on his bench, trying to get his cushions into a comfortable arrangement. Finally about two in the morning he gave up the attempt, got up, went to the window, and stared out at the stars.

Erica joined him.

'You should be asleep,' he said.

'So should you.'

'Never mind. The first French village we come to, we'll hire a room and sleep for twenty-four hours.'

They stood side by side looking out of the hut's window. After a moment Mitch put an arm around her shoulder. Nothing more happened. But Erica felt very close to him in those long hours that passed before dawn crept over the mountain sky.

Breakfast was brought by a different soldier. 'Where's Patric?'

'Off duty.'

'What's happening?'

'Nothing much. Sarge is still waiting for a reply from Paris. Sorry, monsieur.' He moved to the door. 'Need anything? Cigarettes?'

'What I'd like is a shave and a chance to brush my teeth.' Mitch glanced at Erica. 'How about you?'

'Oh, heavens, yes, a wash and chance to do my hair!'

The private hesitated, then grinned. 'I'll see what I can do.'

He returned as they were finishing the bread and coffee. 'Sarge says you can use the facilities. Ladies first, eh?'

He let her take toilet articles out of her travel bag in the car. Eyeing its meagre contents he said, 'You travel light, you and him, eh?'

'Only because we have to. Monsieur Harrowford and I lost everything when the *Portland* went down.'

She saw him make a *moue* of sympathy, then he led her to

a canvas shelter behind which she found a trestle table with a bowl of water and a towel. Beyond that was another canvas shelter, clearly the latrine.

The hardest part of this wash-and-brush-up was combing her hair. Because she hadn't been able to afford a hairdresser in Bilbao she'd grown it long, and now it was in a terrible tangle. When at length she left the washroom, quite some time had elapsed, but it was still only a little after seven.

Too early for the Paris offices to be functioning. And yet the sergeant was standing outside his office holding out her papers.

'We can leave?' she asked in surprise.

'Yes, mademoiselle, I've decided to take an initiative. Who knows how long it might take for an answer from Paris?'

'Oh, thank you, sergeant!'

'As soon as Monsieur Harrowford has made his ablutions, you are free to go.'

'It's very good of you—'

'Nonsense, I shouldn't have suspected you in the first place,' he said, his round face going pink with embarrassment. 'These stupid politicians, eh? They issue instructions: "Be vigilant", "Look out for spies". All nonsense.'

'In our case, yes.' She smiled at him. 'But you couldn't be sure of that.'

'I was uncertain, it's true. But you know what Monsieur Harrowford told me last night, there comes a time to stop being cautious. And I have decided not to be cautious about you.'

By seven-thirty they were ready to go. 'Good luck with the bridge,' Erica said to the sergeant as they moved off through the opening in the barrier into France.

'Goodbye, monsieur, mademoiselle. Good luck.'

Outside on the road there was a contingent of early travellers waiting to enter Spain: lorries with produce, private cars, horse-carts, foot passengers. They stared as the frontier post was opened before the official hour to let a decrepit old Citroën drive through.

Erica drove along the edge of the queue and at last to an open stretch of road. For a time they had the right-hand side of the road to themselves. But at last the time came when the road joined a major route. They had to decide which way to turn.

'What direction?' Erica asked.

'We'd have gone to Bayonne or Hendaye if we'd gone through Irun, wouldn't we? I don't know how far that is.' Mitch looked around at the valley, green fields sloping up to rocky outcrops. 'What does the signpost say?'

She peered up at it. 'Lourdes,' she reported.

Mitch laughed. 'It's a sign,' he said. 'The haven for the walking wounded, like me. Let's head for Lourdes.'

In Lourdes they learned there were no consulates. They stayed one night to rest, in a hostel intended for pilgrims, each in a dormitory containing six beds. Next day, after consultation at the Mairie, they decided the best place to go was Marseilles. The petrol in the Citroën having run out, they sold it for a lot less than Erica had paid for it. With the money, they took the train to Marseilles.

And there, after holding out as long as he could, Mitch collapsed.

Chapter Thirteen

Erica blamed herself bitterly. She should never have listened to Consuelo. What if the Nationalist authorities at first imagined Mitch to be a former member of the International Brigade? With the help of the consuls they could have explained themselves.

Yet . . . there had been rumours of swift judgement and execution; there might not have been time to make explanations. And conditions in Bilbao had been so bad: almost no food, infrequent supplies of water and electricity, strict curfews.

And she'd had no warning of how difficult the journey to France would be.

The doctors at the Hôpital Sainte Vierge were soothing. 'Damaged lungs . . . Ah, yes, that explains Mr Harrowford's pneumonia. It is always a risk in such cases. Not your fault, mademoiselle.'

'I had no idea he had pneumonia.'

'No, why should you? A high temperature, yes, but the weather has been hot, and of course weakness, fatigue, both of those are natural while travelling in hard conditions.'

'But he'll get better?'

'Now that he is in hospital, we have no reason to doubt that with good nursing . . .'

But it wouldn't be done quickly. The pneumonia had to take its course, the temperature had to be brought down, the pulse rate had to be reduced, and all this would end with a crisis in perhaps four or five days. There was no medication that would help. Only expert nursing and patience were of use.

Erica walked to the hospital every day along the busy Boulevard de la Corderie, jostled by shoppers, whistled at by sailors, but oblivious to it all. As soon as the doors were opened for visiting she would hurry along the cool polished corridors to the ward. On the second day she wasn't allowed to see Mitch.

'What would be the use, mademoiselle,' said the nursing sister with calm kindness, 'he wouldn't know you and besides, it would merely upset you.'

She stayed, however, sitting in the waiting room watching the sisters in their starched, winged coifs moving to and fro like creatures from some medieval legend, trying to read their gentle but impassive faces. At the end of visiting hour they sent her away.

Next day was the same, but on the fourth day she was allowed to enter the ward. Curtains had been drawn around the bed. 'He's not going to die, is he?' she gasped, in terror at the sight.

'No, no, but he has been very ill, mademoiselle. He needs peace and sleep.'

She was shown to the bedside, allowed to stand within the curtains. The figure in the bed didn't stir. She took his hand and pressed it. The sister shook her head, detached her grasp, and led her away scolding gently. 'He sleeps now, very deeply.

The crisis is over and he should do well.'

'Oh, thank God!'

'Yes, indeed, every day we thank Him,' said the nun in smiling agreement.

On a hot and drizzly Thursday at the end of July she entered the ward. The curtains had been drawn back and Mitch was awake. But his voice was thin and faint when he spoke.

'I'm not going to say "Where am I?". They already told me.'

'You gave me a fright, Mitch.'

'I passed out, right?'

'On Marseilles station.'

'Oh, great. Always go for the big play.' He closed his eyes then reopened them. 'How long am I in here for?'

'A couple of weeks, they say.'

'And where are you staying?'

'Don't worry about that, I've got a room at a little hotel near St Victor's Basilica.'

'Say, Marseilles is a bad place for a girl on her own.'

'It's all right, Mitch, the American consul recommended the hotel, it's quite respectable.'

'The consul's paying?'

'For the hospital and everything,' Erica said, waving it away. In fact, the consul wasn't paying for the hotel, since Erica was a British citizen and not within his competence. But now that Mitch was off the danger list she could think of herself a little and go to see the British consul for help.

A week later at the hospital Dr Berrault asked to speak with Erica. 'We have of course made a full examination of Monsieur Harrowford. We knew he was experiencing severe headaches and so we asked about this and he told us of his spinal injury. As Dr Achener has a special interest, we took some X-rays. Dr Achener says he believes the headaches are due to chips of bone pressing on the nerve sheaths at the site of the damaged vertebrae. He could improve matters.'

'Improve them? In what way?'

'He could remove the chipped bone and thus free the nerve sheaths. This would probably make it much easier for Monsieur Harrowford to walk and almost certainly improve the headaches.'

'That would be wonderful!' cried Erica.

'Of course, mademoiselle. But you see . . . It is an expensive procedure.'

'Oh.'

'We gather that you and monsieur lost everything in the sinking of the *Portland*?'

'I'm afraid so.'

'No funds at home?'

'Very little.' She didn't explain that, as a professional gambler, Mitch needed most of his money with him to use at high-stake poker games. In his wallet at the time of the bombing Mitch had had the equivalent of about a thousand pounds sterling. Where that had gone, there was no way of knowing – to the bottom of the sea with the *Portland* probably, for he was fairly sure he'd left it in his jacket pocket in his cabin.

'Well, mademoiselle, Dr Achener has a space in his schedule for the operation which he will hold for a day or two. We are now at the beginning of August. Naturally, my colleague has gone on holiday for August. This would give

Mr Harrowford time to make a full recovery from the pneumonia. The operation could be carried out in September. But only if you can let Dr Achener's secretary know by the day after tomorrow that it is to be undertaken.'

'I see. What sort of fee are we talking about?'

'It will be several thousand francs. And then of course Monsieur Harrowford would need a period of convalescence afterwards. Interference with the spinal column is not a minor intervention, you understand.'

'I understand.'

'Shall I tell him you will let him know?'

'Yes, thank you. Does Mr Harrowford know about Dr Achener's interest?'

'*Bien sûr.* He is very hopeful. He will tell you all about it when you see him.'

'Thank you, Dr Berrault.'

The first thing Mitch said when she reached his bedside was, 'Did Berrault tell you about this guy Achener?'

'I've just been talking to him.'

'Achener says he could get rid of the headaches. I'd give a lot to get free of them.'

'Of course, Mitch.' Today he looked so much better, his colour improved and his skin less waxy but, even more encouraging, there was a light in his eye again. She understood, just from seeing him, how much he longed to have the cause of the headaches taken away.

'Would you talk to the consul? If he'd advance the money—'

'Yes, I'll go straight there when visiting hour is over.'

'And listen, honey, it doesn't mean *you* have to hang

around Marseilles. You go back home, you've been through enough—'

'Don't talk rubbish, I couldn't possibly leave you here in hospital.'

'Nonsense, they're taking good care of me.'

'But you wouldn't have any visitors.'

'I'd survive, I'm used to being on my own.

'You mean, you don't want me hanging around?' she said, hurt.

'Now I didn't say that, Erica,' he said, and put out his hand to catch hers. 'I'd miss you, you know that. But your mother must be going out of her mind with worry.'

'I sent her a cable when we got to Marseilles and I've written by ordinary mail. She knows I'm safe and sound. So don't let's have any more nonsense about breaking up the partnership.'

He still didn't have much energy and so he gave up the argument. If truth were told, he was glad to have lost it. Mitch Harrowford had grown very fond of his partner in his own undemonstrative way.

Erica went to see the American consul, a man in his mid-fifties, whose main interest in life was his thesis on the flora of the Mediterranean. He heard Erica out while she related the offer made by Dr Achener, but was shaking his head before she had finished.

'I don't think that's possible, Miss Tregarvon. I've no funds at my command for a thing like that.'

'But aren't you supposed to look after the well-being of American citizens abroad?'

'Certainly, and when Mr Harrowford's life was in danger

during the pneumonia attack I guaranteed to defray his
hospital expenses. And shall do so until he's discharged on
that account. But as to having unnecessary operations—'

'Unnecessary? How can you say that? The damaged
vertebrae cause him terrible headaches, he can hardly see or
stand up while he has them.'

'But he could go home to the States and have the operation
done.'

'Well, I . . .'

'He has money in the States to pay for such an operation?'
Erica made no reply.

'He doesn't?'

'The point is, Dr Achener is offering to do the operation
now, within a few weeks. If you'd advance the money—'

'Miss Tregarvon, I *can't*. I don't have funds for anything
like that.'

'But couldn't you ask? I mean, telephone the Embassy in
Paris?'

'It wouldn't be any use.'

'But couldn't you just try? Explain how important it is?'

Under the appeal of those gold-flecked eyes, Thomas
Baddingly melted. 'Well, I'll give it a try,' he said, and picked
up his phone.

There were the usual delays in getting a non-local
connection. When at length he was put through he was
transferred from department to department in the Embassy.

Erica only heard his end of the conversation. He
explained that an American citizen had the opportunity to
be operated upon by a specialist for a condition brought
on by spinal injury. He mentioned the cost. Would the State

Department make the money available?

'No. I'm informed not. No, sir, no relatives here. A young lady . . . Er . . .' He glanced at Erica. 'Fiancée?'

She shook her head. 'Business partner.'

'Business partner,' repeated Mr Baddingly into the phone, his brows arching over in surprise at her response. 'What business?' He looked at Erica once more. At her reply, he covered the mouthpiece with his hand. 'I can't tell the Under Secretary you're in business to play bridge.'

'Why not? It's what we do.'

'But bridge is just a game.'

'So is baseball, Mr Baddingly, but people make a living at it.'

Baddingly sighed. Then he said into the phone, 'Miss Tregarvon says they make a living playing bridge.'

The voice at the other end of the phone erupted into annoyance and went on for some time. The consul said, 'Yes, sir,' and 'I see,' and 'I'll tell her that.' Finally he hung up. 'The answer's no.'

'So I gathered,' she said wearily.

'You have to see it from our point of view, Miss Tregarvon. The US is in the grip of the Depression. The State Department has limited funds at its disposal and quite a lot of that has to be used in countries like Spain and Germany, where our citizens are in considerable danger from the actions of the dictators.'

'I'm aware of that.'

'We could repatriate Mr Harrowford. We could make a passage home available to him once he's recovered from pneumonia. I'm sure your consul will do the same for you.

But as to advancing money for prolonged medical treatment, and with small chance of being repaid—'

'We'd repay you.'

'If some senator challenged us to account for our actions, it could look very bad. There are other people with better claim.'

'All right, I understand,' Erica said, getting to her feet. 'I'm sorry to have taken up so much of your time.'

She went out into the hot sunshine of the late afternoon. She was very tired, very thirsty. She sat down under a café's canopy to drink a *citron pressé* while she thought about what to do next.

It was no use approaching the British consul for help. Mr Wentworth had already advanced her some money for her immediate needs and told her there was a passage to Southampton ready for her. When she said she'd no intention of leaving Marseilles and that in any case her home was in the Bahamas, he looked at her as if she was insane. He certainly wouldn't advance any money for the medical needs of an American. Nor would he advance any more for her day-to-day living.

She could ask her mother for money. But Amy Tregarvon only had the small salary she earned as hostess at the hotel in Nassau. As to savings . . . It was unlikely she had any, Amy had never learned to save.

Erica sat there examining every angle in her mind while the working day of Marseilles ended and the home-bound clerks and officials began to drop in for an aperitif. When at last she walked along the Rue Sainte in the shadow of the frowning walls of St Victor, her mind was made up.

There were two things she had to do. The first was to sell the remaining links of the gold necklace to pay for the operation on Mitch's spine. The second was to find a job in Marseilles. Luckily, though the fee sounded huge when counted in francs, when converted into sterling it was not nearly so daunting. And all during the Depression, gold had been getting good prices because people had put faith in that rather than paper currency.

Next morning she asked the hotel manager for advice. Did M. Souppran know of an honest jeweller or goldsmith?

'For a repair?' he asked, eyeing Erica's shabby clothes and thinking that she couldn't possibly have any jewellery to repair.

'Something like that.'

'Hmm . . . M. Deseubec is not dishonest.'

'Where can I find him?'

'Rue des Paniers, off the Canebière, close to the harbour.'

'Thank you, monsieur.'

M. Deseubec wasn't dishonest, but neither was he soft-hearted. He examined the necklace through his loupe, tested it with acid to ensure that it was gold, weighed it, and then asked how she came by it.

'It was a birthday present some years ago.'

'Have you any proof that it is yours?'

'No, but it is mine, I assure you.'

'Why have some of the links been taken out near the clasp?'

'Because I needed to sell them.'

'Why didn't you go back to where you sold them, to sell what is left?'

'Because I sold them in Bilbao.'

'In Bilbao? How many links did you sell and how much was paid?'

'I exchanged the links for a car, so as to get away from the Spanish Nationalists,' Erica said. She held out her hand. 'If you think it's stolen, give it back. I'll take it elsewhere.'

'Don't be in such a hurry,' the jeweller said crossly, 'I didn't say I wouldn't buy it.'

He gave her what she felt was a fair price and as he handed her the money he added, 'Got away from the *Nationalistas*, eh? A bad lot, I hear. Well done, mademoiselle.'

She went to a café, asked for a *jeton*, and called the telephone number given her by Dr Berrault. A woman's voice announced that this was the office of Dr Achener.

'I was told to let you know whether or not the operation for Monsieur Harrowford was to be scheduled.'

'For whom?'

'Harrowford, Mitchell Harrowford.' She spelled the name.

'*Ah oui, l'américain. À ce moment à l'hôpital Sainte Vierge. Oui, madame, j'ai trouvé le cas.*'

'I was asked to say whether or not—'

'*C'est décidé, oui? Bien, je l'ai noté.*'

They exchanged a few details, such as the address where Erica could be reached, the probable date of the operation. Erica hung up. When she turned back to the counter she ordered coffee and picked up a morning newspaper from the rack.

With this she settled in a corner of the café to examine the *annonces classées* for a job. She soon found it wasn't going to be easy. France was beginning to feel the effects of the Great Depression which had held first America and then

Britain in its grip for some years. She saw few jobs advertised and knew she didn't have the qualifications for most of them.

'*Serveuse . . . sténographe . . . vendeuse . . .*'

Vendeuse. It couldn't be difficult to sell things. She noted the address, but when she got there half an hour later she discovered it was a leather-goods shop in one of the best shopping streets of Marseilles. They wouldn't even let her inside the door in her second-hand skirt and blouse.

So first things first. She must spend a little of the money from the jeweller on a decent outfit. Nothing expensive, just something with a little more style than a shabby brown skirt and a shapeless white blouse.

In the working-class area near the port she found a dress shop, where she bought a green cotton dress printed with daisies. She bought a straw handbag and some matching sandals from a stall in the market. She bought shampoo, a lipstick, and some scented soap in a chemist. Then she went back to the Hotel Nevette, washed her hair, twisted it up into a tight coil at the back of her head, and while it dried had a bath with the scented soap.

Then she put on the new dress, unpinned her hair so that it fell in loose thick waves, tethered it in two big combs above her ears to let the tresses just brush her neck, and was to some extent satisfied. Carefully she applied the lipstick. Then she surveyed herself.

Not smart, but not dowdy. Clearly not rich, otherwise she'd have silk stockings instead of being bare-legged. But on the other hand, not the poorest of the poor because she smelled deliciously of gardenia.

Erica went out to make her way back to the Rue St Ferreol.

It was now four o'clock, post-siesta time, but still very hot and sticky. She didn't want to spend money on a taxi so went to wait for a bus. While she waited, she gazed across the street at a capacious old house that stood back behind a row of potted palms.

On a painted board above its doorway she read: *Club de Jeu Zèbre. Ouvert le soir 22h à 4h. Adhésion 100fr.* On the door a paper was pinned.

There was no bus in sight. Erica sauntered across the street to look at the gaming club. The paper pinned to the door was a notice of some kind.

She walked up the three steps to the door to read the notice. '*Recherche croupier, expérience pas moins de trois ans, bonne présentation, salaire à plaire, s'adresser au directeur l'après-midi entre 16h et 18h.*'

Vendeuse, sténographe, croupier. She knew nothing about selling goods nor about typing. But she knew about cards. She had more chance of being a croupier than of being a salesgirl.

She rang the bell. There was a long pause. Then a little door in an upper panel opened, and a tanned face looked out at her. '*Et vous voulez?*' said a feminine voice.

'I want to apply for the job.'

'The job?'

'Croupier.'

'Ah? I see. A moment.'

In somewhat longer than a moment the door was opened. It was quite clear to Erica that the woman had been having a nap. She was now dressed in a print silk dress but with rumpled hair and in bedroom slippers.

'Yes?' she said.

'I saw the notice on the door. Has the job been filled yet?'

'We-ell . . .' She stood back to eye Erica. 'You're not French.'

'No, English.'

'You've worked in a gaming club? A casino?'

'No, but I've played cards on most of the ocean liners.'

'*Vraiment?*' she said, looking sceptical. 'How long?'

'Ever since I was a child. Professionally, the last five years.'

'Hm. How old are you?'

'Twenty-seven.'

'Your name?'

'Erica Tregarvon. And what's yours?'

'*Comment?*' said the other in surprise. 'Ah . . . well, I'm Mme Fréjus, I'm *sous-chef*. The manager is M. Kassilis, he isn't here at the moment. Come into the office, the light's better there.'

Erica followed her from the dim hall to the office, which was down a passage at the back. The room was darkened by its shutters which Mme Fréjus threw open. Late afternoon light flooded in.

Madame walked round Erica like a sculptor surveying his subject. 'Nice figure, a bit thin but that's quite fashionable. Good legs, natural hair. It is natural, isn't it?'

'Yes, and so are my teeth. Is there anything else you'd like to know?'

'Has spirit, that's good, but mind, you can't answer back to the guests, they come here to enjoy themselves.' Mme Fréjus nodded to herself. 'Nice perfume – gardenia, isn't it?

Terrible dress, where on earth did you buy that, in a church bazaar?'

'If I get the job I'll buy a better dress,' Erica said. 'Is it my turn now?'

'Your turn?'

'To survey the terrain and ask questions.'

'Depends what you ask. Go ahead.'

'What's the salary?'

'M. Kassilis will discuss that with you. There's also a commission of two and a half per cent on stakes of over 10,000 francs. That's 250 francs if a player stakes—'

'Thank you, I can do arithmetic. What are the hours?'

'Ten at night till four in the morning. It says that above the door, doesn't it?'

'Every night?'

'Well, there's a rota for one night off in ten but if you work instead you make better money. Of course if a client gets off on a winning streak, he'll tip the croupier quite generously. And it's up to you whether you accept any of the invitations that come your way.'

'Invitations?'

'Oh, come along, you're not so innocent as all that, are you? If so, I'd advise you not to apply for the job.' She paused and said, 'In any case . . .'

'What?'

'Kassi was really advertising for a man.'

'It doesn't say so on the notice.'

'No, and we do have girls. There are seven of us altogether, under Kassi, me and three girls and three men not counting the barman. What games can you run?'

Erica had never in fact run a gambling table, although she'd visited casinos. She said at hazard, 'Vingt-et-un and baccarat.'

'Can you run roulette?'

'I've never done it, but—'

Mme Fréjus shrugged. 'I know what you mean, any fool can run roulette.'

There was a little pause.

'When will M. Kassilis be here?'

'What's the time? Oh, in about an hour, I suppose. He likes to be here a few hours ahead of opening to make sure the bar's properly stocked, and he does accounts and so forth. What do you want to do? Do you want to wait or come back later?'

Erica had really nowhere to go. It would probably be too late in the afternoon by the time she got to the Rue St Ferreol, the shop might be closing. And there was no evening visiting hour at the hospital today.

'Where can I wait?' she asked.

'Oh, I was just going to have some coffee and a bite to eat. Come on, we'll go in the kitchen.'

The kitchen was a cool stone-floored room in the basement. There was an ancient gas cooker, an enamel-topped table, a sink and a few saucepans. 'We sometimes heat up some soup,' explained Mme Fréjus, 'or make a cup of coffee. Just for ourselves. The customers only get drinks and salt crackers.'

She was smiling to herself now, a plump capable woman with the sleeves of her silk dress rolled up. Erica sat down at the table while the coffee was made in a jug. Madame produced some bread and pâté.

'Help yourself. Do you want milk in the coffee? It's in the

larder, I fetch it myself so I know it's fresh. What's your name again?'

'Erica Tregarvon.'

'Married?'

'No.'

'Boyfriend?'

'Well . . . yes . . .'

'Not sure, eh? Aren't they the limit! Mine, the one at the moment, he's married. I never know when I'm going to see him. Is yours married?'

'Oh no.'

'Well, you'd better tie him down as soon as you can. Though why I say that I don't know because the chap I married, he took a train to Antwerp one day and I haven't seen him since!' She laughed heartily.

They sipped the excellent coffee while Mme Fréjus talked. It was clear she liked to talk. It also became clear she was more or less the moving spirit of the club. M. Kassilis ran it from the financial viewpoint, and seemed to be answerable to some sort of syndicate of owners, but Mme Fréjus – Céline – supervised the cleaning, looked after the staff, got rid of drunks, and kept the police in good humour. And something else became clear. If Erica wanted the croupier's job, she could have it. Céline had taken a fancy to her and what Céline said was the law.

So it proved. When M. Kassilis arrived, short, very dark and in immaculate white stiff shirt and dinner jacket, Céline said airily, 'Oh, here's the replacement croupier, Kassi.'

'Oh?' said Kassi, surveying Erica. 'Not in that dress.'

'Of course not. She's got other things, haven't you, Erica?'

'Yes, madame,' lied Erica.

'When can you start?'

'As soon as you wish, monsieur.'

He smiled, a gleam of white teeth, not exactly friendly but at least approving. 'Tonight?'

'Oh . . . Well . . .'

'It's all right, I'll see to everything,' Céline put in, with a little jerk of the head to her that said, Leave it to me. 'Usual salary, Kassi?'

'Why not?'

'Right. Come along.'

She shepherded Erica to a room upstairs on the second floor, where it became clear that Céline often slept on the premises. 'Has to be someone here at all times, a courier comes to collect the takings during the day, never know when . . . Well, here you are.' She opened a cupboard whose shelves were piled with clothes. 'Pick something out.'

'But Céline!'

'Oh, they're not mine! No, several sizes too small for me, eh?' The other woman laughed heartily. 'No, no, left behind by some of the girls. They take off, you know, some high-roller offers them a trip to Paris or even further, and off they go at a moment's notice, the fools. Just pull things out and have a look.'

The clothes were almost all evening wear. Some were things Erica wouldn't have been seen dead in, all glitter and sharp colour and smelling of cheap scent. But there was a dark green chiffon that had a good designer label.

'How about this?'

Céline eyed it. 'Mm . . . Belonged to Malou . . . Erich

Greismann bought that for her. Yes, she was about your size. All right, take it home, run an iron over it. Shoes . . . are there shoes to match?'

There were not. In the end they had to settle for a pair of high-heeled black sandals. 'You'll buy your own, of course. You need shoes that fit. Standing for hours at a gaming table is hell on the feet. Well, be back at nine-thirty, right?'

'Right, Céline.'

She hurried back to the Hotel Nevette, borrowed an iron from the chambermaid, pressed the dress lightly, and put it on. The mirror in her room was not of the best but even so her reflection startled her.

It seemed to her that the last time she'd worn evening clothes was aeons ago, in a different life.

Yes, in a different life. Now she was a working-girl, with a weekly wage. No more the easy life of shipboard, no more luxury hotels.

But that was all right. As long as she could fulfil her responsibility to Mitch, and be there when he needed her, nothing else was important.

Chapter Fourteen

It seemed even the great Dr Achener could make mistakes. The first operation wasn't a success and there had to be a second. This achieved the hoped-for result – better control of the muscles of the legs and a diminution of the headaches. Yet to Erica it seemed to leave Mitch with poorer general health.

It also cost more money, so that the sum intended for convalescence had to be used up. When Mitch eventually left hospital he had to come straight to the Hotel Nevette. Erica had arranged to have a larger room on the ground floor, which they shared.

Everyone at the Club Zèbre took it for granted that they were living together as lovers. But it wasn't so.

At first Erica felt that the affair never got started because Mitch was still convalescent and then, when he began to improve, she decided the lack of response was due to the strange hours she worked. Mitch was asleep in the night-time when she was awake, and awake in the daytime when she had to sleep.

Also, at first, they quarrelled a lot. She'd told him she'd found a job at the Club Zèbre, and hadn't corrected him when he took that to be a respectable club for travellers and big-game hunters. When, on coming out of hospital, he discovered she worked in a gambling club, he was quietly furious.

'You'll tell them you're through!' he ordered.

'I can't do that, Mitch, we need the money.'

'You shouldn't have to work at all.'

'It's not as bad as you're thinking. Céline keeps everything respectable.'

'Erica, I may have been sick but I haven't lost my wits. I've been around gambling clubs, I know what they're like.'

'All right, it's not ideal, but I haven't any training for—'

'You haven't any training for being a floozy and you're not going to go on with it.'

It was the kind of fight that took up a lot of energy and caused a rise in temperature, neither of which Mitch could afford. When he had to give in in sheer exhaustion, Erica expected to kiss and make up, and perhaps more. But it didn't happen. They apologized and kissed briefly, and that was that.

One evening, when a friend had given Erica a bottle of good wine, they had dinner together as usual at a nearby restaurant and then came home to share the wine. They sat in the hotel's small, dusty garden, under the welcome and unexpected warmth of a winter sun. They were at ease, close together on the wrought-iron bench. Sometimes she rested her head on Mitch's shoulder. She was in a mood of dreamy longing.

When she went in to change into her evening frock before going to the club, she made an opportunity to come out from behind the screen, which separated her corner of the room from the rest. She was wearing only bra and panties. The excuse was that she'd left her hair combs on the garden seat.

Mitch was still sitting on the bench, legs outstretched, the last of the wine in his glass. She leaned out.

'Hand me my combs, Mitch.'

He turned his head, saw her, stared, then his face went almost blank. He picked up the combs and brought them to the open window. Now, she thought. If he doesn't grab me now, he never will.

He handed her the combs. He leaned close, gave her a kiss on the cheek. 'You'll be late for work,' he said, then turned back and sat on the bench.

Erica did up her hair and put on her dress. She found she was on the verge of tears but why, she wasn't sure.

Mitch became resigned to her job at the club, especially after he met Céline and one or two of the other girls. They would sometimes drop by to visit Erica at the Nevette. They were so utterly ordinary when off duty, taken up with knitting patterns, or recipes for Christmas, that it was impossible to think badly of them. If one or two of them accepted 'invitations', that was their own business.

Mitch tried to add to their income when he could. He gave English lessons to one or two of the hotel residents, and sometimes played poker with them. But he wasn't so sure of winning as in the past. And the long sessions in smoky rooms weren't good for him. His cough troubled him more and more.

One morning when Erica came home from the club she found their room empty. It meant that Mitch was in on a game in M. Souppran's apartment. Indignant – because it was after four o'clock in the morning – she went marching upstairs to break it up.

'*Oh, mon Dieu, quelle belle sauvage!*' the others

murmured as she swept in and snatched the cards out of Mitch's hand.

'You ought to be ashamed!' she raged at Souppran. 'You know this is bad for him.'

'But, mademoiselle, it's just a little New Year party.'

'He's not going to see many more New Years if you let him sit coughing in a room like this.'

'Shut up, Erica,' Mitch said.

'I won't shut up, and anyhow—' she threw down his cards face upwards – 'you're out of the game.'

'Ah, *regardez*! Fours! Not a bad hand!' There were shiftings and mutterings, and it was clear as Mitch rose to his feet that he'd been bluffing them out of their money.

Outside he said to her in a tight voice, 'Great. There was a pot of over three thousand francs there.'

'It's not worth three thousand francs if you're going to spend the next two days in bed.'

'I'm not going to spend two days in bed, dammit!' But the cold anger in his voice was broken up by a fit of coughing.

'Oh no. You'll just have a little coughing fit and that'll be the end of it. But we know better. Mitch, show some sense! No matter how much money you stand to win, it's not worth it if it makes you ill.'

'It's not making me ill. Why do you always have to be so bossy?'

So they had another row, and this time they were so upset over the things they'd said that they ended up with their arms about each other and she thought they would make love. But no, once again it simply seemed to die away, that mood of longing.

'Is it . . . Is there something wrong with me?' she faltered when he drew away.

'Of course not. You're a gorgeous kid.'

'Then why . . . I mean, is there a reason?'

He sighed, and went to lean against the edge of the window. 'You mean, do I prefer boys?'

She hesitated. 'If it's that, Mitch . . . I wouldn't mind, really . . . But I'd rather know.'

His little disclaiming laugh was cut short by a cough. 'It's not that, honey. It's just that I don't seem able to love anybody, not that way and not even you.'

'But why, Mitch? You're fond of me, I know you are.'

'You're the tops for me, kid, you know that. If I could go head over heels for anyone, it'd be you, no doubt about it. But you know . . . I had kind of a dismal time as a kid. I was brought up in a boys' home. I lived through a lot there. I told you once I got out to earn my living by playing cards as soon as I could . . .'

'I remember.'

'Well, if I ever had the ability to really love anybody, it was knocked out of me in that home. I learnt not to feel anything too deep. So that's the way it's been ever since and, honey, I'm not going to change now.'

'But Mitch—'

'It's best, sweets, it really is. You could do a lot better than me, why should you get involved—'

'But I *am* involved, Mitch!' She was going to say, 'I love you!' but caught the words back. It would only embarrass him, it would make him feel she was always expecting more from him than he could give. Nothing is worse, she warned herself, than a demanding woman.

And in any case, she wasn't sure she really loved him, certainly not in the eager, generous way she had loved Bart Crosley. For Mitch she felt something different, rather a protective, watchful affection. Whether passion would ever have turned it into something more, she couldn't be sure.

After their experiences in Bilbao Erica had begun to take more interest in politics. She read the newspapers and listened to the radio. She knew that General Franco had taken the whole of the Basque region through which she and Mitch had travelled, and grieved for the fate of those generous, independent people. In the spring of 1938 Franco moved on to take the eastern half of Spain.

Worse than that, other dictators in Europe were flouting international law and annexing pieces of other countries. During the spring of that year, German forces marched into Austria. Next, the Germans in the Sudetenland of Czechoslovakia were demanding the right to join with the German Reich. Diplomats and statesmen flew from capital to capital for conferences, troops were put on stand-by in France and Britain, sandbags were filled to protect buildings from bomb-blast, air-raid shelters were dug.

Erica's mother wrote anxiously from the Bahamas. Why was Erica lingering on in France when everything there seemed so dangerous? Why didn't she come home? When Erica replied that she was saving up for the tickets and they would travel as soon as she'd got enough put by, her mother replied rather tartly that she didn't see why Erica shouldn't come alone. 'After all, dear, it's not as if you're anything more than business partners.'

Erica smiled as she read the sentence. What Amy Tregarvon would say if she knew her daughter was actually sharing a room with the man, she dreaded to think. But Amy had never fully approved of the relationship with Mitchell Harrowford. To her he was a man she'd seen in the past on ocean liners, a man beneath her social notice.

The political trouble in Europe seemed to die down. The British Prime Minister went to Munich in September to sign an agreement with the dictators of Germany and Italy. 'Peace for our time,' he announced when he flew home.

Leonide Kassilis announced one evening in early October that he was leaving.

'Leaving? Leaving the club?' asked Céline in astonishment.

'Leaving the country. I'm going home to Greece.'

'Kassi! Have you lost your mind?'

With a grim smile he began to take personal things out of his desk drawer to put in a briefcase.

'Trouble with the bosses?' asked Hélène. It was known that the bosses were part of the Marseilles underworld, apt to be tetchy if profits dipped.

'No, it's nothing like that. They know I'm going, they're sending another manager, he'll be here tomorrow.'

'Kassi, what's this about?' Céline demanded, standing over him, arms akimbo. In her long black dinner dress and black evening gloves, she looked like an avenging angel.

'There's going to be a war,' Kassi blurted. 'I don't want to be here when it starts.'

'Don't be silly!'

'It's not silly. That man Hitler, he's not going to be happy

311

until he's got the whole of Europe under his thumb.'

'No, no, that was all sorted out at Munich last month.'

'If you believe that, Céline, you're simple-minded. The Boches are going to march into France.'

'But even if they do,' said Martin, the head croupier, 'they'll be blocked in Flanders, like last time.'

'No,' began Erica, then stopped.

'What d'you mean, no?' Céline challenged. 'The Maginot Line will stop them dead.'

Erica was shaking her head. She was remembering Bilbao.

Kassi watched her and smiled his grim agreement. 'The Maginot Line won't stop them!'

'It'd better! What do we pay our taxes for, I ask you?'

'If there's a war, it would be different from last time,' said Erica. 'This time they'd use bombers to destroy the bridges and railways and factories.'

'Oh, come on, that's nonsense.'

'She's right,' Kassi said. 'No barriers on the ground are going to stop them if they want to come. And they want to come, I can read it in that man's eyes. That's my job, isn't it, to know when a gambler is going to take the plunge? So I'm leaving. I'm going home. Nobody is going to want to invade Greece. Greece has got nothing except ruined temples and olive groves.'

Everyone except Erica tried to dissuade him. For her part, she could understand his feelings. Life at the club was hard, a world turned upside down, day for night. There was no security in it, it might be the subject of a wrangle between two gangs of criminals at any moment. And the world outside the club was full of threats.

To make matters worse, Mitch was having a severe bronchitic attack. The mistral was blowing, making the whole of Marseilles miserable. From the north it came, straight down the Rhône Valley, bringing with it cold and damp and low skies. The Hotel Nevette, never the most comfortable of homes, seemed chilly and draughty. The meals brought in from the restaurant two doors down arrived cold and unappetizing. Mitch couldn't eat, couldn't rest for coughing, couldn't even sit out in the sun to ease the pain in his chest.

To let him have the room to himself, Erica went out for a long walk. She put on the old English flannel coat that had been many times cleaned and pressed since its soaking in the harbour at Bilbao, tied a scarf around her head, and trudged off.

As always, she headed for the sea. The sea had been so much a part of her life that she was never easy without a glimpse of it each day. Today the view was dismal – the masts of the yachts at the moorings were like needles wreathed in drizzle, the Château d'If was scarcely visible, the Gulf of Lyons beyond was hazed with fog. The sound of ships' sirens could be heard from the sea roads beyond.

The sound always stirred Erica. It reminded her of sailing from many a port in days gone by. Those journeys had taken her to pleasant harbours, romantic cities under soft tropical skies. How she longed to be among those warm seas, on some palm-fringed shore! Not in this workaday city with winter coming on and the mistral blowing.

There had been a letter from her mother that morning. 'Thank you for my birthday present, it's a very pretty colour and I can use it as a light wrap for the evenings. A few friends gave me a little party but I missed you. I wish you'd come home. When you first went off on your own I expected you to be back every couple of months or so but now time is going on and on. And another birthday gone by, I'm not getting any younger, dear.'

The words lingered in her mind. Poor Amy. Nature had never intended her to cope entirely on her own. Erica ought to go back. And certainly a day like today, with its dreary skies, made Marseilles seem unfriendly. She loved the Marseillais, with their sharpness and their no-nonsense outlook, but they weren't her own people. And it must be worse for Mitch because he didn't really speak the language well and had little chance to make friends.

She left the Vieux Port and walked on, letting her mind wander back to other times, other places. She pictured the *Langrovia* with all its luxuries, the Esmeralda Hotel in Miami, the British Colonial in Nassau where she had left her mother.

If only they could go there . . . It would be so much better for Mitch. The climate would help his bronchitis. There would be no threat of war in Nassau. Her mother was there, lonely despite the fact that she had made friends.

A sudden longing to see her mother welled up. Her eyes filled with tears. She had to pause and lean on a stanchion while she wiped them away.

All year she'd been trying to put aside a little money, for the passage across the Atlantic. And suddenly now she felt the urge that had overcome Kassi – to get away, to go now, because it might soon be too late. If war came to Europe, it would be almost impossible to get a passage home.

When she looked about, she found she'd walked to the

docks on the commercial side of the city. To her it was a familiar scene experienced often when she travelled on the great ships: lorries lumbering down to the quays, porters with motor-powered trolleys moving goods, the usual racket of loading and unloading; the sound of gantries squeaking, cranes shifting crates, donkey engines straining, chains running through spiracles.   —

She walked along the sea wall, unnoticed in the hubbub. Soon she left it behind her for the quieter quays where ships lay at anchor, loading finished, waiting for sailing orders, waiting for the tide.

She saw the name. '*Carico*, Buenos Aires.'

That had been Bart's ship. There had been a time when she'd followed its career in the shipping pages. But after a time the name had vanished and she guessed it had been laid up because of the Depression. And then she'd ceased to look for it. What had been the use? Here it was, at the Marseilles Docks.

She went down from her viewpoint on the sea wall to the quay. The ship towered over her, hatches closed, a faint smoke coming from the funnel; ready to leave when the hawsers were cleared from the bollards and the anchor was raised, ready to head out from the Gulf of Lyons towards the wider world.

A sailor was leaning over the rail, supposedly on watch, half-mesmerized by the slight movement of water between ship and quay, a cigarette between his lips.

'Hi there!'

He straightened. 'Señorita?'

She hadn't meant to speak to him. But now he was staring

down at her, she might as well ask. 'Is there a Mr Hobart Crosley aboard?'

. 'You wish to speak to him? A moment, señorita.' Before she could stop him he had vanished, glad to be doing something.

She stood a moment staring up, and then embarrassment overcame her. What on earth had made her ask for Bart? And if he were aboard, what would she say to him should he come? She was about to hurry away when the man reappeared.

'The captain says he will be with you in a moment, señorita. Would you care to step aboard?'

'The captain?'

'You asked for Captain Crosley, no?'

'No . . . yes . . . Mr Crosley is captain of the *Carico*?'

'But of course, señorita. Since a year.' The sailor came down the steep companionway that linked ship with shore. He put a hand under her elbow to guide her steps as she mounted to the gate for boarding. He handed her to the deck. She glanced about. Clean decks, neat paintwork, ropes tidied, tarpaulins tied. Just what she would have expected of Captain Hobart Crosley.

He came out of the doorway above, to look down at the visitor. 'Who is it?' he called. Then he came to the bridge rail. 'Who's that?' he said, on a different note.

'Bart?' she called.

Chapter Fifteen

He came down the stairway in the practised swoop of the lifelong sailor. He grabbed her, hugged her, and swung her round.

'Erica! Erica Tregarvon! What are you doing in Marseilles?'

He'd made her breathless with his bear hug. He let her go so that she could reply, and for the first time took a good look at her.

'Good God, Erica, what's been happening to you?'

He saw her try to laugh. 'Do I look as bad as that?'

'No, of course not!' But yes, she did. Where had she gone, the vivacious, lively girl he'd loved? The lustrous chestnut hair was hidden behind a blue headscarf, the lithe body was muffled in a coat that should have been given to the rag and bone man. There was no tan on the magnolia skin. Instead she was pale as if from a life spent too much indoors, and careworn, with a frown mark between the wide arched brows.

The seaman who'd brought her aboard was watching all this with curiosity. No good for discipline, Bart reminded himself. 'Come to my cabin,' he urged, putting an arm about her shoulders. 'You look as if you could do with a drink.'

He watched her survey his cabin and was glad it was like the rest of the ship – absolutely neat, well-maintained, but brightened by a few personal touches. He ushered her to the only chair, by the desk. He had drinks in a cupboard above it, for visiting directors and the pilot after he'd shepherded them out into the seaway.

She took the brandy he poured and sipped it. He was studying her over his. She tried a smile but it faltered.

'Oh, I'm so glad to see you!' she cried.

'I'm *astonished* to see you. I thought you were cruising up and down the Americas.'

'No, the last trip was to Cairo for a bridge tournament but the ship was sunk at Bilbao.'

'The *Portland*?' Every ship's captain knew about the *Portland*, had tried to learn lessons from her unexpected fate. 'So what then – you got ashore at Bilbao?'

'Yes.'

'Your mother was with you?' he asked in sudden anxiety. He had always liked Mrs Tregarvon.

'No, she began to feel the life was too much for her. She's in Nassau now, more or less permanently.'

'But the sinking of the *Portland* was last year, Erica.' Why was she still in Europe, why did she look so down on her luck?

Sensing his scrutiny, she unfastened the headscarf and shook her hair free. How beautiful it was, he thought, a rich deep brown, shining in soft waves about her shoulders. As if she could read his thoughts, she ran her fingers through to tidy it a little, but it might have been merely to give herself a moment to collect her thoughts.

'Well, we couldn't get out of Bilbao. There was a sort of siege. When the *Nationalistas* marched in we got permission to leave so we drove into France. And then ... well, you see ... I'm with someone now, Bart. And he got ill, and had to have an operation, and ... well ... we haven't quite made it back home so far.'

Why should he feel a little sinking of the heart at her words? If anyone had asked him he'd have said he never gave Erica Tregarvon a thought these days. Yet to hear her say she was 'with someone' was an unexpected jolt.

'How are you managing, then? For money and all that kind of thing?'

'I've got a job. We're saving for the trip home.'

'Wouldn't the British Embassy—'

'They'd repatriate me to Britain. But Mitch is an American. And I really want to get to the Bahamas, not to Southampton.' She sipped the brandy to break the thread of reportage, then, resuming, said, 'That's enough about me. What have you been doing?'

'Well, as you've gathered, I made it to the top.' He laughed at his words. But though the captain's cabin was only the room of a second-rate merchantman, he felt pride in it. 'Of course things are pretty tough in the shipping world. Trade's in a terrific downturn. But I've got a reputation for running an economic ship, fast turn-around, no unnecessary harbour dues, that kind of thing. A lot of ships' captains have had to take a spell on the beach but I'm not too worried. The big anxiety at the moment is the way the Germans are carrying on. A war would make sea trade a real cliff-hanger. But if it comes, I'll go in the Navy.'

'Do you really think there'll be a war?'

He thought of the cruisers he'd seen patrolling around Kiel.

Rumour had it that the German Navy was building submarines as fast as possible at Kiel but didn't want it known. Bremerhaven, too, a lot of secret activity there.

'I wouldn't hang about in Europe without a good reason,' he advised.

She sighed. It seemed to him she agreed with the advice, but she changed the subject. 'How long are you in Marseilles?'

'Only a few more hours. I'm waiting for the pilot to come aboard.'

'Am I keeping you from—'

'No, no, paperwork is all up to date, loading certificates all in order. Nothing much to do except count the crew coming back from shore leave and welcome the pilot.' He offered to take her glass for a refill, but she shook her head. 'What brought you down to the docks?'

'Oh . . . Nostalgia? The big ships always make me think of happier times.'

'Erica,' he burst out, 'what's wrong? You seem so . . .' He didn't know how to express it. 'Well, unlike yourself,' he ended lamely.

'Oh, the world's changed and so have I,' she replied. She kept her eyes on her hands, folding and refolding the blue headscarf. 'I sent Mother a silk square like this for her birthday. You can tell by her letter of thanks that she doesn't like it. But it was all I could afford.' She smiled at him, and he could see the tears behind the smile. 'But everybody's hard up these days.'

'This job you have, it doesn't pay much?'

'It's all right. But you see . . . Mitch can't do much. He has chest trouble.'

Bart immediately decided he didn't like Mitch, who was clearly a layabout sponging off Erica. It was all wrong. She was bound to the man, that was clear, but why should she have to support him? Why should she be made pale and wan by living with a fellow like that? It would be far better if they went home to the other side of the Atlantic. This chap was an American. Get them both over there, and Mitch could go home to wherever he came from and Erica could go to her mother on New Providence.

'Have you got any money put by?' he asked.

'Some.' She stared at him. 'Why?'

'I've a friend whose ship is sailing day after tomorrow – for Trinidad. It's a cargo ship but has passenger accommodation. I think van Kreg is a bit short on passenger bookings. How would it be if I got you aboard?'

'Oh, Bart!' Her face lit up.

'You'd have to pay, but I could arrange a bargain fare. And of course it's cheaper on a cargo vessel. You know that, of course.'

'Yes, of course.' She had jumped up, smiling now, with no tears to mar it, her gold-flecked eyes alive with hope. 'Oh, it would be so lovely just to be at sea again! And I'm sure it would be good for Mitch. Mother was always in better health when we were at sea.'

I'm not the least bit interested in Mitch's health, Bart thought to himself. But let him benefit from the sea air, Bart didn't mind, so long as Erica Tregarvon could be restored to her mother and some chance of ease and comfort.

'Leave it with me, will you? I'll get in touch with van Kreg and see what can be arranged. I shan't be in port much longer, I'd better make it snappy.'

'And in that case, I must go. I've got to be at work in a couple of hours.'

'You're working at *night*?'

'Yes, in a club.'

'Erica!'

'Never mind,' she said with a laugh in her voice, 'it looks like I'll be leaving it soon!'

'I should damn well think so!' He was surprised at how shocked and angry he was. 'Have you a telephone number where you can be reached?'

'Yes, at the club, it's called the Club Zèbre but they don't really like the croupiers to leave the tables.'

'For God's sake, Erica, you're not working as a croupier?'

'Yes, I am, don't start making a fuss about it, it pays the rent!' Now he'd made her look miserable again. He could have kicked himself.

'I'm sorry, of course if you say so it's all right. Is there another number to call?'

She gave him the number of the club and of the Hotel Nevette. He wrote them down. 'Look, I'll get on to van Kreg as soon as I can. You should get a call either tonight or tomorrow. All right?'

'More than all right. Thank you, Bart.' She kissed him on the cheek. He was about to put an arm around her but she had immediately stepped back. Of course. Someone else's girl now.

He saw her down to the quay. 'Goodbye for now, Erica.'

'Shall I be seeing you in the future?'

He shrugged. 'Depends on the cargo. But I have to admit

I'm not likely to get anything for the Bahamas. Still, I do get shore leave and I expect I could fly from BA to Miami. I might drop in. You'll be at Nassau?'

'Yes, ask at the British Colonial.'

'Until then.' He took the hand she offered. What he wanted was to take her in his arms and kiss her but she'd put on her Miss Erica Tregarvon armour. They shook hands almost formally. He stood watching as she walked away between the pools of light shed by the loading lamps.

Why had he ever let things die away between them? He could excuse himself by saying he'd had very little to offer her, but at least it was more than her present partner. Why had he been such a fool? He shook his head at himself and went to a dockside café to phone van Kreg.

When Erica got back to the hotel it was past seven in the evening, already dark. They usually ate at seven-thirty in the restaurant, two doors along from the Nevette. When she got indoors, Mitch was waiting in some anxiety. 'Where have you been, honey? You've been gone over four hours!'

'I went for a walk—'

'In this weather?'

'Oh, listen, Mitch, something wonderful's happened. I met a man I used to know – he was an officer on the *Langrovia*—'

'The *Langrovia*?' Mitch echoed. 'I sailed on her once, let's see, nine years ago?'

'Yes, Mother and I remember seeing you—' She broke off. It all seemed so long ago, unreal, like something on a cinema screen. 'You wouldn't know him, Bart Crosley.'

'No, I can't say I—'

'He only joined the crew later. He was a fourth officer or something when we knew him.'

'Aha,' Mitch said, with more lightness than he'd shown for days. 'One of your old flames, was he?'

It made Erica catch her breath. 'Mother warned me never to get involved with the ship's officers,' she said with a laugh.

'Sound advice. I hope you took it. So you met this fourth officer from the *Langrovia*?'

'He's got a ship of his own now, the *Carico*.'

'Never heard of it.'

'No, it's only a middle-size merchantman. But that's not what I want to tell you, dear! Bart says he can arrange a cheap passage for us with a friend of his, a Captain van Kreg.'

'Passage? Where?'

'Trinidad!'

'Trinidad?'

'Just think, Mitch, it's only a short trip from Trinidad to New Providence! We could get a local flight to New Providence. In a week or two we could be there.'

'Do I want to be on New Providence?' Mitch inquired, looking doubtful.

'Of course you do! My mother's in Nassau, and she'll help us find somewhere to live, and I can get a job.'

'Whoa, whoa, hold your horses! You're taking it for granted that we're going to be welcome.'

'Of *course* we'll be welcome.'

Mitch was half-shaking his head. 'I don't know so much. Your mother doesn't like me.'

'Mother's never really met you.'

'Look, Erica, don't get carried away by the chance of going

home.' He caught himself up. 'No, it's great for you, you should go.'

'I'm certainly not going without you!'

'But what about your mother? I've always felt she thinks I'm several rungs below you on the social ladder.'

'Oh, nonsense, and anyhow does that matter? We'll sort that out when we get there. You do want to go, don't you?'

'To Trinidad?' He was thinking that at Trinidad he could say goodbye. No need to turn up with her in Nassau, embarrassing the hell out of everybody. He'd find some way of getting to the States on his own.

'It'll be so lovely, Mitch! Blue skies, warm seas, no mistral . . .'

'Everybody speaking a language I can understand.'

'Rum punch.'

'No French bread.'

'Don't you like French bread?'

'I hate it. Boy, wouldn't it be great to have a hot-dog with a soft roll!'

'And fruit so cheap you can buy a basketful for a shilling.'

'And waiters who actually smile at you.'

'A chambermaid who lets you leave your clothes on a chair.'

'A room that doesn't make you feel like climbing the walls.'

'Mitch! Is that how you've felt?' she cried, stricken.

'No, no, baby, it's been fine, it's been great.'

'But you've hated it.'

'Well, yeah,' he said with a rueful laugh.

'But Mitch dear, why didn't you say something?'

'What good would that have done?'

'Well, we could have moved on.'

'That's what we're doing now, isn't it?' he said.

'You don't think I'm being too bossy, planning all this?'

'For once it's okay for you to be bossy!' And they threw their arms around each other and waltzed about in delight.

While they ate dinner they were eagerly looking ahead to the journey. Now that they were going to leave, each confessed to the other, sometimes with chuckles, sometimes with a sigh, how much they hated the life they'd been leading. Erica admitted that she'd had to be rescued more than once by Céline from over-eager admirers. Mitch said he was sick to death of Mme Souppran, whose economy measures included switching off the electric fan on even the hottest summer day and making misshapen tablets of soap out of the remains of old ones.

The following morning, Erica got home as usual about four-thirty. She slept until eight, rose quietly so as not to wake Mitch, and was just about to go out to the café for breakfast as usual when she was called to the telephone. The telephone was in the hotel foyer. Mme Souppran hovered, eager to hear what the call was about.

'Yes?' said Erica. 'This is Erica Tregarvon.'

'Mme Tregarvon? I hope this is not too early to call you?' A youngish voice, speaking French with a strong Dutch accent. He had pronounced her name as if it were French.

'Not at all. Who is this, please?'

'My name is Schelmer, second mate on the *Iridea*, acting purser. Captain van Kreg asked me to speak to you about passage to Trinidad?'

'Yes, that's right.'

'For you and Monsieur, is that correct?'

'Yes.'

'The Captain says he would be glad to accommodate you. Captain Crosley has already discussed this with you?'

'Yes, he and I had a chat yesterday.'

'You understand we are sailing tomorrow? You can be ready at such short notice?'

'Oh, yes, indeed.'

'Well, that is most satisfactory, madame! We will complete the formalities when you come aboard. You have passports and the necessary fare?'

'Of course. What time would you like us there?'

'If you and Monsieur could come not later than four in the afternoon? We sail at seven. Dinner in the passengers' dining saloon will be at eight. And by the way, you realize, I'm sure, the *Iridea* is a cargo ship, the life is fairly informal. No need to dress for dinner, although the gentlemen are asked to wear jacket and tie.'

'Thank you, I understand.'

'Then I shall welcome you aboard tomorrow afternoon, madame?'

'I look forward to it.'

'Thank you, Mme Tregarvon. *À demain*.'

She disconnected. Mme Souppran was fidgeting about behind the reception desk. 'I can tell by your face it was good news, Mlle Erica?'

'It certainly was.'

'I'm so glad. Something pleasant? A party?'

'A little better than that. But I must go, madame, Jules

will have my breakfast coffee ready.'

At the café she could hardly eat or drink for delight. Other regulars glanced at her with interest; she seemed aglow with pleasure.

When she got back to the Nevette, Mitch was up in his dressing-gown. It always took him a long time to get going in the mornings. At sight of her as she burst in, he knew there had been a phone call.

'It's arranged, then, is it?'

'Oh, Mitch!' She threw her arms round him and gave him a hug. 'Tomorrow at four.'

'In the morning?' he cried, pretending to be horrified.

'No, silly, in the afternoon. Departure at seven, dinner at eight. The ship's called the *Iridea*.'

'May God bless her and all who sail in her.'

'Isn't it great?' She laughed. 'Mme Souppran was eavesdropping, dying to know what the call was about.'

'Did you tell her?' At her headshake Mitch said, 'Let's go and tell her now. And while we're at it, let's return that terrible cake of mottled soap she dished out on Saturday.'

He didn't want Erica to go to the club that night, but to send word that she was leaving. 'But I've got money owing to me, Mitch,' she protested. 'And besides, I'd like to say goodbye to the others. Céline's been very kind to me.'

'Well, I'm coming with you. And you're just going to collect your money and leave. I never approved of that place.'

'All right.' No harm in giving in to his prejudices now. Soon the Club Zèbre would be a memory.

Céline was sad when she heard the news. 'Ah, *ma p'tite*, I shall miss you,' she sighed. 'But you are going home, *n'est-*

ce pas? One can't begrudge you that. Ah, Monsieur Harrowford, remind her to write to us, eh?'

Erica had expected some reproaches about leaving them at such short notice. But apparently the new manager had a girlfriend he wanted to install as croupier, so there was no problem. Erica collected her pay packet and left.

'Goodbye, Club Zèbre,' she said, turning at the foot of the little flight of steps to survey the façade.

'Goodbye and good riddance,' snorted Mitch, and hurried her away.

Packing was soon done. Shortage of money had prevented them from buying much except necessities in the fifteen months they'd spent in Marseilles. At three-thirty they said their farewells to M. and Mme Souppran and such of the residents of the Hotel Nevette who were there. Because the mistral was still blowing and a grey drizzle was falling, they allowed themselves the luxury of a taxi to the quay.

The purser was waiting at the head of the gangplank to welcome them aboard the *Iridea*. Others were coming aboard too, luggage was being carried to cabins or stowed in the hold.

'If you would come to the purser's office, monsieur, madame? This way.' He offered them chairs, smiled, asked if they would like tea, and when they declined got down to business.

'Your passports?' He looked expectantly at Mitch, and seemed a little thrown when Erica produced hers from her handbag.

He opened both and looked at them. He murmured, 'English ... American ...' Then he turned a startled gaze on them and spoke in English. 'But . . . sir . . . madam . . . I mean Miss Tregarvon . . . I am so sorry . . .'

'What?' asked Mitch in surprise.

'You are not man and wife?'

'Obviously not.'

'But . . . But . . . I was informed . . . At least I thought it was so. I am so sorry.'

'About what?' Mitch demanded, cool annoyance in his tone.

'There is only a double cabin available.'

'That's quite all right,' Erica said quickly.

'No. No, I am afraid not. It is quite impossible. It is against company rules for an unmarried couple to share a cabin.'

'What?'

'It is a regulation. Perhaps you have not travelled much by sea.'

'Oh, God,' groaned Mitch.

It was true. They both knew it. How often had they seen a businessman and his 'secretary' on board ship, each with a separate cabin while everyone else on board knew they were lovers. Quite impossible to allow them to share a cabin! It was the same in hotels; couples indulging in clandestine affairs had to register as 'Mr and Mrs Smith'. Shipboard was even more difficult because passports had to be produced.

Dismay flooded through Erica. The disappointment was so intense that her brain seemed to turn to ice, she couldn't speak, couldn't react. Then she glanced at Mitch, and saw how grey and ill he suddenly looked. The shock for him had been even greater. Until that moment she'd no real idea how much he longed to get away.

It wasn't fair that the chance should be snatched from him like this! 'Wait!' she exclaimed. 'There's been a misunderstanding.'

'I'm afraid so, mademoiselle. I very much regret—'

'No, just a minute. You see . . .'

'Yes?'

'M Harrowford and I aren't married, that's true. But . . . we *wish* to be married. We wish the captain to marry us at sea.'

'Miss Tregarvon!'

'When I said it was all right – about the double cabin – that was what I meant.'

'Erica—' Mitch began.

'It's my fault, I should have asked Captain Crosley to explain it to you, Mr Schelmer,' she went on quickly, overriding the protest. 'Of course we shouldn't expect Captain van Kreg to carry out the ceremony until we've cleared harbour.'

'No,' said the purser faintly, 'it must be in international waters.'

'And the captain would be busy with his duties until later, of course. We thought it might be done after dinner, didn't we, dear?' she said to Mitch, taking his hand and pressing it hard.

'You're talking hooey, Erica—'

'Hooey?' said Schelmer.

'That's an Americanism, you wouldn't know it,' Erica put in, 'it means I'm letting myself be carried away with my romantic notions. It's quite true, I do get romantic ideas. It was my suggestion we should be married at sea, we could

331

just as easily have had the ceremony in Marseilles, all our friends at the Hotel Nevette wanted us to, didn't they, Mitch darling?'

'Erica,' breathed Mitch. The act she was putting on had him almost reduced to silence.

'I'm talking too much, aren't I? I'm sorry, dear. It's just that I'm so happy! You understand, don't you, Mr Schelmer?'

'Oh, of course,' said the purser, rising gallantly to the occasion. 'May I excuse myself for a few minutes? I have to ask the captain if he is willing to undertake this office.'

'Certainly, I quite understand. Do tell Captain van Kreg that he will be giving us a wonderful start to our married life, Mr Schelmer.'

As soon as the door closed behind him Erica burst out, 'Now, Mitch, don't say you don't agree. We'll lose the berth otherwise.'

'But goddammit, you can't do this!'

'Why not? You asked me once, remember, on board the *Providence*.'

'Yes, and you said you didn't want to get married.'

'Well, I've changed my mind! I want to make this trip as Mrs Mitchell Harrowford.'

'It's crazy! We'll just have to wait for another ship.'

'We *can't* go back, Mitch,' she pleaded. 'We've turned our back on the past, we can't change our minds now.' She couldn't let them go back to that life, to the weary nights at the Zebra Club, to a room where he felt like climbing the walls.

'But it's such a big step to take.'

'Darling, we've been living together for over a year –

everybody's treated us like a married couple.'

'But we're not, and it's no use kidding yourself about it. I'm not husband material.'

'Oh, for God's sake, Mitch, it's only so that we can travel on the ship. Nobody's asking you to make a career of it! If you like I'll go to Reno and get a divorce in a month or two!'

That gave him pause. He frowned.

'Don't worry about it,' she urged. 'Let's just go through the ceremony and be Mr and Mrs Harrowford until it suits us to change again. Let's go forward, Mitch – I can't go back, I *can't*!'

She was used to watching him in a bridge game, thinking back over the cards that had been played, assessing what was to come. She could see him accept the idea. He said nothing for a moment and then sighed. 'Well,' he murmured, 'I'd better go ashore again, hadn't I?'

'What for?'

'The ring, honey, the ring. If we'd been planning a romantic wedding at sea, we wouldn't have forgotten the ring.'

'Oh, Mitch!' She laughed uncertainly, and touched his cheek with her hand. 'Always planning two moves ahead.'

The purser came back smiling. Captain van Kreg had never conducted a wedding ceremony but had always wanted to. He'd be delighted to marry Miss Tregarvon and Mr Harrowford. As the bride had so intelligently foreseen, after dinner would be the best time.

'That would be marvellous,' cried Erica, clasping her hands and giving the purser a starry-eyed gaze, still acting her part.

Mitch said he had to go ashore – he'd forgotten to make an important phone call.

'Certainly, no problem,' said Schelmer. 'If you would be so good as to settle the account for the tickets before you go.'

'Of course.'

They were shown to their cabin, much plainer than that of any other ship in which they'd sailed, but quite comfortable. Mitch dropped a kiss on her head and hurried off, leaving her to unpack.

When he came back he brought a plain, inexpensive wedding band in a box. He also brought a corsage of orchids.

'Mitch!'

'A bride has to have a bouquet.'

It was wildly extravagant, but she was so touched by the thought she was almost in tears.

At dinner at eight, it was clear that other passengers had heard the news of the wedding. There were six of them, an Italian tobacco merchant and his wife, three Frenchmen who travelled in various commercial goods, and a student from the Hague. In honour of the occasion, English was to be spoken. Captain van Kreg, whom they now met for the first time, had ordered champagne. Not very good champagne, but better than anything they'd been able to afford for months.

'A toast,' cried the Captain, raising his glass in a massive hand. 'To the bride-to-be and the groom! Best wishes and a long life.'

'Thank you, thank you.' Neither of the happy couple seemed capable of making response to the toast. But then, it wasn't to be wondered at. So unusual, so romantic. Everyone smiled on them as they sat silent and embarrassed at the dinner table.

Afterwards everyone assembled in the lounge – necessarily

a small room, for most of the space aboard was taken up with cargo and the machinery for handling it. Mr Schelmer had agreed to act as best man, Signora Travoriano was delighted to act as matron of honour. Captain van Kreg came in in his best uniform; he was carrying two heavy volumes. One was the prayer book of the Dutch Protestant Church, the other was a bound copy of company regulations. He looked like a bear about to perform a circus trick with them.

'Ladies and gentlemen, I never had to do this before,' he began, looking down at them from his great height, 'but I took a look at the rules and I think I know what to do. Of course I can't carry on like a preacher, but it says in the rule book I can "make use of such phrases as are appropriate to the solemnity of the occasion, so long as the official questions are included and the marriage is duly registered". One problem is that the only prayer book I've got is this one–' he brandished the missal – 'so I'll have to translate as I go along. Clear?'

'What does he say?' Signora Travoriano whispered in Italian to her husband.

'What does it matter?' he whispered in reply. 'It isn't a proper marriage anyway without a priest.'

'I had the devil of a job finding the form to be signed that makes it legal.' He beamed. 'But my first mate knew where they were so it'll be registered and everything. Everybody ready?' Van Kreg looked about, then fixed his delighted gaze on the bride and groom.

Erica touched the orchids at her shoulder. Then she turned to look questioningly at Mitch. If he were to say now that they ought to call a halt, she would agree – almost thankfully, for now that it was about to happen she didn't know whether it was right.

Mitch drew in a breath that was half a question, half a sigh. Then as if they were sitting opposite each other at the bridge table he gave the faint smile that always meant, Play your card.

'Ready,' Erica said.

'All right. Ladies and gentlemen, we are gathered together on the bosom of the ocean to unite this man and this woman in holy matrimony . . .'

Chapter Sixteen

Amy Tregarvon was in a transport of delighted excitement. She was going to see her darling child again after an absence of almost two years. And not only that: Erica was coming home as a bride.

Amy had readied the rented bungalow in East Bay Street for the newly-weds. She had harried the cleaning woman, stood over the gardener, supervised the unloading and stacking of food stores, personally arranged the flowers. And now here she was at the airport, with a hired car waiting, far too early.

Generally in times of stress, Amy would sit down and force herself to concentrate on a game of patience. But there was nowhere at Oakes Field to lay out the cards. She paced about, pausing now and then to look at the newsstand, her eye skimming over the headlines. She tried never to pay attention to the news, it always seem to be bad these days. 'War Service Register: Figures Published.' 'Italy Denounces Agreement.' What did it all mean?

Much more important to her was the weather. She looked out at the sky: blue with white cottonwool clouds, promising perhaps a refreshing rain shower later; the temperature was about eighty degrees. Better than last month, when the tail end of some late hurricane weather had brought high winds that bent the palm trees at right angles and took the shingles off a few roofs.

She'd worried about Erica on board the *Iridea*. Not a big ship, likely to be tossed about more in high seas than the great liners she was accustomed to. But Erica had always been a good sailor. And though some ships had been in trouble there had been no word on the radio bulletins about the *Iridea*. And of course she'd had a cable from Erica when they disembarked in Trinidad so she knew they'd arrived safely.

Then the delays, the awful delays. Problems about air tickets. The little airlines that flew between the Caribbean islands had only a limited number of seats, usually booked well in advance. In the end the travellers had had to fly from Trinidad to Havana, from Havana to Miami, and now from Miami to Nassau, a round trip of three days extra.

Never mind, once they were home in the bungalow they could have plenty of rest and comfort. The furnishings were so nice – almost like an English cottage, chintz and mahogany and a fireplace, not that anyone would ever light a fire in it. Amy was sure the newly-weds would like it. At least, she was sure Erica would like it.

About Mitchell Harrowford she was not so sure.

A little bubble of indignation rose within her. She didn't even know the man! Her own daughter married to a man she'd never really met. Then she caught herself up and scolded herself. Erica knew what she was doing. Erica was her father's child, sensible, capable, not likely to be carried away. And of course she hadn't been carried away, she'd known Mitch a long time, been partners with him.

Partners with him: Amy had always been careful not to

ask herself quite what that meant. Well, whatever it had meant in the past, now everything was respectable and nice: they were married. No one in Nassau could point a finger.

The public address system croaked into life. The flight from Miami was approaching Oakes Field. A moment later she heard the propellers. Clasping and unclasping her hands, Amy hurried to the entrance to watch the twin-engined aeroplane touch down and taxi to within walking distance of the airport building. Its engines died and stopped.

The staircase was wheeled up to the plane. The passenger door opened. People began to emerge. An elderly couple, she knew them by sight, Mr and Mrs Carruthers coming back from a visit to relations in Florida. A group of men together, businessmen with briefcases, talking back and forth up the steps as they came. Hurry up, urged Amy mentally, I want to see my little girl.

Three girls home from school for the Christmas holiday. A very young couple, clearly honeymooners. Mr Gadley who ran the catering at the Yacht Club. A young woman – Amy raised a hand to wave but no, it wasn't Erica, this was a girl being greeted by a young man off to Amy's right.

And then at last, moving slowly, Erica . . . looking back . . . her arm extended as if she was holding someone's elbow . . . and equally slowly a man. They came down the airline boarding stairs carefully.

'Erica!'

Her daughter turned halfway down the steps, saw her. For a moment she stood still. She raised a hand, but immediately turned her head to look back at the man behind her.

Amy trotted across the tarmac. By the time she'd gone

halfway they had got to the foot of the steps and were coming towards her. Amy stopped, staring at her daughter.

How changed she was! Thinner, pale, clad in a cotton print dress that had seen better days, a travel bag over one arm and the other tucked in the arm of her husband.

He was nothing like the man Amy recalled. Still tall, of course, but a little stooped somehow. A white suit, rather crumpled, but then they'd been travelling. And yet it wasn't that.

He's ill, thought Amy. My poor girl, she's married to a sick man!

'Darling!' she cried, and hurried the last few yards to throw her arms around Erica. They clung to each other, half-laughing, half-crying. By and by they let each other go, and Amy turned to her son-in-law.

'So this is Mitchell,' she said. 'Welcome to Nassau.' She held out her hand and offered a cheek to be kissed.

'Thank you, Mrs Tregarvon.' He shook hands and kissed her. His lips were dry and hot. He's got a fever, thought Amy.

'This way, this way.' She urged them into the airport arrivals lounge, where the minimum of formalities was carried out; Nassau prided itself on being welcoming to its visitors. Within minutes they were out, their scant luggage had been brought to the car, and the chauffeur was driving them past the whitewashed stones of the airport road and past the golf course towards Nassau.

'I hope you'll like the house I've rented for you,' chattered Amy. 'It's one of Sir Harry's properties. I've had the essentials delivered, milk and bread and so on. The cook isn't very experienced but you can train her up as you want her. Neginah, her name is, I think it's Biblical—'

'Mother,' said Erica, taking her hand and pressing it, 'calm down.'

'Yes, darling.' Amy drew a breath. 'I'm sorry. I'm terribly nervous. You must forgive me, Mitchell,' she said, smiling at him across her daughter. 'I've never been a mother-in-law before.'

'That makes us equal, I've never been a son-in-law.' She thought his voice sounded strange, rusty, not quite hoarse, but as if he had trouble producing it. His breathing seemed uneven.

'Did you have a good voyage?'

'Not very.'

'I got quite bothered about the reports of the storms. But you never were upset by bad weather, dear,' she said to Erica.

Her daughter gave her a rueful smile. 'That was in the old days, Mother, when we were on shipboard most of the year. Mitch and I had been ashore for about eighteen months, we'd lost our sea-legs. We were terribly seasick.'

'Oh, my darling, I'm so sorry!' She felt relief, all the same. Seasickness was nothing, an ailment you recovered from within days. Yet its aftermath might perhaps make them look so wan.

She and Erica kept up a conversation during the drive. It struck Amy that her daughter was very reserved about their life in Marseilles but both women had had years of practice at chatting about very little: shipboard chat, inconsequential information about themselves that they exchanged with fellow passengers.

Mitch took almost no part. Amy saw that he was looking avidly out of the car window at the passing sights, almost as if he were drinking them in.

She too glanced out. What did he see? Dense greenery under a sunny sky, casuarina trees with their tresses of fronds moving a little in the sea breeze, the cheerful blaze of bougainvillea, pink-walled houses with cared-for lawns and fountains, space, warmth, luxuriant flowers, a look of ease and indolence.

'I hope you'll like it here,' she murmured.

'Oh yes, Mrs Tregarvon, I think I shall.'

Neginah, as instructed, had refreshments ready. The travellers elected to change into fresh clothes before sitting down to tea and scones. Their bags having been carried in, Amy paid off and tipped the chauffeur. When she turned back into the bungalow, Erica had come out of the bedroom and closed the door.

'Mitch is having a rest,' she said. 'He won't bother with tea.'

'Erica, my love,' Amy burst out, 'what's wrong with him?'

'I don't know. He's been ill before but not like this. It was the bad weather, you don't know what it was like, Mother,' Erica said, closing her eyes and putting a hand to her forehead as if she couldn't bear to remember it.

'You mean a bad voyage could make him like that?'

'All the passengers were seasick. You know how we've smiled when we've seen people looking under the weather?' Amy nodded, and Erica shook her head. 'I'll never do that again. I recovered after a couple of days but not Mitch. He had a bronchial attack. He's had chest trouble ever since he was injured on the *Portland*.'

'Oh, that terrible war! How *could* they bomb a passenger liner?'

'Mother, worse things than that happened,' Erica said. 'We were lucky, we survived. But Mitch was really badly hurt and he's never been well ever since.'

'My angel, he'll pick up here. I've found the climate here agrees with people who have chest trouble, though I'd have thought the South of France—'

'Marseilles isn't "the South of France" in that sense, Mother. It can be smoky and dirty there. In the end we felt we had to get away. And I practically forced Mitch to take this berth on the *Iridea* and now something has happened – I know it has – he's much worse than before.'

'Darling,' soothed Amy, putting her arms round her. 'Don't. Don't blame yourself. I'm sure you meant it for the best.'

'Oh, of course I did! I felt we absolutely *had* to get out of Marseilles.'

'Had to get out? I don't understand, Erica. I thought you were so happy there, with a nice job and everything.'

Erica shook her head. Her weary expression told it all.

'But your letters—?'

'Never mind, Mother. That's all gone by now. We're here, in a place where I'm going to make everything right again. Mitch will get well – I'll look after him – I'll get a job—'

'Oh, my poor little girl,' cried Amy, and put her arms around her daughter and wept into the thick waves that curved against her neck.

Neginah came to the door to ask whether she should bring

in the tea. 'Gone get too strong if you doan drink it, mam.'

'Yes, thank you, Neginah.'

Mother and daughter sat down at a little table laid with silver and china. A plate with a doily and homemade scones had the place of honour. The mere Englishness of it made Erica smile. Her mother, watching her, relaxed. Everything was going to be all right. The poor child just needed a few days' rest and some motherly looking after.

But everything didn't turn out all right. That day went by in its gentle way, and on the following Amy insisted on taking Erica out to buy some clothes. Mitchell opted to stay home and rest. A chaise longue was put out for him in the back garden, the houseboy was instructed to see he had iced drinks or coffee from time to time.

The shops in Bay Street were well-stocked in anticipation of Christmas tourists. The two women dallied in Jaeger and Liberty. It did Amy's heart good to see how her daughter began to come alive in these surroundings, delighting in trying on soft silk blouses, fine leather shoes, absurd little hats.

They had drinks and a snack in the bar of the Royal Victoria Hotel and then went on to the hairdresser. Here Erica's long thick tresses were brought into order and refashioned in an upswept, cool style beginning to be called the Edwardian look. Amy insisted on buying creams and lotions for her. With a boy trotting after them with their purchases, they turned for home just after two.

Amos the houseboy opened the door for them as they set foot on the veranda. 'Mam,' he said with anxiety, looking first at Amy and then at Erica, 'Mister ain't so good.'

'What's happened?' Erica exclaimed, and ran past him to

the living room. But Mitch wasn't there, nor was he in the master bedroom.

Now she knew where he was, because she could hear him. The sound of a paroxysm of coughing came from the back garden. She ran out of the bungalow. Mitch was sitting on the chaise longue, feet on the ground, body bent over as he fought for breath.

'Darling!' she cried. She knelt beside him, one arm over his bent back. But there wasn't anything she could do. He rocked to and fro, and glimpses of his face showed him as deathly pale, lips drawn, eyes straining, struggling to draw air into his lungs.

'Erica,' gasped Amy as she reached them. 'Whatever is it?'

'I don't know. He was like this on the ship. Nothing seems to help. Mitch, Mitch darling . . .'

Time passed, and with it the attack. Breath began to rattle in and out of his throat. Erica helped him sit up, then got him settled on the chaise longue propped up with pillows.

Any drew her away. 'We'd better have the doctor.'

'Do you have someone we could call?'

'Of course, Dr Commager, I play bridge with him.'

'Would you ring him?'

She hurried away to put the call through. Since William Commager's surgery was only a few doors up the street, he was there in ten minutes. They met him on the outer veranda to explain the situation.

'Some kind of attack, it comes on when he's been coughing a while. He simply can't get his breath, I think he feels he's going to suffocate.'

'How long has he had the condition?' Commager asked. He was of the opinion the girl could do with some medical attention herself, she looked so shocked and pale.

'It's fairly recent, but he's had the cough since he got pneumonia last year.'

'Ah! Made a good recovery, did he?'

Erica recounted the story of the shipwreck, the injury to the spine, the operation that wasn't quite successful the first time, the lack of complete recovery since that time.

'I see.' The doctor stroked his fleshy throat. 'Well, let's see what we can see.'

He motioned to Amy to stay indoors and allowed Erica to conduct him out to the back lawn. Mitch was half-sitting, half-lying on the chaise longue, head back, eyes closed. He opened his eyes at the sound of footfalls.

'Well, young man,' Commager began, standing with his hands behind his back and staring down at his patient, 'I hear you just gave everybody a thorough-going fright.'

'Gave myself one too,' Mitch said with the shadow of a grin.

'It's happened before, I gather.'

'Too often.'

'Shall we go inside and try to find out what's wrong?'

'I suppose we'd better.' He tried to swing his legs round to stand up. It took him two attempts. When Erica made as if to help him, Commager laid a hand on her arm to prevent her.

Once he was upright, Commager offered his arm. After a moment Mitch accepted it. The two men walked slowly towards the bungalow and then indoors. Erica followed after but at a gesture from the doctor joined her mother in the sitting room.

About half an hour went by. Dr Commager's tall stout figure finally appeared in the doorway of the sitting room.

'Doctor!' Erica sprang up, scrutinizing his expression. She read nothing good there. 'Tell me.'

He sat down in one of the chintz-covered armchairs, sighing. 'I could do with something to drink,' he said.

'Of course!' Amy rang for Amos, who was sent to fetch iced tea.

'Let me get this straight,' Commager began. 'Your husband was injured when the ship was bombed.'

'Afterwards, when he was about to jump from the rails.'

'Was he struck by something heavy?'

'It was a bench that had come loose. You know the kind of thing on a ship – made of slats of wood held together with iron bands.'

'And then he had pneumonia.'

'Yes, from being in the sea after being hit, I suppose.'

'What did the hospital say when they discharged him?'

'They said there was a partial fracture of two of the vertebrae. They said it wasn't too important, but then of course they were desperate to get rid of him because the wounded were being brought in from the fighting on the outskirts of Bilbao.'

Amos arrived with the glass of tea on a salver. Commager seized it, gulped down a mouthful, sighed, and wiped his mouth. 'Another please, Amos – more ice next time.' He turned to Erica. 'Did they mention anything about his lungs?'

'They said they had patched him up.' She cast her mind

back to those dangerous days. 'That he would suffer from shortness of breath. That he oughtn't to exert himself.'

'Hm . . . Well, from what I can hear through the stethoscope, they tacked together a very dodgy lung. I dare say they had no alternative. Well, that's all right, a man can manage quite well after that, but you see, during one of these recent coughing attacks the remains of that lung collapsed. He can't get enough air when he coughs.'

'Can something be done to improve the condition?' Erica asked anxiously.

'Oh, of course, we can reinflate the lung. It's a fairly simple procedure and if it had been done as soon as the collapse took place, he wouldn't have been through these terrors he's been undergoing. But you must understand . . .'

'What, doctor? What is it?'

'All this has placed a terrible strain on his heart. I'd like an electrocardiograph. We can do it at the same time as we inflate the lung.'

'That means hospital?'

Commager smiled. 'He said he'd had enough of hospitals. That's all very well but some things can only be done in hospital. I'll see to it straight away if I may use your phone.'

Arrangements were soon made; Mitch was driven to the Collins Avenue Clinic. 'This isn't exactly a joyous homecoming for you, honey,' he said with a sigh as Erica parted from him at the door of the ward.

'Never mind, we'll have plenty of time to be joyous once you're better.'

'I feel such a *nuisance*!'

'Of course you're not a nuisance!' She kissed him on the

cheek. He patted her shoulder. Amy, watching, thought it less than passionate. But perhaps you couldn't expect passion at such a time.

Within a week the lung had been put back to normal and the electrocardiograph had been taken.

'I have to tell you,' Dr Commager began, 'that it's not good. I'd imagine things have been going wrong for a couple of years now – the pneumonia may have started it off. But events in the past few months have made it a lot worse, particularly for the right side of the heart. Coughing fits in which he thinks he's going to die, the heart hammering away because it has to keep going, but it's under tremendous stress . . . Well, there you have it.'

'What does it mean, Dr Commager?' Erica asked.

'A very easy life.' The doctor leaned forward to study her as he spoke. 'Your mother told me you have only just married, Mrs Harrowford. This is a difficult thing for you to have to cope with all at once. But you've got to ensure your husband keeps calm. He's got to try to avoid starting up the bronchial trouble – coughing fits are bad for him in more ways than one. Luckily the climate here is beneficial, and I'll give you a mixture to relieve his bronchitis whenever it looks like being troublesome. But on the whole the recommendation is, make him take it easy, live one day at a time and live it quietly.'

Erica sighed. 'I blame myself. He wasn't happy in Marseilles but at least he wouldn't have had all this extra trouble if it hadn't been for being so ill on board the *Iridea*.'

Dr Commager patted her hand. 'It would have happened anyway. His lungs are under strain all the time and anything could have brought on collapse after he had a bad coughing fit. Children sometimes get lung collapse, you know, when they have whooping cough. It's not rare. Of course children don't usually develop a heart condition. It's just rotten bad luck it happened this way for your husband, and on his honeymoon trip too.'

Mitch came home to the bungalow from hospital, life began to develop its own quiet rhythm for them. Christmas came and went with the usual Bahamian Junkanoo festivities. As the year of 1939 began, Erica had a conference with her mother.

'I've got to get a job, Mother. We can't go on living off you.'

Amy would have liked to wave away all financial worries. But the truth was, her savings had not been great and were now much reduced. She was forty-nine years old, and knew quite well that she couldn't go on for ever as a hostess at the hotel. They would want someone younger and more active.

And this had already given her a thought. 'Why don't you take over my job at the Colonial, dear?'

'Take over your—? But what about you?'

'Dear heart, I'm getting too long in the tooth for it,' she said with a wry smile. 'The American visitors particularly, they like young people around them. And I'm not really very good at it. I get upset if things go wrong, if transport doesn't turn up or luggage goes astray. I think I've only hung on to the job this long because everybody knows Lady Oakes takes an interest in me.'

'Oh, Mother . . . you always talk about yourself as if you can't do anything.'

'I was spoiled,' Amy sighed. 'While we had money and

your father was in charge, I got used to letting others do things for me and I've never really come to terms with it the other way round. But you seem to know how to do it. I've watched you with Mitch, you just cope, somehow.'

'But I couldn't push you out of your job.'

'I'd be glad if you did! You see, Mrs Liddell has asked me if I'd like to go in with her in her flower business.'

'What sort of flower business? In a shop?' Erica asked, trying to envisage her mother selling bunches of ixora.

'Not exactly. You see, now there are several flights a day to Miami and connections on to the rest of the States, Mary Liddell's worked up a business sending flowers by air. The tourists arrange to have bouquets sent to friends at home, Mary notes it all down, and the flowers are specially packed and sent first-class airmail. It's surprising, she's doing very well.'

'And what would you be doing? Packing up flowers in boxes?'

'Of course not, Erica, you know how butter-fingered I am. No, Mary just wants someone to stand in for her when she has to go out or something. Take orders in her absence, answer the telephone, that sort of thing.'

It sounded like a sort of glorified office girl. 'Wouldn't you have to take a big drop in income?'

'Well, yes. And I'd lose my room at the Colonial. But I thought . . . perhaps you wouldn't mind . . . I could move in here.'

'Here?'

Amy blushed. 'I don't want to intrude on newly-weds, dear, but really there's plenty of room, isn't there? And if you had to stay late at the hotel, I'd be here with Mitchell.'

In the short time since their arrival, Amy had got over any prejudice she might have had against Mitch. In the first place he so clearly thought the world of her daughter. And in the second place, though often very unwell, he never complained. And in the third place, he seemed to take to Amy. It was difficult to be stand-offish to a man who so clearly liked her.

'Well,' said Erica, 'we're talking as if the Colonial's bound to take me on.'

'But they will, you'll see.'

So it proved. Eric Staithe, who had replaced McDermot as manager, heard them out with a mixture of amusement and relief – amusement that Mrs Tregarvon seemed to think the job could be handed on like an inheritance, and relief at the thought of getting rid of her. She was kind, she was sweet, but she was not well-organized. He had often been on the verge of telling her to show some sense, but then always restrained himself at the recollection that Sir Harry Oakes's wife might not like it.

'If you really want to resign, Mrs Tregarvon . . . ?' he murmured, fingering his foulard tie.

'I think I'd better, don't you?'

'And I'd be very grateful if you'd give me a try, Mr Staithe.'

'I see no reason not to. You say you'd rather not live in, though?'

'If you've no objection. I live just down the road, you know.'

'Quite convenient.'

'That would mean no deduction from salary for board and lodging, of course.'

Ah, thought Mr Staithe, this one has her head screwed on the right way. He began to think he might be making a very good move if he took her on. Good staff were very difficult to come by. Most of the white women on New Providence were the wives or daughters of merchants, who thought it beneath them to work in a hotel, or to work at all. He often had to hire people from Florida, who came and went like birds of passage. Someone with a mother and a husband here was more likely to stay.

'Let's say we'll give it a trial,' he said, and opened a drawer to find a copy of the hotel rules. 'One month's approval on either side, starting next Monday. What do you say?'

'Thank you, Mr Staithe.'

Mitch raised no objection to the British Colonial. He'd been there for a drink – what resident of Nassau had not? – and knew it to be thoroughly respectable and decent. Not a bit like the Club Zèbre in Marseilles. Erica's hours might sometimes be difficult, but that had always been so when they played cards on cruise ships. And he knew only too well that they needed the money.

Mitch was accepted easily into Nassau society. He was the son-in-law of Mrs Tregarvon who, in her turn, was the friend and protégée of Lady Oakes. True, he didn't have any money, but once he was made a member of The Club – the bastion of male influence on New Providence – he proved to be worth cultivating. Quiet, reserved, but Lord did he play a good game of poker when you could tempt him into it.

Mitch allowed himself to be tempted from time to time

even though he knew Erica disapproved strongly. But the card room at The Club wasn't particularly smoky, open to a veranda looking out to sea. And everyone stayed up late in Nassau, because that was when the air was at its coolest and freshest.

He won money most of the time. If he was on a losing streak, he quit the game. No one held it against him. After all, the poor fellow didn't have much in the way of funds, didn't own any property in the Bahamas, and clearly suffered from poor health. And of course he had a pretty wife. It was worth knowing Mitchell Harrowford just to be able to drop in on him at home and chat with his wife.

Erica threw herself into the job at the British Colonial Hotel. By the end of the month's approval she'd already proved her worth by inaugurating 'Bridge Tea' one afternoon a week for the ladies of Nassau, setting up a morning bridge class in the ballroom (which would otherwise have been wasted space), suggested a 'Bridge-and-Fashion' evening, managing all this while carrying out the ordinary duties of the role.

She enjoyed the work too. Her confidence began to come back. Her health, too; she had time during the intermittent duties of the day to swim, to stroll about getting to know the pretty town, to sit with Mitch in the garden or on the veranda, to chat with his friends.

The only thing that troubled Erica was to find that Timothy Perriman was still around. She was startled to see him one morning at the hotel reception desk. Busy signing in, he didn't notice her as she crossed quickly from the stairs to the breakfast room to collect a group of visitors for a motor tour of the island.

When she got back at lunchtime, she asked the duty receptionist: 'Was that Mr Perriman I saw this morning?'

'I expect so,' the girl said with a shrug. 'Just off the early flight from Miami, I suppose. You know him?'

'Does he come often to Nassau?'

'Oh, three or four times a year. He usually stays at the Fort Montagu but it's got the decorators in at the moment.'

Erica nodded and let the matter drop. That afternoon, on her way home to check everything was all right with Mitch, she dropped in at Flowers for Friends, where Amy was now employed.

'Can I help you? Oh, it's you, dear. Are you off home? Fetch me a hankie on your way back, will you? I've lost the one I came out with.'

'Mother, Timothy Perriman is staying at the Colonial.'

'Is he?' Amy said, with no apparent interest.

'He seems to be in Nassau quite regularly.'

'Yes, so it seems. He's got business interests here, he and Harold Christie often have their heads together.'

'You never mentioned it in your letters.'

Amy gave her a glance of surprise. 'I didn't think you'd be interested. You and Mitchell had teamed up by then. Anyhow, we only ever nod to each other in passing, I never know quite how to react to him after . . . you know . . . that awkwardness between you.'

'I suppose not. It gave me a bit of a shock, seeing him.'

It gave Timothy a shock when he saw Erica. Although he'd once sent out the word that he wanted to know anything about the activities of Erica Tregarvon, that was two years ago. And now, of course, she was Erica Harrowford. He had seen the name on the hotel brochure on the dressing table in his room, never suspecting it was Erica: Social Hostess, Mrs Harrowford.

Should he speak to her? Or simply nod in passing? He'd kept his distance from the mother: polite bows to each other, sometimes holding a door open for her. Best not to be offhand with her because Lady Oakes took an interest in her, and Timothy was trying to work up a friendship with Sir Harry Oakes. But with Erica, should he make some move?

At The Club he picked up the gossip. Mrs Tregarvon's daughter had come home from Europe with this fellow, not too chipper it seemed, had to go into the Clinic almost as soon as he got here. Decent enough chap, the girl seemed devoted to him.

So that was all. She'd come home to mother because she had a sick husband. Nothing to worry about. Better to speak to her, be on friendly terms. He sought her out in her little office at the hotel when he came in from a business conference next day.

'May I come in?' he said, putting his head round the door.

'Of course. How do you do, Timothy. I saw you around yesterday.' She rose from her desk but didn't come round to shake hands. She was surprised how little he'd changed. Still immaculately turned out even in the midday heat of a May day in the Bahamas, still with perfectly barbered dark hair and those light grey eyes like glacier ice.

He said, 'You look well, Erica.' And she did. More of a woman now. Less rounded, less lively, yet with character and dignity.

'Thank you, I'm fine. You're here on business?'

He nodded. 'And you're a resident in Nassau now, I hear?'

'Oh yes. Mitch and I have a place on East Bay Street. Are you staying long?'

'A few days. How's your mother?'

'Oh, enjoying life. She lives with us, of course.'

'Lives with you? You mean she doesn't have a room here in the hotel any more?' he said, at once alert.

'No, that went with the job.'

He saw the faint frown, and knew he'd sounded too interested. All the same, there was a chance now. Never could get at Amy's possessions while she lived in at the hotel, never could find out what she'd kept of the things that had belonged to Lindon Tregarvon, the vanished husband.

'I heard at The Club that Mr Harrowford isn't too fit. Nothing serious, I hope?'

'He just has to take it easy, that's all. Is there anything I can do for you? Did you come to ask for information or—'

'No, no, just to see you and have a chat. For old times' sake.'

'How kind. But if you'll excuse me, I have the Bridge Tea to organize for later.'

Although perfectly polite, she couldn't have made it plainer that she wanted rid of him. He moved back to the door. 'Might see you around?'

'Yes, quite likely.' But she sounded as if she'd rather not.

He had things to do, messages to deliver, plans to further. Although at the behest of Giancarlo Manzini, business manager of the Bassania brothers, he had by now bought considerable amounts of property in the Bahamas, it hadn't yet achieved the desired result. Harold Christie reported that the Legislative Council was adamantly opposed to the building of a casino.

'It's Sir Harry,' he explained. 'He's the Big Noise in Nassau, no two ways about it.'

'But surely he could be outvoted?'

Christie made a grimace. 'You'd have to work damned hard to get the other members to vote against him. Oakes has got all the money in the world. And he's used it well. He's done a lot of good in the Bahamas in his domineering way. He built the airfield, provides employment, it's difficult to argue against him.'

'My clients are used to getting what they want, Harold.'

'But so is Oakes! Look, tell Mr Manzini I'm doing the best I can. This is a long-term thing, we've always known that.'

'How long is long?' Timothy asked coldly, but knew there was no answer to that.

On Saturday evening there was a dinner-dance at the British Colonial. After making sure that Erica was on duty there, Timothy sauntered along to The Club for a drink with friends. It was easy enough to suggest dropping in on Mitchell Harrowford, just to keep the poor fellow company. He and Harold Christie and Norman Simmons strolled along East Bay Street in the cool night air.

If Amy Tregarvon was surprised to see Timothy, she hid it well. She welcomed the visitors when the houseboy showed them through to the back veranda, switched off the radio to which she and Mitchell had been listening.

'How nice to see you all! Timothy, what a surprise! Come in, come in. Amos, bring the drinks tray.'

Mitch got up to shake hands with the new arrivals. He was introduced to Timothy, gave him a smiling greeting. Timothy smiled back. It was clear to him that Erica had never so much as mentioned his name to her husband.

They settled down with drinks, everyday gossip was exchanged. Before too long the idea of a bridge game was suggested. 'Just one rubber,' said Simmons, 'what do you say, Mrs Tregarvon?'

'No, no, there are five of us, that would mean one left out.' Her hostess instinct was against it.

'I don't mind not playing,' Timothy volunteered. 'I'll just go out into the garden and smoke a cigar, if that's all right?'

It had been made known that smoking wasn't allowed in the house, it was bad for Mitchell. Anyone who wanted to smoke had to go outside. Amy smiled at him for his thoughtfulness, ordered Amos to set up the card table, and they all settled down around it.

Timothy went out into the garden. He took out a cigar and lit it. By and by its aroma was floating up to the veranda, but not enough to cause offence. What nobody knew was that Timothy had left the cigar burning on the rim of a clay flowerpot.

He crossed the back lawn in the darkness, went round the side of the house, and in through the open front door. Amos appeared. 'Can I get you anything, sah?'

'How about a cup of coffee?'

'Ready in a moment, sah.'

As soon as Amos had withdrawn Timothy inspected the living room. It was a big room, something like the main room of an English country house with its chintz-covered sofa and its cabinet of fine china. The main contents showed the taste of the former owner, who had had to return to England unexpectedly and from whom Harry Oakes had bought the house.

But like any living room, it had its personal belongings. Amy had collected a few things since coming to Nassau: presents from Mrs Oakes at Christmas, a painting of Christ Church Cathedral by a friend. But Timothy was interested in the mementoes of her past. They were ranged on the chimneypiece of the fireplace in which a fire would never be lit.

A photograph of the *Margravine* cut out of a yachting magazine and framed locally. Another of the *Langrovia* by the quay at Southampton. A small cedarwood box brought back from a long-ago cruise. A fan bought in Tokyo. A small silver cup, and a triple folding photograph frame of silver.

A sound at the door made him turn away. Amos appeared with a small silver coffee pot on a tray together with cup and saucer, cream and sugar. He set it down, poured the coffee. 'Cream and sugar, sah?'

'No thanks, just black. That'll be all.'

When the man had gone, Timothy went back to the mantelpiece. He had hoped to see those personal belongings of Lindon Tregarvon. His card-index mind had always retained the memory of Amy's words. 'He's sent me some of Lindon's things . . . His hairbrushes, that folding photograph frame.'

He picked up the cup, read the engraving with contempt: 'Winner, New Providence Invitation 1929, Lindon Tregarvon.' He put it back in its place. What stupidity. A rich man, as Tregarvon then had been, racing his yacht, risking his life, to win a trumpery thing like that.

But it was the photograph frame that mattered. At Amy's words so long ago in that dismal little seaside hotel, a visual image had flashed into his mind: Lindon Tregarvon putting something into the back of the frame. Timothy had entered the saloon of the *Margravine* at that moment. Tregarvon had set the photograph frame down rather quickly. Whatever he had put there, it was not to be seen. But Timothy had made a guess.

Just before he opened the saloon door and came in, he'd heard the click of a cupboard lock. There was a cupboard in the walnut panelling of the bulkhead which Tregarvon used as a safe when aboard the *Margravine*. It was a secure place, a secret place, the keyhole disguised in the burl of the polished walnut, unnoticeable unless you knew it was there. Timothy was sure that he had heard that cupboard being locked.

And in that cupboard had been papers: important papers. After Gaynor Medcalfe bought her, Timothy had gone aboard the *Margravine* in search of them after the scandal. But he'd had very little opportunity during the sailing race at Montauk to find the cupboard, and when he did, it was securely locked. He tried to prise it open with a knife, but it was impossible.

He'd consoled himself for years with the thought that no one but himself knew the cupboard was there, the cupboard with its documents so important to Lindon Tregarvon that he'd been prepared to skip bail to fetch them. The man who bought the boat, Gaynor Medcalfe, clearly never suspected its presence. And what if it *had* been noticed? No one could open it without the key.

Timothy Perriman picked up the silver frame. From it the photograph of a wedding couple smiled out at him, Lindon and Amy Tregarvon over thirty years ago. To one side of the main photograph was a picture of a baby; Timothy remembered that this was the little boy Neville, who had died young. To the other side was a little girl in a sailor blouse, smiling, assured even at the age of four. Erica Tregarvon, now Erica Harrowford.

He turned the triple frame over in his narrow hands. His fingers felt along the edges of the divisions, feeling for something.

'Timothy! What on earth are you doing?'

He whirled.

Erica was standing in the doorway, staring at him.

He found he couldn't say a word. He seemed powerless under her astonishment.

Amy came from the veranda. 'Darling, I thought that was you I heard. How nice! Have you finished for the night?'

'I didn't know you had company, Mother,' Erica said, her eyes still on Timothy.

'Isn't it kind? Timothy and Harold and Norman dropped in. We're in the middle of a hand of bridge.'

'Timothy didn't play, I see.'

'Darling, what's the matter? You sound a bit odd.'

'I'm all right. Go back to your bridge game.'

'Oh, Timothy, you've been looking at our family photographs! Do you remember?' She took the folding frame from his hands, opened it out to set it in its place on the mantelpiece. 'It used to stand on my husband's desk in the *Margravine*.'

'I remember, Mrs Tregarvon,' he said faintly. Stupid, stupid fool! Why was he always so overthrown when things took an unexpected turn?

'Neville was always very delicate. He'd have been almost thirty if he'd lived.' She roused herself. 'I see you got some coffee. Would you like something to eat?'

'No, in fact I think I'll get back to the hotel. I've got some phone calls to make.'

'So soon—?'

'I'm afraid I must. See you again soon, I hope.' He made a sketchy bow that included Amy and her daughter, then made his escape.

'Well,' said Amy, 'that was a rush!' She glanced about.

'What are you looking for?'

'He went out to smoke a cigar. I'm sure he didn't have time to finish it.' She failed to find it. 'Oh, well, perhaps it went out. Are you home for the night, Erica?'

'Yes, the dance is in full swing, Mr Staithe said I could go. Mother, how long had Timothy been here?'

'What? About twenty minutes, half an hour, I think. Are you coming to say hello to Norman and Harold?'

'In a minute.'

Amy nodded and went back to the game. When she'd gone Erica stood for a moment frowning, studying the dark green satin of her evening shoes. Then she nodded to herself and took the folding frame off the mantelpiece.

She sat down with it on the sofa, the skirts of her lace evening dress floating to settle about her. She turned the frame over, as she'd seen it in Timothy's hands, and felt as he had along the edges of the folds.

What? What had he been seeking? She could feel nothing. Rising, she went to a lamp, switched it on, and examined the back of the frame under its light.

The frame was of embossed silver, in a luxuriant pattern of dolphins and conch shells. The backing of each section was a rectangle of fine wood. Just like any other picture frame – wood backing, photograph in its mount, glass, and then the frame which clipped together to hold it firm. The lower edge of the central section of the frame seemed slightly more worn than the rest. She held the frame with one hand, put thumb and forefinger on the worn part, and rubbed. Nothing happened. She pressed.

The tiniest of gaps appeared between the embossed frame and the backing. It was merely an eighth of an inch. She let go the frame, the aperture closed.

She bent forward under the lamp, tilted the frame, and once more pinched the worn part. The gap showed itself again. And this time she could just glimpse something else, something that glinted a little.

She turned the frame upside down, pinched the worn part, and shook. A minute steel key fell on to the parquet floor.

Chapter Seventeen

Erica and Amy sat on the sofa in the living room. It was a little after one in the morning. The visitors had left, the servants had departed to their own quarters, Mitch had gone to bed. They were staring at the key, which lay on a low table in front of them.

'What is it *for*?' wondered Erica.

'One of the clocks?' Her mother looked vaguely round at the furniture.

'No, Amos winds up the clocks, the key to each of them is inside the clockcase.'

'An attaché case?'

'Whose?'

'Well, one of the men, Norman, Harold – perhaps it fell out of their pocket.'

'Could be, but I don't think so.'

'Why not?'

'Because I found it inside the photograph frame.'

'I beg your pardon, dear?'

'Inside the folding frame.' She nodded towards where it stood on the mantelpiece.

'Don't be silly, Erica.'

'It's true.'

'But . . . how could that be? I've never noticed it, and I've picked up that frame often enough, heaven knows.'

'It was hidden.'

'Hidden?'

'Inside the bottom part of the frame of the centre photo.'

'Erica, don't be absurd. The frame fits close against the photo.'

'Yes, but it's an embossed design – the dolphins and shells stand out.'

'Yes, but it's solid silver.'

'No it isn't. Don't forget, it's a folding frame meant for travelling. It was made to be lightweight. The silver must have been moulded somehow over a solid shape – a piece of wood, maybe with the dolphins and shells carved on it. Anyhow, there are hollows which seem to hold a little air, and when you pinch the outside edge of the frame, it gapes a little on the other edge.'

'But, good gracious, I must have "pinched" it a dozen times accidentally.'

'But you have to hold it in a good light to see the gap, Mother. And then if you turn it upside down and shake it, the key falls out.'

Amy rose, picked up the folding frame, held it under the lamp and, according to instruction, pinched the lower edge of the entire photograph.

'Oh . . . Yes . . . I see.' A little taken aback, she carefully set the frame back on the shelf. 'So you picked it up because we'd been talking about it when you came in. And happened to find the gap.'

After a moment Erica said, 'Yes.' She didn't want to

mention that she'd only examined the frame because Timothy had been doing so.

'Then . . . you think, you think that key has been there since . . . since . . .'

'Yes, that's what I think.'

Amy sank down again on the sofa as if her legs had ceased to hold her up. 'Then it isn't a key to anything here?'

'No.'

'It . . . are you saying it belonged to your father?'

'Yes.'

And then almost together they repeated, 'But what is it *for*?'

'Did you ever see him use it?' Erica asked. 'For a case, or a document box, or anything like that?'

'No.'

'Think, Mother.'

'No, I never saw it,' Amy said with a reluctant shake of the head. 'But don't forget, dearest, I wasn't in his confidence where business was concerned. If it has anything to do with business, it's quite likely I never saw him use it. I never even knew the code for the safe where he put my jewellery at night.'

It was only too true. He had once given her the combination because while he was away for a day or two she would have occasion to wear her diamonds. Amy had written the numbers on a slip of paper and tucked it in a corner of her dressing-table mirror where any would-be safecracker could see it.

'I have a feeling it has to do with business,' Erica murmured.

'But even if it does, my love, what difference does it make? Everything to do with the Tregarvon Shipping Line was taken

367

away and dealt with by the men who dealt with the bankruptcy . . .'

'The receivers.'

'Yes. And if they found a document case or a safe-box they didn't have a key to, they'd just have someone break it open. Wouldn't they?'

'I suppose so.'

Amy began to cry. 'What's the *use* of it?' she gulped, seeking about for a handkerchief. 'Why do we have to find it now? Shall we ever know if it was a key to something important?'

'Don't, Mother,' Erica said, putting an arm around her and patting her shoulder. 'It's only a key.'

'But it's hidden in a safe place. I somehow feel he meant to come back for it.'

'Now, now, don't upset yourself.'

At length Amy calmed down. Erica made hot milk drinks for both of them. They said goodnight and made for their bedrooms. Amy stopped to watch her daughter go quietly into the room next to the master bedroom.

She longed to ask, Why do you and Mitchell have separate rooms? She wanted the answer to be, Because he's ill. But she had a feeling that wasn't what she would hear. She was sure her daughter and her husband loved each other, but it wasn't the love Amy had shared with Lindon Tregarvon. Poor child, she thought. Life hasn't dealt with her kindly.

Erica didn't sleep much that night. She was thinking about the little key. But her thoughts seemed to be in a jumble.

It was not until the following month that they were put into some sort of order for her, and that was with the help of Bart Crosley. She had written to let him know that she had arrived safely in the Bahamas and that she was now married. Bart replied with congratulations and to say he would drop by to see her when he could, bringing her wedding present.

At the beginning of June he turned up, by air from Buenos Aires via Miami. He registered at the British Colonial though Erica and Amy had tried to persuade him to stay at the bungalow. Bart had his reasons. He didn't want to be under the same roof with the man who'd stolen Erica Tregarvon from him.

However, he had to accept a dinner invitation for his first evening in Nassau. He brought the wedding present with him. It was an exquisitely carved scrimshaw sailing ship. 'It's old,' he explained, 'the chap in the shop said the date's probably around eighteen hundred.'

'It's beautiful! Isn't it, Mitch?'

'Sure is.' He ran his fingers over it. 'Ivory?'

'No, the dealer said he thought it was walrus tusk.'

'Thanks a million. It deserves a place alongside the other family treasures.' Mitch placed it carefully between the photographs of the *Margravine* and the *Langrovia*.

'I know this old girl very well,' Bart said, touching the photo of the liner. 'And this is the *Margravine*, eh? A lovely boat.'

'So I hear. I never saw it,' Mitch said.

'Oh, she was a beauty! I wonder whatever happened to her?' sighed Amy.

'She was sold on to somebody who changed her name and re-registered her, I expect,' Erica said.

Neginah the cook had excelled herself in preparing a special meal. They sat now in the living room, the windows open both sides to the veranda and the sweet night air.

Bart had been interested to see at last the fellow on whom Erica had thrown herself away. He was more or less determined to dislike Mitchell Harrowford on sight. Yet strangely enough, he couldn't.

The man was so clearly ill. The pale skin, the slow movements, the occasional struggle for breath, the coughing fits that he tried to suppress . . .

And he thought the world of Erica. That was evident in his every glance at her. You couldn't really hate a man who loved Erica.

He found himself growing quite friendly with him. They would go out for a stroll together while Erica was on duty at the British Colonial, a contrasting pair, one so clearly fit and full of life, the other so thin and lacking in energy.

'What actually is wrong with Mitch?' Bart asked Erica one evening when she joined him for a moment in the hotel after dinner.

'It's his heart. It's made worse by the fact that he's got damaged lungs due to being hit when the *Portland* went down.'

'Life really changed for you when the *Portland* went down . . .'

She shrugged and half-shook her head. 'You should have seen me when I was a London debutante! Life changed for me almost as soon as I'd backed out of the Throne Room.'

'Because of that business with your father? I suppose it's something you can never forgive him for.'

She hesitated and then said, 'I've hired that investigator again.'

'What, the one in Miami?'

'Clarbrook, yes. At least, it's one of his "associates" who's on the job.'

'What brought that on? I thought you decided you couldn't waste any more money on trying to find him.'

'It was the strangest thing, Bart. I found a key.'

'A key to what?'

'That's what we don't know.' She told him the story of the tiny key in the photograph frame. 'Mother's got no idea what it's for and neither have I. But somehow, it seemed to bring him so close.' She shivered.

Bart put his hand over hers. 'It scared you?'

'Not the key itself. But the reason I found it.'

'Meaning what?'

'I walked into our living room one evening at an unexpected hour and found Timothy Perriman feeling round the edge of the photograph frame.'

'Perriman! Perriman's here?'

'Now and again. He's got business friends here. I don't quite know who, he and some of the Bay Street Boys get together in the The Club.'

'Why would Timothy Perriman be fiddling about with a photograph frame that didn't belong to him?'

'The only thing I can think of,' Erica said with a troubled frown, 'is that he knew something was hidden in it.'

At that moment Mr Staithe the manager strolled through the dining room and by a passing glance made it clear that he thought Erica should be elsewhere.

'I must go,' she said, getting up from the table. 'I've got people waiting for me in the card room.'

'I'll walk you home when you're finished,' Bart said.

'Oh, you don't need to bother—'

'No bother.'

Somewhere around midnight the bridge games broke up. Erica found Bart waiting for her in the foyer. They set off together down Bay Street with a salty breeze blowing off the sea in their faces. Erica in her high-heeled evening slippers had to take two steps to every one of Bart's.

'I've been thinking about what you said,' he began. 'About Perriman searching for something. Seems to me if he knew where it was, he might have known *what* it was. In other words, he hoped to find a key.'

'But a key to what, Bart?'

'That we don't know. But if you think about it, we can perhaps make a guess where the key belonged.'

'Belonged? I don't understand.'

'Timothy Perriman was looking for it. What have you told me about Timothy Perriman?'

She considered. 'That he was my father's personal secretary. That he helped wind up his affairs after he went away. That he . . .' She paused. She'd never told Bart about Timothy's proposal of marriage and didn't intend to. 'I don't know what else,' she ended.

'I'll tell you what else you told me. You hired Clarbrook to see if he could find a trace of your father. Clarbrook started with the idea of looking where your father seemed likely to go, which seemed to be the *Margravine* berthed here, at Nassau.'

'The *Margravine*!'

'What did Clarbrook find? Timothy Perriman had been looking for the *Margravine*.'

'Yes, he went to Long Island, to Easthampton—'

'Went sailing aboard her, though you told me he hated sailing.'

'Yes, and he talked about her almost as soon as he saw us, that first time—'

'So,' said Bart, 'don't you think it's possible – it's even likely – that the key he wanted to find fits something aboard the *Margravine*?'

'Bart!'

'It's just a thought.'

'But . . . but I'm sure you're right!' She hugged his arm. 'I think that's why Timothy proposed to me.'

'He did what?'

'Oh!' She hesitated then laughed. 'I never meant to tell anyone about that. Only my mother knows. He proposed to me and when I refused he told me I was making a big mistake because nobody else would have me.'

'Erica . . . He didn't.'

'Oh yes he did. His view was that being the daughter of Lindon Tregarvon was a terrible handicap and it would be better to become Mrs Perriman. Besides, marriage was the only way to avoid starvation since nobody was ever going to give me a job.'

'He sounds a charmer!'

'I couldn't understand why he was asking me if he thought I was such a burden. But now I begin to think . . .'

'It was because he wanted to look for the key?'

'I suppose he knew or guessed that Father's personal belongings would be sent back by the new owner. I mean, after all, who wants a folding photograph frame with pictures of somebody else's family? It was a fair guess Mr Medcalfe would send the things to my mother.'

'But he didn't get a chance to look for the key.'

'No, because of course we were living in a hotel. Our things were mostly packed up in a trunk in the basement. No chance of getting to see our belongings. If I'd accepted the offer of marriage, I suppose he'd have had a chance to look for the key because it was his idea to have Mother live with us.'

'But that didn't work.'

'No, so for some reason he went after the *Margravine* on his own. Why did he go after the *Margravine*?'

'That's a puzzle. If he knew you and your mother had the silver frame, he knew you had the key, even though you yourselves weren't aware of it. Yet he went to the *Margravine*, without the key . . .'

'I don't understand it. If the key opened a box or a case, that might have been on the boat. But Mr Medcalfe didn't send us anything like that.'

They walked on a few paces. Bart stopped almost in mid-stride.

'It's a fixture,' he said.

'Sorry?'

'A fixture. Something built-in. Good God, Erica, you know what life on shipboard is like. Anything that can be built-in is built-in. Beds fold up, bottles fit in racks. The key you found in the photograph opens something on the *Margravine* that is a fixture. I'll take a bet on it.'

'You know,' murmured Erica, 'I believe you're right. But even if it's true, we'll never know why it was so important to Timothy. Because we don't know where the *Margravine* is.'

'Where is the key?' he asked.

'The key? We put it back where we found it.'

'Do you think that was wise, Erica?' he queried, a little alarmed.

She sighed. 'Perhaps not. But Mother said . . . she felt . . . she felt that Father might come back one day to look for the key where he had hidden it. So she asked me to put it back. And I did.'

'Do you really think he'll come back for it?'

'Who knows?'

'Do you want him to?'

She hesitated then burst out in a voice thick with emotion: 'Yes, I want him to, I want him to! Mostly for Mother's sake because despite everything, she still loves him!'

'And for yourself. How do you feel about that?' Bart asked quietly.

'I'm not sure. For a long time I hated him—'

'Erica!'

'Yes, it's awful, isn't it – my own father. I hated what he did to us, leaving us in the lurch, leaving us to go under. But now, you see—' She broke off. 'I've done some silly things myself by now, Bart. I realize that we can't always be sensible and clever and in control. I can understand now that he might have been overcome by panic – felt he had to get away.'

She was thinking of her own impetuous decision to leave Marseilles, of the way she'd talked Mitch into agreeing. And of the madness of the marriage at sea. Not that she regretted it now; she felt Fate might have decreed it so that she would be there to look after Mitch. Yet she had made some wild decisions; she could understand that Lindon Tregarvon might have done the same.

'But I still think he ought to have got in touch,' she went on. 'I was sure he really loved Mother. How can he leave her still wondering what became of him?'

'Perhaps he really will come back for the key. Perhaps her instinct is right.'

'I hope so. I never thought I'd ever hear myself say so, but I hope he comes back to us.'

'So the key's in the frame again. On the mantelpiece where I saw it?'

'Yes.'

It didn't sound safe to Bart, but he didn't want to argue, nor to alarm her. Perhaps it was all a fuss over nothing. Yet it was strange that Timothy Perriman should still be looking for a key that clearly had something to do with Lindon Tregarvon, so long after Lindon Tregarvon had disappeared.

Bart delivered Erica to her door with the slightest of goodnight kisses. On the walk back to the hotel he thought about her and her mother. Each in her way was a survivor. Amy Tregarvon would survive because the charm that had won Lindon Tregarvon brought her friends who would want to help her. But Erica would fight and struggle for herself against all odds; she was her father's daughter.

The end of his vacation drew near. Bart was out for a stroll in the coolness of early morning. He was admiring the last shreds of buttercup-yellow sunrise cloud when he saw

Mitchell Harrowford coming slowly towards him along the shore.

The man walked as if he were a hundred years old, with an unacknowledged weariness. Although he was as neatly turned out as always, his clothes hung on him.

'Good morning,' Bart said with more cheerfulness than he felt. 'I didn't know you were an early riser?'

'I used not to be,' Mitch said, 'but I don't seem to sleep much these days.'

They walked a few paces together. Clearly trudging in the sand was tiring to Mitch. Bart espied an upturned fishing boat, and there they settled themselves.

'You'll be leaving soon, I gather,' mused Mitch.

'Yes, the *Carico*'s refit will be finished at the end of the week.'

'Will you head back this way again?'

Bart studied the question. Was it a simple inquiry or was Mitch asking whether he ought to think of him as a rival?

'I might,' he said in a neutral tone. 'It depends.'

'I wish you would,' said Mitch.

'What?' He couldn't keep his startlement hidden.

'Yeah, you probably think I want to see the back of you. But I don't.'

'How am I supposed to take that?'

'Look, I may be sick but I'm not stupid. I can see you love Erica and I'd wager more than ten to four that she loves you.'

'But she's devoted to you.'

'Yeah, yeah, same goes for me, I'd do anything for her. But that's not what I mean. I'm no good as a husband, you must have guessed that—'

377

'Look, it's not my business.'

'But I want it to be your business! I want you to take care of Erica.'

'Take care of her?' Bart said, totally at a loss.

'When I'm gone.'

'Gone? Where are you going?'

'To that great bridge game in the sky, my friend.'

'Oh, come on, Mitch!' Bart protested. 'That's no way to talk!'

Mitch picked at a piece of seaweed that had dried on the keel of the boat. He kept his eyes on it as he went on. 'I talk this way because I'm anxious about Erica. I want to get it straightened out before I go.'

'But there's no need—'

'Oh yes there is. I'm not long for this world, *amigo*. Every day is more of a drag to me. One morning I'm going to wake up and find myself in the obituary column.'

'Now that's absolute nonsense—'

'Not from what I gather from the doc. I don't talk about it to Erica, but let's you and me not skirt round it diplomatically, Bart. I don't think I've got another year to go, and when the time comes Erica is going to be devastated.'

'There you are, I told you she loves you.'

'I don't argue with that, but what's going to do her the most damage is the sense of guilt. She'll feel if she hadn't made me leave Marseilles I wouldn't have got this sick. But it was going to happen anyhow, she just never knew how bad I was before we made the trip. I want you to help her get over it, Bart.'

Bart was too stunned to make any response. The other

man had clearly thought a lot about what he was saying, it wasn't a spur of the moment plea but something gone over and over in his mind.

'I'm right, you're the one she'd turn to, aren't you?' Mitch insisted.

'Well . . . I don't know . . . If I were here . . .'

'Try to be here, Bart. Try to come to her when it happens.'

'Dammit, don't talk like that! You're practically talking yourself into the grave!'

Mitch smiled, his pale features creasing up in genuine amusement. 'You mean you want me to keep hanging on so that the two of you never get together? Come on, don't be silly. Erica and I should never have got married in the first place. I haven't any real right to her, but she's too decent to have an affair while I'm still around. From the way she spoke about you when you and she met up again in Marseilles, it was an easy guess something had happened in the past.'

'But that was years ago.'

'Yet here you are, all the way from BA to see her.'

'Well . . .'

'I've a feeling she really belongs with you. I just got in between you without meaning to. Don't get me wrong, I've given Erica all the affection I'm capable of, I'd do anything to make her happy. And setting things up so you'll be around when I'm gone is one of the things I feel I have to do.'

'Mitch, I don't know how to answer you,' Bart said in dismay.

'You do love her?'

'Of course.'

'Be there for her. That's all I ask.' They sat in silence. 'Is it a deal?'

'It's a deal,' Bart said. And though each of them was shaken by the conversation, they shook hands almost as if they'd concluded an everyday arrangement.

Chapter Eighteen

Mitch died at the end of August.

July and August were very hot months on New Providence Island. The hotels always closed down except for a skeleton service for the locals, because the tourists dwindled away to almost nothing. Erica's job was suspended, the Flowers for Friends shop closed down until October. By then the heat would have diminished, the humidity would be more bearable, and the hurricane season would be more or less over. Employees in these establishments had to have saved enough money to see them through until the tourists reappeared.

Amy Tregarvon had become accustomed to the weather. She'd learned the tactics of the habitués: do nothing energetic, move about as little as possible, stay in the shade if you have to move, keep up the level of fluid consumption to replace sweat, and don't get into arguments.

A routine of this kind was ideal for the playing of cards. Friends would gather in each other's homes for indolent sessions of bridge, whist or cassino.

At one of the games evenings, Mitch excused himself to go to his room.

'He all right?' asked Mr Simmons, after a sip at his iced lime juice.

'It's the heat,' Amy said.

Everyone nodded. 'The heat' was the reason for missed appointments, family rows, the poor programmes on the radio, migraines and broken fingernails.

Mitch didn't return. When the guests had gone Erica tapped on the door of Mitch's room and went in to ask if he wanted anything, a drink or something to eat.

She found him sitting in a cane armchair under the electric fan, looking haggard. 'Good heavens, what's the matter, love?' she cried, hurrying to him.

'Lord knows. I feel rotten.'

She put out her hand to touch his cheek. His skin was burning. 'You've got a temperature.'

'I sure have, and a terrible headache.'

'Like the ones you used to have?'

'No, this is an all-over headache, not just one side – but I've got pains in my back, Erica.'

She knew it must be bad because normally he never talked about himself or his pain. 'I'll call Dr Commager.'

'No, don't bother him at this time of night, it's just some bug. I'll be better in the morning.'

But though it was very late she paid no heed. She was sure something serious was wrong.

'Sand-fly fever,' Dr Commager said when he'd completed his examination. 'You've been on the beach?'

'Yes, of course, it's one of my favourite places.'

'Without putting on any protective cream.'

'Lord, doctor, a man can't go around smelling of citronella all the time.' Mitch tried to summon a smile but it was almost beyond him. His voice sounded as if it came through layers of paper.

'Bed,' said the doctor. 'Plenty of fluids, milk and soda water. I'll send you a mixture to take. Have you any phenacetin?'

'No, only aspirin,' Erica supplied.

'Have you taken any?' Commager asked Mitch.

'Yes, three, since about eleven o'clock.'

'Very well, you can have two more now and I'll send some phenacetin tablets with the mixture. Now get to bed and take it easy.'

As Erica saw him out he said, 'It looks like a bad attack. Make him rest, try to keep him cool. I'll come back in the morning.'

Amy was still up, waiting to hear the verdict. 'Sand-fly fever, that can be bad,' she said from the experience of her three years' residence. 'Sometimes it can take a fortnight to get the better of it and then people usually feel very low for a week or two.'

Erica knew something about it too because she'd seen people at the hotel laid low. The main complaint with them was that it was wrecking their holiday. But true enough, after a couple of weeks they were generally up and about again.

The duty messenger came from the doctor's house with the medicaments. Mitch took a dose of the mixture, not even protesting at its camphorish taste. Erica helped to settle him under the mosquito net, adjusted the electric fan, and sat down in a chair to read.

'Go to bed, honey,' Mitch commanded. 'You don't want to sit up all night.'

'But you might want something.'

'Go to bed! It's just a fever. All I have to do is sweat it out and there's no way you can help by sitting at the bedside.'

'But I really feel—'

'Stop fussing, Erica, you'll keep me awake sitting there watching me.'

She smiled and gave in. And for that she never forgave herself, because when she came into his room about five hours later, at eight next morning, he was gone.

'You mustn't blame yourself,' Dr Commager said when he arrived as he'd promised. 'His heart just gave out under the strain of the fever. There's nothing you could have done.'

'I could have called you—'

'I don't think you'd even have known, my dear. He went quietly in his sleep. I'm very sorry, very sorry indeed. But there was always the chance of something like this.'

Everyone was very kind. They roused themselves from the lethargy of the hot weather to send messages of condolence, to offer any help that might be needed. Poor girl, a bride of only a year, and now a widow. They turned up for the funeral although it was one of the hottest and most uncomfortable days of that weary summer.

But even though they were genuinely concerned for her, other and greater matters were calling away their attention. Three days later Britain declared war on Nazi Germany.

'What do I care!' Erica raged when she heard the news. 'Let them kill each other if they want to! My husband's already dead.'

'Erica, my darling—'

'Don't tell me I'll get over it, Mother! I don't want to hear it.'

'I know you don't, child. But you will,' Amy sighed. 'Loss

becomes bearable. I know, I've been through it.'

At the words, Erica threw herself into her mother's arms. The two women clung to each other in something like desperation. Although Amy had never imagined herself in the role of comforter and supporter, she tried now to be both for her daughter, who was usually her tower of strength.

A week or two had gone by before Erica could rouse herself to the task of clearing out Mitch's few belongings. Three or four sets of tropical whites, some shirts and shoes, most of it dating from their arrival in Nassau and nothing going back beyond the sinking of the *Portland*. So little, for a man who had travelled the world for almost a quarter of a century.

In a little box of woven palm leaves where he had kept his cuff-links and shirt studs, Erica found a folded sheet of paper. She opened it out. It was covered with Mitch's spidery writing. She sank down on the bed to read it.

Dear Erica

If you're reading this it means it's pm – post mortem. Don't cry too much over me, honey, it would be a waste of tears.

I want you to know that you made my life different from the moment you came into it. You know the saying, lucky at cards, unlucky in love – that was always how it was for me, I never seemed to be able to feel anything much for any of the women I've known. And there have been a few, who mostly gave up, baffled.

But with you it was different. I didn't have to keep my guard up with you. That's not to say I'd ever have been able to open up entirely – I was too accustomed to the shell I'd grown, I don't think I could ever have abandoned it.

But I've loved you, Erica, as far as I was ever able to love anybody. And I'm grateful for what you gave me so unstintingly, even though I felt it was wasted.

Go on with your life, be happy.

From your old partner, Mitch.

Much later Amy found her, the letter in her hand, the tears still wet on her cheeks.

Amy sat down beside her on the bed and took her hand. The sight of the tears was a relief to her. Until now Erica hadn't wept. Instead she seemed to have been protecting herself with a wall of suppressed anger and self-reproach.

Yet afterwards, when the tears had dried, the self-reproach returned. Erica couldn't forgive herself for bringing Mitch to Nassau, for being so sure she knew what was best for him. It was her fault he had been exposed to the fever that in the end exhausted his damaged heart.

Nassau began to seem like a prison to her. The heat was oppressive, the people unimportant. She longed to get away. But where could she go? Back to the life of the cruise ships? That was hardly feasible. American cruise companies were still in action yet there was a feeling that the high seas were no longer safe, even for ships acknowledged to be 'neutral'. The ships of the ocean were hunted these days by submarines. Passengers were nervous, trade even on neutral shipping declined.

Besides, she couldn't leave her mother. Amy, like herself,

was at present unemployed. She would only be back at work with Flowers for Friends when and if the tourist season revived in October. All that seemed left was the listless social life of the colony: a few pupils who wanted to improve their bridge, a small tournament run by the British Colonial Hotel for the residents of Nassau – hardly enough to keep her mind occupied.

Into this season of doldrums came Timothy Perriman. It was startling to see him on the island at such a time. He must have very good reasons for coming in the discomfort of the late summer heat.

In fact Timothy was there because of the outbreak of war. His employers had been made anxious. The Bahamas were British territory. Would there be some sudden requisitioning of foreign-owned property? Some ban on non-British investment? The Bassania brothers and their partners had made long-term plans for the Bahamas, which they didn't want to see abolished by some war-time decree. They sent him to make some discreet inquiries.

Timothy's first impression was that the white islanders were too busy being 'patriotic' to bother about who owned what. They'd formed various committees to show support for the Allied cause, they'd 'adopted' one or two warships for whose crews the ladies of Nassau were now knitting scarves and balaclavas. As to the black population, it hardly seemed to know a war had broken out anywhere.

Timothy judged it best not to intervene and remind the Bay Street Boys, the businessmen, that quite a lot of terrain, both on New Providence and Grand Bahama, was now owned by American companies. He tactfully let his business activities drop and turned instead to private matters.

He knew, because he'd made it his business to know, that Erica Harrowford was now a widow. The news had pleased him. He'd never liked Mitchell Harrowford, who had had a way of looking at him that made him feel uneasy. But more than that, Erica was now on her own again, without the protection of even an invalid husband.

Timothy understood that it was no use trying to make any kind of personal advance. But there were other ways of getting close to her.

He watched for an opportunity to chat. One evening when she was tidying up after a long bridge session in the card room of the British Colonial, he joined her. 'Things are pretty slow around here these days,' he remarked.

She'd been aware of him, hovering beyond the door of the card room while the last rubber was under way. She straightened from gathering up the cards. 'It's always quiet in the off-season,' she said.

'But is there going to be an "on-season"? Now that there's a war on?'

'Who knows?' She went back to her task. The electric fan whirred, a faint sound of music came from the ballroom where a few enthusiasts were still dancing.

'What do you think of doing now?' Timothy asked, studying her as she moved quietly around the card table.

She was still a very attractive woman – more attractive now, perhaps, than in the days when nothing had marked her young, fresh features. Now she had a rather thin face, tanned by the sun that couldn't be avoided in the Bahamas. Her eyes seemed larger, the lashes darker against the golden skin. Her chestnut hair was piled on top of her head for coolness, held in place by a pair of coconut-shell combs. The evening gown was one he'd seen her wear before – pale green silk chiffon, high-waisted and with a square neckline. Only a discerning eye would have known it was the fashion of some four years earlier.

Erica made no response to his question. She didn't see that it was any business of Timothy Perriman's what she thought of doing. In any case, she didn't know. She couldn't seem to see her way ahead any more. The decisiveness that had always been one of her characteristics seemed to have deserted her.

'You know,' Timothy went on, 'I've got friends who might very well finance you if you wanted to set up in business.'

That startled her so that she turned, the packs of cards in her hands, to look at him. 'Business? What business?'

'Well, what you're good at. The game of bridge.'

'I don't understand why anyone should want to finance—'

'Bridge is getting to be really big,' Timothy interrupted. 'Everybody in America seems to want to learn these days.'

'Oh, in America.'

'Yes, it's big business, there are bridge schools in all the cities, all the resorts. How would you like the backing to set up a school of your own, Erica?'

There wasn't a doubt that she was interested. She set down the packs of cards. 'Bridge isn't ever going to rouse the same amount of support as horse-racing or the numbers game, Timothy. Why should your friends take an interest in it?'

She saw his narrow face flush at the words. The light grey eyes flashed for a moment with something that might have been resentment. 'My friends are interested in making money,' he said in a level tone. 'People with money are interested in bridge. It's as simple as that.'

'I saw your friends at that New York restaurant, remember?' She gave a little shrug. 'Still the same, are they?'

'They've got funds to invest, Erica. Banks and finance corporations are eager to do business with them. Money's money, whoever owns it.'

Once he'd said it he realized it was a tacit admission that his friends weren't respectable. He was annoyed. Why was it that in trying to deal with Erica Tregarvon he kept on making clumsy mistakes? Was it because memories of the past unnerved him?

He went on. 'You could move out of Nassau, if you wanted to. I imagine you only stay on here because you and your mother feel indebted to Lady Oakes. Well, you could make a fresh start with money from an independent source. You could go to Miami, or Palm Beach, or any mainland city you choose.'

'The mainland?'

'Why not? You don't want to hang around in the Bahamas for ever, do you?' Yes, get her away from the Bahamas, from Nassau, from any chance of ever picking up the trail of the *Margravine*.

It fitted in so well with her mood, with her longing to escape the claustrophobic atmosphere of the little town, that she was tempted.

'What do you say?' he urged.

'I don't know if I'd want to start with money from the friends I saw in New York, Timothy.'

'All right, let's say I advance you the money myself.'

'Oh no.'

'A loan, a personal loan. You could pay me back at an agreed interest. Strictly a business loan.'

'But it might be quite a lot. The lease of a suitable place, alterations perhaps, decoration, advertising . . .'

'Naturally. I wouldn't want you to have anything second-rate. You could fly to Florida, pick out a likely base and talk to the real estate men.'

'There's a restriction on air travel now that we're at war.'

'Oh that . . . I'll get permission for you, don't worry about that.'

Although he didn't know it, he'd made her wary again. He could get permission for her to fly out of Oakes Field, without any problem, it seemed. This on an island where petrol and air fuel had to be imported and were now about to be strictly rationed. Would he get her travel permission through these dubious friends of his? Would she be somehow indebted to them? The thought alarmed her.

'Think it over,' he said, feeling that to be too eager would only put her off. 'I shan't be leaving until the day after tomorrow. Come back to me with your ideas and we'll talk them through, get some idea of costs.'

'I don't know, Timothy. I've never been in debt to anybody before—'

'Don't think of it as a debt, think of it as a joint investment. You invest your experience, I invest my money. That's fair, isn't it?'

'I suppose so.'

He left it at that. His business instinct told him now was

the time to break off. He had sensed that she longed for change, for a new start.

But business negotiations are generally about money. For Erica, money, though important, wasn't the first consideration. There were other factors.

First was the feeling of mistrust that always arose when she dealt with Timothy Perriman. It seemed to her that he was always trying to manoeuvre her in some way. Right back to that first embarrassing, awful event, the proposal of marriage. Timothy hadn't really wanted to be married to her, he'd wanted to . . . what? To be in control of her, perhaps.

After that he'd kept reappearing in her life. She didn't believe for a moment it came from any feeling of affection. For some reason he wanted to maintain contact.

Now he was offering favourable terms so that she could start her own business. And it was true, she would be glad to go somewhere and start afresh.

But did she want the help of Timothy Perriman?

She longed for someone with whom to discuss it. But she couldn't talk about it to her mother. She had a feeling Amy Tregarvon quite regretted the fact that she'd refused Timothy years ago. But then Amy didn't really know Timothy – to her he was still the young man her husband had trusted, now so successful, so highly regarded.

Late that night, home from the hotel, Erica sat down and wrote to Hobart Crosley.

She poured out all her feelings, her anxieties and uncertainties, her longings and regrets. Her grief over Mitch, her sense of loss, her uncertainty about the future, her doubts about Timothy Perriman, the ache of loneliness that never seemed to go away. 'Where are you?' she wrote. 'Are you far away? I need you, Bart. Where are you?'

About three in the morning, exhausted, she went to bed.

Next day she reread the letter. It made her ashamed. One long whine about herself and her problems. She tore it up and threw it in the wastepaper basket.

All the same, she'd never written to Bart to tell him of Mitch's death. She sat down again at the bureau and this time wrote a sensible, brief letter. She ended it with the words, 'Mitch spoke about you quite often after your visit. I want to thank you for spending time with him while you were here. Perhaps one day you'll be back. It would be nice to see you, Bart.'

This letter she posted. When it would reach Bart she'd no idea. He and the *Carico* might be the other side of the world for all she knew.

But writing to him had cleared her mind. She knew beyond a doubt that she couldn't accept any help from Timothy Perriman. His offer seemed generous, perhaps too much so. It was somehow suspect.

She sent a note to him at the hotel to say that she'd decided against accepting. She avoided the hotel until she heard that he'd left for Miami. She never mentioned the matter to her mother.

All the same, the idea of setting up a school was a good one. With the advent of the cooler weather she set about it in a small way. She made an agreement with the hotel for the hire of a room, advertised in the *Tribune* and the *Guardian*, and found to her delight that the bored inhabitants of New Providence were quite pleased to have something new to do.

There were, moreover, a few servicemen posted to the islands in 1940. In Europe there had been what the newspapers dubbed 'the phoney war': nothing was happening between the Allies and the German forces. Then in late spring the Nazis began a drive which took them straight through into northern France, conquering Holland and Belgium en route.

The British forces fought a rear-guard action until they reached Dunkirk. Ships of all kinds plied to and fro across the Channel ferrying them to the comparative safety of the South of England. Thereafter the War Cabinet had to reorganize. And so, men were sent abroad to train or to guard vulnerable terrain. A few of them came to the Bahamas, where their coming generated trade, entertainment, activity of all kinds.

From this Erica and Amy benefited. With more money around, people felt inclined to spend. Life became a little easier from the financial point of view. And even when the hot weather began to return in July, the British servicemen refused to be daunted. They moved about the colony, playing scratch golf, attending the races at Hobby Horse Hill, sailing their hired boats among the Out Islands.

A letter came from Bart at last. Its envelope bore the marks of much travel through sorting offices and mail checks.

Dear Erica

After being delayed a long time at the shipping office in Buenos Aires your letter reached me here. Your news came as no great shock to me. Mitch had told me he didn't think he'd last long. I'm very sorry he's gone, he was a good man in his own detached way.

I'd come to see you like a shot, but as soon as war broke out I volunteered for the Navy. My address is now 'somewhere in England', a naval training camp. When I've finished the course I hope to muster as a lieutenant and see something of the war at sea, but it's in the lap of the gods, or the Admiralty, which is the same thing.

(Here a government censor had blacked out several lines on grounds of national security.) . . . So you see I can't say for sure where I'll be posted. I'll only say that I hope very much the powers-that-be may send me in your direction. Write to me through the Forces Post Office using the above address, though in the nature of things I may have moved on by the time you get this.

Erica's mother could see at once that something wonderful had happened. Her daughter was almost incandescent with happiness. 'A letter from Bart!' she cried, flourishing it. 'Oh, Mother, at last – news of Bart!'

'That's lovely, dear,' Amy agreed. 'How is he?'

'Well, he doesn't actually say! But he's joined up, he's in the Navy. Here, read it. Oh, it's so great to be in touch with him again.'

'Yes, dear, I see it is,' Amy said with amusement.

Of course it was necessary to reply to the letter at once. It had taken months to reach her. What must he think of her for not responding? She wrote almost joyously, telling him what she was doing, what life was like in Nassau these days, laughing over the idea that now she would have someone to knit for. 'I've never learned to knit, isn't it awful how my education was neglected?' She and her mother put together a parcel of the good things still easily obtainable in Nassau, like candied fruit, American candy bars, cigarettes. For the first time they felt they belonged to the earnest committee of ladies who collected 'comforts for the troops'.

Towards the end of July the ladies of Nassau had others things to think about. There was something in the air. Everybody could sense it. A few of the menfolk – members of the Executive Council – seemed to know what was happening, but they wouldn't tell. Then the Governor of the Bahamas, Sir Charles Dundas, was transferred to Uganda, before his term of office had expired. What did it mean? Was he in disgrace? Had there been a scandal?

About the middle of August, when the heat was at its most intense and normally the Bahamians would have been taking it easy, little groups could be seen talking earnestly with their heads together. Then the news leaked out. Strange news, incredible news.

The Duke of Windsor had been appointed the new Governor of the Bahamas.

At first no one believed it. Nazi propaganda, silly American inventions.

But no, it was true. Bunting began to go up in Bay Street, flags were brought out and run up on flagstaffs, garlands were made to drape shop windows. The Duke was coming, and with him, perhaps more important to the American journalists who descended on Nassau, the Duchess!

It was impossible not to be involved in the event. The whole of Nassau went into a fever. Erica and her mother turned out on the appointed day, into the stifling heat of the waterfront, among the purple bunting and palmetto wreaths. Like everyone else, they had put on their best clothes. Absurd, to stand in a crowd under the blazing sun, in silk dresses and big hats and high-heeled shoes. And for what? To welcome a man who was being sent to the place where he could do the least damage, it seemed.

The gossip went that the Windsors had been saying tactless things about a negotiated peace with the Nazis. They had been in neutral Portugal, they had been at parties enjoying themselves with Nazi diplomats while France fell and British forces barely escaped across the Channel. The War Cabinet in London had decided to put them out of circulation, in a safe place. So they had been sent to the Bahamas.

The destroyer HMS *Excalibur* nosed into the bay. From it the new Governor and his wife, escorted by a small group of naval personnel, transferred to the *Lady Somers*. As the ship approached the home slip, the distinguished passengers could be seen on the bridge picking out the landmarks of New Providence: the pinkwashed Governor's mansion, Fort Montagu, the Courthouse.

The crowd moved nervously. Important people began to arrive: Sir Harry Oakes, chief benefactor of the islands; Harold Christie, the biggest of the property dealers; others of the Bay Street Boys and their families, eager to shake the hand of the former Prince of Wales.

The *Lady Somers* inched up to the jetty. The gangplank

was put in place. The new Governor appeared on deck, his wife at his elbow. He took his first step on to the gangplank. The crowd raised a ragged cheer.

In a few moments he set foot on his new kingdom: a vast expanse of ocean scattered with lovely islands, the chief of them New Providence, which was to be his home now, totally unimportant to the world at large. A strange ending for the man who had once been, briefly, King of the United Kingdom, Emperor of India, ruler of Canada and Australia and a thousand colonies spread over the globe.

Members of the Executive Council approached to shake hands and offer loyal greetings. The Windsors advanced into the shade of a canopy to have introductions made to other members of the community. Some paces after them came members of the escort carrying portfolios and personal luggage for the Duchess. Behind them again came a small group of naval officers.

Because in the shade of the canopy the Duke and Duchess were no longer visible to her, Erica turned her glance on the uniformed men descending the gangplank.

And her heart nearly stopped.

Third in the procession was Hobart Crosley.

Chapter Nineteen

Erica clutched her mother's arm. 'Mother!'

'What?'

'Mother, there's—'

But the officer had moved with the others to form a group further along the quay. His face was hidden now.

Illusion. Because she'd wanted to see him, she'd conjured him up.

'What, dear? What is it?'

'Nothing. I thought I saw someone I knew.'

Amy glanced about. 'Well, of course, Erica.'

The ceremony of swearing in the new Governor took place. The Duke and Duchess were driven to Government House, which, according to later rumour, they instantly rejected as a dwelling-place. Too dingy, too comfortless. Rumour said the Duchess had asked if they could transfer to the Duke's ranch in Canada until redecorations were carried out. Rumour said they were refused. So for their early months in Nassau the Windsors were destined to stay in houses lent by the Bay Street Boys.

But for that first day a patriotic enthusiasm prevailed. Parties were being held to celebrate the arrival of a prince of the blood. Erica and Amy had invitations to several. They had tea with the Eaglestons and cocktails with the Marshes.

Then for the evening they went to the British Colonial, where the manager expected Erica on duty as hostess. There was to be a special Welcome Our Governor dinner with toasts, a dance afterwards, a cabaret, streamers, balloons, and a late-night champagne buffet for those prepared to stay the course.

As Erica and her mother came out of the cloakroom after leaving their wraps, the reception clerk beckoned. 'Mrs Harrowford, I have a note for you,' she said.

'Really? Someone asking for a table to be set up—'

'No, no, a black boy brought it. I think it's from the boat.'

'What boat?'

'The *Lady Somers*.'

Erica frowned in perplexity, then a glorious premonition swept through her. She seized the envelope from Alice's hand. One glance told her she was looking at Bart's writing.

'I did see him!' she breathed.

'Who, my love?' her mother asked.

'Bart! It's from Bart!' She tore open the envelope.

'Dear Erica,' she read, 'I hope this doesn't give you a fright. I'm here in the Bahamas. On duty for the next few days but as soon as I can I'll come to see you. Love Bart.'

'I did see him! It really was Bart!'

'Darling, you're not making sense—'

'Read it, read it! He's here in Nassau.'

Well, no, he wasn't in Nassau. When on the following Thursday he arrived at the house in East Bay Street, it was with a guarded explanation of his presence. 'Oh, I'm just tagging along after the Duke,' he told them as they hugged him and fussed over him.

Later, when he and Erica were out for a walk under the

shade of the trees around Fort Montagu, he explained a little more. 'I couldn't say anything in front of your mother,' he began. 'Nor can I say too much to you either, darling. The long and short of it is, Mr Churchill thinks he's been a little too clever in getting rid of the Duke.'

'What does that mean, getting rid of him?' she asked in astonishment.

'Well, he was an embarrassment. And it seems he had some strange friends in Lisbon. So Winston's sent him to the Bahamas where he'll meet only stuffy British colonials. That was the theory.'

'Mmm . . .' said Erica. 'There are some strange men among the stuffy old colonials, I can tell you! And there are also some friends of American gangsters.'

'It's not American gangsters the Foreign Office is worried about, it's the danger of a Nazi raid.'

'Here?'

'Why not here? There aren't any defences, now are there? All the German Navy has to do is send a U-boat and land a party of determined commandos. How would it look if the Duke of Windsor got kidnapped?'

Erica stared but somehow couldn't take it seriously. Bart, seeing her expression, grinned. 'Well, yes,' he agreed to an unspoken comment, 'it *is* a bit absurd. But the Admiralty felt it had to take some precaution so they sent a bunch of us to patrol the waters around New Providence.'

'Good Lord! You're not expecting to have to deal with a U-boat?'

'God forbid,' Bart said. 'No, you can tell it's not taken too seriously or they wouldn't have sent a bunch of new boys like us. We're going to patrol in an MTB.'

'What on earth's that?'

'A motor torpedo boat. The only one with any experience of the craft is the commander. I'm here because I know the waters from previously having been on the big liners, as if navigating a liner was anything like dashing about in an MTB. But there you are, that's the Admiralty for you.'

'I don't care how foolish it may be,' Erica declared. 'I'm just glad you're here.'

'I'm not exactly "here",' he said. 'We're based on one of the small islands. I'm not allowed to say which one, so don't ask.'

Erica laughed. 'If it's a secret, it's probably known all through Grants Town and in every fishing village in the islands,' she told him. 'The Bahamian fishermen know almost everything that's going on out there.'

'Really?'

Her words clearly made him thoughtful. In the succeeding weeks she realized that he was taking pains to become friendly with some of the black islanders.

Bart found this difficult. The black Bahamians were good-natured and easy-going towards him, but they weren't accustomed to being treated as equals. The relationship between black and white had always been that of servant and master. The Bahamians seemed not to hold this much against the British colonists, yet they would seldom be totally open and honest with them. And who, thought Bart, could blame them?

However, if an officer from a little naval post on one of the uncomfortable Out Islands wanted to drop into their villages during Junkanoo and join in the festivities, that was all right. Particularly if he bought drinks and liked to chat.

They told him such things as were common knowledge among the black population. For instance, the big rich Scandinavian who owned Hog Island had built some very strange radio equipment into his house. For instance, though several of the islands between Grand Bahama and New Providence had been sold by the Bay Street Boys of Nassau to seemingly respectable clients, the real owners were former gangsters; the islanders knew they were gangsters, because they had worked for them during Prohibition. For instance, cargoes still came in by night to unfrequented spots and were ferried on. To whom? Well, it wasn't healthy to inquire too closely into that.

The report that Bart sent to the Admiralty by the middle of 1941 was greeted with some alarm. It was quite clear that security in the Bahamas leaked like a sieve. Nor could it be improved without sending many patrol ships. And was it worth it? If drugs were being smuggled into Miami now instead of liquor, should the Admiralty care? If dirty money from Cosa Nostra bosses was being laundered by the banks in Nassau into clean British sterling, did it matter to the British government?

And did any of it endanger the Duke of Windsor?

They instructed their special intelligence officer aboard the MTB *Striga* to continue with his news-gathering as and when his patrol duties allowed. 'Thank you very much,' muttered Bart to himself on receiving this order on a hot and sticky day in July. There was nothing he wanted less than to visit yet another mosquito-infested island on the outer rim of the Bahamas. Gathering information had to be done in his spare time. It meant he very seldom got to Nassau to attend to his own affairs.

The difficulty was that he couldn't explain his long absences to Erica. Other members of the crew of the *Striga* were able to drop in at the hotels for relaxation and entertainment. Erica must wonder why he had less leisure time than the rest. But his role as intelligence officer was known only to his commander and the Admiralty.

He saw Erica when he could. He wanted very much to spend time with her, to try to restore the relationship between them to what it once had been. After those few magic days in Curaçao, now so long ago and far away, no other woman had ever been able to take hold of his heart.

Yet Erica was different now, and so was he. Erica had been through tragedy, had married and lost a husband, who clearly had meant much to her. She wasn't the eager, ardent girl he had initiated into the mysteries of physical love. Nor was he the ambitious young ship's officer of his twenties, with no one but himself to consider.

The time might come, the chance might present itself, to rebuild the bridge that they had allowed to disintegrate. In the meantime Erica seemed to be glad to see him when he called, and that was enough for now.

He came to her one day with surprising news. 'I don't know whether you'll want to hear this or not, Erica,' he said with some hesitation.

It was late September of 1941. The temperature stood at eighty-eight degrees. A storm during the night had brought winds of almost hurricane force but now the wind had dropped and for a short time a pleasing freshness breathed through Nassau. Erica, in a cotton dress and sandals, was sitting on the veranda of the British Colonial, planning a beginners' tournament to entertain her bridge students.

'Sit down, have a drink,' she countered, smiling up at him from under the fronds of the meloncillo vine. 'You look all hot and bothered in that starchy uniform.'

He sank down in the adjoining lounger, tossing off his uniform cap. Erica beckoned a waiter. When Bart had ordered she said, 'Now, unbutton that ferocious collar and relax. What's this I may not want to hear?'

'I think I've found the *Margravine*.'

'What?' She sat up straight. The tray on which her plans and lists had been laid out slipped from her lap. She stared at Bart.

She had gone pale. He said gently, calmly, 'Take it easy. I knew it would be a shock to you.'

'The *Margravine*?'

He nodded.

'But Bart, how can you be sure? You've never seen her.'

'I've seen that photograph on your drawing room mantelpiece.'

'But you've never really *looked* at it.'

'Oh yes I have. Besides, how many looks does it take for a seaman to know the outline of a ship or a yacht? Her silhouette is unmistakable: a two-masted brigantine with a two-spar mainmast that looks like steel and with a yard for a topgallant.'

'Yes,' she said in a faint voice.

'I've only sighted her. I haven't been up close but I asked

around.' He paused. 'Do you want to hear this?'

'Yes,' she said again.

'As far as I can gather the man who first bought her sold her to buy something faster.'

'Yes, I knew that much.'

The waiter arrived with his drink. He took a moment to sip and rearrange his thoughts. 'Well, she was sold to a white skipper trading perishables between Eleuthera and out as far as Inagua. I'm told he used to take butter and cream in the refrigerator to rich yachtsmen who could afford such luxuries.'

'Oh yes,' Erica said with the shadow of a smile, 'we always had good things in the refrigerator.'

'Then I gather she went for a short time to a Cuban businessman who used her for entertaining but he damaged her somehow and got rid of her. She seems to have been patched up and sold on several times. In the end she was bought by a black Bahamian on Stocking Island to rent out for fishing trips.'

'And where is she now?' she whispered.

'She's pretty derelict, Erica. Her name's been changed to *Perlina*.'

'Is there anyone aboard her?'

'Oh no.' He leaned forward to take her hand. 'She's lying in six feet of mud snarled up among mangroves, as far as I could see. No duckboards laid down to get to her from shore, and to reach her from sea you'd need to pick your way along tricky channels. It's a creek on the north side of an islet about sixty miles out that doesn't even seem to have a name; the nearest inhabited island is Panago and that's not very big. The people call the islet Diggo.'

'You mean she's just lying there?'

'It seems so. From what I can gather, some bunch of rollicking tourists hired her out for fishing a couple of years ago and ran her aground in bad weather. They got off in the dinghy after some problems. They compensated the owner so it wasn't worth anyone's trouble to pull her off and refloat her even if they could. From what I could see she's stuck fast. Since then I gather anything worth taking off has gone: furniture, the fridge, the auxiliary engine.'

For a moment she said nothing. Then she murmured, 'Poor thing. What an end for her.'

A great sadness had filled her as she listened to Bart. She'd always somehow felt that if she could find the *Margravine* it would lead her to her father. Every hint she'd ever had of his intentions when he left the house on that fateful evening seemed to imply he was heading for the *Margravine*.

It was a revelation to her to realize she'd always been hoping that somehow, somewhere, she would get news of him. All these years, even when she'd been telling herself she blamed him, hated him, she'd still wanted to see him again. She saw him now in her mind's eye: handsome in his business suit, his skin glowing with health, his eyes alight with interest, a smile on his lips, that aura surrounding him of success and assurance. Oh, where was he now? Where, in all this wide world, had he gone?

Bart was speaking to her again. 'What did you say?' she faltered.

'I asked if you'd like to go and see her?'

'Oh no! Not in that state!'

'All right.' He pressed her hand.

She got to her feet. 'I'm sorry, Bart, I've got to go.'

'I shouldn't have told you—'

'No, no, it's nothing like that. I've just remembered I have some phone calls to make from my office.' She hurried away, leaving her tray of papers scattered on the veranda.

Once in the little room she called her office, she locked the door, sat down at her desk, laid her head on her arms and burst into tears.

Poor *Margravine*. Poor beautiful, graceful creature. Broken and despoiled, she lay somewhere out there in the turquoise blue of the Caribbean like a crushed dragonfly on a robe of satin. That one last memory, that one last hope, was gone.

When she thought it over later she decided not to tell her mother. If it affected Erica so much – she who kept telling herself she was strong, sensible, capable – how much worse it would be for Amy. No, better not, it could do no good, and might actually do harm. She would banish the whole thing from her mind.

Easier said than done. From then on not an hour of her waking life passed but some wayward memory of life aboard the *Margravine* would flash into her mind. At night her dreams were haunted by visions of the graceful prow plunging in among the sharp coral rocks, breaking and shattering, boards floating away, the spars tumbling into the angry waves, the sails drowning and being dragged down among the sticky mangrove roots.

When Bart had a day's leave about a week later, he dropped in at the house in East Bay Street. It was the lunch hour. Amy was home from her flower shop, Erica had returned to the house to change for a social afternoon at the hotel. He stayed to share a meal with them and afterwards walked with Erica to the British Colonial.

'You know what you told me last week?' she began.

'I was a fool to tell you. It bowled you over.'

She summoned a smile. 'I admit it hit me harder than I expected,' she said. 'I think I made a bit of a fool of myself, running off like that.'

'Don't be silly. You had every reason to be upset.'

She stopped to turn and look up at him. 'It's nice of you to understand.'

'Of course I understand. If I heard a boat of mine was in a mess, I'd cry my eyes out.'

'No you wouldn't,' she said, but she laughed.

After a moment they strolled on. 'What I was thinking,' she resumed, 'was that I . . . I . . .'

'What?'

'You asked me if I'd like to see her.'

'Yes?'

'Well, I would, Bart. I know I'm never going to rest until I see her.'

He nodded. 'I'd feel the same myself.'

'Is she . . . very awful?'

'Well, she's no oil painting, I'm afraid. And if you're thinking about salvaging her, don't bother. It would cost the earth and wouldn't be worth it.'

'No, I wasn't thinking of putting her back in order. I just feel . . .'

'What, Erica?'

'I need to say goodbye to her.'

'All right, I'll take you. But it can't be until the good weather comes back. It's a good four hours out to the islet and four back so I don't fancy getting caught in a mini-hurricane.'

'No, of course not.'

'I have a three-day pass due to me. Let's say I apply for it for the end of October. How about that?'

'All right, that gives me plenty of time to make arrangements at the hotel.'

At this time Nassau was buzzing with activity. The War Cabinet had decided to send RAF recruits to the Bahamas for training. Airstrips, barracks and offices were about to be built. The Bay Street cabal was delighted; money would flow into New Providence again after the awful tourist slump that had come with the outbreak of war. The Royal Victoria Hotel, which had closed because of the lack of customers, was about to be reopened.

Cynics said that there was always talk of 'rejuvenation' when the cool season began at the end of October. It would be the same now – a lot of talk but with no real action. In this they were proved wrong. Before the end of October construction machinery imported from the United States was being unloaded at the docks.

At a jetty some way along from the port, Erica embarked on her trip to Diggo Islet. Bart had hired a motorboat with the requisite amount of fuel; some slight black-market dealing had been involved.

The day was fine, the sea was calm. They headed out towards Sail Rock and the Exumas. Erica knew the waters from having in the past been on boating parties during the

Out Islands Regatta. This trip was totally different. She was filled with a wrenching muddle of emotions: longing to see the yacht on which she'd spent so many happy days, curiosity as to how it came to be there, dread of the memories it would evoke.

Bart respected her mood. With scant conversation they forged across the shimmering water. They stopped in the lee of Highborne Cay for lunch, which Amy had lovingly packed for them in a wicker basket lined with palm leaves: cold chicken, salad, fresh fruit and cheese, white wine which they cooled by hanging the bottle over the side in the sea.

Bart eyed Erica. She was very pale under the light tan. 'Would you rather we just head back?' he asked.

She shook her head.

'She's just a hulk now, you know. Do you really want to see her?'

She couldn't explain to him the urgent need to see the boat. She gave a shrug that would have seemed almost ill-natured, except that he understood her unhappiness.

They headed off between the cays. 'There,' Bart said at about two in the afternoon.

The glitter on the water was intense. Even under the striped canopy of the motorboat she had to shade her eyes to see the land rising to greet them.

'Panago,' he said. 'Diggo is to the east, about a mile.'

The heat shimmer made it impossible to see the islet. She knelt on the leather seat, straining to glimpse it. The channel lay quite close in to Panago. Some of the island's inhabitants came down to the beach to watch, thinking the motorboat was about to put in. Bart waved a greeting, pointed to the right, and waved goodbye as they left the landing stages behind them.

In a short time Diggo became plain, a lumpy rock with a green tuft of trees, like a stumpy shaving brush whose bristles had gone mouldy. Shards of sharp stone rose up to greet them as they approached. Bart cut the engine down to a murmur, just enough to give him seaway. He let the current drift them along the edge of the rim of coral rock until they were on the northern side. Here narrow creeks ran into the land. The shift and eddy of the water gave them away, but they were masked by the overgrowth of mangrove.

'There,' Bart said again, pointing.

Following his hand, she saw them – the masts of the *Margravine*, standing up like pencils from among the greenery. Under the strong afternoon sun there was a faint glint on them although seabirds had fouled the once-cared-for metal. The *Margravine* had had masts of a special alloy, a new idea to help give her the advantage of bearing canvas under poor conditions, to put her ahead in a race. Erica gazed at the masts. After a moment she heard Bart speak in a voice that meant he was repeating a question.

'What? Oh, yes, unmistakable. I gather quite a lot of yachts have metal masts now but when the *Margravine* got hers it was an innovation.'

They idled on the water. 'Did you get closer before?'

'A little. Do you want to go in?'

She nodded, unspeaking. He increased engine power a little but was very cautious as they edged into the little curve. 'Don't want the bottom ripped out,' he murmured, 'especially since this isn't my boat.'

To reach the entrance to the creek needed careful manoeuvring. At length, after more than a quarter of an hour, they were alongside a barrier of mangrove roots that ran across its mouth. Beyond, it was possible to make out the shape of the former brigantine, run up into the harsh rocks of the islet and with a hole in her prow through which murky water lapped.

Erica stood up in the motorboat, steadying herself by grasping a branch of mangrove tree. '*Perlina*', she read from the ill-painted nameboard.

Perlina, a stranger. Dressed up in thick green paint, her metalwork wrenched off to make a handrail on some island jetty, planks from the cabin roof gone to make an island chicken coop.

'Can we get aboard?'

Bart shook his head. 'I don't know how. We certainly can't get up to her in this boat, the mangrove won't let us through. There used to be some way of boarding her because so much has been taken off her, but I don't know if it can still be done, and if it can I don't know where to land without being stove in.'

'I see.'

'We could go and ask on Panago.'

A pause. 'Yes, let's do that,' she said.

Bart reversed the motorboat and with infinite care edged them out of the creek-mouth. When he had leeway he turned, then headed gently off. As they approached Panago the same little crowd gathered to wave their passing, but cheered with delight as instead they headed in to the beach.

'Man, we thought you made an out when you pass by first

time,' remarked a helper as they landed. 'Why for goodness was you sailin' off to Diggo? Far better to pass at Panago.'

Everyone gathered round to shake hands. Bart singled out an elderly stout man with whom he'd talked on his previous visit. 'We went to look at the *Perlina*,' he explained.

'Nuthin' there now.'

'Erica, this is Hosiah Gorley. Hosiah, Mrs Harrowford used to sail in the *Perlina* in days gone by.'

'Oh me Gard!' exclaimed Hosiah in surprise. He gave a wry smile. 'She come down in the world since then, for sure. You care for to come along and have some refreshmen'? Thirsty work, sailin' this weather.'

He led them without more ado to his house, where his wife had run ahead to prepare for the visitors. She had shooed a little mob of children out of the way to clear their path. As they were shown into the cool of the cabin she was already laying a white cloth on top of a crate to act as table. A little girl fetched cups from a hanging cupboard, her eyes all the while on the two white people. Something to boast about to her friends; the two strangers had come into *her* house for drinks.

A concoction of rum and fruit juice was offered. Erica accepted it with thanks, because to refuse would have been bad manners, but took only a sip. She waited while Bart went through all the preliminary chat about the weather, sea conditions, the morning's catch of fish, and what the 'royal man' was doing these days.

At length it was possible to come back to the *Perlina*. 'We were close enough to read her name,' said Erica. 'Is there any way of getting aboard?'

Hosiah exchanged a glance with his wife. 'Lila don't like me to go there,' he said. 'Some good crayfish around there but it's a bitch place to take a boat.'

'If'n he go there, I feel for sure he get a cut. I don' go there but I hear the rocks is cruel,' Lila put in.

'For true,' Hosiah agreed. 'Sharp as swords.'

'But people have been aboard her, salvaging.'

'Not soon time,' Lila said, shaking her head. 'Mangrove grows, channels close up.'

'Uncle Porter was on the deck before storm-time,' piped up the little girl.

'Hush you, now, Mimmy, Uncle Porter never been on.'

'For true he been on. Afore storm-time.'

Storm-time was the hurricane season. It meant Uncle Porter might have been on the *Perlina* in June or thereabouts.

'How did he get aboard, Mimmy – do you know?'

Dumbstruck at being directly addressed by the white lady, Mimmy shook her head and looked at her toes.

'Could we speak to Uncle Porter?' asked Erica.

'Porter's off on the far side presently,' said Hosiah. 'Sparkin'.' He smiled. Erica guessed he meant Porter was with his girlfriend.

'Does he live here? Will he be back?'

'For sure, but who know when?' Lila said with a little toss of her head. 'Own brother to me but I never know where he is or what he's do. He come and go. But if'n you care to stay, he be back some time this afternoon I 'spect, he plan some night-fish with the pitch-oil lamps.'

On the islands 'this afternoon' meant evening, some time after about five. Bart looked at Erica. It was her decision. If

415

they wanted to get back to Nassau today they ought to set out soon, but if they waited for Porter it meant they couldn't return until next day, unless they cared to navigate by night in these chancy waters.

'Could we wait, Bart?'

'If you want to.'

'Well, man, that's great, you can talk us about the royal man and he wife. It true she got a di'mond crown?' asked Lila.

Erica laughed. 'Not that I've ever seen. But then I don't go to events at Government House, Lila.'

Lila began to question her about the 'grand life' in Nassau. Erica answered to the best of her ability. The children peeked in at the door and the windows to see the visitor's dress and hear her strange accent. Meanwhile Bart was dealing with the more mundane matter of overnight accommodation.

They could sleep aboard the motorboat. The leather-cushioned seat would make a passable bed, but only for one. Bart would have to sleep in the well of the boat on the planks. Moreover, to avoid the sand-flies, they would have to motor out into the bay. When Hosiah heard this he absolutely refused to countenance it.

'Man, you can sleep in Porter's place. He house is empty—'

'But he'll want it for himself.'

Hosiah winked. 'Porter he won't be back till dawn,' he said. 'You think night-fish with oil lamps is goin' to fetch him away from that sugar-sweet girl? Naw, he'll come astrollin' back when she send him, and I 'spect she won't part with him come-along dawn.'

Thus it was that after a long and noisy meal at the home of Hosiah and Lila, in which most of the village took part, they were shown to the house of Porter McCabe. It proved to be a cabin of coral rock and palm leaves, open on one side to the sea, covered only by a rattan blind. The main room was surprisingly neat, with belongings stored in hanging nets and a big gourd of fresh water on the veranda. Behind it was a smaller, narrow room with a table where Porter kept a few cups and saucers and a saucepan.

'But doan you bother to cook breakfast, man, plenty at our place if'n you just stroll along when you wake,' urged Hosiah. He was anxious not to lose any opportunity for talk with the visitors.

When their hosts had reluctantly left them, Bart eyed Erica anxiously. She looked wan and tired. She had taken part in very little of the conversation except when cross-questioned by Lila.

'How's it going?' he asked.

'Oh, Bart!' She threw out a hand blindly.

He took it and drew her to him. 'We shouldn't have come,' he murmured. 'I was a fool to bring you.'

'No, no, I wanted to see her too. And yet . . .'

And yet it had been piercing to see the beautiful yacht brought so low. Gone was all her grace and splendour. And gone with them, finally, was hope.

Despite everything she'd felt there might be some hint, some aura from the past, that would help her to find her father. Now she knew she must give up that hope for ever. If her father had ever reached the *Margravine* he would never have let her come to this pass. She knew now, although how she couldn't explain, that Lindon Tregarvon had never been on board the yacht since the scandal broke in London.

Father would have saved her somehow. She heard herself say the words inside her head and realized that for the first time in years she had thought of him as Father. Ever since he had run away she had tried to distance herself from him, tried not to think of herself as the daughter of this thief, this fraudster.

But now some barrier had broken. She felt close to him again, her father's child, bound to him by a love that had made her childhood warm and safe. Where was he, what had become of him, the man who had given her years of magic? Tears were running down her cheeks. She felt Bart's arms go about her. 'Don't,' he was murmuring, 'don't cry, my poor love.'

Like an incoming tide, need flooded through her. It had been so long, so long, since a man had held her in his arms. She pressed herself against Bart's strong body, trying to draw from him the comfort of belonging. She could hear the throb of his heart, gaining speed, and knew it matched the tempo of her own. When his hand slipped aside the neck of her dress so that he could kiss her breast, she leaned back in rapture.

Then with a shudder of desire they clasped each other. Mouth was hard upon mouth, limbs became bonds to grasp and hold. They made love with eagerness, trying to make up for the long parting, the time of loss and longing. Her tanned legs, her white-skinned body, her glossy hair, they received their due of kisses. In return she caressed and embraced him, accepting and returning his ardour a hundredfold.

On the truckle bed of the island fisherman they found their paradise again.

Chapter Twenty

When Timothy Perriman was notified of Erica's visit to Panago, he wasn't perturbed. So she'd gone on an overnight picnic with some naval type. So what? He'd long ago given up any notion of setting up any tie with her, business or emotional. She quite clearly didn't like him, and although he wouldn't have minded a sample of the delights promised by that firm, strong body, he could always find pleasures elsewhere.

Besides, the sister of one of his important clients was showing an interest in him. From the Sicilian background, with jealousies and suspicions to match, it wouldn't do to be interested in any other woman while Clementina was interested in *him*.

There was a continual flow of information from the Bahamas to Timothy. The intelligence system of the Mafia matched anything the British government could manage even in war-time. When the news came through that Erica's 'overnight picnic' had included a view of a wrecked yacht, alarm bells rang.

The *Margravine*? Could it possibly be the *Margravine*? That almost mystic boat, with its elusive contents. For ten years Timothy had been trying to get at its hidden safe. The closest he'd come was on that dreadful cruise off Long Island when Gaynor Medcalfe, the new owner, had been his host. He looked back on those few days with horror. Seasick, helpless, he'd tossed about aboard the yacht while Medcalfe raced her in some idiot regatta. Only once had Timothy managed to get into the saloon unobserved and alone. But for that short space of time his eyes had been swimming about in his head; he hadn't been able to focus them enough to examine the panelling for a keyhole.

Since then the *Margravine* had drifted out of his ken. Beyond the feeling that she was somewhere in Bahamian waters he'd had no real clue. And what had it mattered, so long as no one with any connection with the Tregarvon case came near her? No one except his former boss Lindon Tregarvon really knew where to look. The panelling in the saloon seemed perfect. Unless you had prior information you'd never suspect there was a safe hidden behind one of the rectangles. Even Timothy himself, though in the old days he'd seen Tregarvon move about in the saloon, was never quite sure on which wall the keyhole could be found.

But someone else who had a reason as serious as his own might make a close examination. And find the keyhole. And then wonder about a key.

There was a key hidden in the folding silver photograph frame. That much Timothy was almost sure of. Once, on one of their cruises, he'd reminded Tregarvon that the company chequebook was needed. At the time his employer had been in casual clothes, without the key-chain that usually hung across from one pocket to the other of his waistcoat. His formal clothes, Timothy knew, were at the yacht club for an event later that afternoon; he'd seen the valet go ashore with the case containing them.

'No problem,' Tregarvon had said. Later he'd gone into the saloon. By and by, the chequebook had been produced, the cheques written, signed and despatched. The only place Tregarvon had gone into was the saloon, so the safe must be somewhere in the saloon panelling. And the likely place for the spare key was in the folding frame; Timothy had gone in later and noted that the folding frame had been moved from one side of the desk-shelf to the centre.

That folding photograph frame now stood on the mantelpiece of the house in East Bay Street. The key was there, he'd felt its presence that one evening when he'd been left alone in the living room. There hadn't been enough time to get it out. But he hadn't been too perturbed about that. Neither Erica nor her mother knew of its existence and, even if they did, they'd have no idea what it was for.

But now . . . now it might be that Erica had found the *Margravine*. And if she had, she might make a search. And find the keyhole. And look for a key. Or even simply have the panel forced open, if that was possible.

Timothy made himself think about it calmly. If the boat that Erica had looked at was the *Margravine* – and that was a big 'if' – did it matter? Nothing had emerged from the discovery, so far as Timothy could hear. She hadn't been thrown into a flurry of activity about it.

Perhaps it had simply been a sentimental journey on her part, a search for something that she'd loved in her childhood. He remembered that she had indeed loved the *Margravine*, though why, Timothy could never understand: uncomfortable, pitching, unsteady. Why would anyone want to go journeying around on a yacht when there were comfortable hotels ashore?

And perhaps it hadn't been the *Margravine*. His Nassau informant reported that they'd looked at a boat called the *Perlina*, a hired craft used by deep-sea anglers. Wrecked now, it seemed, and a dreadful mess to look at. Didn't sound like the *Margravine*.

Here Timothy was hampered by an inborn lack of imagination. He could only think of the *Margravine* as he had last seen her, in the proud hands of Gaynor Medcalfe. He couldn't conceive the misfortunes that might befall even the most beautiful of creatures.

It was a lack he was unaware of. He thought of himself as a consummate schemer, forward-looking, foreseeing accurately the reactions of business opponents, sensing forthcoming changes in the business climate. In this he was right. But he wouldn't acknowledge to himself that the unexpected always threw him. Now, for instance, the idea that Erica Tregarvon might have found the *Margravine* threw him into a muted panic. How could anyone have imagined such a thing after all these years?

Yet there might be no need to worry. Nothing had come of the discovery, if discovery it was. All the same, it would be nice to get hold of that key. If any opportunity should arise, he would seize it.

The opportunity came, totally unexpectedly, and yet, because he'd had some time to prepare for it, quickly seized.

There was a riot in Nassau. The Americans were getting more forcibly into the war. To enable their allies to keep air watch over their coastal waters, the Bahamian government was building airfields. Workers were imported from Florida, workers were hired from among the Bahamians.

Unfortunately the wages paid to the workers were very unfair. Black Bahamians got less than a quarter of the money given to the white drivers of diggers and bulldozers.

Unrest began over minor matters. There were no buses to take the labourers the eight miles to and from the construction site. There was no food available at midday so men had to bring it with them, but, alas, they also brought bottles of home-brew. Wages were paid out, as was usual, on Saturday, but the men were only paid for work from Wednesday to Wednesday, a system they couldn't understand and which made them feel they were being cheated.

Moreover, the workpace was much harder than the Bahamians were accustomed to. Sun and heat were recognized by local employers as serious factors and the pace had always been regulated by the need to rest, to replace lost moisture by plentiful breaks for drinks. The bosses at the airfields weren't accustomed to taking time out just because it was hot, and besides, there was a war on, they were building an airfield for warplanes, not a luxury hotel. They closed their ears to what the black workers considered reasonable demands.

But the worst was, a black Bahamian truck driver was paid a shilling an hour: a white American was paid six shillings.

On a hot Saturday in June, when meagre wage packets had been opened and deductions for 'rain time' had been angrily noted, patience ran out. A meeting was held outside the office of the labour supervisor. No sense could be made of his explanations. There was argument, the police arrived, a warning shot was fired. The meeting broke up in alarm.

Black drivers gave lifts to black labourers. They drove into Nassau. There they seemed to disperse to their homes, but in fact many of them went to the local bars to drown their sorrows.

Next morning they came to the gathering point in Nassau where they were usually picked up by trucks for the journey to the airfield. But on this morning they simply refused to board the trucks.

A black lawyer, regarded by the Bay Street Boys as 'representative' of these unskilled, uneducated labourers, arrived to make a speech. He explained that wages were a matter for negotiation, that work must continue on the important construction project. When he left, the four hundred men who had heard him were little the wiser. They decided to strike.

At the airfield, those from other districts had arrived but had refused to begin work. Once again the police were called. This time the police captain withdrew to the offices of the construction site to call the Commissioner of Police for reinforcements. But before they could arrive, the men were marching from the airfield on Nassau.

Timothy Perriman was staying at the time at the Prince George Hotel. His Mafia clients controlled the trade union of the white construction workers, so Timothy was here to check that the union members were being paid according to the negotiated terms. The noise of a singing, shouting crowd drew him to the window.

He was astounded to see a mob of men armed with sticks and machetes being herded by a cordon of police along Bay Street. As he watched the mob was forced past the Prince

George, on along towards the British Colonial. Men stumbled and were trampled upon. The singing gave way to angry howls. And he heard the sound of breaking glass.

With a frown he drew back from the window. He paused. Then, with a little suppressed smile, he went to the telephone.

It so happened that Erica and her mother were in the British Colonial Hotel that morning, replaying the winning hand of a national bridge contest as a teaching session for their bridge school. When one of the hotel staff ran in to say that a rioting mob was headed towards them, most of those present panicked and ran.

Erica didn't at first believe the story. There had been other foolish rumours, notably that a German U-boat had landed a party of commandos to kidnap the Duke of Windsor. But this time the rumour proved to be true, for the sound of the mob began to be audible.

'Oh, good heavens, Erica,' gasped Mrs Tregarvon, 'we'd better take cover!'

'Where, exactly?'

'Well . . . Upstairs?'

Erica couldn't see the sense of that. If the crowd were actually intending harm to the hotel guests, they would look for them in the public rooms and then, if they didn't find them, upstairs. So the best way to go was out the back on the ground floor. But the bridge players who had first run off in panic now came back to say that some of the rowdies were already round the back of the hotel, carrying away cooking equipment and food stores.

Erica looked around the room. There was little there worth looting. Chairs and curtains and sun blinds, card tables, packs of cards, a big glass jug and a set of punch glasses. If they wanted those they could easily carry them off without doing any harm to the room's occupants.

'I think we should just sit still,' she suggested.

'But they're coming!'

In the end, they were not. The police forced most of the rioters down side streets. This was quite good tactics if the only aim was to save the British Colonial. But of course some of the men simply ran along the back alleys, turned another corner, and came back into Bay Street at a different point.

Most of the shops in Bay Street were wrecked and looted. All the bars had been raided for their stores of liquor. Men were rushing everywhere without sense or direction, some of them too drunk to know where they were. Shots were fired, but by whom no one could tell.

By noon the contingent of troops brought to the island for the protection of the Duke of Windsor was turned out to help quell the uproar. The Duke, as it happened, was absent – in Washington with his wife. The Cabinet sent him an urgent telegram, though what exactly the Duke could do if he returned was not clear. Somehow it seemed his fault that rioting had broken out, the tone being that he left Nassau, next thing Nassau was under siege. He must come back and put a stop to it.

There was no stop to the unrest. Although the violence had been cleared out of the centre of Nassau, Grants Town was on fire. Hesitant, still frightened, the white population came out of hiding to see the damage done to the white quarter. The main street, once thought of as the Bond Street of the Caribbean, was in ruins.

Erica and Amy Tregarvon picked their way through the wreckage as the late afternoon sun was waning. They walked slowly to East Bay Street, sighing at every broken window, every overturned car, pausing to commiserate with friends who had suffered looting. There were personal belongings and occasional pieces of furniture scattered about in the road. Yet as they reached their own district things seemed less disturbed.

When they reached their own house they stopped short, taken aback and afraid to go in. The front door had been smashed open, then jammed back in place.

'Amos?' called Erica, mounting the steps of the veranda. 'Neginah?'

There was a faint sound from inside the house. Against the sunset she glimpsed a shape moving. She drew back, alarmed, but in a moment the maid Neginah spoke from behind the broken door. 'That you, Miz Harrowford?'

'Neginah! Are you all right?'

'Sure thing, but if'n you wan' come in, Miz Harrowford, you gots to go round the back.'

'It's all right, Mother,' Erica called to Amy. 'Neginah's inside.'

Still unsure, Amy followed her daughter round the side of the house and to the kitchen door. Neginah was waiting there with her hand on the door knob. As soon as they were inside she closed and bolted the back door. 'What happened, Neginah? Were you here?'

'I wuz gettin' lunch ready. Amos he out the back cuttin' me some greens. There was these five wild men – them banged on the front door, shoutin' and ravin' an' I din know what to do so I ran out to Amos and we's hid in the arbour an' them wild men they smash the door – I heard um.' Her voice climbed in terror at the memory.

'Take it easy, Neginah,' Erica soothed. 'Sit down, take your time. They didn't hurt you?'

'No, Miz Harrowford, Amos and me, we stayed in the arbour quiet as mice. I whispers to Amos, they got to be robbers come rob the place. But they doan do that, Miz Harrowford.' She threw out her hands to take in the kitchen. 'They jus' take the cool wine from the icebox and they loll 'round drinkin' and bangin' on the cookpots, and then after a while they go in the livin' room, and they smash up somethin' – turns out it wuz the china cabinet. And then they run out across the back garden, laughin' and ravin' an' carryin' on.'

'They didn't take anything? Did they go upstairs?'

'No'm, they just sat in the kitchen suppin' the wine an' makin' a fuss with the pots. Lord good to me, I wuz shakin' all the time, an' Amos, he kep sayin', should he creep out and run for the police, but I sez, no way you can leave me here alone with um, and I sure doan run for the gate while those men sittin' there lookin' out the kitchen windows.' Neginah wrung her hands. 'I was frightened, Miz Harrowford. Mebbe I shoulda run with Amos. But my legs wouldn't take me no step.'

'You did quite right, Neginah,' Erica assured her. 'There was no sense taking risks. But where's Amos now?'

'We heard from Miz Doonan's cook next door, she say Grants Town got fires ev'where, and Amos, he brother lives in Grants Town so he gone to find out. I told him he should stay till you come again—'

430

'No, no, he was naturally anxious about his family. So long as you're all right, Neginah . . .'

'I'm fair, Miz Harrowford, but I got no lunch nor no supper in the pot.'

'That's all right.'

'It true they's broken up shops in Bay Street? It true the soldiers come out to shoot at the crowd?'

'We don't know what happened, Neginah. Mother and I were trapped in the Colonial. But Bay Street is in a terrible mess.'

'Prophets in Israel! Bay Street broken up?' To Neginah it was like hearing that the Bank of England had fallen down.

'Have you had anything to eat since it happened?' Amy asked. All her life she'd made it her business to see that the household staff were looked after.

'No, Miz Tregarvon, I haven't had a morsel.'

'Come on then, Neginah, you make us all a cup of tea and a sandwich. Mrs Harrowford and I will take a look at the rest of the house.'

This was said with more hardihood than Amy actually possessed. When it came to the point, she let Erica go upstairs to examine the bedrooms. Erica crunched her way over the broken glass of the china cabinet in the living room to go upstairs. But nothing there had been disturbed so far as she could see.

When she came downstairs, it was to find Mrs Tregarvon standing with a piece of broken china from the cabinet in her hand. But she was staring at something else.

'What is it, Mother?' she asked in alarm.

'Look.'

Erica turned her glance where the finger pointed. The mantelpiece above the unused fireplace was empty.

Mere trifles. A photograph of the *Margravine* cut out of a yachting magazine, a photograph of the *Langrovia*, a cedarwood box, a Japanese fan, a small silver cup, and a folding silver photograph frame with family snapshots. But they were all gone.

They called Neginah to show her the empty shelf. She stared, then shook her head. 'I din notice that, Miz Tregarvon. I s'pose I only had eyes for the cabinet bein' broke.'

'Why did they have to take those things?' Amy wailed. 'They aren't worth anything! Not to anyone except me!'

'Now, Miz Tregarvon, doan you take on—'

'You don't understand, Neginah! That was the only photograph I had of my baby boy who died.'

Neginah burst into tears. The two women sank down on the sofa, Neginah with her apron over her face, Amy with her hands clutching a broken statuette against her cheeks.

Erica fetched the tea that Neginah had made, made them drink some with plenty of sugar. She found some biscuits to go with it. They sat trying to comfort themselves for this terrible day.

But Erica's mind was already busy. Why should the 'wild men' have come to their house when the riot seemed to have died away some distance off? Why, after breaking in, had they done nothing but amuse themselves in the kitchen? Why not ransack the house? And why, when they at last made off, should they take not the silver from the dining room, not the brandy decanter, but the inoffensive little items from the mantelpiece?

It seemed almost like deliberate spite against her mother. But nobody in Nassau disliked Amy Tregarvon.

After a troubled night, Nassau woke next morning to the problem of explaining what had happened the day before. What exactly *had* happened? Who fired the shots? Had anyone been hurt? Who had led the riot, stirred up the unrest? And what had been its cause?

These were the same questions being asked by the Bassania organization. Timothy Perriman had a hard time giving the right answers during a long, angry phone call from their local boss in Miami.

'Nobody seems to know exactly what started it,' Timothy reported. 'Our men say the Bahamians were furious about the difference in the wages.'

'So what are those guys being paid, then?'

'Somewhere between a quarter and a sixth of what the white men are getting.'

Alfredo Capelli, startled, blew out a breath. 'Gee, we'd no idea the differentials would be so high. Look, damp this down, Perriman. We don't want anybody looking too closely at the negotiations.' No indeed, some very large bribes had been involved so that their men would get the jobs.

'It's not up to me to damp it down, Mr Capelli. It's Sir Harry Oakes and Christie and the rest of the big names here. They're meeting now to establish what happened, and the Duke's supposed to fly in later today.'

'Can you get to him? Talk him into seeing it as a race riot?'

'Get to the Duke?' Timothy echoed, aghast. 'Absolutely out of the question! The troops are out, there's tight security everywhere for the moment.'

'The other guys you mentioned – Sir Harry and this Christie and so on – can you talk to them?'

'And say what? That we should regard yesterday as a racial problem?' Timothy shook his head as if Capelli could see him. 'It wouldn't work, Mr Capelli. The last thing they want is a suggestion of racial trouble.'

'Listen, Perriman, I sent you there to take a look at how things were going. Things ain't going so well, it seems to me. It's up to you to sort it out.'

'But Mr Capelli—' But the phone had been put down at the other end.

Luckily the reporters who now descended on Nassau from the mainland like a flock of vultures provided a get-out. Someone decided the Nazis were to blame. *Agents provocateurs* had been at work, undercover agents who wanted to prevent the building of the airfields needed by the American Air Force. That evening Timothy was able to ring back and report that a good explanation had been found, which would prevent any acute examination of the wage negotiations.

'Not bad,' murmured Capelli. Timothy heaved a great sigh of relief.

Now he felt free to pursue his own interests. And chief of those was to find out how the Tregarvons had reacted to the burglary of their house.

It was perfectly in order for him to drop in on them. Everyone in Nassau was dropping in on everyone else, inquiring how they'd fared during 'the revolt'. It would provide conversational material for months, the story altering and evolving all the time until some of the population would be certain they'd actually seen swastika flags among the rioters.

The front door of the Tregarvons' home was still jammed shut. A neatly typed notice apologized and asked visitors to go round the back. Timothy did so, to find the kitchen door wide open so that friends could come and go at will. The sense of crisis had evaporated already.

Amy Tregarvon was delighted to see Timothy. There were a couple of other visitors to whom he was introduced, members of the school of bridge. Erica was offering drinks, her back to him, so that she was able to avoid shaking hands. What was he doing here? Why should he care how they'd got on during the riot? His presence, as always, sent a prickle down her spine.

'I see your front door was damaged.'

'Oh yes, when we got home yesterday. Timothy, you can imagine how scared we were.' Amy babbled on, giving a vivid picture of their return, of Neginah's terror, of their relief in finding no great damage. 'But I do wish they hadn't taken my photographs!' she lamented. 'That was the only photograph I had of poor little Neville. He was so delicate, you know, we were almost afraid to have the photographer come and take the picture because it meant an upset and he wasn't used to upsets.' She wandered off into memories of the lost son, so greatly loved and carefully tended, whose life had been so short.

Timothy already knew all about Neville, he'd heard it a thousand times while he was in Lindon's employ. He'd never been interested and even less so now.

He had come to get specific information. First he needed

to know whether the Tregarvons had realized the burglary had been specially set up to get the folding photograph frame. It seemed not. They were puzzled, it was true, and he meant to speak severely to his friends here who had recommended the men. He'd instructed them to smash the place up a bit, act like rioters, not sit about drinking wine and banging on some pots.

The next thing he needed to know was whether Erica had found the *Margravine*. He had the folding frame, he had the key and he knew what the key was for: the hidden safe on board the *Margravine*. What he now wanted to know was: had Erica's trip to Panago brought her to the *Margravine?*

It took him a long time, but little by little he edged the conversation away from yesterday's dramas. He began to talk about plans for the forthcoming months, the hot season. 'I suppose there's not much chance of getting permission to leave for cooler climates,' he mused.

'Oh no, "Is Your Journey Really Necessary?", you know,' said Mrs Givens, as if she had just invented the well-worn war-time slogan. 'We must all help to save fuel. Of course we realize, Mr Perriman, that you travel on important business.' She knew Perriman hobnobbed with the Bay Street Boys.

'I expect a little will be allowed for some sea trips,' Timothy said. 'I've heard it's cooler on some of the Out Islands, because the breezes set in that direction.'

'New Bight is cooler,' suggested Sam Merton. 'If I liked, I could go out to the New Bight under sail. Nobody could say I was wasting fuel.'

'But the German U-boats?' shuddered Mrs Givens.

'Does anyone know if there actually are any U-boats? I think I heard you'd made a trip a little while ago, Erica. Did you see any periscopes?'

Startled, Erica looked at Timothy. He was gazing nonchalantly past her, as if the question were totally unimportant. But she sensed he was after something.

'Oh yes, you went out towards Exuma, didn't you, Erica? Or was it Eleuthera?' Sam Merton recalled.

'It was only a picnic with a friend,' Erica said. 'Nothing much.'

'Did you land anywhere for the picnic? I often think the sand-flies make it uncomfortable if you want to picnic on a beach.'

'Yes, we landed. We stayed overnight, as a matter of fact.'

Everyone in the room was perfectly well aware of the fact. All the students of the bridge school knew that Erica Harrowford and Bart Crosley were absolutely mad about each other, and if wedding bells didn't ring quite soon it would be a wonder. But Erica had no intention of talking about it in front of Timothy.

'What sort of a place was it?' Timothy inquired. 'Decent beach? Did you swim?'

'No, we didn't.'

'Anything worth seeing? A waterfall? A lake?' Mrs Givens took it up.

'No, Panago isn't big enough for anything like that. In fact, I think they have a problem with fresh water.'

So the information was correct. The island she had visited had been Panago. But where was the yacht? And was it the

437

Margravine? There was no way he could ask the question directly.

'I suppose it's another of those islands where there's supposed to be buried treasure,' he said with a chuckle.

'Or a Spanish galleon,' added Merton, just as Timothy knew he would. In the Bahamas, if you talked about 'treasure', it immediately evoked the words 'Spanish galleon' or 'pirates' hoard'.

'No, nobody mentioned anything to us about buried treasure,' Erica said. 'Would anyone like another drink?'

Glasses were held out, but the subject refused to be changed.

'Of course there's treasure out there,' Merton said. 'Any amount of ships have gone down in the past, and let me tell you, quite recently too! During Prohibition, many a little boat was lost because it was overloaded with rum barrels.'

'I suppose there are plenty of little boats among those rocks?' Timothy asked.

But Erica refused to make any response.

He didn't know whether it was significant or not. If she had looked at a wreck, as his informant said, it was quite likely she wouldn't want to speak of it in front of her mother. But would that mean she'd found the *Margravine*? Or would it just mean she had looked for the *Margravine* and been disappointed?

Later, as Erica prepared for bed, she thought about the chat over their drinks. Was she mistaken or had Timothy been fishing for information?

She had not gone back to the *Margravine* the morning after their stay on Panago. Uncle Porter, who might have shown them the channel of approach, had never shown up, detained, no doubt, by the charms of 'that paradise girl'. Bart had to get back to Nassau: he only had a forty-eight-hour pass.

So she hadn't boarded the *Margravine*, nor would she. She'd decided it would only make her cry. And besides, these days she had better things to think about.

For the first time in years she was looking to the future with complete confidence. She was in love, deeply in love, with a man who loved her. When they could spend time together, she was happy as she had never been before. As yet they could make no plans because the war made claims on Bart, allowed them little chance to think about their life as it might be. But she knew she was luckier than many another woman who was parted from her man for months, perhaps years, at a time. Though she and Bart only saw each other briefly and infrequently, each moment was a glimpse of heaven.

For this reason she was unwilling to waste time on unimportant matters. Yet the visit from Timothy troubled her, and she spoke to Bart about it when next they could meet. They had dinner together at the Prince George, in a sheltered alcove where they could hold hands.

'He was trying to find out which island I'd been to. What business is it of his?' she remarked.

'It's odd. He's a strange chap.'

'You can say that again! Why does he keep on popping up in my life? Why should he bother to call on us to see if we were all right? He's usually off in The Club with the bigwigs.'

'I've no idea. It's true that he's hand in glove with some of the Bay Street Boys.' Bart hesitated. 'Erica, this is confidential, but since he keeps coming into your affairs, perhaps it's permissible to tell you. Intelligence is keeping an eye on Timothy.'

'Intelligence? You mean, he might be a spy?' Erica burst out laughing. 'Not Timothy Perriman! He's not the type.'

'What type is that?' Bart inquired mildly.

'Well . . . Surely a spy's got to be prepared to face danger? I don't think Timothy's very brave.'

'You don't have to be brave to spend money in The Club and butter up the Bay Street Boys.'

'But what could he get from them?' she insisted. 'The only thing he'd want to spy out is a business opportunity.'

'Exactly. The story is, he's trying to persuade the Bahamian government to allow a casino to be built here.'

'That's ridiculous. Everybody's far too busy building airfields.'

'Oh, I don't mean now. It's for the future, when the war's over.'

'But that's very long-term, Bart.'

'The people he's dealing for are the sort who plan for the long term. They're the kind who might be on the side of the Nazis if they thought they'd get favourable treatment from them after the war.'

'None of the Bay Street Boys is pro-Nazi.'

'Are you sure? I don't hear that they're particularly liberal in their outlook.'

'Well no, they're a bit tight-fisted, but . . . Sir Harry Oakes, for instance, he'd be dead against a casino or anything like that. He even thinks I'm a bit of an adventuress because I play bridge for money.'

Bart shook his head. 'I'm not joking, Erica. There are some very unsavoury characters trying to get a hold in Nassau. They usually get what they want in the end.'

'But why should British Intelligence care about the business plans of these unsavoury types?'

'Because pressure is being put on the leading members of the community, on people like Sir Harry, and Harold Christie, and Sands, and – this is where Intelligence gets worried – on the Governor.'

'On the Duke?' Erica said, startled.

Bart shrugged and ended the conversation with, 'Just take care around Timothy Perriman, that's all.'

For the moment there was no need. Timothy had gone back to the mainland.

The rainy season went by with its usual listlessness and languor. During September the temperature began to go down and those lucky Bahamians who had had permission to travel to cooler latitudes returned to Nassau. Sir Harry Oakes and his wife and family came back from Canada.

Once they were settled in their house up on the ridge, the Oakeses usually gave a party. So Erica was surprised when she received a telephone call from Lady Oakes asking her to call the day after their arrival. She accepted the invitation with some curiosity. It must be that Eunice Oakes wanted her to arrange some bridge parties for her. Although Lady Oakes was kindly disposed towards them, they seldom encountered each other socially these days.

When she reached Wimbourne she was ushered into the drawing room. Lady Oakes joined her after a very short wait. 'I'm sorry not to have been here when you were shown in,

Erica. You know what it's like when you just get back, everything's at sixes and sevens.'

'Not at all,' Erica said meaninglessly. Something about her hostess troubled her. The older woman, though her usually stalwart, capable self, looked distressed.

'Please sit down, my dear. Would you like some refreshment? Lemonade? Coffee?'

Erica settled for lemonade. Lady Oakes fussed about while they waited for it to be brought, her tall figure like a moving pillar in the cool shaded room. She only subsided into a chair when the maid came in with the tray. What *is* wrong with her, wondered Erica. Usually she's so calm.

When they had received their drinks and taken a few sips, Lady Oakes laid aside her glass.

'My dear,' she said, leaning forward, 'I have something very serious to show you.'

Erica's eyes went wide with surprise. 'To show me?'

'Harry and I discussed it. We thought it best to bring it with us and for me to show it to you in person rather than post it to you with a letter.'

'What, Lady Oakes? What are you talking about?'

For an answer Eunice Oakes picked up a folded newspaper from the table next to her chair. Its leaves stirred a little in the current of air from the electric fan. 'Look at this.'

At a loss, she took the proffered newspaper. It was folded open so that a small news item low on the front page leaped into prominence. 'MISSING FINANCIER FOUND?' cried the headline.

Missing financier? Erica's heart gave a lurch. Her father? Her father, safe and sound in South America! Her eyes leaping from sentence to sentence, she read: 'The skeleton of a man has been found during the reopening of a disused quarry. It seems the man fell to his death some years ago. From an inscription inside the case of his pocket-watch the body is thought to be that of Lindon Tregarvon, the shipping tycoon. Lindon Tregarvon failed to respond to his bail in 1932 and it was thought he had fled the country. It now seems probable that he met with an accident.

'The quarry was being reopened for storage purposes, otherwise the body . . .'

The words blurred before her eyes. The world went blank.

Chapter Twenty-one

Erica heard Lady Oakes calling in alarm. 'Nancy, Nancy!' Someone, presumably Nancy, began to chafe her hands. The breeze from the electric fan grew stronger, as if it had been moved closer.

She opened her eyes. Eunice's daughter Nancy was bending over her in anxiety. The butler was holding the fan over her head. Lady Oakes was offering a crystal glass.

'Erica, my dear girl! Can you hear me? Erica, wake up!'

'Ye-es,' she whispered. 'Yes, I'm all right.'

'What a fright you gave us! Here, drink this.'

'No, I—'

'Drink it, my dear, it will do you good.'

She sipped the brandy. Nancy slipped a cushion behind her head. She lay back in the cane chaise longue, trying to grasp at the wisps of memory that seemed to drift in the air around her.

Her glance fell on the newspaper on the floor. Her eyes focused on it. She sat up. 'Oh!'

'My dear, keep still. You've had a big shock.'

'Did I . . . Did I really see that? My father?'

'Yes, I'm afraid so.' Lady Oakes wasn't one to shirk the inevitable. 'Now lie back, take a moment. There's no hurry.'

'But my mother!'

'Yes, she will have to be told. But it can wait a few minutes.'

'It's waited long enough,' Erica said with a bitterness stronger than the voice in which she uttered the words. 'Almost a dozen years.'

'Beaufort, get Mrs Harrowford more brandy.'

'No, no, thank you.' Erica struggled from Nancy's retaining touch on her shoulder, sat up. 'I must go home.'

'Not yet—'

'I'm all right. Really, I'd rather.'

'But you haven't recovered.'

'Mummy, she wants to be alone!' seventeen-year-old Nancy broke in, impatient at the lack of understanding, bright-eyed with tears of sympathy.

'Oh, of course. How tactless of me.'

'Not at all, Lady Oakes. You've been very kind.'

'Beaufort, have the car brought round.'

'No, I'd rather walk, thank you.'

'You're not fit—'

'Please, the fresh air will do me good.'

'Are you sure, dear?'

'Yes, yes, I'm quite sure.' Kind though they were, she could hardly wait to get away from them.

Eunice walked with her to the door. 'Now, Erica, if there's anything we can do.'

'You've been more than kind already.'

'Nonsense, we only did what we could. But there's more to be learnt about this business, Erica. A paragraph or two in a skimpy war-time newspaper – that's not much to go on. Would you like Sir Harry to have inquiries made?'

'Could he do that?' she asked, startled.

'Of course. You know there are diplomatic channels open to him that might not perhaps be available to you.' This meant that Sir Harry would have a word with the Duke, and the Duke would send word to someone in the government in London, and whatever could be learned from Scotland Yard would be passed on.

'Oh, thank you, Lady Oakes, thank you, you're so kind!'

'Not at all, not at all,' Eunice Oakes said, blushing as she often did when her good works were acknowledged. 'You had better take the newspaper, hadn't you?'

Reluctantly, Erica accepted it. To her it seemed an enemy because it had brought such terrible news. But her mother might need to see the words with her own eyes before she would believe it.

In this she was wrong. Amy Tregarvon sank down on the sofa as her daughter told her what she had read in the *Globe*, going pale, shivering with reaction. Tears brimmed over her lashes, she began to sob. And yet she accepted the news at once.

'I *knew* he never intended to just leave us! I knew, I knew! Oh, Erica, he never meant us to suffer as we did! Only death could have prevented him from looking after us. I should have *known*!'

Mother and daughter sat, arms around each other, tears mingling, memories tumbling in their minds. Erica recalled the many bitter things she'd said about her father – how he had abandoned them, had been callous, thoughtless, cruel, a thief and a murderer and a swindler. She longed to take back each searing word, each angry, self-centred thought.

All that day and the next they were very quiet, speaking to each other only when they had to. They were like two invalids coming back into the world after a long illness. They must be careful in case they brought on a setback. Everything looked different, required effort and thought.

Bart arrived in the evening of the second day. He was taking documents to Government House, so could only stay a moment. Erica took him out in the starlit garden to tell him the news, unwilling to subject her mother to a public rehearsal of the circumstances.

'In a quarry?' Bart echoed, aghast. 'Where, for God's sake?'

'We don't know yet. Sir Harry Oakes is trying to find out more for us.'

'All this time, while you were having that Miami detective look for him.'

'Yes, all this time, Bart. And I thought he was hidden safely away with some secret store of cash in Venezuela or Chile.'

'But you know, Erica . . . we've discussed this, we've wondered if he left home to make his way to the Bahamas.'

'That's been one possibility.'

'Trying to get to the *Margravine*.'

'Yes, perhaps.'

'Well, a quarry is usually out in the country somewhere. What was he doing there? And how did he get there?'

'What do you mean?'

'Presumably he didn't walk there?'

'Well . . . no . . . I suppose not.'

'Did someone drive him there? If so, who?'

There was a long silence and then they both said together,

in a low tone, 'Timothy Perriman?'

Erica began to shudder. Bart put his arms around her. 'Don't, darling. It's all right.'

'No, it isn't, it isn't! He frightens me!'

'But he's not here now. It's all right.'

'He'll come back. He keeps coming back. And he's always *there*, somehow sneaking into my life, keeping tabs on me . . . I feel it, Bart, he's somehow *watching* me.'

He stroked her hair and soothed her, almost as if she were a child in need of comfort. By and by he said, 'I've got to go, I'm due back at the base as soon as possible. But I'll try to get some time off. I'll be back as soon as I can. We'll go to the Prince George, talk it all over.'

When he returned a few days later, Sir Harry Oakes had been able to pass on some notes from a report that had come in the diplomatic bag to Nassau.

'The quarry is in Hampshire, it's called Hilliston Quarry,' Erica reported. 'It was closed in 1929 when the Depression caused a slump in house-building. It was being reopened to store ammunition. There isn't a railway station nearby nor a bus that passes close. The nearest town is about five miles off.'

'But there's a road, obviously?'

'Yes, the road used in the past for the trucks taking away the stone. I gather it's a track, really.'

Bart hesitated. 'There's been an autopsy?'

'Yes, but nothing much could be learned,' Erica said steadily. 'Very little but bones inside a suit of clothes, damaged by mildew and . . . and rats . . . and things like that.'

'Signs of assault?'

'There were broken bones, but that could have happened in the fall.'

'They're not suggesting he took his own life?'

'Sir Harry says they're treating it as a murder inquiry. Father had packed a bag with a few clothes. There's no sign of it but of course it could have been stolen. But the main objection to accident or suicide is that they feel he didn't walk there. He was wearing town shoes, in fact evening shoes: thin black leather. Enough of them has survived to show that he certainly didn't walk to the quarry over rough tracks. Scotland Yard is more or less satisfied that he drove there.'

'But if he drove himself, where's the car?'

'Exactly. Someone took him there and then drove away.'

Neither of them said *afterwards*. After Lindon Tregarvon had been pushed over the edge of the quarry.

Erica and Bart were in their usual quiet corner of the Prince George's restaurant. A silver coffee pot and a tray of candied fruit lay between them on the white tablecloth but neither paid any attention to them.

'They're treating it as a murder case?' Bart mused.

'Yes, but Sir Harry pointed out that they won't be giving it any priority. "There's a war on", and so forth. More important things to think about than the death of one man more than ten years ago.'

'Your mother's taking it very well.'

'She's almost happy,' Erica said. 'My father's reputation has been cleared, at least in part. He didn't skip bail, he didn't abscond, he didn't leave us in the lurch. As far as Mother's concerned that means he's entirely innocent, even of the insurance fraud.'

'Perhaps he is,' Bart said.

'Oh, if only we could be sure!' cried Erica, throwing up clenched fists in a gesture of frustration.

'Certainty is difficult but, you know, Erica . . . It looks as if someone lured him out to that quarry and pushed him over. He told your mother he thought he could find documents that would clear his name. Perhaps that's why he was killed – to prevent that.'

'He told Mother he wanted to get to the *Margravine*. But we've seen the *Margravine*.' She sighed. 'If there was ever anything there, it's gone now.' At last she began to pour the coffee, now tepid. It was scarcely worth drinking but she was thirsty. She felt almost as if she had a slight fever. Talking about her father's death gave her this feeling; it made her sad, troubled, full of self-reproach.

Bart was silent for so long that she had to prompt him. 'What are you thinking?'

He took her hand. 'Think back. You remember the key you found in the photograph frame? I said it looked like the key to some small fitment aboard ship. Just suppose, Erica . . . Just suppose that the fitment is still there?'

'Bart!'

'Some place where your father kept papers when he was on the yacht?'

'There was a place! I think it was in the saloon, a sort of safe. Oh, I don't remember!'

'Would your mother know?'

'Oh, Father never told her anything about business matters. I don't think she'd know. But I'm almost sure, almost certain, there was a panel in the saloon that opened. Her jewellery went in there when she wasn't wearing it.'

'As soon as I can,' he said, getting to his feet, 'I'm going to ask for a couple of days' leave and we're going back to Panago to ask Uncle Porter how to get aboard the boat. And we'll get that key and take it with us.'

'Yes!' She too had risen, had started to gather up her handbag and make for the doorway of the restaurant. Then she sank back in her chair.

She'd gone so pale that Bart stooped over her in alarm. 'Erica, for God's sake, what's wrong?'

'The key,' she said. 'The key.'

'What about it?'

'It was in the silver frame.'

'Yes, I remember.'

'Bart, that was almost the only thing stolen when the rioters broke into our house!'

Bart too sat down once more. He was shaking his head in consternation.

'Tell me again,' he said. 'About the break-in.'

'Neginah told us the men broke the front door down. They sat in the kitchen drinking the wine from the icebox. She said they clashed the lids on the pots and pans, and sang and shouted.'

'But didn't break up the kitchen or steal the food stores?'

'No. After a while they went back through the house. She's sure they didn't go upstairs. She heard something smashing. When she and Amos plucked up courage, they found the kitchen messed up but not damaged. The china cabinet in the living room had been tipped over. The only things taken were the mementoes on the mantelpiece.'

'Erica,' Bart said slowly, 'that's what they came for.'

'What?'

'It was a put-up job. Somebody took advantage of the rioting to have those things stolen.'

'But why, Bart, *why*?'

'Because the key was in the frame.'

She frowned and shook her head. 'But the key's no good without the safe, Bart. And if the safe exists it's probably on the *Margravine*.'

'Yes.'

'Well, nobody knows that except us.'

Bart took a breath. 'Timothy Perriman knows.'

'Timothy knows?'

'He was your father's confidential secretary, yes? Worked with him on business affairs when the family travelled.'

'Oh yes. He did.'

'He's very likely to know the safe exists. And he was looking for the *Margravine*, wasn't he? Your detective established that for a fact.'

'Yes, that's true, he went aboard her. But if he was trying to get to the safe he had no chance; they were being tossed about by a Force Eight gale. And if he's been looking for her since then, Bart, he didn't find her. We did.'

'Quite right. And were asking questions on Panago, weren't we? Asking how to get on board the *Perlina*.'

'But, I don't see . . .'

'You say you've had the feeling Perriman is watching you. Perhaps that's true, Erica. Perhaps he's always been afraid you'd get to the *Margravine*. Because there's something in that cupboard he doesn't want found.'

The thought was too frightening to contemplate. She shied away from it. 'He couldn't have found out about our seeing the *Margravine*. We never mentioned that name to anyone.'

'No, but we went and looked at a boat. You told me he was curious about where you'd been, what you'd done.' Seeing her frown in perplexity he went on. 'Someone drove your father to the quarry and drove away again. It must have been someone he trusted, don't you think? Because he was probably on his way to a port to get on board ship for the Bahamas, so someone offered to drive him, and took a little detour by an abandoned quarry. Who would he have trusted, Erica?'

Her pale lips formed the name: Timothy.

'Who asked you to marry him so he could keep an eye on you? Timothy Perriman. Who went looking for the *Margravine* on Long Island? Timothy Perriman. Who did you find examining the silver frame? Timothy Perriman. Who might have had the frame stolen after he heard you'd found the boat? Timothy Perriman.'

'You're saying . . . you're saying he wanted to prevent the contents of that safe from being found.'

'Because they probably clear your father of the insurance swindle. And who do you think they might incriminate?'

'No . . .'

'Somebody arranged that cargo fraud, somebody arranged to sink those ships. Lindon Tregarvon disappeared and was declared bankrupt, but who had enough money all the same to start up in business in New York? Timothy Perriman.'

'I can't bear it,' Erica gasped. 'My father *trusted* him.'

The more fool he, thought Bart, but didn't say it aloud.

'Why would he do such a thing?' Erica insisted. 'My father was always good to him.'

'Envy? Spite? Greed? Any one of those or all three,' he replied. 'Believe me, darling, in my job with Naval Intelligence I come across men willing to sell out anybody for a few hundred pounds. I can imagine Timothy seeing how easy it would be to take advantage of your father's trust.'

'Oh yes,' she broke in, seeing it as if it were yesterday, 'especially during that last year or so when I was being launched into the London season. Father paid a lot less attention to business, he left a lot to Timothy.'

'So there you are. He had motive and opportunity.' Bart paused. 'I'll give him this, murder probably wasn't any part of his plan. With luck, the insurance fraud might never have been discovered.'

'That's right, it only came to light because two men from one of the sunken ships appeared somewhere in Australia talking too much.'

'There you are then. Without that, Timothy would have bided his time, given up his job with the Tregarvon Line, and set up for himself without ever having to take desperate measures. But when your father was accused and thought he might clear himself by means of some papers he'd left on the *Margravine*, Timothy couldn't take the risk.'

Erica shuddered. 'I might actually have married him. Mother wanted me to.'

Bart jumped up and pulled her to her feet. 'Come on, let's get out of here.'

When they were out in the starlit night, he took her in his arms to hold her close. 'Let's forget all those sad things,' he said. 'I've only a few more hours before I have to go back to base. Are we going to waste them making ourselves miserable?'

'No, no, darling, of course not.'

They went to the room he had taken in an inexpensive hotel close to the waterfront. In each other's arms they forgot the past, they didn't try to plan the future. They lived only for the present and the moments of joy they could give to each other.

A couple of months later a little packet arrived for Amy Tregarvon. It came via the diplomatic bag from London. Inside the little cardboard box were the belongings found on the body in the quarry. With trembling hands she took out a crocodile-leather wallet with a gold fastening, the white five-pound notes made green with mould. There was a gold Waterman fountain pen, his gold and mother-of-pearl studs and cuff-links, and his watch and chain.

Erica sat at her side watching the items appear one by one. Neither woman could speak at the sight of these little mementoes of the man they had both loved.

Then Erica drew in a startled, trembling breath. She reached out to pick up the gold watch and chain from her mother's lap.

Attached to the chain was a tiny key.

Chapter Twenty-two

Timothy Perriman had a good network of informers in the Bahamas. It was a leftover from the days of Prohibition, when any little piece of news might help avoid confiscation of cargo.

Yet it wasn't a perfect network. Particularly where news of Erica Harrowford was concerned, informants didn't take him quite seriously. So he had a thing about this pretty lady. So what? That wasn't business, that was pastime.

So it took a long time for the news to filter through about the discovery of Lindon Tregarvon's body. When it came, it came in fact from one of his most highly placed gossips, one of the Bay Street Boys. On a trip to Washington, after dinner and over the brandy, the Honourable Harold Christie remarked, 'I heard a strange thing from Sir Harry the other day. That little fluttery lady who helps run the flowers by post?'

'Yes?' Timothy said, pausing with the snifter halfway to his lips.

'Seems her husband's dead after all, not missing.'

There was a long silence. The Honourable Harold didn't notice it because he was selecting a smoke from his cigar case. He was pleasantly full after a meal that had paid scant attention to war-time rationing.

'How . . . how did that come out?' Timothy asked.

'Er . . . let me see . . . I think Her Ladyship noticed it in one of the British newspapers they get shipped out to them. Harry likes to keep his eye on everything, you know, reads newspapers like you and me read menus.' Christie laughed, puffing at his cigar. 'If I remember rightly, they found a body in a lake or a mineshaft or something. Turned out it was poor little Amy Tregarvon's missing hubbie.'

By now Timothy had recovered himself enough to talk about it naturally. 'Upset her, I dare say?'

'I s'pose so. I wasn't in on it at all. I don't think anybody knows about it really except Eunice – you know how she interests herself in everybody else's affairs. Good works, she calls it.'

Christie went on to talk about Lady Oakes, whom he rather liked although he thought her too upright. He was sorry for her; her daughter had made the entire family look foolish by marrying that ne'er-do-well de Marigny.

There was no way to reopen the subject without attracting Christie's sharp attention. But alarm bells had begun to ring for Timothy.

He sent messages of complaint to his watchers. Why hadn't he been informed? What had happened since?

Well, thought the watchers, if he's really willing to pay money for titbits, let's supply some.

The result was a great deal of gossip about Erica and Bart. They'd been seen about together a lot since the turn of the New Year. Now, Lieutenant Crosley wasn't around any more. There was a lot of naval activity, something fishy seemed to be going on among the Out Islands. Miz Harrowford hadn't taken up with anyone else, she was busy with the business of earning a living. Was this what Mr Perriman wanted to know?

In part, yes. But for Timothy the important item was added in pencil to the badly typed report. 'Amos Powell, house-servant to Miz Tregarvon, says she was mighty upset when she got a package, something to do with old times back in England and was sent by special messenger from Government House.'

Timothy was so alarmed that he made a direct telephone call to the chief news-gatherer. What had the package contained? He would pay a bonus for fast information.

The man who collated the news and gossip was a bar owner called Barka in Grants Town. Amos dropped in when he visited his parents on his evenings off. Nothing easier than to edge the conversation round to the day when the package had arrived. In the early hours of the morning, when the bar had closed, Barka made a collect call to Washington.

'Mr Perriman? You said, call you soon's I got the word. That package Miz Tregarvon got?'

'Yes?' Timothy gasped, sitting up in bed wide awake.

'Jes' she husband things – messy wallet all et up by ants, watch and chain, cufflinks. That what you want to know, sah?'

'Yes, thank you, Barka. Yes, you've done well. There'll be a hundred dollars next time I see you.'

When he had put down the receiver, Timothy Perriman dragged himself out of bed. He was shaking. He could hardly tie the sash of his dressing-gown.

He went into the living room of his Washington flat, collapsed into an armchair, stared into the darkness.

As if thrown by a projector on to a screen, he saw the watch and chain, Lindon Tregarvon's watch and chain, the chain draped across the fine worsted of his evening waistcoat. It had been there when Timothy pushed him into the quarry.

He hadn't meant it to happen quite like that. He'd meant to knock Tregarvon unconscious with the heavy torch he carried, and then search the body before tumbling it over the edge.

But he never expected in the first place to have to take emergency action. His plan had always been to carry out a few clever swindles and squirrel the money away for the future. Then, one day, he'd regretfully tell Tregarvon that he had the offer of a good opening in the States, take his leave with handshake and handsome farewell cheque, and set up for himself in New York. No more kowtowing to a man who had less business flair than he had himself, no more putting up with the mother's prattle and the daughter's uppishness.

The first spanner in the works had been when the engineer and first mate of the *Ganymede* turned up in Darwin drunkenly boasting about easy money. Then a hue and cry was raised to find the captain of the *Lariette*. Only the faintest rumours had reached Timothy. He was no more prepared than Tregarvon for the sudden arrest on that cold Sunday evening in January.

Timothy had been very frightened. Yet at first everything seemed to go well from his point of view. Tregarvon was arrested, Tregarvon was held to be the criminal. What was more, the man was too devastated to think properly.

All his friends distanced themselves from him. Except, of course, the good and faithful servant, the personal secretary, Timothy Perriman. Timothy was there to help the detectives look for documents, to unlock safes and drawers for them, all the while protesting the innocence of his employer.

Having no one else to turn to, Tregarvon talked to Timothy. With growing alarm Timothy noticed that the ship-owner was beginning to think more and more of the insurance documents he'd signed one evening while on holiday in Nassau.

'I'm damned sure I never assigned the cargo of the *Ganymede* to be handled by Fairforth Freighters,' Tregarvon began to murmur. 'There was something a bit tricky on one of their contracts a while back . . .'

'I don't remember, Mr Tregarvon.'

'Oh, you *must* remember, Timothy! We talked about them. Something about a cargo going missing in Pernambuco and the goods turning up in San Francisco . . .'

'No, I can't recall that, sir.'

'I'll tell you what I think, Timothy, I think there's been a switch of papers somewhere down the line. Or somebody in my organization has been paid to type in a different firm on the top copy.'

'Oh, no, sir, surely no one would do such a thing!'

'For money, Timothy, for money . . . Well, if I can only find my personal copy of the contract, it'll show that I never signed with Fairforth Freighters.'

That had been in the early afternoon of February 1st. Timothy had helped Tregarvon search for the copy of the bills of loading and the contract. They weren't to be found. Timothy murmured that he supposed the police had taken them.

There the matter rested. Next day Lindon Tregarvon arrived at his office with a look of renewed hope. 'Timothy, I don't think I ever brought those papers back to London. I think they're still aboard the *Margravine*!'

All day they talked it back and forth, while still making desultory searches in unlikely places in the office. At last, when his employer decided to call it a day and go home for dinner, he said, 'I'm going to trust you with a secret, Timothy. I've decided to make a break for it and get out to Nassau. I *know* those papers I left on the yacht will prove I never entered into any arrangement with Fairforth Freighters, and that will prove that someone in my offices is the one to blame for the fraud.'

'Mr Tregarvon! You can't mean you're going to skip bail?' That had never occurred to Perriman. He only knew the other man as a wealthy ship-owner, he had never seen the adventurous fast-moving merchant-seaman he used to be.

'Yes, I am. I've got friends in the yachting world, I'll get someone at Itchenor to motor me over to France and get a ship there for the US. From there it's only a hop, skip and a jump to Nassau and the *Margravine*.'

'But sir—'

'Don't look so shocked, Timothy. It's against the law, I admit, but if it brings the real culprits to justice, that makes it all right.'

Timothy's brain, never at its best in an unexpected drama, at last began to tick over. 'But your wife and daughter—'

'I shan't tell them. I'll be there and back within ten days, I hope.'

'But . . . but . . . How will you get away?'

'Tonight, after dinner. I'll change and eat dinner as usual and then I'll say I've got work to do at the office. I shan't take the car, don't want the chauffeur to know. I'll take the train to—'

'Is that wise, sir? Suppose someone recognizes you? Your picture's been all over the papers.'

'I'll take that chance.'

'Wouldn't it be better if I were to drive you, Mr Tregarvon?'

'Oh, I couldn't ask you to do that.'

'But I want to, sir. After all, if it's going to sort out this mess and get back your good name—' He broke off, gazing fervently and loyally at Tregarvon.

Lindon Tregarvon was touched. Much though he liked and trusted Timothy, he'd always thought him a bit of a stick. It was a surprise to find him willing to get involved in something risky. Even more surprising, on the drive towards Itchenor, Timothy came up with something more. 'I was thinking, Mr Tregarvon, about your passport.'

'I've got it with me,' Tregarvon replied, touching his breast pocket.

'Yes, but what I mean is, it may not attract the attention of a purser aboard a French ship, but an American immigration officer – he might have read something in the papers – English language, you see, whereas a Frenchman . . .'

Out of this muddle his employer picked up the danger. 'It's possible, but it's a risk I have to take.'

'No, sir, not at all,' Timothy rejoined. 'I have a friend who lives in Hampshire – a farmer, looks very much like you – I think if we dropped in on him en route and offered him a lot of money, he'd lend it to you for a couple of weeks.'

'Good Lord, Timothy!'

'I know it's illegal, Mr Tregarvon, but after all—' With a gesture of one hand, he indicated the car and their journey through the dark countryside. 'And John needs money.'

'Well blow me down,' Tregarvon said, reverting to old slang in his amazement. The conservative, upright Timothy. And when you came to think of it, he was right. No sense in using his own passport and risking discovery before he got as far as the *Margravine*. 'Where's this farm, then?'

'It's off the main road about twenty miles further on. John lets me go shooting on his land from time to time.'

And so in due course he had bumped the car along the dark track to the quarry he had noticed more than once on shooting trips. 'We have to walk from here, sir,' he said at last.

They got out. Timothy led the way with his torch along the path to the quarry edge.

'Bit neglected, isn't it?' remarked Tregarvon, feeling the pebbles scarring his evening shoes and the brambles catching at his trouser legs.

'Well, I told you, sir, he's hard up these days.'

He reached the rim of the great opening in the earth. 'Here we are,' he said in a welcoming tone, as if he'd set his hand on a gate at last.

In the darkness Lindon Tregarvon stepped up to him. But something in the quality of blackness – the darkness of winter night sky rather than the darkness of an unlit house – must have warned him. He turned as he joined his secretary, with a question on his lips. 'Is the house—?'

Lindon Tregarvon never finished the sentence. Panicked, Timothy struck him as hard as he could with the torch and as he fell shoved at him so that his victim couldn't aim a blow. He heard the thud of the body hitting a boulder at the quarry's rim, the thrashing and tearing as it went down through the weeds and thorns, the faint sound as it hit rocks and water below.

For a long time Timothy crouched trembling on the edge of the abandoned quarry. He had lost the torch but found it again, still switched on, among the coarse grass. He directed its beam downwards into the chasm.

There was nothing to be seen. Even if the bushes had been broken they had mostly sprung back again after the body's passing. Timothy stood there, listening. He was waiting for Tregarvon to cry for help. For almost an hour he stood there, waiting, listening. But no voice drifted up from the depths. Tregarvon was dead, or unconscious.

And if he was still alive but injured, a night out in this bitter cold would soon finish him.

Only a long time afterwards did Timothy wish he could have made sure Tregarvon was dead and then searched the body before toppling it into the quarry. By then the key on the watch chain had become important. He had tried to buy the *Margravine* but had been too late, and then when he finagled a sea-trip aboard her he'd been able to find the safe among the wall panelling, but couldn't open it without a jemmy.

Later he'd taken steps to obtain what he thought of as the only existing key, the one in the photograph frame. He had it now. But now the Tregarvon family also had a key, the one he should have taken from the watch chain.

Would they do anything with it? If only he knew whether

Erica and her boyfriend had actually found the *Margravine*. But it wouldn't do to make a trip out to Panago and board the wreck. It would attract too much attention, because there was a lot of attention focused on the islands.

There was always talk about buried or sunken treasure in the Bahamas. There was also a continuing fear that landing parties might try to capture the Duke of Windsor. Strange vessels had been seen slipping in and out of quiet coves. Some thought it was something to do with Wenner-Gren, a Swedish millionaire, owner of Hog Island and known to be a Nazi sympathizer. Others maintained it was Sir Harry Oakes sending his cash out of the British domain, to be changed into American dollars or Swiss francs – or better yet, gold.

The result was that the small naval force had been put on alert. It was no longer possible to make holiday trips by boat. Only valid traffic such as fishing or the transport of goods and mail was permitted.

This heightened attention to the traffic among the islands didn't suit Timothy's present employers at all. They did in fact use the Bahamas for the laundering of Mafia money, and they didn't want official attention drawn to it. He was instructed to go to Nassau. He was to find out whether Wenner-Gren was at the bottom of the suspicious activity, in which case nothing could be done. But if it proved to be Sir Harry Oakes up to some buccaneering trick, Perriman was to persuade him to stop.

'And how am I supposed to do that?' he asked Giancarlo Manzini, the Bassania brothers' business manager.

Manzini was used to asking questions, not answering them. 'You'll think of something,' he said in his cold, passionless voice. 'But whatever you think of, make sure it works.'

Perriman was under a lot of strain when he arrived back in Nassau. He had been given an order in no uncertain terms. He didn't know how he was going to carry it out. Besides this, he had his own worries . . . If that boat really were the *Margravine* . . . But there was no way to find out.

As if that wasn't enough, it was the beginning of July and the heat was growing intense in the Bahamas. Everyone alike suffered from the heat. But one other inhabitant of Nassau shared with Perriman his anxieties about the wreck out on Diggo.

Erica Harrowford wanted to get out to the *Perlina*. She had the key of the safe. If she could only get aboard to check that the safe was still there! If the panelling hadn't been stripped out for other use, if the saloon hadn't been vandalized, she might find whatever it was her father had been in search of.

One day, the alert out among the islands would be over and Bart would get some leave. They would go out to the wreck and together they would find the safe.

But the alert about suspicious shipping was replaced by another, even more dramatic.

On the morning of July 8th, 1943, Sir Harry Oakes was found murdered in his half-burned bedroom.

Chapter Twenty-three

The reaction to the news was disbelief.

Elderly heads were shaken, men at The Club gathered in groups. 'Utter nonsense! There's never been a white man murdered in Nassau!'

But as the morning wore on, disbelief was replaced by stunned acceptance. It was true. Harry Oakes had been found with his skull bashed in.

The blows hadn't utterly killed him. While he was still alive but unconscious, someone had doused the body and parts of the room with some kind of liquid fuel and set it alight. The fire hadn't taken much hold, though it had leapt out for a while to the hall. The walls there showed hand prints, bloody hand prints, the rumour said.

The body was found by his friend the Honourable Harold Christie, who had slept all night as a guest in a room two doors along the landing. He had heard nothing, but it had been a night of violent thunder and lightning.

The house had been otherwise empty: Mrs Oakes and her children had gone for the summer to their cool northerly house in America; the servants always left at eleven o'clock; the nightwatchmen were off duty because there were few people in the house.

The richest baronet in the British Empire, a friend and

associate of the Duke of Windsor, had been murdered in his beautiful tropical mansion. Naturally the world's press were avidly interested. It made a nice diversion from the war. They descended on Nassau like a huge flock of vultures, despite war-time security and travel control.

Every policeman and serviceman in the Bahamas was put on duty to keep order. The alert about unidentified shipping was forgotten as the authorities grappled with the aftermath of the murder. 'It's just possible you'll be called on for some help,' Bart Crosley was told by his ship's captain. 'They seem to be making an unholy mess of the murder inquiry.'

Rumours arose, caused argument, fights, dissent. One faction declared Oakes had been murdered by order of the Bay Street Boys because he was a friend of the black Bahamians, paying fair wages promptly, whereas others wanted to keep wages low and irregular. Another faction was convinced Wenner-Gren and his pro-Nazi friends came into it somewhere. A third muttered that it could have something to do with the Mob – Oakes had been firmly and loudly against the introduction of gambling, whereas the Mafia, typified by Meyer Lansky, a well-known mobster in Cuba, wanted to extend their hold in the Caribbean.

Then of course there was Harold Christie, apparently overwhelmed with grief at the death of his friend. 'He was there, wasn't he?' said the gossips.

Someone else who was there – but only on the day *after* the murder – appealed more to the investigators. They arrested Sir Harry Oakes's son-in-law, Nancy Oakes's newly wed husband, Freddie de Marigny.

'Do you think they've got the right man?' Erica asked Bart when he came to the house in East Bay Street one hot and sticky evening later in the month.

'Well, they certainly got quick results,' he replied with a shrug.

'Bart dear, you say that in a casual sort of way,' Amy Tregarvon protested. 'Think of poor Lady Oakes. Her husband dead, and now they're saying her own daughter's husband did it. She needs to have the right result, not just a quick one!'

'Well, the "right" result varies, depending on who's in charge.'

'But how can you say that? The police are—'

'The police are led by the Duke himself. His big mistake was to call in those two incompetents from the Miami Police Department to help him.'

'Yes, that does seem rather strange,' Erica put in.

'Strange? It's brainless! The Duke knows nothing about criminal investigation, the men from Miami know nothing about local conditions, and the scene of the crime wasn't made secure at once.' Bart's professional instincts had been offended by the ineptness of the whole thing. 'The evidence could easily have been tampered with.'

'But who would want to tamper with it?' Amy cried. 'We all want to bring the murderer to justice.'

Do we? At Erica's shake of the head, Bart closed his lips on the words. There was no point in upsetting Mrs Tregarvon, who grieved on behalf of the Oakes family as if it were one of her own who had died.

Later, when Erica went with Bart to the gate to say

goodnight, she asked what he really thought. 'Do you think de Marigny did it?'

'Erica, fifty per cent of Nassau wants him as the murderer because they never liked him. He's a foreigner, a womanizer, and a business competitor. He stole a march on them by marrying into the Oakes family. Forty-five per cent want him as the murderer because it's the most convenient way of sweeping the whole thing under the carpet. About five per cent are really interested in the truth.'

'That doesn't answer my question. Do you think he did it? Over some family disagreement?'

'No.'

Erica hesitated. 'Do you think it was Harold Christie?'

'That's possible. But if he did it he wasn't alone.'

'What makes you say so?'

'The fuel that burned the room was brought to the scene from outside. It seems to have been some sort of petrol-based product and no container's ever been found. The implement with which Sir Harry was beaten over the head was brought in from outside, and *that's* never been found.'

'Christie could have had those things with him in his car when he drove to Westbourne for the evening's card game,' Erica suggested.

'That's true. And he was seen later driving in Nassau though he denies having left Westbourne, so he could have gone out and dropped the container and the weapon in the sea. But I don't see Christie as a man of violence.'

'No,' she agreed, thinking of the affable manner, the indolence, the love of the social whirl she'd seen in the man. 'But he and Sir Harry Oakes were very bound up in business matters. They could have . . . I don't know . . . quarrelled over money.'

Bart had given the matter a lot of thought, piecing together what he'd heard on his Intelligence grapevine, what the gossips said, what he'd guessed. Nobody had asked him for his opinion. Quite the contrary, he'd been warned off by a message from the Admiralty: 'On no account are Naval Intelligence facilities to be offered or utilized in the inquiry concerning the demise of Sir Harry Oakes.' Which seemed to imply either that the Admiralty were miffed with the way the Duke of Windsor was behaving, inviting in his friends from the Miami police, or else they knew something was rotten in the state of Denmark and didn't want to be involved.

Because, after all, Sir Harry the victim, Harold Christie the sleeping witness, and Freddie de Marigny the arrested man were all part of the Duke's social circle in Nassau. What was more, there was very good evidence that Sir Harry, Christie and the Duke were engaged in investing money in Mexico, contrary to the law against exporting sterling. How very embarrassing if *that* came out during the murder inquiry.

But though he'd been warned off, it didn't mean Bart's brain would stop working. 'Christie went to Westbourne for a card party,' he mused as he stood at the gate with Erica. 'He stayed on after the others left. What if he'd arranged for some business associate to join him – to discuss money matters with Sir Harry?'

'But it would have been very late, Bart.'

'Perhaps it was the kind of discussion that could only take place when everyone else was asleep in bed. You know all this alarm over unidentified craft out among the islands . . .'

'You think it's got something to do with that?'

'Well, maybe it's just a coincidence that there's been all this clandestine activity at sea. There's no way of knowing what the boats were carrying. But just let's suppose it was money.'

'Money? You mean actual cash?'

'He had a lot of it, Erica. Sir Harry, I mean.' He didn't mention to Erica the suspicion in high places that Sir Harry had been buying property in Mexico – that was classified information. 'Suppose Christie was joined by some colleague to discuss Sir Harry's little games. Maybe they wanted a share in whatever he was up to, or maybe they wanted him to stop. Suppose the colleague brought a strong-arm man with him to give some power to the persuasion. And suppose things got a bit out of hand.'

'That's a lot of guesswork, Bart.'

'Of course.' But the tone in which he said it made her think it was more than that.

'If there's any evidence of the kind you've been "guessing" at, Bart, oughtn't it to go to the police?'

'What, those two idiots from Miami?'

'But darling, if what you've been saying is anything like the true story, Freddie de Marigny ought not to be under arrest.'

'But first you have to convince the authorities to listen to it. And the authorities have made up their minds they're going to try de Marigny for the murder.'

After a long, slow course through the magistrate's court, the case against Alfred de Marigny was opened on October 18th, 1943. As Bart had foretold, the evidence had been so botched up that the defence made the fingerprint expert look a fool. Worse, they made it look as if de Marigny had been framed. The jury brought in a majority verdict of Not Guilty.

Giancarlo Manzini rang Timothy Perriman. 'I thought you said the French guy was sure to take the rap?' he said in his cold, unemotional voice.

'That was the general opinion, Mr Manzini.'

'So what happens now? Are we going to have *more* trouble?'

'I don't believe so—'

'You don't believe so? Now isn't that comforting. I told you to deal with the problem, not make it worse.'

'It'll be dropped,' Perriman replied with eager conviction. 'I tell you, no one in the islands wants any more snooping around by police. And the Duke of Windsor is still convinced de Marigny did it, no matter what the jury said. He's ordered him to leave the colony, or at least the Acting Governor's issued the order on his behalf – the Duke's in New York.'

'The Nassau police—'

'Excuse me, Mr Manzini, but the Nassau police can't do anything. The detectives from Miami messed up all the evidence, not that there was much.'

'There shouldn't have been any!'

'I agree, of course, but things can get a bit out of hand.'

'Not in our organization,' Manzini said. He allowed a moment of silence to ensue, pregnant with menace. 'Well, okay, you're supposed to know the local situation. If you say there isn't going to be any after-effects, I take your word for it. You better be right, Perriman.'

'Don't worry, Mr Manzini. It's all over.'

* * *

So it seemed. De Marigny left the island as commanded. An uneasy sense of release followed. The mysterious flitting of vessels in the island channels had ceased. There was a general stand-down of forces to the normal level. Leave was granted to weary men.

Bart Crosley got a four-day pass. 'What shall we do with all this unwonted freedom?' he inquired. 'Apart from seeing each other every available minute, I mean.'

Erica laughed in delight. It was months since they'd had more than a few minutes' conversation, a snatched embrace. 'Well, we could swing in the garden hammock. We could attend Mrs Montagu's treasure hunt party. There's a rally to encourage investment in War Bonds—'

'It's all too much. I don't know how I'd survive such a hectic pace.'

'There's one thing I really would like to do, Bart,' she said uncertainly.

'What's that?'

'I'd like to get out to the *Perlina*.'

The desire to get aboard the wrecked yacht had never been far from her thoughts ever since she saw the little key on her father's watch chain. But war-time regulations and then the three months of strict security after the murder of Sir Harry Oakes had made it impossible.

'I was expecting that,' Bart said.

'Do you think we could do it? Go out, get hold of Uncle Porter, and get aboard the boat?'

'I don't see why not. The strict embargo on pleasure craft has more or less been lifted. I don't think I could get fuel, but

476

we could borrow a sailing boat, go out and back under windpower. Stay overnight on Panago.'

'Would you like that?' she said, smiling.

'If I remember our last visit correctly, it has its attractions.' He paused. 'But it upset you a lot, all the same, Erica. Are you sure about this?'

'I have to know if there's anything there, Bart. I owe it to him.'

'I understand.'

There was no difficulty borrowing a sailing dinghy. They set off in the early morning of a November day, with a good north-westerly breeze to help them.

Uncle Porter was at home when they stepped ashore at Panago. He came down with the rest of the village to greet them. 'Man, I heard all about how you wanta look at the wreck. Sorry I missed you last time, but you know how it is about t'ings of the heart.' He rolled his eyes expressively as they shook hands.

'We quite understand,' Bart said. 'What we'd like, if you can spare the time, is to be taken out to Diggo and shown how to get up close to the *Perlina*.'

'That's what I heard. Well, sure can't do it now – tide's all against it for the rest of the day. You care to stay on till next-a-day?'

'We would like that very much.'

'Aha!' said Uncle Porter with a knowing look.

There was a long leisurely meal after the sun went down, and a long evening of music under the stars. Guitars and drums throbbed, voices rose and fell. 'Kingfisher, you feather's bright and fine, But not so beauty as that girl o' mine.'

The fragrance of bauhinia and puoi flowers drifted on the air, mingled with the scent of the salty wood embers of the cooking fire. The moon rose, a silver sequin on a blue velvet cloak.

It was a night made for lovers. The singing group around the fire thinned as couples quietly stole away. Erica and Bart sat for a long time with their fingers entwined, savouring the moment to come.

At last they too rose to make their way to the borrowed hut. The moon sailed over the island, silent among the drifting clouds that now and then masked her. The sea murmured, the breeze whispered among the palms, the cicadas trilled. In the darkened fishing village, other sounds were too secret to merge with the muted chorus of nature. The quickened breath, the murmur of love-words, the cry of passion.

Next morning at dawn the village was awake. Uncle Porter, tall and angular in his well-washed whites, awaited them on the shore. 'Well now, I got to do the steering when we gets close,' he remarked as they set out with Bart at the helm. 'No offence, man, but you could end up with a coral wedge t'rough the bottom of the boat.'

'Just give the word when you want to take over.'

They reached Diggo in about twenty minutes. In the rays of the morning sun it was more difficult to distinguish the spars of the yacht among the greenery of the mangroves, the angle of light was against it. They lowered sail. Bart rose from his seat by the rudder. Uncle Porter took his place.

'What you gots to understand is,' he observed, 'that they's four problems – the mangro' roots, the coral edges, the current, and the openin' you got to find. Once you find the openin'' that's one problem behind you. But the other t'ree is gonna take up all your mind. So pay heed, and when I tell you to fend off or bow the head, you do it quick. Here we are, we reach at the openin'.'

The way in was much further away from the wreck, along the coast of the islet, than they would have expected. They edged their way in, using oars to 'fend she' when Porter called. They inched along, the water surging round the dinghy as tide and current eddied into the creek. Soon the mangroves were meeting overhead, making the light dim and green. The water swirling around the dinghy was darkened with mud. Insects sang in the dank air. To Erica, it was detestable.

But she hadn't expected it to be a garden fête. Shivering in her cotton skirt she braced herself against fear. Her father had never been afraid; she couldn't let him down.

The channel opened and closed among the mangrove roots. How Porter had ever found it, she couldn't imagine, but then the hope of goodies aboard the wrecked yacht had been a big incentive.

What they were doing was picking their way among scattered coral rocks which had collected enough soil to attach the hungry roots of the mangroves. The leaf-cover overhead made it like a journey through a twisting tunnel.

At length something of a paler green flickered in an opening among the trees. 'That she,' Porter said, pointing. But it was gone again as they took another twist in the passage.

And then they were drawing up against a big rock. Porter tied the painter to a shaft of coral. On the other side of the rock was the *Perlina*, wedged like a beached porpoise. Porter leapt on to the coral, using a foothold already known. Poised on top, he leaned down to help Bart follow him and then both helped Erica ashore.

'Watch out, she slippery with weed, and this old coral sure is sharp. Mind you knees.' It was a timely warning for she'd almost lost her footing on the weed. Keeping close to their guide, they took a few steps along the crest of the sharp rock, which brought them alongside the remains of the *Perlina*'s bows.

Porter paused. With irony he said, 'If'n you heard she a treasure ship, now's disappointment time.'

Truly, the yacht was dismaying to see. She was resting in among the dead coral uneasily. Erica could hear the faint grinding as the wood was rolled back and forth with each wave. Erica made a sound of distress, turning away too sharply, almost losing her balance.

Bart grabbed her to steady her. Porter said, 'You know this boat?' His dark eyes examined her.

'I used to know her,' Erica said in a choked voice. 'When I was a little girl.'

The fisherman nodded. 'I'da be the same if mine was spoiled-up on the rocks.' He gave a little invitational gesture of the hand. 'You say you want to go aboard.'

'Is it safe?' Bart said, and with good reason, for some of the deck planking had gone, either wrenched apart and floated off by the tide, or stripped off by salvagers.

'Oh, sure, I been aboard many a time. Though doan know how many more times afore a storm take she.' He sighed. 'Sure like to get those masts off before she go down. Good strong metal, one ud make a great wireless mast for Panago. But you need a chainsaw to cut it out and we ain't got one.'

As he was speaking he was leading the way aboard, through the gap in the battered deck-rail, along a safe stretch of decking, so that in a moment they were standing amidships.

'And what now?' Porter inquired.

'Can we go down into the saloon?'

He hesitated. 'Well, sure, but it a dreary place. Not like when you was a little girl, Miz Harrowford.'

'I don't expect it to be. But can we go?'

'Yeah, follow me, but step careful. The companionway got slime and there's crabs and things.' He glanced at her footwear, clearly thinking it a pity that her boat-shoes would be spoiled.

Erica was wearing a blue cotton skirt with a loose short-sleeved blouse, and canvas shoes. She had a pink bandanna to tie back her thick chestnut hair and folded into this was the watch chain with the key.

With Bart's hand under her elbow, she followed Porter down the slippery steps to the saloon. There was about eighteen inches of water there. The light coming in at the empty portholes was filtered by the leaves of the mangroves. The effect was green, sombre, dismal.

To look for a little keyhole they needed a light. Bart had brought a Service knapsack with a torch, a claspknife, and a few other items. He brought out the torch, switched it on. Most of the panelling had been removed from the walls of the saloon, and of course all the planks of the seating, the squab cushions, the centre table, the carpeting – anything moveable.

Something had been immoveable and had been left. A square of panels at about eye level on the aft bulkhead had apparently been too difficult to prise off. 'Ah,' said Bart, and trained the light on it.

They splashed across the room. Close up, there was nothing to be seen but a quadrangle of mildewed walnut panelling made up of four carved, decorated squares. Porter ran his fingers round the sides of it, feeling curiously for an aperture into which he could put his fingers so as to pull, to see if the wood was loose. But the panels fitted too closely against the bulkhead.

'That's some piece of carpentry,' he said, in a tone of admiration.

'Let's see . . . Erica, hold the torch a minute.' Bart in his turn stepped up close. He too ran his fingers over the panelling, but not around the outer edge. He was feeling for the keyhole. After a moment he drew back. 'Nothing,' he said.

'It must be there,' Erica said insistently. 'Why else is that square of panelling so securely fixed that it hasn't been dragged off?'

She handed the torch to Porter. She started at the bottom edge and let her fingers run gently and slowly over the carving. Nothing. Tendrils and knobs that felt like fruit, fish with fins and curving tails . . . She had a sudden vision of the panelling in its hey-day. It represented a sea cavern with seaweed waving in the current, and the fish in motion through it, and in the centre . . . In the centre where these four squares remained, there had been a mermaid combing her hair. Holding up a mirror, to see her reflection.

'Just a minute,' she whispered. She felt her way among the carvings, her eyes closed, recalling the picture in her mind. She found the mirror, a little oval mirror held aloft. And in the middle of that little mirror, she felt a tiny aperture.

'Bart . . .'

'You've found it?'

'I think so. Just a minute.' She stood back and with trembling hands untied her bandana. She unfolded it, took the key between the finger and thumb of her right hand, and with her left found the mirror once more.

She inserted the key, and turned.

Nothing.

'What's the matter?' Bart asked.

'The key's in the lock, but it won't turn.'

'Try again.'

'I'm trying. I'm afraid to turn too hard – the key might snap, it's so delicate.'

'Hang on,' said Bart. In the reflected light on the water, she could make out that he was feeling about in the knapsack. 'Move aside a bit.' She did so. And then in the light of Porter's torch she saw that he had produced a tin of grease. 'Take the key out,' he said. When she did so, he smeared some of the grease on it. 'Now try it again,' he said. 'Move it about a bit, let the lubricant get into the lock. After all, it hasn't been turned in over twelve years and part of that time it's been here in the damp and wet.'

Obediently she stood moving the key in and out, and then trying to turn it. Bit by bit it moved more easily. Porter was standing by holding the torch over her shoulder, whistling to himself between his teeth. The sea water slapped about their legs. It was cold. Her fingers began to fumble as they lost warmth. The key slipped and was almost lost in the water but she caught the watch chain, retrieved it.

Holding back her frustration, she let Bart once more put a drop of grease on the tiny barrel of the key. Almost without hope she put it back in the lock and turned.

There was a click.

'Oh me Gard!' cried Porter, throwing up his hands so that the torchlight flittered along the ceiling. 'She done it!'

'Good for you!' Bart exclaimed. 'Hold the torch steady, Porter.'

The key had turned, but the panel remained closed. Erica pulled on the key. The door of the safe moved a little, but not enough. She pulled again, but it wouldn't budge. Bart took out the claspknife, slid its blade under the lower edge of the door, and teased it open. The hinges squealed.

'Come over this side, shine the light in!'

Porter obeyed.

The inside was a metal-lined cube, about twelve inches on all sides. There were several things lying on the shelf. One was a small rectangular box which Erica instantly recognized as the container for her mother's ruby bracelet, long forgotten. The others were documents, folded foolscap sheets lying loose or in envelopes. With a cry of joy Erica drew them out.

'This what you was lookin' for?' Porter said in amazement, directing the torch beam on the mildewed collection.

'Yes, oh yes! This is what my father meant to bring back to London, to prove he wasn't guilty!'

She began to peel them apart, to see what they were. It was impossible to discern much in the gloom of the cabin, even with the torch's help.

'Let's get on deck into the light,' suggested Bart.

Porter led the way, clicking off the torch. Erica followed

next, with Bart's arm guiding her because she was using her hands to hold the precious papers. A heavy scattering of raindrops greeted them, the warning of a coming squall.

Porter came to a sudden halt on the deck. Erica stumbled, almost bumping into him. Bart stepped closer. 'Careful,' he said. Almost as one they urged Porter forward so as to come out into the daylight.

'I'll take those,' said a voice.

Beyond Porter's angular frame they saw a newcomer.

Timothy Perriman.

Chapter Twenty-four

Perriman's hand reached out to seize the papers. Bart moved between Erica and Perriman. There was a jostle, a stumble. Perriman went down on the deck. Someone moved forward to help him up – a black man, unseen until now. With a snarl Perriman shoved the helping hand aside. He scrambled up. His thin frame straightened, his fist went into his jacket pocket. And came out, holding a gun.

For one moment there was utter stillness. It was as if a camera shutter had opened and closed, fixing them in eternity. The stocky black man drawing back against the ship's rail; Perriman with his angry face; Porter rigid, staring; Bart with a question on his lips; Erica clutching the documents against her breast. A dull steely gleam from lowering clouds lit the scene. Heavy drops of rain had begun to fall, but no one noticed. All were transfixed by the gun.

'Give me the papers,' Perriman said between stiff lips.

'No!'

'You think you have a choice?' He motioned with the pistol.

Erica had recovered from the first numbing shock. Her mind was racing now. 'It's so important to you to get them? You've been after them for years, haven't you!'

'Hand them over.' He moved closer, fingers tightening on the gun.

Bart eyed it. A .22, a pocket gun, but big enough to do damage at close quarters. And the man was desperate enough to use it. 'Give him the documents, Erica,' he said.

'That shows proper respect.' It was a sneer of triumph as he snatched the folded papers. A wayward gust of wind flapped them as he took them, turning back one sheet. Erica glimpsed one word. *Ganymede*.

The *Ganymede* had sunk, cargo and crew. Only two men had remained alive. For this, her father had been arrested as a murderer and a swindler. This freight contract would have proved his innocence.

'It *was* you,' she said in a stifled voice, staring at Timothy. 'It was you who defrauded the insurance company. Somehow those papers prove it.'

'Very clever,' said Perriman. He said it with irony, but Bart could see he was shaken. The fingers tightened on the gun.

Quickly, to deflect his attention, Bart said, 'How the devil did you get here?'

'In a boat, of course.'

'But how did you know where to come?'

'By following you.'

'But how—'

'Money well spent,' Perriman said with satisfaction. 'All these years, a few dollars here, a few dollars there, but I've always known what Mrs Harrowford – ' he gave a mock bow in Erica's direction – 'was up to since she came to Nassau.'

'I knew it,' Erica breathed. 'I could feel it, eyes watching me . . .'

'Why did you have to come to the Bahamas?' Perriman

interrupted, in something like indignation. 'I didn't care what you got up to in France or Spain. But I couldn't have you sneaking around the Bahamas.'

'Too risky, eh?' Bart said. 'Too close to the *Margravine*.'

'Oh, by the way, I have to thank you for that,' Perriman said, smiling. '*I* would never have recognized this mass of rubbish as the *Margravine*.' He glanced about at the ruined wheelhouse, the gaping planks.

The rain squall, which had passed, returned. Raindrops pattered on the papers he was holding. He tucked them into the breast pocket of his jacket.

'What are you going to do with those?' Bart asked.

'I'm going to have a little ceremonial bonfire this evening. It's taken me years to get them. I want to give them a good send-off.' Perriman's even teeth showed in a grin of enjoyment.

'What do they prove? That you tricked Lindon Tregarvon?'

'Oh, not for the first time, I assure you. I had a good thing going with Fairforth Freighters.'

'You sound as if you're proud of it,' Erica said, shaking her head in dismay.

'Cleverer than your old man, wasn't I?' challenged Perriman. 'Small things at first, but then when His Lordship began to get immersed in all that rubbish about the London Season, it got easy to bring off bigger things. I got quite good at forging his signature on substitute papers.'

'And all the time he trusted you . . .'

'He need never have known a thing about it if those two fools hadn't been shooting their mouths off in Darwin,' he protested, as if anxious they should see that it wasn't his fault his plans had gone awry. 'When that happened I thought my number was up, I can tell you. But you see, here I still am, and the world thinks it was the great Lindon Tregarvon who carried out the shipping fraud.'

'It wasn't just fraud! Men were drowned on the *Ganymede*!'

'Well, yes, but that was the captain's fault – he bungled things.'

Porter stirred from his trance-like silence. He flung out an arm in accusation. Rain splashed against the brown skin. 'You sayin' you let men get drowned fo' money?'

'What business is it of yours?'

'I live on the sea, man! I bin close to drownin', I know how it like. You a real bad hooky-worm!'

'Shut your mouth—'

'Who you to tell me "shut my mouth"? Sneak up on us, follow me track in the channel, you think you so clever you, but you just a nuthin', couldna got here without some blackfellah brung you in his boat—'

'Who you callin' blackfellah?' snarled the Bahamian by the rail. 'Ignorant islandman! Watch your mouth!'

'What you help him foh? Got no sense, you? Hear me now, he say he kilt seamen – that you kind of friend?'

Timothy Perriman waved the gun. 'My kind of friend because I pay him,' he said.

'Well, I ain't you friend, and when I get back to Panago I'm goin' send a message to Captain Sears of the police, tell him I—'

'You what?' parried Timothy. 'You listened to some foolish talk—'

'No, hear me now, man,' said the boatman who'd brought Perriman. 'It's not just this stupid fisherman. There's Miz Harrowford and—'

'Well . . .' Timothy held up a hand for silence, gave it some thought, hunching his shoulders and letting them drop. 'Who says they're going to get back to Panago?' A long pause. The rain pattered on the decking, on the figures who stood in confrontation.

'What are you going to do?' Bart said. 'Shoot three people?'

'Why not?'

'Come on, Perriman, how are you going to explain three bodies with bullet-holes in them?'

'Who's going to find them?' Timothy said.

On hearing that Erica and Bart had set off for the Out Islands his one thought had been to follow, to find out where the yacht was beached, to get to the safe on the *Margravine* ahead of them. Easy enough in Groby's fast motorboat, he'd thought. They'd sighted the wreck last evening and landed on Curpa, the largest island next after Panago. But no one on Curpa could tell him how to approach the wreck on Diggo. 'You gots to ask Porter McCabe on Panago,' he was told. But Panago was where Erica and Bart had gone.

The only course had been to lay off in Groby's motorboat until they saw the dinghy sail into the opening among the rocks then follow, inch by inch. The tension had been high. Groby had been complaining all the way about the damage done by the mangrove roots and the coral to his sparkling boat.

But they'd made it, they'd found the channel and the

tethered dinghy. No one aboard the yacht, it seemed. Where had they gone? It had been quite a shock when Porter emerged from the companionway of the saloon.

So now here Perriman stood, face to face with three people who knew that he had come to get the freight contract, who had heard him boasting about getting the better of Tregarvon. Why had he boasted? Because he'd wanted to triumph over them. Stupid, stupid . . . Now they couldn't be allowed – simply couldn't be allowed – to get back to Panago or to Nassau.

'I don't have to explain any bullet-holes,' he said with an inward surge of relief as his brain presented him with a way out. 'A storm's coming up, you can feel the wind rising. After you're dead we'll just load you into the dinghy, tow you out to deep water, and sink you for the fish to deal with. Lost at sea in a storm. Very sad, but it happens all the time.'

'Hey!' said Groby behind him.

'What?'

'You never said nothin' about another killing.'

'Shut up, Groby.'

'Look at me here! I didn't hire out to kill nobody!'

'What's the matter? You finished off quite a few in the old days.'

'Mr Perriman, that was during the Prohibition. That was business.'

'Well, this is business, Groby. You won't be out of pocket, I promise.'

'How much will you have to pay him?' Bart inquired. 'A hundred? Two? And when he comes back next week and the week after, saying his conscience is bothering him and he feels he ought to go to the police—'

'Groby knows better than to blackmail me,' Timothy said with a smile. 'Don't you, boy?'

Groby glowered but remained silent.

'So that's how it is, is it?' Bart said. 'He gives the orders, Groby, and you have to take them. He's in with the bosses.'

'I've got friends,' Timothy agreed.

'Miami gangsters? Currency smugglers? Mafia?'

'Mind your own business.' But there was surprise in the rejoinder.

'Oh, you haven't gone unobserved, Perriman. We know quite a lot about you.'

'We? Who's "we"?' A tremor of real alarm ran through Timothy. For years he'd been in control, unassailable. Now this light-o'-love of Erica's hinted he was somehow vulnerable.

'There are people in Nassau who take quite an interest in you, my friend.'

'If you mean the police, forget it! We've just seen how the police handle an inquiry. Arrest the wrong man, bungle the court case, and then have him booted out when he's found not guilty.'

'You know de Marigny was the wrong man, do you? Inside information?'

'Never mind about that!' Why was he letting this man bait him? He was in charge. He was the man with the gun.

Yet it wasn't as easy as he'd thought. He had to shoot three people. Well, all right. Pull the trigger three times. But suppose the shots didn't kill them? The man who provided the gun had warned him it was too small to be the most effective weapon.

Shoot each of them twice? Yes, that was the way. Shoot Bart Crosley first – he was the most likely to cause trouble. And then the fisherman.

And then Erica.

Why not? He'd never liked her. Bossy little kid, walking past him in her father's office as if he didn't exist, turning down his marriage offer because he wasn't good enough. He'd show her.

He stared at his victims. The rain was blowing across the deck, soaking them all. Porter stood stoically, arms folded so that his drenched shirtsleeves clung to his body. Crosley was a little in front of Erica, trying to shield her from the squall and from Timothy. The cotton blouse clung to her breasts, her long chestnut hair was moulded against her head, the rain had gilded her cheeks like some precious oil. A fine-looking girl, but her time was up. And for her lover too – this was lights out. His finger tightened on the trigger.

'Wait!' exclaimed Bart. 'Perriman, don't do it! You'll never be able to live with it.'

'Why not?' Erica said bitterly. 'He's done it before.'

Groby gave a grunt of surprise. 'How you know that? The Oakes trial didn't prove a thing! Nothing to link us—'

'Shut up, you fool!' Perriman snarled.

'So you think I'm talking about Sir Harry Oakes?' She was too concentrated on what mattered in her own past to spare a thought for the Oakes murder. 'No, I'm talking about my father.' She raised her head, looked clear-eyed at Perriman as she levelled the accusation. 'You killed him, Timothy!'

The breeze seized her words and swept them out among the mangroves, over the coral rocks, out to the turbulent sea.

Timothy shrugged. So she knew, but what did it matter? The sound of her voice had soon been lost, and the bodies too would go, weighted to sink among the dead coral, where the fish and the crabs would pick the flesh from the bones.

Erica understood that death was near. Oddly enough she felt regret, not fear. Regret that she would never be able to tell her mother that her belief in Lindon Tregarvon had been justified, never be able to clear her father's name, never tell Bart how much she loved him, never bear his children.

She was to blame that he was here, about to share her fate. If she had not wanted to open the safe in the *Margravine*, he wouldn't be here now. Yet perhaps there was the slightest crumb of comfort in that: they were to die together, and if there was an afterlife, perhaps they would enter into it together.

Bart was still standing a little in front of her, trying to shield her from the sight of Perriman's gun. She leaned against him so that her body weighed heavy on his back. She wanted to transmit the message: if it has to come, at least we're together. He put a hand behind him so that it cupped her elbow. He pressed it. A faint thrill of hope ran through her. Bart was telling her, It's not over yet.

Perriman saw the movement of Bart's hand. 'Keep still,' he snapped. Crosley was the dangerous one. Finish him off first. Try to do it with one shot, straight to the heart.

Timothy edged a little closer.

It was the chance Bart had been waiting for. He kicked forward and upward, knocking his gun hand up. Dockyard bruiser tactics, no Queensberry rules.

Perriman gave a yell of pain. The gun went sailing through the air.

It landed on the deck beside Erica. Groby, coming out of a moment's trance, lunged for it. Erica kicked the gun into a gap in the deck-planks. It vanished into the cabin below.

Bart had Timothy down, trying to hit him hard enough to knock him senseless. Timothy, no fighter, was grappling for his life. With a strength that came from desperation he convulsed and thrashed, wrenching himself sideways on the slippery surface. The deck under his body gave a great lurch. The incoming tide shoved against the *Perlina*. The wind mounded up the water, hurling a great wave among the rocks.

Bart lost his hold on Perriman. The other man slid away on the slimy planks. Once more the sea surged in the spell of the wind, the yacht heaved, crunched into the crags, tilting.

Erica lost her footing, stumbled into Porter; they went crashing down together in a tangle. Groby threw himself on a stanchion so as to cling on.

Timothy Perriman slithered sideways to the edge of the deck. There was a gap where the rail had been looted. He went through the gap, shrieking, grasping at the raindrops.

The wreck shivered under the assault of the waves. The timbers were awash with sea water and rain. Bart scrambled up, helped Erica to her feet, dragging her to the wheelhouse for a handhold.

'Get off the boat!' cried Porter, running like a dancer over the gaps in the planking. 'She givin' up!'

Groby was hanging on to the stanchion for dear life. He lumbered after Porter, on to the rocks on which the *Perlina* was grinding. Bart heaved Erica ashore where Porter was waiting to grab her. He followed, falling, gashing his knees on the sharp rocks. Blood tinged the muddy surface.

They looked back for Perriman. He was in the water on his back. Bart jumped to the outer rocks, as if to dive in for him. Porter clutched his shirt.

'Don't, man, don't! Water only four feet deep, mebbe three feet! Bash you brains out on coral if you go in there!'

'But he's—'

'He's dead, man. Look!'

Pulled back into safety, Bart looked. Timothy Perriman was lying not in the water but on it.

He had gone over backward on to a bed of coral rock. One shard had pierced between his shoulders like a sword.

About noon, after the squall was over and the sea was calm, Uncle Porter came back to Diggo in Groby's motorboat, with some companions from Panago. They had brought with them a raft of driftwood. On this they delicately poled their way among the coral and recovered the body of Timothy Perriman.

They also took what was worth taking from the remains of the *Perlina*, now in two pieces with her masts in the water. 'Come back some time with a chainsaw,' Uncle Porter remarked, 'get those spars for a wireless mast.'

In the pocket of the dead man were some papers, soaked and half-illegible. But there was enough there to show that they were the bills of loading for the *Ganymede*, signed by Lindon Tregarvon but not made out to Fairforth Freighters.

'I don't understand,' Amy Tregarvon said, when Erica and Bart tried to explain it to her.

'Don't you see, it's proof that the contract was altered after his signature and presumably without his knowledge and consent,' said Bart. 'And of course we've got Uncle Porter and Groby to make statements witnessing what they heard Perriman say. That he'd forged your husband's signature on substitute papers. Mr Tregarvon intended to send the cargo by a different freighting firm, one that he knew was honest. Perriman altered the papers to allow the cargo to be handled by a firm who stole the cargo and shared the loot with him.'

'But the insurance . . . I thought it was an insurance fraud?'

'The ships had to be sunk so that their cargo would be reported lost at sea. The insurance was legitimate but your husband had no idea the ships were sunk to conceal the theft of the cargoes.'

'I see.' But it was clear Amy did not see. Besides, her mind was taken up with an analysis of last night's bidding in the bridge tournament. Of course Mrs Earle should have played that King of Spades earlier but having lost that, why hadn't she blocked Willie Darnley's entry to dummy?

'Mother,' reproached Erica, 'aren't you interested in proving Father's innocence?'

Amy smiled. 'I don't have to prove it, darling, I always believed in it.'

That was true. Erica could only kiss her and leave her to her mental rerun of last night's bridge.

'What will happen about the Oakes case?' she asked Bart later as she went with him down to the jetty.

'Nothing, I imagine.'

'But Bart, from the way Groby reacted he thought I was accusing Timothy of killing Sir Harry. And he not only seemed to be agreeing that he did, he said there was nothing "to link *us*" with it – in other words he was there, he could be an eyewitness.'

'And there's the snag in the idea of reopening the case. Groby isn't going to make a statement admitting he was there.'

'But *we* heard him say so—'

'What's the famous quote from Dickens? "You must not tell us what the soldier said, it's not evidence." In other words, hearsay isn't admissible.'

'You seem to know a lot about what's evidence and what isn't?'

'Gathering evidence is one of my jobs, Erica. That's what Intelligence does. But some is legally admissible and some isn't.' Bart sighed. 'In any case, nobody's going to reopen the Oakes case even if Groby were willing to testify.'

'But Bart—'

'Timothy Perriman was a "businessman", right?' he interrupted. 'Whose business did he look after?'

'Well, I don't know . . . I told you, I thought he was connected with . . . what do you call it . . . the Mob?'

'The Mob, Cosa Nostra, the Mafia, whatever. That seems to be true, from all we can learn. Well, the big boys in the Mafia have strong underworld links in Italy.'

'Yes?'

'And the Allied Forces are at this moment fighting their way up through Italy against strong German opposition.'

'Yes?'

'Do you really think the American government wants to antagonize the Mafia bosses at a time like this? One word from the big boys in New York and Chicago, and all the cooperation the forces are getting from the Italian population in Salerno and Sicily would stop as if it were turned off at the tap.'

'You mean nothing will be done about the Oakes case because the Mafia might object?' she demanded, aghast.

'More or less.'

'But that's—'

'That's politics, Erica. Besides, I don't know that the police would get much out of Groby about the Oakes murder. He's a lot more scared of the Cosa Nostra bosses than he is of the police. Without his testimony, there's no case against Perriman as far as the murder of Harry Oakes is concerned. Besides, Perriman's dead. What's the good of stirring up a hornet's nest when the suspected murderer's already paid the price?'

Erica was silenced. They strolled on, letting their thoughts drift back over the events of the last few days, weighing up what had been gained and what lost.

Timothy Perriman was dead. The murder of Sir Harry Oakes might for ever remain a mystery because of that. But on the credit side, Lindon Tregarvon's fate had been explained and his name would be cleared at last.

When they reached the jetty, the dory was waiting to take parties back to base on Spessu Island. One or two crewmen were already aboard.

'I've got to go,' said Bart.

'Yes.'

'What's the matter? You ought to be smiling. Your father's reputation will be restored.'

'I can't help remembering that Timothy . . . that Timothy was his friend, someone he liked and trusted. And now Timothy's been proved a traitor and a murderer. And he died so horribly, Bart. I'll never forget the look on that face, turned up to the dark skies and the falling rain.'

'Don't dwell on it, Erica love. Perriman brought his own death on himself. And he deserved to die.'

'I know that. It's just—'

'What?'

'One minute he was so *alive*, so in control, the next he was nothing – just a collection of flesh and bones swaying on top of the coral.'

Bart could think of nothing to say. In most things he could try to offer comfort, justification, support, but against the realization of mortality, there was no comfort.

It seemed Erica's own thoughts had taken the same turn. She managed a wavering smile. 'At least I can say one thing for sure. That scene aboard the *Margravine* showed me what really mattered in this world.'

'And what was that? Your father's good name?'

She sighed. 'After all the years when I hated him for making it a name to be sneered at, and then the months when I realized he wasn't to blame . . . No, after all, when Timothy had his finger on the trigger, the only thing that mattered was that you and I had had such a short time together.'

He smiled. 'That ought to count when you think about what I asked you. I'll want an answer when I get back.'

'When shall I see you again?'

'Soon as I can manage it. A week or two. I've got to go, Erica, I'm holding up the duty boat.'

He bent to take a kiss of leave-taking. Her response surprised him. She answered him with passion, holding him close, trying to seal into her body some of his human warmth so as to see her through until they could be together again.

There was a murmur of approval from the seamen in the boat. Bart let her go, stepped down, smiling back up at her as the boat made way.

Erica stood on the jetty watching it sail out of Nassau Harbour. She had stood here before to watch him return to duty. But this time it was different. Bart had asked her to have an answer ready when he came back. The question had been, Will you marry me?

The answer had formed itself in her mind as she kissed him goodbye.

The disgrace that had shadowed her life had been wiped away. She could admit to being her father's child without a sense of shame. Bart's career could not be harmed by marrying her, she was no longer someone over whom a question mark hovered. She could go to him as his wife with no sense of doubt, no fears from the past.

Life wouldn't be all roses, even so. War still raged elsewhere, Bart might be summoned away where death and destruction reigned. All the more reason to seize their happiness, cherish it, enjoy it.

The answer he had asked for would be ready when he returned. She would say yes with all her heart.

Author's Note

The murder of Sir Harry Oakes in Nassau during World War II and under the governorship of the Duke of Windsor remains unsolved to this day. The solution offered in this novel is only one of many that have been proposed.

EDITH PARGETER

She goes to War

It is 1940. Catherine Saxon is on her way to join the Women's Royal Naval Service at its Quarters in Devonport. She isn't quite sure why she joined up in the first place. A journalist on a local paper, her brief had been to cover gossip and fashion, so she was hardly in the front line! But join up she did, and her impulsive decision is to have undreamt-of consequences...

Sent first for basic training as a teleprinter operator, Catherine is surprised to find she enjoys the camaraderie of her fellow WRNS and quickly grows to love the beautiful Devon countryside. A posting to Liverpool comes as something of a shock, but she soon acclimatises to the war-torn city, and it is here, one fine day in early spring, that she meets the man who is to have such a profound effect on her life.

Tom Lyddon is a veteran of the Spanish Civil War and his political beliefs strike an immediate chord with Catherine. In wartime, the usual stages of courtship are dispensed with, and she readily accepts Tom's invitation to spend a few days with him in the blissful solitude of the North Wales countryside. Their idyll ends when Tom is recalled to active service abroad, and then all Catherine can do is wait – and hope – for her lover's safe return...

Also by Edith Pargeter from Headline
The Brothers of Gwynedd Quartet, The Eighth Champion of Christendom,
Reluctant Odyssey, Warfare Accomplished,
and, writing as Ellis Peters,
A Rare Benedictine, The Hermit of Eyton Forest, The Confession of Brother
Haluin, The Heretic's Apprentice, The Summer of the Danes, The Holy Thief,
Brother Cadfael's Penance, City of Gold and Shadows, Death Mask, Death to the
Landlords, Flight of the Witch, Holiday with Violence, Mourning Raga, Never Pick
up Hitch-hikers, The Assize of the Dying, Funeral of Figaro, The Horn of Roland,
The Piper on the Mountain, The Will and the Deed

FICTION/GENERAL 0 7472 3277 6

More Enchanting Fiction from Headline

PAMELA EVANS

TEA-BLENDER'S DAUGHTER

As a provider, Henry Slater can't be faulted; he is the owner of a successful tea-trading company, and his family enjoy a comfortable lifestyle near Ravenscourt Park. But love has never been on offer to his children, Dolly and Ken – Henry is above such things.

For all Dolly's intelligence, her father refused to let her stay at school beyond the official leaving age, and she now works at Slaters and is expected to marry Frank Mitchell, her father's deputy. But during the General Strike, Dolly is rescued from a riot by Bill Drake, a factory labourer, and embarks on an illicit affair with him. Just as they agree to elope, Henry discovers their relationship and devises a plan to part them forever.

Stunned by what they both believe is rejection, Dolly marries Frank, and Bill joins a rival firm, coldly setting out to marry the boss's daughter, whilst determining revenge against the Slaters. As the years progress, they accept that the past is behind them. Until the end of the Second World War's rationing heralds new opportunities – and a merger between the rival tea companies...

Don't miss Pamela Evans' other warm-hearted, London sagas available from Headline:
LAMPLIGHT ON THE THAMES, A BARROW IN THE BROADWAY,
STAR QUALITY, MAGGIE OF MOSS STREET, DIAMONDS IN DANBY WALK
and A FASHIONABLE ADDRESS

FICTION/SAGA   0 7472 4491 X

A selection of bestsellers from Headline

THE CHANGING ROOM	Margaret Bard	£5.99 ☐
BACKSTREET CHILD	Harry Bowling	£5.99 ☐
A HIDDEN BEAUTY	Tessa Barclay	£5.99 ☐
A HANDFUL OF HAPPINESS	Evelyn Hood	£5.99 ☐
THE SCENT OF MAY	Sue Sully	£5.99 ☐
HEARTSEASE	T R Wilson	£5.99 ☐
NOBODY'S DARLING	Josephine Cox	£5.99 ☐
A CHILD OF SECRETS	Mary Mackie	£5.99 ☐
WHITECHAPEL GIRL	Gilda O'Neill	£5.99 ☐
BID TIME RETURN	Donna Baker	£5.99 ☐
THE LADIES OF BEVERLEY HILLS	Sharleen Cooper Cohen	£5.99 ☐
THE OLD GIRL NETWORK	Catherine Alliott	£4.99 ☐

All Headline books are available at your local bookshop or newsagent, or can be ordered direct from the publisher. Just tick the titles you want and fill in the form below. Prices and availability subject to change without notice.

Headline Book Publishing, Cash Sales Department, Bookpoint, 39 Milton Park, Abingdon, OXON, OX14 4TD, UK. If you have a credit card you may order by telephone – 0235 400400.

Please enclose a cheque or postal order made payable to Bookpoint Ltd to the value of the cover price and allow the following for postage and packing:
UK & BFPO: £1.00 for the first book, 50p for the second book and 30p for each additional book ordered up to a maximum charge of £3.00.
OVERSEAS & EIRE: £2.00 for the first book, £1.00 for the second book and 50p for each additional book.

Name ....

Address ....

....

....

If you would prefer to pay by credit card, please complete:
Please debit my Visa/Access/Diner's Card/American Express (delete as applicable) card no:

Signature .... Expiry Date ....